WHAT PEOPLE ARE SAYING ...

Dr. Bernard Helgman's world spirals inward like a chambered nautilus shell. On the outside he is shiny perfect, but inside he is tormented by memories, confusion, and remorse. David Tannenbaum's exquisite novel, *Out of the Depths*, explores the many losses of a Holocaust survivor—and his lonely struggle to find a meaningful "after Auschwitz" life. When Helgman is accused of unspeakable crimes, his carefully-constructed shell shatters and he must once again endure the unendurable. My heart is broken. Days after finishing this book, I'm still pondering—and crying.

~ JOYCE FAULKNER Award-winning author of *In the Shadow of Suribachi*, *Windshift*, and *USERNAME*

David Tannenbaum weaves pathos, humor, and tragic love into one man's powerful story of survivor's guilt ... a guilt so deep it refuses to stay hidden behind the paint of a clown's face. Forced to assist the SS doctors who carried out gruesome concentration camp experiments, Helgman's face was often the last his fellow Jews saw before they succumbed to the atrocities inflicted upon them. Set aside some time and a box of tissues ... you'll need both.

~ STEVE HATHCOCK South Texas Historian

Many people are unaware of the extent to which the guards and administrators in the German concentration camps used Jewish prisoners to help run the camp, keep order among the prisoner population and carry out other tasks. *Out of the Depths* is a story, set in post-war America, of a reconstructive surgeon, Bernard Helgman, who, as a little more than a boy, had found himself side-by-side with Nazi doctors as they carried out their horrific medical experiments. Tannenbaum masterfully shows us the inner turmoil that Helgman suffers every day of his life as he struggles to come to terms with what he did, or didn't do, in the Auschwitz infirmary. It's fiction, but it could have really happened just as Tannenbaum relates it.

~ LEONARD FELMAN Author of *Lifelong Learner*

OUT
OF THE
DEPTHS

DAVID HARRY TANNENBAUM

Library of Congress Cataloging-in-Publication Data

Names: Harry, David, 1939- author.

Title: Out of the depths / David Harry Tannenbaum.

Description: Pittsburgh, PA : Red Engine Press, [2016]

Identifiers: LCCN 2016026362 | ISBN 9781943267071

Subjects: LCSH: World War, 1939-1945--Atrocities--Germany--Fiction. | War criminals--Germany--Fiction. | War crimes investigation--Fiction. | Surgeons--Fiction. | Guilt--Fiction.

Classification: LCC PS3608.A783855 O88 2016 | DDC 813/.6--dc23

LC record available at https://lccn.loc.gov/2016026362

Cover Layout ©2016 Ana (Kat) Gally

Background image: Joel Saget /AFP/ Getty Images

Red Engine Press

Pittsburgh, PA
Printed in the United States.

DEDICATION

This book is dedicated to those who died at the hands of the Nazis and to those who managed to survive. May their memory be a blessing and may their lives be an inspiration for their descendants and for all of us.

This book is also dedicated to the men and women of the Armed Forces of every nation, then and now, who put their lives in harm's way so that others may live in freedom. A special thanks goes to those who liberated the concentration camps, giving life to those who faced near certain death. May God bless the veterans, their families and their loved ones. Our world would not be the same without you.

DISCLAIMER

The characters and events in this story are entirely fictitious. Any similarity to anyone, living or deceased, is purely coincidental. Life in the camps was so appallingly horrible as to defy even the most active imaginations.

Life expectancy for those who were not selected for immediate gassing was three to six months. Even those who were treated "well" lived only a few months longer. I have attempted not to trivialize the calamity or the experiences of those who suffered horribly and died in the camps. I hope I achieved that objective.

FORWARD

by
Rabbi James A. Gibson
Temple Sinai, Pittsburgh, PA
Spring, 2016

More than 70 years after the Holocaust, we still suffer from its trauma, either through direct memory or simply its legacy.

It has become a template upon which we tell our own stories of love, desire, betrayal, faith, commitment, and revenge. The smaller dramas of our lives today are intensified with the Holocaust as a backdrop.

The most authentic books and movies that draw on the Holocaust refuse to draw black-and-white judgments about event and behavior. We are gripped by the struggle of Jewish Kapos or Sonderkommando members. We realize that each decision they made to live might have required yet another betrayal of themselves or their people. Even the members of the Jewish Councils (Judenrate) that helped the Nazis with their meticulously planned murder of entire Jewish communities were neither wholly good nor wholly evil.

Today we view all who cooperated with the Kingdom of Night (as Elie Wiesel terms the Nazi world) as collaborators, worthy of contempt, beyond forgiveness. But honesty requires us to see their acts through the lens of ambiguity, even though judging them would be far easier. Ambiguity demands that we evaluate people and their behavior without the cheap comfort of moral certainty.

That is what David Tannenbaum asks of us in his compelling novel, *Out Of The Depths*. His protagonist, Dr. Bernard Helgman, carries an impossible burden; he is ceaselessly haunted by what he was forced to do to survive in the most notorious of the camps, Auschwitz. By becoming a healer he struggles to give his life meaning in the wake of atrocity. By selfless application of his world-class surgical skills he seeks to counterbalance any wrongs—real or imagined—that he may have committed in the camp. He not only heals children's bodies through his skill as a doctor, but he also heals their souls through his exquisite talent as a clown and magician.

One would think that years of healing and saving lives would attenuate the memory of trauma and the guilt that attends it. But we discover that it does not. Memory, guilt, shame and even passion will not be silenced so easily. Author Tannenbaum brings Dr. Helgman into full confrontation with all of his deepest drives and passions, from intense love to the deepest hatred and every emotional note in between.

Forced to confront his past, desperate to hold on to his present, terrified for his future, Dr. Helgman's world comes to a knife's edge. There he experiences a long-suppressed desire for intimacy as well as for revenge. The memories and legacies of the Holocaust are inescapable. Is Helgman forever doomed to remain their victim, even though he is thousands of miles and decades away from the heart of death called Auschwitz? Or can he somehow break free? Painful though it may be, immersing ourselves in that struggle is why we read novels like this one.

Strap yourselves in and hold on to your hats. The rollercoaster ride is about to begin. David Tannenbaum offers us a ride we could not have bargained for. See you on the other side.

PROLOGUE

1947

Dr. Seymour Katz, Chief of Surgery at the University of Pittsburgh Medical Center, again studied the papers on his desk, not so much for what they said, but for what they didn't say. Sitting stock still across from him was a young man, barely out of his teens who, but for the paperwork, Katz would have pegged as being in his thirties. The hardened eyes alone proclaimed a man even much older.

"So you're from Germany," Katz finally said, moving on with the interview. "Liberated from Auschwitz."

"Birkenau, actually. Two years ago last week."

"And so where were you between then and now?"

"Switzerland. In a rehabilitation center."

"You were one of the lucky ones then. Many who were liberated didn't make it that far. Is that where you learned English—in Switzerland?"

"Yes, sir," Bernard Helgman answered, careful not to react to being labeled *lucky*.

"You don't have much of an accent."

"My father also taught me as a young boy," Helgman volunteered.

At the mention of his father, Katz noticed an ever so brief softening around his visitor's eyes. "And now you're twenty one?"

"That is correct."

"And you want me to take you on as a surgical resident despite your age?"

"That is what I want. Yes."

1

"I can hardly believe you have even a basic medical education, what with being in the camp and your age and all. But these papers show that you do."

"I can assure you, sir, I'm qualified," the young man replied matter-of-factly. "I learned from medical books in the camp infirmary. And then I helped the doctors in the rehab hospital and pretty much lived in the hospital medical library."

"I presume you were malnourished when you arrived. How could you find the strength to study medicine while you were recovering?"

"I wasn't as bad as the others." Helgman hoped Katz wouldn't delve into why that was the case. Nor did Helgman tell Katz that he had also learned magic—this from a magician who came to the hospital to cheer up the patients —and that he was well on his way to becoming an accomplished illusionist.

Katz turned the pages of the file, found what he wanted, and pulled the sheet toward him. "Your test score results." He tapped the paper. "The same tests all of our medical school graduates take. I must confess I rarely see scores like these. You must have had some teacher. Was your father a doctor?"

"A lawyer."

"What about surgical training?"

"Some." The boy looked down at his feet.

Katz stood. "Come with me," he said. "Let's see how much hands-on surgery you've had. I know what you've learned from books."

Katz led the way to the basement anatomy lab, while replaying in his mind the circumstances under which this man, this boy actually, had come to him. A colleague had conveyed a message that an anonymous person—who insisted on remaining anonymous—promised to donate millions of dollars to the medical school, provided Katz accepted the boy into a surgical residency. Not a man to be bought off, Katz promised himself that if he had even the slightest doubt about the boy's surgical potential, he would not accept the proposition, despite the boy's unusually high test scores—and despite the money.

Two hours later, Katz had his answer. He was excited to realize that he could adopt this young doctor as his protégée and steer him to greatness.

Now all he had to do was deal with the paperwork required by the Pennsylvania State Board of Medicine. Being chairman of that board made that task easier than it might otherwise have been.

BOOK
ONE
1956-1957

ONE

Stephanie Grenoble and Bernard Helgman first met during the Thanksgiving weekend. Their meeting was accidental, Stephanie having come home to Block Island at the last minute. It wasn't until much later that Stephanie came to suspect, and ultimately confirm, that she and Helgman had met many years earlier under circumstances intentionally shrouded in mystery.

Stephanie was Radcliffe yearbook editor and she had intended to spend a long quiet weekend in Boston designing the pictorial layout that was due before the Christmas break. But pressure from her family finally persuaded her to travel to the family home on Block Island to attend the traditional family Thanksgiving dinner with her mother, father, and her Uncle Dieter. Aunt Gretchen, Dieter's wife of more than fifty years, had died in the spring and this would be Dieter's first Thanksgiving without her. Stephanie keenly felt the burden of being the only child of the two families and this year it manifested itself in the guilt she was experiencing with her decision to remain in Boston.

Her guilt, however, was tempered by her relationship with her uncle Dieter—a relationship that had become strained of late. Stephanie had long wanted to join the family shipping business, Green Lines Shipping, but Dieter had denied her every request. "It's a rough and tough business," he'd always said. "No place for a girl."

Otto Grenoble, her father who was president of the company, had pleaded her case several times. But Dieter, who was chairman, remained adamant.

Stephanie's mother had called yesterday—the fourth time in a week—and the message was not subtle this time. "You should be here." Her mother's tone was a combination of demanding and begging. "My brother is without his wife. I know you and Dieter have differences, but he loves you.

You can go back to Boston on the Friday morning ferry. Thanksgiving won't be the same for any of us without you."

Earlier in the day Dieter himself had called, something he rarely did. He all but demanded her presence at Thanksgiving dinner. "Bring your project with you," he urged. "The salt air will clear the spider webs. You'll think better."

"I need time to myself." Stephanie treaded lightly with her uncle despite her anger. Thanksgiving was important to him, she knew, because he was a naturalized citizen and this was an American holiday. America had taken him in after the war and he was indeed thankful. To this day he refused to discuss exactly how he had managed to take the shipping line with him when he fled from Germany to Greece—and then, when the war ended, to the United States. Stephanie's father cautioned her against pressing the question.

"We owe our lives to him—my life, your mother's life, and even yours. Your Uncle Dieter has forbidden discussion of Germany and our business there," her father said, "and we must respect his wishes."

Earlier, when her uncle had been on the line, in an attempt to sound reasonable, she'd said, "This project I'm working on is very important. It is part of my writing composition class grade and anything less than an 'A' ruins my chance for valedictorian. I may even need an 'A+' to make it."

"I'm deeply disappointed in your decision." Dieter brushed aside her reasons for remaining in Boston during the break. "It'll not be Thanksgiving without you here with us." Dieter did not take kindly to what he regarded as Stephanie's disobedience and his tone of voice made that all too clear.

Now, with the dorm mostly empty, it was actually too quiet to concentrate on the yearbook. Stephanie found her mind replaying conversations she'd had with her father. One of them particularly stood out. They had been sitting at a Boston wharf café the previous July when her father casually mentioned he was taking time off from work. "I'm going out to the cottage a month or so early this year," he said. "I can use a little R&R." Replaying both the words and the images, she realized that he'd seemed tired. In fact, he had wound up taking off the entire summer and didn't come back to work until late October. This now troubled her.

Rest and recuperation from what? It was useless to ask because health and business were topics that her parents and uncle refused to discuss with her.

Perhaps the insistence that she come for Thanksgiving was their way of telling her something. On impulse, she checked her watch, making a fast calculation as she did so. With luck, she could still make the late afternoon ferry from Point Judith.

Stephanie heard the ferry's one-minute warning whistle just before she turned the final bend to the wharf. The Golden Eagle rocked gently, straining against its dock lines as it waited impatiently for the last of the commuter cars to be driven aboard. The Eagle was Stephanie's favorite ferry, the very same one she had ridden on her first trip to Block Island eleven years earlier at the age of nine.

"Slow down, Miss Stephanie," a deck hand shouted as she ran across the gravel parking lot. "We ain't never left you before, have we?" His leathery face, missing all its front teeth, broke into a smile. The man's callused hand was locked around a docking line leading to a massive bollard. "Saw you drivin' in, Missy, and you still goin' way too fast. Better slow yourself down. We ain't fixin' to leave for at least another five seconds."

"Must have left school early, Mr. Griffith," she said, her own smile broadening further than his. "Can't imagine how I allowed so much extra time."

"Picked a nice day, you did. Water's cooperatin'. Light's good. Not much chop. Bein' a nice ride."

The whistle sounded and Griffith flipped the line over the bollard. The ferry slowly backed away from land, gaining speed as it moved down the river leading out past the long jetty and into the sound. The ship's motion grew more pronounced as the boat moved further offshore. The breeze continued to freshen and Stephanie soon pulled a sweater from her bag and slipped it over her head.

Griffith appeared with a hot chocolate, something he always did when she rode with him across Block Island Sound. Stephanie held the steaming cup between her palms, finding comfort in the rich aroma.

The jetty receded into the distance and the Golden Eagle now rose and fell in a comforting rhythm. White gulls, their wing tips mottled brown, hung suspended behind the vessel as if waiting for a handout.

As usual, the motion of the ferry relaxed her. She allowed her head to rest on the back of the stern-facing bench, the salt air working its invigorating magic. One by one, the gulls peeled off until only a single bird, its eyes focused directly on Stephanie, hung in the air. Then, with a dip of its graceful wings, it too disappeared, precisely as the land behind the ferry fused with the water into a single dark silhouette framed against the late afternoon sky.

Soon they would approach what she always thought of as the point of no return, the place where she could not see land in any direction. Stephanie walked forward knowing it would be a while before Block Island would be visible ahead, but not taking any chances of missing the island's bluffs as they first appeared in the far distance.

The water reminded Stephanie of many hours spent standing in her father's office overlooking Boston Harbor watching the ships move in and out. They came from strange and exciting sounding ports, their horns and whistles calling attention to themselves, their flags proclaiming their foreign pedigrees.

She had studied the wall charts and knew the shipping capitals of the world long before she learned all of the U. S. state capitals. From the shipping news, she kept track of ship arrivals and departures. She never missed the opportunity to take up binoculars and, watching the harbor entrance, announce in her deepest little girl voice, "The steam vessel Anastasia, fifty days out of Tyre, now entering Boston Harbor!"

She would then laugh at her own silliness, with the office staff joining in.

Now Stephanie refocused her attention on the horizon just in time to see the dark shape ahead morph into a land mass colored with the familiar hues of the bluff. Her beloved Block Island was rising from the water to meet her.

As the ferry passed through the breakwater into the harbor, Stephanie thought of her uncle Dieter and visualized him standing on a ledge atop the bluffs at sundown as he did every day when he was on the island. Many a time she had hiked up to talk with him on the bluffs, high above the Atlantic, looking down on the waves pounding the rocks and, later, watching the light fade over the water. For as far back as she could remember, Stephanie's best conversations with her uncle had been there on the bluff. It had been at those times that she found him accessible, a wholly different person from his normally closed-off self.

And then there were times when the two of them would just stand there, her uncle lost in faraway thoughts and Stephanie looking down as a bird would, watching the surf crash against the rocks, throwing spray upwards toward her. Then, looking up, she would see the gulls soaring gracefully in an updraft, twisting their wings ever so slightly to send them plunging downward to snatch a morsel from the sea. The violence, the serenity, the continuum of nature, all played out for her on the bluff.

"Nice weekend, Missy," Griffith called, interrupting Stephanie's reverie as she stepped onto the wharf. "See you lost in thought. Take a load from your mind out here, you hear? And don't be eatin' too much of that ole bird."

"Thanks, Mr. Griffith. You too. Hope the weather holds."

"Oh, it will, Miss Stephanie. At least till Sunday. Can't go promisin' no further than that. No ma'am, I can't. But Turkey Day, now that'd be a promise."

"You've always been right. Best weatherman I know."

"I calls it the way it is. No reason for foolin' nobody with fancy talkin'. No hot dog and beer forecast like they does on the radio."

Walking across the parking lot, Stephanie's thoughts again turned to her uncle. There was still enough time to catch up with him, she realized, but only if she hurried.

TWO

A second passenger from the ferry also made his way to the wind-blown bluffs, as unaware of Stephanie as she was of him. He had spent the ferry ride much as Stephanie had, huddled in self-reflection. Had Stephanie noticed him, she would have observed a man with his head down, apparently asleep. On closer inspection, she would have noticed his fingers opening and closing rapidly. She would also have seen a man almost double her age with a ruggedly-handsome face. She would have described him as agitated and very troubled.

This wasn't the first ferry ride to Block Island for Bernard Helgman. His previous trip was to satisfy himself that the Dieter Schmidt he had located after some quiet detective work was the same Dieter Schmidt who had turned over a child, who had been called Max, to the Gestapo in exchange for exit visas for himself, his wife, his sister, her husband, and their daughter. He was now absolutely positive that this Dieter Schmidt, now of Block Island, Rhode Island, USA, was the man responsible for all that had happened to young Max in a German concentration camp.

Helgman lost track of the number of times he had forgiven Schmidt, only to wake in a cold tormented sweat. Nightmares were coming more regularly of late and were keeping Helgman awake for longer stretches of time. He could only believe that his torment would continue until Dieter Schmidt owned up to what he had done.

For months, Helgman contemplated taking his own life, several times even filling a syringe and lining up the needle against an artery. At each moment of decision, the deformed face of a child he had recently repaired appeared in his mind's eye. Without his dedication and skill, children like them would live their lives with deformities. He just couldn't countenance that. So each time he threw the lethal syringe away.

Today was the day. Helgman had learned from his previous visit that the old man meditated daily on a deserted bluff. In his fantasy, it would be a simple matter to come up from behind, shove the bastard off the rock ledge, and retreat to the ferry. Easy. The world would be a better place without people like Dieter Schmidt.

The summit was now only yards ahead of him and Schmidt had just disappeared over the crest. Helgman held fast to his resolve to confront Dieter Schmidt and insist that he face up to the terrible wrong he had done to the young Max. He rushed forward, pausing for only an instant before going over the top and down toward the target of his hatred.

THREE

"Stephanie!" It was the voice of her parents' next-door neighbor, a bag of groceries in each hand. "I thought you weren't coming home this year. Your mother's been so disappointed. Just this morning she—"

"She still doesn't know," Stephanie said, upset at this kink in her plans. "I had school work, but decided to come at the last minute. How are you getting along, Mrs. Davis? Sorry about your knee. Mother told me."

"It's actually much better, thanks. I can go shopping myself now, but only if I don't buy too many heavy things."

"Can I carry something for you?"

"My car's just over there. If you'll load these bags for me, that'll be nice. And then can I drop you home?"

"No thanks. I prefer walking."

"Just over there" was a block and a half away. Once the bags had been loaded, Stephanie wished the woman a Happy Thanksgiving.

"Thank you. It'll be nice," the neighbor replied. "I have to hurry home and put my pies in the oven. Phil's coming tomorrow. Want to stop by? He'll be here till Sunday."

Philip was the eldest of the family's three sons. The last time Stephanie's mother had spoken of him, she reported that he had a drinking problem. Philip Davis was the last person in the world Stephanie wanted to see. "No thanks," she replied. "I'm going to spend the time with my parents. Maybe next visit."

Stephanie checked her watch and saw she could still make it to the bluffs before Dieter started home. She turned off the road and hurried across a barren field, the summer corn stalks plowed under. She came out of the field nearly halfway up the hill and followed the familiar landmarks until reaching the intersecting main path leading to the bluffs.

Her uncle, she knew, would be on the far side, out of view, most likely staring down at the water, absorbed in thought.

A man walking briskly appeared from her right. Stephanie stopped in anticipation of him turning down the path in her direction. Instead, he moved toward and then over the summit and she followed at a distance. Something in his purposeful stride seemed menacing and she watched him carefully. She made him to be about age 35 possibly 40, dark hair and around six feet tall.

Her uncle was exactly where she had expected him to be, his head bent forward apparently unaware of the stranger behind him. The man was a fair distance behind Dieter and standing stock still, except for his hands which were alternately clenching and opening.

The stranger turned slightly, displaying the profile of a strong, handsome face. Stephanie was struck by his rugged good looks and felt foolish for having suspected him. Embarrassed about intruding on his private space, she waited to see what would happen. Her foot slipped on the incline, sending a trail of stones down in his direction.

Responding to a pebble hitting the back of his ankle, the man turned on his heels and saw Stephanie. He started back up the hill toward her. Not knowing his intentions, she ran up to the summit and then back down the path.

But Stephanie wasn't fast enough and the man knocked into her as he rushed past, sending her sprawling into a jagged rock formation at the side of the trail.

A conversation Stephanie had overheard years before forced its way into her consciousness. "It is so peaceful on this island," her uncle had said to her father. "I hope to live out my days with no more violence."

Stephanie had no idea how that conversation was related to what had just happened, but she felt a connection.

Still on the ground, Stephanie's thoughts were interrupted by a realization that the stranger was coming back toward where she lay. He quickly closed the distance between them and she was again transfixed by his handsome face, framed by bushy eyebrows. His piercing steel gray eyes, which she had previously only caught a glimpse of, suggested a keen intellect.

"I'm sorry." The man reached down to help her up. "Lost in my own thoughts, I'm afraid."

His voice was soft, almost too soft. She recognized a faint German accent, identical to what she heard at home. Stephanie said nothing, and did not reach for his hand.

"Guess I didn't expect to see anyone on the trail." His eyes locked onto hers and held fast, as if he were trying to see into her mind.

She knew she should be frightened, but nothing in his manner provoked any feelings of fear. *Speak up or remain silent? Am I in danger? What about Uncle Dieter?* Playing for time, Stephanie allowed the man to pull her up.

The stranger then turned as if intent on going back up the hill. Finding her legs, Stephanie took a quick step forward but lost her balance again. This time her head hit the edge of the rock formation and blood gushed from a deep cut across her forehead. A shadow passed over her and now her senses were on full alert. She cringed, expecting something to happen.

She raised her head just in time to see the man jam a hand into his coat pocket and pull out a white cloth as he advanced toward her.

Concluding that the man intended to gag her, Stephanie's previous sense of disquiet turned into adrenaline-fueled fear. She resolved to kick him when he got close enough and then run for help. She timed his movements, but he suddenly arrested his forward motion and her foot only grazed him.

"Listen. No, I mean, I'm sorry I scared you!" The tall stranger waved the small handkerchief as a flag of truce. "Here, you can wipe the blood yourself," he said, holding out the handkerchief.

Stephanie tentatively reached for the handkerchief and, as she did, the man bent close and peered. "That laceration will definitely require sutures," he announced.

"I can take care of myself," she shot back, standing to face him. "Just leave me ... us ... alone!"

"Sorry," he said, "but without proper suturing you'll have a permanent scar." The man studied her a moment, then added, "Here, put my jacket on." She was shivering, more from the anticipated violence than from the chill in the air. "Is there a doctor in town? Can't do much out here."

Stephanie brushed past him and walked to the top of the hill. Dieter was sitting on the rock where she herself always sat when they were together, oblivious to all that had gone on just over the crest of the hill behind him. She wanted to go to him, but how would she explain the gash on her forehead without telling her uncle about the stranger? Better to leave it alone, she concluded, until she had time to think it through.

Her head throbbed. She felt dizzy, nauseous. Her knees buckled and she began to fall, but the stranger came up from behind and was there to catch her.

FOUR

"What'd you say?" The man sat down beside Stephanie.

"Doc McGee is the only doctor on the island," Stephanie said, slowly starting to stand. "The dizziness is gone, but I feel—"

"No, don't try to get up just yet. Give it a moment."

Stephanie continued to stand up anyway and the stranger grabbed her arm. "Let's get you over to this Doc McGee and get you fixed up."

"He can patch a scraped knee or a leg, but not much else. He's been trying to retire for years but they can't get anyone to take his place."

"Let's go anyway. If he can't deal with it, I will."

"*You* will? I don't even know who you are," she protested.

"Oh, sorry. My name's Bernard Helgman. I'm a surgeon. Pediatric reconstruction. Mostly burn repair."

"And I'm Stephanie Grenoble. This is all so strange. I don't think I should—"

"Come," Helgman managed. "Time is wasting. We need to get to McGee's office before they close. We can talk later."

Dr. McGee was currently making a house call, his nurse explained. She examined Stephanie's forehead and agreed that sutures would be required. "You'll have to go over to the mainland to get it done. Won't look pretty if Doc McGee does it. His eyesight's not what it used to be."

"I'm a reconstructive surgeon," Helgman said. "Bernard Helgman. Let's get her into a treatment room and I'll do it."

"Absolutely not," the nurse shot back. "I can't—"

"You can call my office and my nurse will ... better yet, you can call my hospital."

"Absolutely not," the nurse reaffirmed her position.

"If you don't, as you just said, this young woman will have a nasty scar. I can't believe you want that."

"She can take the ferry over—"

"Please. Just call the hospital. Here's the number. Ask for the administrator, Stanton Preston."

The nurse studied Helgman a long while and then relented. "You win. Miss Grenoble's family will never forgive me. The two of you just wait right here." She disappeared into a back room, and when she returned, simply said, "Follow me."

The nurse ushered them into a treatment room and busied herself laying out sutures, dressings, a large syringe and a bottle labeled Xylocaine. That done, she retreated to the door where she planted her feet, intent on remaining in the room.

Helgman scrubbed at the sink, then turned to Stephanie. "One stick and that's all you'll feel."

"The way my head's throbbing, I won't even feel that."

"I can't promise to make your head feel any better, but at least you won't feel anything I do. Just hold still."

Helgman worked carefully but quickly and soon stepped back. "Good as new," he pronounced. "You'll barely see the scar when it heals."

The door opened and McGee entered. The nurse introduced Helgman to the old doctor, quickly explained what was going on, and then slipped out. McGee picked up a magnifying glass and studied the sutures. "Well done, lad. Well done! Never seen a stitch like this in all my years. Don't reckon there'll be any scar, not even a line. You're lucky Miss Grenoble. Thought I'd about seen it all."

"Learned from the best," Helgman replied, while dressing the wound.

A few minutes later Stephanie and Helgman were on the walkway leading from McGee's office when a ship whistle blew two piercing blasts. "Is that the ferry leaving?" Helgman asked.

Stephanie nodded.

"I had planned to be on that ferry," he said. "And it's the last one, right?"

"Afraid so. Sorry." She didn't sound sorry at all.

"Well then I'm stuck," he said with an air of resignation. "Where can I find a room?"

Stephanie pointed across the winding street to the Old Island Hotel. It was a visitor favorite, with its wrap-around porch, comfortable lobby, and year-round wood-burning fireplace that conveyed Old World comfort. "They'll make room for you," she said. "You're not the first person to miss the last ferry."

"This is not good. I have a perform—I mean I have to be at the office in the morning."

"Haven't you lost track of the date, Dr. Helgman?" Stephanie asked. "Tomorrow's Thanksgiving. Isn't your office closed until Monday?"

"I have ... Oh. Of course," Helgman replied. "Don't know what I was thinking. And please," he added, "call me Bernard."

"Okay, Bernard then."

This last gesture, combined with the fact that he had been nothing but solicitous of her since their first encounter on the bluff, caused Stephanie to decide that the disquiet and nagging suspicions she'd had about Bernard Helgman were the product of an overactive imagination. He was a doctor, after all, and a very accomplished one, too, as Doc McGee had confirmed.

With uncharacteristic boldness, she met his overture with one of her own. "Listen," Stephanie found herself saying, "since you've got some time off, why not stay at least until Friday? In fact, I can be your tour guide. We can go where the locals hang out, walk along the beach, watch the breaking waves. Come," she urged, without waiting for an answer. "I'll walk you over to the hotel."

As predicted, the hotel had a room for Helgman. "Let's have a coffee on the porch," he suggested, after he had checked in. "It's not too cold is it?"

"Sounds nice," Stephanie said. They took coffee from an urn standing on a table in the lobby and then walked out onto the porch, where they sat at a small table at one end.

"You didn't say whether you'd stay and let me show you around," Stephanie said after they had sat in silence for a moment. "In fact," she added, "if you stay tomorrow you can have Thanksgiving dinner with us. My parents live in Boston, but they have a home here as well. I'm a senior at Radcliffe and I'm home for the holiday. And my uncle Dieter is here too."

Helgman's face set hard. *Dieter? Damn!* He made a show of thinking over her offer before answering. "Thank you. It's very kind, but Thanksgiving with your family is out of the question."

"No really," Stephanie insisted. "My family loves to have company. It would be great."

"I can't," Helgman replied. "Listen, I have to tell you something."

"Tell me what?"

"Your Uncle Dieter. He's Dieter Schmidt, right?"

"Yes, but how would you—"

"No, listen," Helgman repeated. "It was no coincidence I was up on the bluff when I was. I know your Uncle Dieter and I knew he'd be there."

Stephanie's eyes went wide. She sat motionless trying to absorb what Helgman just told her. Helgman, for his part, waited for her to respond.

"*What* did you say?" It was all she could manage when she found her voice.

"I know him," he repeated. "We've known each other since ... since Germany."

"So then you and my uncle were friends?"

Helgman's eyes went hard and his jaw drew tight. "Friends? Not friends. In fact, I have only the bitterest of feelings toward him."

"Then what were you doing up there?" Stephanie was still trying to make sense of all this.

Helgman debated how much he should tell her. This, after all, was Dieter's niece so he knew who she was, but obviously not the other way around. The year was 1941, he was fifteen and had been living with Dieter and Gretchen as their supposed son, Max. It did not surprise Helgman that the woman now sitting across from him, the woman who would have been three, perhaps four, at the time, didn't know who he was since they had been in each other's presence only a few times in the year that he had lived with the Schmidts. How Dieter had explained Max's disappearance he could only guess. Perhaps she'd been told that Max had been killed by the Gestapo. But it really wasn't important what he'd said. Max was gone from their lives, abandoned to the Nazis as the family's ticket to freedom. Helgman needed more time to think this through.

"It's a long and painful story," he said finally, "Maybe someday we can discuss it, but can we just leave it for now?"

"I suppose." Stephanie was disappointed that he wouldn't confide in her now, but she was determined to change that.

"Good. Thank you. Can we talk about you now? You're at Radcliffe. But what else?"

"You know it's funny," Stephanie replied. "Yes, Radcliffe. In one sense, my life seems so full, always running here and there, doing this and that. But whenever I've tried to summarize myself it always comes down to name, rank, and serial number. But here goes."

In spite of herself, Stephanie found she could talk to this man as she'd never spoken to anyone before. After an hour, Helgman said, "You better get on home before they send out a search party for you."

"Actually, no one even knows I'm here. They wanted me to come out, but I had work to do and told them no. But I changed my mind and caught the ferry on the spur of the moment." Stephanie paused and studied a sea gull for a long moment before continuing. "I don't know how to say this, so I'll just blurt it out. It's weird, but I feel I've known you all my life. You're easy to talk with and you're not ... not obsessed with cars and sports."

"You're right. I don't care one bit about things like that. But how'd you know?"

"It's just a feeling. Is that strange to say after just a few hours?"

"I suppose, but—"

"Things happen for a reason. I really believe that. I've had such a good time. I've enjoyed our time together—despite the stitches. I'll come by for you later, about nine. We can talk some more. The island's a special place at night."

He stood. "Not tonight, I'm afraid. In the morning you can show me around before I leave."

"Okay." Stephanie was disappointed. "I'll come by at eight thirty. You can take the noon ferry."

Helgman watched as Stephanie's silhouette dissolved into the distance. Since leaving the camp, this was the first woman he'd ever been able to speak with on a personal level without his stomach knotting up. He felt a connection and found himself wanting—hungering—to know her better. However, the camp had left a terrible legacy, the inability to have a normal sexual involvement with a woman. Pursuing a relationship with Stephanie, he knew, could only lead to frustration and pain for both of them. Yet....

Helgman lay in his bed listening to the gulls cawing in their endless circling overhead, screeching in playful flight as they waited for darkness, safety, and ultimately, rest. He envied their freedom to soar, to be free, to move with the wind currents. He craved a freedom like that for himself. But the only kind of freedom he ever achieved was a false one; when he painted his face and then peered out at the world over a clown's nose.

FIVE

It was early, the sun just beginning to spread light on the water. "I'll be back after lunch, Mother," Stephanie said at breakfast. She hoped her mother's sensitive antennae did not pick up the excitement rising within her. "What time's dinner?"

"Usual Thanksgiving time, three thirty, and ... " Hilda Grenoble paused.

"And what?"

Stephanie's mother let out a heavy sigh. "Something's not right here," she began. "You didn't come right here when you got off the boat. Maybe you went to the bluffs, but Dieter says he didn't see you there. You acted so strange at dinner last night and you won't explain that bandage on your forehead." She paused yet again as Stephanie buttered her toast for the second time.

"It's nothing, Mother. I already told you. I tripped when I got off the boat. It's nothing. I stopped at Doc McGee's and his nurse cleaned it and put the bandage on."

"Really, now." Hilda remained unconvinced.

"Listen, Mother," Stephanie snapped, instantly sorry for the outburst. "I'm upset enough and I don't want to talk about it."

"Upset about what?"

"You know," she replied, stalling to give herself time to think. "My ... my future. I've been trying to figure out how to convince Uncle Dieter to let me work for Green Lines."

Hilda took a deep breath. "I'll speak to him myself, if you want."

"No, Mother, please stay out of this. If you must know, I was going to the bluffs to speak with Uncle Dieter. That's where I fell."

"Oh. Well, you can talk to him tomorrow then."

"Anyway, why does he get all the say and not Father?"

"Leave it alone, my dear. Please. It's ancient history."

"I'm not a baby anymore! Don't treat me like one!"

"The past was an unpleasant time for us. People did things they ... they may now regret. Survival was what mattered. Survival at all costs. We are paying the true price for our survival now." She touched Stephanie's shoulder. "Enough of this. Let us speak of pleasant things."

"Yes, let's. I met Mrs. Davis yesterday in town. Did she tell you?"

"That's how I knew you were on the island. Imagine how I felt when you did not come home. She—"

"I told you I fell."

" ... told me you were seen with a man at the hotel."

"A friend."

"So bring your friend home so we can all—"

"Mother!"

"You're so sensitive. Why?"

Stephanie didn't respond at first. Part of her wanted to confide in her mother about this attractive man. Did her mother believe in love at first sight? How would Stephanie know love when she felt it? She had certainly never experienced anything like this before. What might her mother know about Bernard and her Uncle Dieter? One thing she knew for sure: she had hardly slept last night planning her day on the island, imagining the feel of sand on her bare feet, Bernard's arm around her waist, even at one point, envisoning herself in a white dress arm-in-arm with her father.

And then she decided. "Mother, can't a person have any privacy?"

"He's gone Steph," the hotel owner, a longtime friend of the family, announced when Stephanie walked briskly into the lobby. "Up early and took the ferry at first light."

"I didn't know—"

"New this year. Can't imagine many people using it on Thanksgiving, but the state has a new policy. Ferry's gotta keep its schedule, no matter what. Even Christmas."

Stephanie tried to hide her disappointment, but her shoulders slumped anyway.

She walked the island from end to end, kicking at the sand she loved, angry with the waves splashing her feet, even throwing a stone at a silvery gull. The first stone she had ever thrown at a living creature.

Stephanie barely knew this Bernard Helgman, but she found him to be incredibly complex—more so than any person she'd ever known. She couldn't stop thinking about him, recalling the texture of his skin, the scars on his face, the gentleness of his touch. She tried to convince herself that this man could not be the real source of her turmoil—that her disquiet was all about Dieter and his refusal to allow her to follow her dream.

But deep within her—in that place where emotion trumps rationality—she knew that the real source of her agitation was Helgman, not Dieter.

***

"Hey!" Stephanie called out when her roommate, Nancy, slipped into their dorm room just after Sunday night curfew. "I need your experienced advice."

"Let me pee first," Nancy replied. A moment later, she was sitting cross-legged on her bed while Stephanie paced the tiny room. "Let me guess. It's a guy, right?"

"He's older than me and ... well, I only met him over the weekend. I've only actually known him a few hours."

"Oh, the love at first sight thing! Well, why not? What's his name?"

Stephanie wanted to say "Bernie," but Bernie didn't seem to fit. "Bernard," she answered. "He's a doctor. But here's the strange thing. We only spent a few hours together and yet ... yet, I feel I've known him my entire life."

"Anything to do with that bandage on your forehead?"

Stephanie didn't want to talk about what happened on the bluffs, so she evaded the question. "He was born in Germany and there's something wrong from the past between him and my uncle. He looks older than he actually is."

"So what's the problem? Oh ... " Nancy broke into a knowing grin. "Was it something *else* at first sight?"

"Uh-uh." Stephanie closed her eyes, and involuntarily shivered as she again imagined Helgman's gentle touch. "Nothing like that happened. But truth be told, Nan, I would have if he'd even so much as hinted. I never felt like this."

Stephanie threw herself on the bed next to her roommate and everything that happened on Block Island spilled out.

When Stephanie finished, Nancy gave her assessment. "Girl meets boy. Boy seems interested, but really not. Girl is broken hearted. It's the story of life, my friend. Get over it."

"I wish it was that easy." Stephanie fought back tears. "I don't even really know him. I don't even know where he lives. That's so stupid, right? I feel like a love-struck teenager. But truth is, I can't get him out of my mind."

"How many times have I told you? You can't live with 'em and you can't live without 'em."

"You, my dear friend, are no help. I'm dying here and all I get are trite comments."

"You want something profound? Try this, *my* dear friend. You need a man." Nancy patted the bed. "I've been telling you that all semester. But no. Not you. Saving yourself for Mister Right. Well, Steph, there just isn't a Mister Right. He doesn't exist."

The semester ended and soon enough a new one began. It was Stephanie's last.

In mid-February, talk turned to late-winter break and the debate over beaches and mountains began in earnest. Places full of people and places isolated from it all. Cold places for skiing and warm places for swimming and water-skiing. And beer-drinking in any climate.

Usually, Stephanie would get excited for weeks before winter break, making meticulous plans but always making new ones at the last minute. Ft. Lauderdale one year, Stowe the next. The previous year she and Nancy joined a group for a week at a new resort in Acapulco.

Nancy called from the bathroom, "You haven't packed a thing and the guys'll be here any minute. We're already late and planes don't wait. Hurry."

"I'm not going."

"What?" Nancy threw her hairbrush into the already over-stuffed suitcase and began forcing it closed. "You're crazy. You know that? Now pack, we gotta go. This is your last winter break."

"It's all so foolish. You're going down there to drink yourself silly. Maybe, if you get lucky, you'll end up with a one-day love affair that'll take you months to get over."

"Look who's talking about love affairs. How long was it? An hour? And you're still in the dumps. Get over it already!"

"I need time by myself. Drink a few for me. I think I'll go out to the island. I need to speak with my uncle."

"That's what you said at Thanksgiving. You need time by yourself. Look what happened. You're driving me crazy. Come with us. You'll meet someone and that'll get your mind off ... *Bernard*."

"Go already," Stephanie replied. "No more lectures. I'm doing a good job lecturing myself."

"Not a lecture, my friend. Just the facts. You don't even know him. He's a dream, a fantasy! Forget him."

"I wish it was that easy. As soon as I think I'm beyond him I feel his hand on mine. So gentle." She stroked the now almost invisible line of the wound that had healed so well. "I know it's corny, but he's part of me."

A horn sounded.

"They're here!" Nancy sat on her suitcase and forced the snaps to catch. The bag looked ready to burst.

"What the hell you got in there? For a person who wears so little on the beach I'd think a handbag would be enough."

Nancy threw a pillow at her. "Last chance. I'll hold them up if you hurry. Throw something in a bag. You can buy what else you need."

Stephanie remained silent.

"Okay. Have it your way. I'll bring you a souvenir." The door closed behind her.

Then it opened again. Nancy poked her head back into the room. "Don't just lay on that bed all week feeling sorry for yourself. If you won't come with us, then go to Dr. Wonderful. He can't be all that hard to find. Get it out of your system once and for all."

SIX

Terror displaced anxious expectation. Certainly it was not the upcoming performance. Nor was it the terrible atrocities he had witnessed behind the barbed wire of the concentration camp. The brutality was forever seared into his soul and never allowed him a moment's reprieve except when he performed for the children. No, the beads of sweat that broke through the layers of greasepaint came from his deep-seated fear that his real identity would surface and all that he had created since his liberation from the camp would be stripped away.

From behind the curtain, he studied the audience of young vulnerable faces, knowing that only a lucky few would be alive a year hence and that some would die within the month. Each young expectant face concealed a private truth behind innocent eyes—eyes that, could they penetrate the greasepaint, would know his own private truth and the profound sadness hidden underneath the red and white makeup.

The children came from their sickbeds, some with tubes still attached, and the voice was that of the hospital's chief administrator, acting as announcer. The clown, lost in his own private hell, rarely listened. It was a world he allowed no one else to enter.

"And now," the chief intoned, "the funniest clown of them all. He doesn't say much. In fact, he doesn't say anything. But he's a clown so funny ... "

Muggs closed his eyes, forcing his mind to focus only on the children.

" ... and here he comes ... Muggs the Clown!"

Little hands went wild. Anxious eyes turned to the curtain. The applause and shouts once again lifted the man from his private world as the mask of the clown locked tightly onto his face. His eyes came alive with the only joy he could ever know as the children screamed his name, their focus turned outward away from their own pain, away from their silent suffering, away from their brave posturing.

Muggs ran to the front of the stage and suddenly his feet flew out from under him. The children gasped, their faces frozen with fright. A rocking chair appeared and Muggs landed upright in its seat sending a pot of flowers flying through the air. He lurched forward out of the chair, skidding across the floor and arriving just in time to catch the pot.

Then there were two flowerpots flying upward, and then three, following each other around in an arc, seemingly never touching his hands. The pots became volleyballs. One of them escaped the arc, flew across the stage, bounced off the chair and hit Muggs in the back of the head. The impact made his eyes cross. Then quarters flew from his ears.

Animated faces screamed in delight.

Muggs tumbled from the stage to be closer to the children, touching them, hugging them, and pulling coins from their noses and ears. A white bird escaped from inside the robe of a bed-ridden child, the girl's smooth scalp gleaming in the lights. The bird flew around the room, landing on the clown's head. The children screamed and pointed, all to no avail. Muggs shrugged in mock confusion and the shouting grew even louder. A boy ran up, pulled Muggs down on his knees, and grabbed for the bird, only to find it gone when he opened his hand.

Muggs worked the room, each patient receiving a gift that magically appeared in a lap, under a gown, or on a shoulder.

He flipped a coin to the head nurse, but her fingers closed on empty air when she reached up to catch it. Muggs strode over and pulled the coin from the startled nurse's ear. The children laughed and pointed at her. The nurse frowned and shook her fist. Birds appeared and just as quickly disappeared. A white dove became a rabbit. Then there were two rabbits. Then four.

The beads of sweat on Muggs's face blended with tiny tears in the corners of his eyes.

Muggs's performance had gone perfectly. The children loved his antics and especially the new trick where the kids poured magic sand into his hand and watched as a red rose grew right up through his fingers.

The hospital was located in upstate New York, a three-hour drive north of the city and this was one of his rare mid-week performances. Helgman had been at that hospital since early morning assisting in the facial reconstruction of a two-month-old girl who had been born without a nose or her left ear. As always, the hospital staff did not know the clown's real name or occupation.

Helgman had taken a motel room for the night, anticipating he would be too exhausted to drive home after the late afternoon performance. His plan was to leave early in the morning so he could be back in time for his morning rounds.

The ringing phone startled him. "Doctor Helgman, this is Doctor Smithington. I understand from your answering service that you are still in town. They gave me this number."

Helgman immediately thought of the infant girl. "Is there something wrong?"

"The little girl is doing fine. But we just admitted a four-year-old white male with first and second degree burns over ninety percent of his body. He was thrown, or fell, into an incinerator. Doesn't appear he'll make it through the night, but I thought—"

"Signs?" Helgman was instantly alert, sleep now far from his mind.

"Heart rate erratic. Pressure seventy over fifty. Temperature one hundred, but spiking. No apparent brain damage, but it's too early to know for certain. Several broken bones."

"Compound?"

"No, thank goodness."

"IV?"

"Started a few minutes ago."

"Please do nothing with his skin until I get there? Eyes?"

"Lashes gone. Eyes clear. We've started ophthalmological pads, changing them at minute intervals."

"Good. Give me ten minutes." Helgman walked quickly to the door, opened it and started down the hall toward the elevator. He had a sudden urge to urinate and knew that once he arrived at the hospital events would move quickly and it might be hours before he had another chance.

Back in his room, he turned on the bathroom light and was momentarily startled to see the face of a clown looking back at him. The big clown nose, the heavy makeup, hat pulled far down over his forehead and generous body padding had all been carefully designed to ensure that no one would ever recognize him. Indeed, for a moment, he almost fooled himself. He quickly cleaned the grease paint from his face, changed into street clothes, and raced to the hospital.

"He's worse than we first thought," Smithington said, when Helgman arrived. "Eighty to ninety percent tissue loss. He's only alive because the super heard screams and pulled the incinerator door open. That cut the flame off."

Helgman followed Smithington to the dressing room where they both scrubbed and changed into surgical gowns. A small figure surrounded by doctors and nurses was visible through a window and, as usual, Helgman paused a moment to reflect on the unfairness of scenes such as this, knowing full well they were repeated daily in hospitals across the country. Helgman silently asked the question he knew had no answer. *What did this innocent child do to deserve what happened to him?* He had first asked this question at the age of sixteen when he had been thrust into the midst of the "experiments." Only then it was the atrocities that were visited on women that had tormented him—as they still did.

Helgman, his mind now focused on the child in front of him, took his place beside Smithington. "Doctor Bernard Helgman," Smithington began, "as many of you already know, is a specialist in pediatric reconstruction. He has developed techniques that haven't yet gained wide acceptance. But his track record is excellent. I've asked for his help on this case and I'll be assisting."

Several pairs of eyes opened wide at this. Smithington was the chief of pediatric surgery and a man renowned in his own right. "Even I can learn from the best," he added, noting the questioning looks. "Now let's get to work and save this boy's life."

Helgman studied the young boy, his eyes taking in every inch of the small body. Then he said, "Even if we save his life, the morbidity in cases like this is high."

"It always is with this much trauma," Smithington answered, puzzled by the obviousness of the statement.

"But it need not be that way. I've been working on a technique to prevent scarring in such cases. It works well. But we have to start immediately. We need skin. Graftable skin. There isn't an inch we can harvest from the boy."

Smithington considered Helgman's request for a moment before responding. "Listen Bernard, I respect you. That's why you're here tonight. But beginning the grafting process this soon isn't, well, it isn't the way we do it here. We should clean the dead skin and—"

"I know it's unusual. But I've developed a process that'll work in this context. We cut the grafts into a mesh that allows the area of the graft to expand ten to one. So fifty square centimeters of skin will expand to cover five-hundred square centimeters of the child, more or less."

"I've never heard of such a thing. I can't allow—"

"As you yourself said, he'll not make it through the night with conventional protocols. If you won't follow my lead, then I don't understand why I'm even here."

Smithington studied Helgman a long moment. "Frankly, I was grasping at anything I could think of. But what you propose is ... is well outside the hospital's surgical guidelines. I can't—"

"Then there's nothing more I can do to help." Helgman turned toward the door. "I'm withdrawing from the procedure. Please excuse me."

"Wait," Smithington said, his eyes focused on a monitor. "What exactly do you require?"

"I'd say about five-hundred square centimeters which will expand to about five-thousand square centimeters. I propose two pieces each approximately sixteen centimeters square."

"That's much larger than we usually use."

"The mesh works better at this size. We'll set up a saline bath to promote skin growth. Scarring will be minimal. He could have tightness in his fingers and joints, but with time even that should resolve favorably. One of your team can repair the ears at a later time."

"He's type AB. That much we know."

"Excellent!" Helgman exclaimed. "That's the least likely to reject. A donor with AB would be best, but either A or B will work. We'll require two donors because of the graft size." Helgman studied the team, making eye contact with each of them. Then he said, "I'm looking for two skin donors. Preferably type AB."

They all became very busy doing their jobs. No one spoke. Eyes were no longer on Helgman. He said, "We can save this boy's life tonight and keep him from being scarred if we act quickly. Now do we have any volunteers? Type AB, if possible. But A or B will work as well."

A few minutes passed without any volunteers.

Then Helgman felt a slight tap on the shoulder. He turned to face a petite woman who had been sitting at a table in the corner of the room monitoring a small screen.

"I'm type AB," she said. "If it'll save his life, I'll do it."

"What is your name?"

"Alice. Alice Wilkinson."

"Okay, Alice, you're one. I need another." He turned to the head nurse and said, "Please arrange for a room for Alice. I'll be removing the tissue from her inner thigh. I require one nurse and a tissue transport." Helgman corrected himself. "Actually, we can use this room. Please bring in a gurney."

"Alice," he said, returning his attention to his donor, "when I'm finished you'll have a bandage on your leg for a few days, perhaps as long as a week. But when you heal, there will be only the smallest of scars. That much I promise."

"Thank you, Doctor. If it saves his life, then it's okay with me."

"I wish everyone had your attitude—and your compassion. We still need one more volunteer. Now, Alice, put on a patient gown so we can get started."

While Alice was changing, the head nurse rushed into the room. "Dr. Helgman," she called, showing the first signs of excitement Helgman had seen from her. "We found a skin graft, type AB, just about the right size."

"Okay. Now we can proceed."

The nurse lowered her voice so only Helgman could hear. "The only problem is that it belongs to Dr. Levinson. For a facial reconstruction tomorrow for some HS."

Helgman looked puzzled. "Hotshot politician," she added. "Dr. Levinson will be on the warpath when he finds the graft gone."

"You can tell him his graft saved this child's life."

"I'm afraid, sir, that'll make no difference to him." She hurried across the room, busying herself counting instruments.

Helgman asked Smithington to authorize the use of the needed skin graft. After several testy exchanges, Smithington held his ground. Helgman stormed from the operating room, threw his mask and gown on the floor, and was halfway across the parking lot before Smithington caught up to him.

"Okay, Bernard, you win. Come back inside and let's finish what we started."

"It's the boy who wins. This is not about me, it's about postponing Levinson's facial reconstruction by a few hours—or even a day. It's a small price to pay to save the boy's life."

"That's why I've agreed to go forward. But there'll be hell to pay."

Harvesting the skin graft from Alice went well. Helgman then fashioned it to his exact specifications before beginning work on the smaller graft that Dr. Levinson had intended to use. When satisfied, he turned to Smithington, "Is the saline bath at the right temperature?"

"It is."

"Excellent. Then I'll work under water. Place him in the tub. Take turns holding his head."

"I've never heard of such a thing," Smithington said. "Your ... your vision will be impaired, the sutures—"

"I'll do it by feel. Do we have enough hands to keep him steady? This will take a while."

"This whole procedure is most unorthodox," Smithington replied, a deep frown embedded on his face. "The Board would never approve."

"They're not here to stop us."

"You're impossible," Smithington said, taking no steps to stop Helgman. "I only hope this works. Tomorrow you'll be back in the city and I'll be alone to face them. I'll be lucky to get away with a reprimand."

Helgman realized his colleague's career was on the line. "I'm sorry to put you in this situation. Demand that I stop the procedure and then walk out when I refuse. I'll take the heat. The staff will be your witnesses."

Smithington paced the room, lost in thought. After a few minutes, he said, "Helgman, I've never met anyone quite like you. If this experiment of yours fails, we're all in deep trouble. Assure me this'll work."

Helgman sighed. "You know I can't do that. The odds are against him. But I can promise you that he won't live without this procedure. That, my dear sir, is a certainty I do know."

"Then let's just make sure the boy lives. It's always easier to explain success than to justify failure. And Helgman—"

"Yes?"

"May God watch over you."

The thought of God watching struck Helgman as strangely odd. Was God watching when the boy fell into the furnace? Was God watching in the dark days of the camps? Was God watching when those women, young girls mostly, had their ovaries and uteruses cut from them? Did God see those women, bloated and in agony, die in Helgman's arms? It was beyond human comprehension to imagine God watching and not taking action to stop it.

Yet Helgman knew something, or someone, was out there watching. His fingers worked the same magic in the operating room as they did when Muggs's performed in the auditorium. Maybe there wasn't a God, but if not, then where had his gifts come from?

SEVEN

Stephanie stepped from the long escalator leading up from the train tracks buried in the bowels of Grand Central Terminal. She paused, allowing the sour smells of the underground to clear from her nostrils.

Gathering her courage, she turned north. She walked briskly up Park Avenue, barely glancing at the people climbing in and out of limousines in front of the Waldorf Astoria.

But her resolve faded as she approached Helgman's office. From what little she could glean on the phone from his receptionist, he worked alone, and only on children. Burn victims usually, along with "accidents of birth."

Stephanie's heart raced as she climbed the stairs to his second floor office. She paused on the landing, taking several deep breaths to calm herself, all the while fighting the impulse to flee. "Make a plan and stick with it," Uncle Dieter had drummed into her. Well, she had a plan and she would stick with it.

Stephanie took one last long breath, let it out slowly, then pushed open the office door. A pleasant-looking woman sat behind a glass partition with only her head showing. She was busy punching numbers into an adding machine. A puzzled expression crossed the woman's face when Stephanie appeared above her.

"I'm here to see Dr. Helgman," Stephanie announced, forcing a smile and trying to sound professional. "Stephanie Grenoble."

The woman continued tapping numbers into her machine, the paper tape spilling over her small desk onto the floor. The puzzled look deepened. "Are you with Drummonds?" Her eyes turned back to her work. "A drug rep? Must be new. I didn't know they hired women. I'm sorry. Doctor only sees reps by appointment."

"I'm a patient of his." Stephanie's determination held fast.

The receptionist's fingers stopped moving and her head came up, her eyes fixed on Stephanie. "There must be some mistake. Doctor only sees children."

Stephanie pulled back her hair and twisted her forehead into the light. He stitched this."

"That's impossible. I know all his patients. He never—"

"Please tell him that Stephanie from Block Island is here. I'm sure he'll want to see how the wound healed."

"I don't understand," the woman persisted. "What is this about?"

"Please just tell him Stephanie from Block Island is here. I'll wait."

Stephanie turned to find a chair. A little girl took her hand. "Here, miss, you can sit next to me. Don't be scared. The doctor is nice. He won't hurt you." The child appeared to be about seven, with big round brown eyes floating in a patchwork quilt face, distorted so much that, but for her clothing, her sex would be indeterminate. The skin was red and blotched, her nose puffed and bruised, her lips almost nonexistent. The skin extending downward from her jaw line and disappearing under her loose fitting blouse appeared to be a jigsaw puzzle in muted colors. Stephanie forced herself not to show how much it horrified her.

"Karen," a woman's voice rang out, "leave the nice lady alone. Sit over here and behave." She turned to Stephanie. "Please don't mind her. She's been through a lot. She's had several operations and we hope not too many more. This visit will tell. That's why Karen is so nervous."

"I'm not nervous, Mother. I want a pretty face just like hers."

"Karen, please."

"My face was pretty." The little girl moved toward her mother, never taking her eyes from Stephanie. "My face was pretty before ... "

"And what happened to your face, Karen?" Stephanie immediately regretted the question. Recovering, she added, "Dr. Helgman will make your face even more beautiful than before. You will be very beautiful."

The little girl's brown eyes sparked. "No one except my parents has said that to me. No one will even look at me. You looked at me. I like you. Will I be beautiful?"

Stephanie didn't know how to answer a seven year old who might never again be able to look at another human without seeing revulsion in their eyes. She managed to say, "Only God knows that for certain, Karen. And besides, beauty comes from the inside. If your heart is beautiful, then you *are* beautiful."

"My bed got on fire. I was sleeping. Uncle Whiskers died."

"She means her cat," the mother explained. "If it hadn't been for Whiskers letting out a screech, Karen would have died as well. We were lucky. The firemen got her out just in time. The doctors at the hospital said she had lost so much skin and the burns were so deep they didn't expect her to live. Dr. Helgman saw her and asked if he could do an experimental procedure. Something to do with mesh. My baby was dying. I told him to do what he needed to do. I just wanted her to live." Tears ran down the mother's face and she wiped them away. "The chief of surgery and the director of the burn unit examined her and both said she would not likely live the night. They sent the chaplain. One of the nurses took me aside and said, 'If anyone can save your daughter, it's Doctor Helgman. The man has a great gift. The best of the best. God himself guides his hands.'"

"Don't cry." Karen patted her mother's knee. "I'll be brave. I promise."

"I'm okay, honey. You *are* very brave. It'll be over soon. And this nice woman is right, dear. You'll be beautiful when it's over." Turning back to Stephanie, the mother said, "He worked on her for twenty-four hours straight! As you can see, he saved her life. He says she'll heal perfectly. He says those creases we see now will allow her skin to heal without overstretching."

"He's a nice man," Karen said. "He'll make me beautiful."

"I know he will," Stephanie said.

The receptionist returned and motioned for Karen and her mother to follow her into the back room. To Stephanie, she shrugged her shoulders and said, "Miss Grenoble, Doctor Helgman will see you in a bit."

Lost in her thoughts, Stephanie did not hear the door open. "Doctor will see you now, Miss Grenoble. Please follow me."

Stephanie sucked in her breath, pulled her shoulders back and marched through the door, following in Karen's brave footsteps.

Helgman came into the room almost as soon as she did, positioning himself inside the now closed door, a file folder in his hand.

At first, Stephanie thought he had not recognized her. But then, softness appeared in his eyes conveying more than words could have. They both remained silent and suddenly Stephanie felt foolish.

It was Helgman who finally spoke. "So, to what do I owe the pleasure?" His voice was soft, professional.

"I came to show you your handy work." She threw back her head. "It's healed beautifully. Just a slight line, but you have to look closely to see it."

Helgman placed the folder on a counter and without a word, pulled her hair back. He studied her forehead for a moment. Stepping back, he said, "By the end of summer, if you keep out of the sun, even that slight line will be gone."

"Out of the sun? And how do I accomplish that?"

"You could stay indoors. A large hat will work. How about a good sun lotion? Using aloe will work if you can find it."

"I won't be unhappy if it doesn't heal any better than this," Stephanie replied, not really focusing on what Helgman was saying.

"Keep the sun away and you'll see noth—"

"You left so suddenly." Her tone was more accusatory than she had planned. "Why? Why did you go so early?"

Ignoring her question, he asked, "Why have you come here?"

"I think you owe me an explanation."

"We spoke for maybe two hours. What's to explain?"

"Like I said, I have to know why you left so suddenly." She felt her face grow hot and knew she was blushing.

"We spoke. Nothing more. I thought it prudent to leave as soon as I could."

"Are you saying our meeting meant nothing to you? If that's true, then I'll go. That'll be the end of it."

Helgman remained silent a few beats too long. "If I'm perfectly honest with myself," he began, his voice now tentative, "then I must say those two hours were extremely satisfying."

His statement sounded more like a confession than an explanation. "We might have been together only a few hours, but it seems like I've known you a lifetime." She gathered her courage. "Let's have dinner, and finish our conversation."

"I really can't. My practice consumes me. I'm sorry Stephanie, it's not as you see it."

"It's only dinner. I'll leave New York in the morning. Scout's honor."

He laughed at her silly salute. "Eight tonight?"

It took her a moment to understand he had changed his mind. "Eight is perfect," she replied, the butterflies again fluttering. "I'll check in at the Pierre. Green Lines—that's the family business—has a suite there," she said by way of explaining why she would be staying at such an upscale hotel.

"I look forward to it."

EIGHT

Eight o'clock came. Eight fifteen. Eight thirty. Stephanie checked the front desk to see if Helgman had called.

No messages. It was difficult for her to remain seated. She walked out of the front door intending to breathe fresh air. Concerned she might miss him, she came back inside and forced herself to sit.

Nine o'clock and the realization came that Helgman had agreed to meet her only so that she would leave his office without a scene. Stephanie felt foolish and angry.

Nine fifteen and she could sit no longer, yet she couldn't leave. The lobby clock seemed to be her enemy.

Nine thirty and she was beyond hunger, and beyond anger. The reality of her foolishness was now clear to her. She toyed with the idea of rushing off to join Nancy in Ft. Lauderdale—a good place to drown her sorrows in beer amid the laughter of winter-breakers.

A shadow fell across her lap, as had countless shadows for the past two hours. But this shadow did not pass.

"Aren't you going to say hello?"

Stephanie looked up and quickly jumped to her feet. Relieved to see him, the words tumbled out. "Were we confused about the time? I was sure you stood me up and I was about to leave. I'm glad you came."

"I called just after eight thirty and left a message with the hotel switchboard. Didn't you get it?"

She grabbed his hand impulsively. He leaned forward as if to kiss her on the cheek but pulled back before his lips made contact.

For her, that was enough. All thoughts from the last miserable ninety minutes evaporated. "You look tired. Are you okay?"

"I must apologize. An emergency came up."

"That must be hard on you. I mean dealing with injured and deformed children. Will Karen be okay?"

"Karen?" Then his face registered recognition. "Oh, right. I guess you met her in the waiting room. I believe she'll live a normal life when she heals. I used a technique I've thought about for years. I've tried it for minor reconstruction, but never before on such a large scale. She's a brave little girl. As a matter of fact, I used that same technique last night upstate and I've every reason to believe it'll work."

"Her mother said you saved her life when other doctors—"

Helgman interrupted. "God saved her life. I just did my part." He smiled as he spoke, but Stephanie sensed sadness behind the smile. "But enough about that. Let's eat."

"There's a great restaurant right around the corner. French if that's okay."

"Wonderful," he said. "Lead the way."

It was only then that Stephanie realized that she was still holding his hand. The warmth felt wonderful.

"This is a fancy place you're staying in," Helgman observed as they strolled toward the hotel entrance.

"I always stay here when I'm in New York. Like I said, the family business pays the bills."

"Well then maybe you should buy dinner."

He was smiling, and for a brief moment, his sadness was gone.

"So tell me about Green Lines," Helgman asked, looking up from his coq au vin.

"We own freighters that travel around the world. We transport cars, grain, oil—pretty much anything."

"And are you planning to join the company after you graduate?"

"I want to, but my Uncle Dieter refuses to let me in."

"Judging from the spark in your eye when you talk about the business, it seems a big mistake to keep you out. That's their loss."

Stephanie decided to change tack. "You said you knew Uncle Dieter in Germany. Isn't that what brought you to the island?"

Helgman nodded and she saw his chin set. But he said nothing.

"How exactly *did* you know him?"

He studied her closely, making up his mind how to answer. "I'm sorry, Stephanie, but I can't talk about it. It's not you ... it's me. I've tried to write to you, to explain, but even in writing I can't. Maybe someday, but not now."

"Are you trying to shield me from something?"

"I wish it was that simple. But in truth, I'm shielding myself. I can't form the words."

Stephanie felt as though he was emotionally pulling away from her, which would be worse. "How about a walk on Fifth Avenue?" She hoped to put things back on a more neutral footing. "It's beautiful out."

"I'd love to, but I'm exhausted. It's been a long day and I have an early call in the morning. But, if you can stay in the city another night, we can go to dinner at a respectable hour, and maybe even see a show. How about I pick you up right here at six tomorrow?"

Despite her disappointment, Stephanie smiled. "Yes, that would be wonderful."

NINE

Helgman's nurse looked up when he came into the office shortly after noon the next day. "Seems you caused a real dust-up at Upstate, Doctor. Preston has already called three times. Wants you to call *immediately* when you arrive." Her eyes rolled. "Made me promise to tell you first thing."

"Any calls from a Smithington?" Helgman asked, ignoring the urgency in her voice.

"No, but a Mr. Jenkins was on the line when Administrator Preston first called. I think Preston said he was the Upstate administrator."

"How's the patient load this afternoon?"

"Annie Garcia is here for her follow up. She's in the exam room. Minor scarring behind her right ear. The sutures over her right eye are ready to come out. After that, it'll be light till two thirty. Then you've patients till five."

"Okay, nothing after five. I'll call Preston after I finish with Annie."

"He's angry. About took my head off! That's not like him."

It was never a good idea to get on the wrong side of the hospital administrator. But Helgman was not without power of his own. His unique expertise drew patients from around the world. And with them came money. The hospital's reputation as a leader in pediatric surgery was now widespread. Helgman knew that in hospital politics money is king. As long as he brought in the money, the worst he could expect was a little static.

Helgman never had a chance to make the call. No sooner had he finished with Annie Garcia than Stanton Preston, all two hundred fifty pounds of him, burst into Helgman's office. He was gasping for air and his face was red. "Those steps nearly killed me!" Preston bellowed before the surprised Helgman could say a word.

Helgman took his seat behind his desk thankful for the barrier. "You didn't come all this way to complain about my steps. So to what do I owe the honor of your visit?"

"I called three times this morning."

"I know, but patients come first."

"Sure they do." Preston rolled his eyes. "Listen, Bernard. They're madder than hell up there. Just what did you do? Paul Jenkins says Levinson's livid."

"What did I do? I grafted a burn victim. To be exact, I saved a four-year-old boy's life."

"To be even more exact, you did it with Levinson's graft. Or should I say Senator Higgins's graft? A little private work Higgins wanted before opening his campaign for President. His campaign people had some elaborate plan to cover the operation by having the senator leave the country, et cetera, et cetera. Now they're screaming that their timing is all screwed up and they want your head. And if that's not bad enough, our hospital is one of many trying for a federal grant for an experimental high-speed imager. Higgins sits on the appropriations subcommittee. You think this helps our chances?"

"Politics is not my problem," Helgman shot back. "The child was my problem. More importantly, how's the boy doing?"

"Holding his own so far. But that's not the point. Protocol says you get permission first."

"Protocol would have killed that boy."

"Never mind. That skin had a more important use."

"More important than what? Saving a child's life? I can't believe you said that."

"Maybe you saved a life, maybe you didn't. Jury's still out on that one."

"You'll see. That boy'll live, despite what the odds were when they called me in."

Preston let out a big breath, slumped into a chair and brought his fingers to the bridge of his nose. "Look, Bernard," he began quietly. "Whether you did or you didn't save a life, you need to watch yourself. You're good at what you do. Excellent results. There's no denying that. But some have taken exception to your methods."

"I do what I have to. I'm sorry if that offends people."

"You've made some powerful enemies, and not just at Upstate. That's never good."

"They're jealous, that's all."

"That, and—"

"And what?" Helgman demanded.

"Look, there's talk of suspending your privileges."

"What?"

"Just talk. Nothing'll come of it."

"Anyway, Stan, back to Levinson. I've studied the senator's face. Frankly speaking, Ben Levinson's not capable of doing what needs to be done. Judging from the graft size, the procedure he planned would have had a negative outcome. Get the senator in here tomorrow and I'll fix him up. Or I'll go back up there and do it. Within a week, ten days at most, no one will be the wiser. Clear it with Levinson any way you want to."

Preston thought for a moment and then warmed to the idea. "But you already used the graft skin."

"He doesn't require a graft. Just a tidy reconstruction."

"What do I tell Jenkins?"

"Tell him Levinson can be part of the surgical team. In fact, he can take full credit for the procedure. You can work it out," Helgman said with a wink. "You always do."

TEN

Late in the afternoon, after aimlessly wandering in and out of several art museums, Stephanie found herself window-shopping in the jewelry district. She glanced at her naked ring finger, feeling foolish as she did so.

"Come inside, miss," a voice said over her shoulder. "We have even nicer goods in the cases."

She turned to see a man in his mid-fifties, dark black hair, black beard, with a black vest over a white shirt. Black pants. Black skull cap. So simple, black and white.

"We have the best prices in the city. Come. See for yourself. Don't be shy."

"I was just passing by. I'm not—"

"You never know. Come inside and I can show you diamonds like you've never seen before. Good prices."

Stephanie backed away. "I'm really not interested. Not yet anyway."

"I've been selling diamonds my whole life and know a diamond shopper when I see one. Come. It's okay if you just look."

Sheepishly, she followed the man inside, where she encountered two other men dressed exactly as he was. "My brothers," the first man explained. "Abe and Shmuel. I'm Ruben. What can we show you?"

"How about a necklace?" Stephanie ventured tentatively, overwhelmed by the jewelry on display. "Do you have necklaces?"

"Anything in diamonds we have. If we don't have it, we can make it for you. You only need tell us what you want. You're at the right place."

Ruben laid out several beautiful necklaces. She tried them on, one by one, and imagined Bernard admiring her. She saw herself walking toward him, his hand extended toward her. He was not looking at the necklace but rather deep into her eyes.

"Miss," Abe said, "may I show you anything more?"

"Oh, sorry. I was daydreaming. No, I won't be buying today, thank you."

"What would a diamond merchant be without dreams? Come back whenever. We can make your dreams come true."

If only you could, Stephanie thought. *If only you could.*

Stephanie took herself down to the Pierre lobby at five fifty five, while at the same time not daring to trust that Helgman would be on time—or even show up. But there he was, exactly at six.

He looked even more tired than he had the night before, but his face came alive when he saw her. "Not late, am I?"

"Not at all. Right on time. Not a common trait in a doctor, I'm coming to believe."

"Was that a left-handed compliment?" He smiled. "Anyway, you look lovely tonight."

"It's this dress I bought today." She executed a quick little twirl as she had for her father when she was little. "Like it?"

"What's there not to like? Ready to go?"

"Ready. Where are we going?"

"I hope you like Greek food."

"I'm not sure I've ever had it."

"There's an excellent little place close to here. It's owned by the father of a patient."

"Sounds exciting."

They walked and talked. Stephanie told him about the different art museums she'd visited, describing some of the paintings she'd seen earlier in the day. "They reminded me of you, Bernard."

"How do you mean?"

"You create faces for children, just like some of the portraits I saw."

"Only God creates. I repair."

"If you insist. But to me you're the ultimate artist—making children beautiful."

"Nature is beautiful, until a mistake happens. My job is to fix the mistakes." Helgman stopped short and pointed to steps leading downward from an eye-level sign reading,

"Athena Grill," and the tag line "Greek Home Cooking At Its Best". He guided Stephanie through a door at the bottom, where they were immediately met by a booming voice attached to a heavy-set man with white hair and a belly hanging over his belt.

"Doctor Helgman! How nice to see you my friend! And you've honored me with a new customer."

"Niklas, this is Stephanie Grenoble. Stephanie, Niklas Hallas, the best Greek chef in New York."

"The doctor exaggerates, Miss Stephanie." Hallas, obviously enjoying the compliment, escorted them to a back corner away from most of the other diners.

"I'm sorry, I have no private rooms," he said, "but this will be private for you. I hope you like Greek cooking."

"My first time," Stephanie admitted.

"You're in for a treat then. Greek home cooking at its best, if I do say so myself." He then turned to Helgman. "Do you want to order, or should I decide?"

"You, please."

It wasn't long before a stream of food started arriving— lots of little plates of different items. Stephanie recognized the stuffed grape leaves, but little else. Hallas stopped by after a while and turned to Stephanie.

"So, was I right?"

"Everything's delicious."

Hallas beamed. Then his face turned pensive. "You know, Miss Stephanie, your friend, Dr. Helgman, is the best doctor in all the world." Hallas wiped his hands on his apron and reached for his wallet, slipping out a picture of a child. Stephanie guessed her age at four.

"Look how beautiful." Tears filled his eyes. "My daughter, Teresa. We took her to many doctors. Many. But none of them held out much hope. Your Dr. Helgman gave her a new life." Wiping his eyes, Niklas turned to Helgman and kissed him on the forehead before retreating to the kitchen.

Stephanie said nothing, waiting for Bernard to fill her in. "Okay. Out with it," she finally said when it became obvious that he had no intention of doing so. "Tell me about Teresa."

"Teresa was one of those accidents of nature. Her nose and mouth were so deformed that her face hardly looked human. She had one ear. She was eleven months old when I first saw her."

"And look what you did!" Stephanie exclaimed.

"It's not as good as it should be. But—"

"She's beautiful! Niklas has every reason to be thankful."

"But I should have done better."

"You really care about her. I see it in your eyes."

Helgman looked away and then quickly turned back. "I care about them all. The ones I've fixed, and—"

"And?"

"And the ones ... the all too many ones I couldn't save."

"Couldn't save? Don't you mean the ones you couldn't fix?"

"No, save."

"Meaning what?"

"The ones left behind. I think about them every day."

Stephanie was confused. Left behind where? The far-away look in Helgman's eyes suggested that "where" was a place a long way off and a time long past. She reached across the table, laying her hand on his arm, knowing she couldn't probe further. Not now, anyway.

They sat that way for several moments, close, yet so very far apart.

"Sorry," he said when his head finally lifted. "The past is so ... the past intrudes at times when ... when I let my guard down. It's something I can't control."

"You must—" Stephanie began, realizing too late that Helgman was again lost to her.

For his part, the women in the camp, and particularly the girls, were now clearly focused in his mind. He wanted to tell them that indeed he was using the gift he'd been given, the gift to be able to fix the ones who were broken and deformed. This was the time to shout it at the top of his voice, loud enough for them all to hear him. He wanted them to know so they could finally be at peace wherever they were. But the victims were without hearing, ash floating in the universe, and would never know. He pounded the table in frustration.

Stephanie, startled, pulled her hand away.

"What is it Bernard? Take your own advice. The past is what it is. Leave it alone."

"That's just it. I can't. I was given a gift, a gift that allows me to repair the victims, fix the mistakes. That's my life."

"You need more for yourself."

Helgman fixed his eyes on her, but said nothing.

Stephanie knew she'd made a mistake.

The silence became uncomfortable. "I'm sorry," she said. "I didn't mean to criticize. I certainly can't presume to judge."

"These children are helpless. I'm here for them. That's my mission." Deep pain filled Helgman's eyes, and his voice became barely a whisper. "I've already let too many people down as it is. I vowed to never repeat the past. And I won't."

Stephanie fell silent.

Helgman's eyes stopped dancing wildly and focused on Stephanie. "I'm sorry. You've brought back painful memories. Memories I've tried to force from my mind."

Stephanie touched his hand tentatively. He did not pull away. "I shouldn't presume to know what you've been through, Bernard. Nor to pass judgment on what you do. I'll stay out of your past."

Now it was Helgman's turn to hold her hand. "With you, I'm vulnerable to the past. More vulnerable than you can imagine."

She felt a slight tremor in Helgman's grip, but did not heed its warning. "Bernard, you're a product of your past. We can work with it, use it. Your life is the past moving forward."

"For some, that may be true. For me, the past is ... is devastating."

She ran a finger along her lips. "My lips are forever sealed on that topic. Promise."

"That's just the problem," Helgman confessed. "To me, you *are* the past. Dieter Schmidt is your uncle. He and I are forever bound together. You and I are bound solidly to the past through Dieter and that fact alone is beyond painful."

She looked directly into his eyes. "What are you saying?"

Helgman's head was down, his eyes closed, his body still. Time stood still even as the warmth of his hand flowed into her. The restaurant noises faded from her senses.

Helgman's hand withdrew ever so slightly and with that almost imperceptible movement, Stephanie knew what was coming. She sat still, waiting for his head to come up. Waiting for him to look at her. Waiting for the inevitable.

When Helgman's eyes finally met hers, they held a depth of sadness and despair that would remain forever locked in her memory.

"We must end this before it goes any further; before it takes us both down." The words sliced into her like a scalpel.

"Please, Bernard." Stephanie fought back tears and struggled to breathe normally. "Let me decide my own fate." She paused to collect herself. "Ever since I met you, you've been in my thoughts. There's a special relationship between us. I've felt it since the very first. We can make it work. I know it."

"What you don't know, my dear Stephanie," Helgman confessed, "is how I've struggled since we met on Block Island. I'm glad you came to see me—but at the same time I wish you hadn't."

"So, why end it?" Desperation crept into her voice. "Why can't we work together to help you put the past behind—whatever it is?"

"That's exactly why I came last night. And tonight. Because I had the same thought. I thought I could force it to work. But I'm damaged beyond repair and you deserve more than I can ever give you. A lifetime of trying can't change it. You deserve a whole man, Stephanie. I'm just a shell."

"Please let me try." Tears streamed down her cheeks. "You're the most wonderful person I've ever met and you ... you might be wrong you know. Even doctors can be wrong." She tried to laugh, but it came out more like a grunt.

"Stephanie, if I could ever love the way it's meant to be, it would be with you. That much I know. But while there are twelve years between us, those twelve years—"

"Twelve years is not so much that we—"

"Listen to me. Because of all that has happened, those twelve years are more than a generation. They're a lifetime. A horrible lifetime. And that lifetime will destroy us both. I can't allow that to happen to you."

Stephanie sat stunned. She was in love with this man. But although she had seen for herself the depth of his emotion, Stephanie could only guess at the horrors of his past.

She squeezed Helgman's hand, savoring its warmth, memorizing its texture. Leaning across the table, she kissed him softly on the lips before he could protest or pull away. Then she stood and walked from the restaurant into the cool night air.

ELEVEN

A month after Stephanie walked out of the restaurant, Helgman's resolve never to see her again had faded. The memory of her smell, the feel of her skin, the pleasantness of her touch, were all too real. The lightness in his step when he thought of her was also real. He thought of calling her, but couldn't bring himself to impose the heavy burden of his life on her, even though she was the only woman—actually the only person—he had ever felt comfortable socializing with. He knew that he was in love with her, but he also knew that he would never be able to fully consummate that relationship.

Helgman had accustomed himself to practice his magic in times of stress. He retrieved a bag of magic paraphernalia from his office desk drawer and extracted a coin, which he then flipped in the air. The coin seemed to land in his right hand. He opened his hand and the coin was gone. He repeated the trick over and over, exercising the dexterity that, in his professional life, set him apart from others.

The repetitive mindlessness of his motions was soothing. Helgman thought back to the man who taught him magic during his rehab in Switzerland. The German-born wizard now regularly appeared on television. He recalled when the teacher had remarked to him, "Such fingers! I should have such fingers. How do you say? Dexterity? With such fingers I'd be world-famous."

"But you *are* world-famous. You're the best there is."

"Bernard." A twinkle appearing in the magician's otherwise dull eyes, "you flatter an old man. I only wish I had your gifts. If you were to ever go into the business—I mean become a full time magician, I'd never get work again."

"It's you who flatter me," Helgman replied.

"Enough talk, young man," his teacher said. "It's time for you to learn a new illusion. Only a few have the skill. Time's passed me by. I don't do it any longer. But you're ready. I only know of three people who have ever performed this trick on stage. It's called the Kaiser Illusion because it was first performed for Kaiser Wilhelm. In his honor it should only be performed with the right hand, since the Kaiser had no use of his left."

Now, thinking about the illusion, Helgman realized he hadn't performed it in over a year. However, the trick required props, and he'd traveled light. The essence of the trick was that one moment he was standing in front of the audience, his hands over his head and with a puff of smoke he was sitting atop a horse, a sword in his right hand.

The illusion brought a smile to his face. He wanted to perform the trick for Stephanie. At the thought of her, his depression returned. On the spur of the moment Helgman ran down to his car and drove the three plus hours to Upstate Hospital to visit the little boy, Leslie, who was still in the intensive care unit. From all reports, he was doing well.

Smithington stopped Helgman in the hallway outside the ICU. "I have to hand it to you Helgman," he began, "I never expected that boy to live. No signs of rejection and everything else is progressing nicely."

Helgman smiled in spite of himself. "Thanks for that," he said. "And thanks again for going to bat for me with the committee."

"All thanks are owed to *you*, my friend," Smithington replied. "You saved my bacon the way you handled Levinson. That was brilliant. The senator is so pleased with the outcome that he's sending patients and Levinson's thrilled."

"All's well that ends well," Helgman said, now growing uncomfortable with the conversation. "I've been thinking of Leslie. What will become of him when he's released?"

"CPS will find a new foster home for him somewhere."

Helgman visualized little Leslie being raised by foster parents. He shuddered as the image brought back memories of his own childhood. Helgman recalled bits and pieces of music; vaguely remembered walking in the woods holding his father's hand, but could not bring to mind how it had felt. And hard as he tried, he could not bring either of his parents' faces into focus. Sometimes, late at night, he would see them, but they were always blurry, as if in a passing dream. One thing Helgman did clearly remember was his birth name, Mordechai Stein. Helgman found it difficult to believe that he really had once been the young boy Mordechai.

The day after Mordechai's fifteenth birthday was the last time he'd seen his parents. They had come into his room after his small party and sat flanking him on his bed. Hugging him with tears streaming down their faces, they told him that he was going to live with his father's former boss, Dieter Schmidt. Mordechai's father had been Green Lines Deputy Director for Legal Matters, a position he'd held for eight years until Dieter was forced to dismiss him two years earlier because Jews could not work in businesses deemed critical to Germany's war effort.

It had become commonplace for Jewish children to be "adopted" by Aryan Germans and so Mordechai Stein became Max Schmidt, son of Dieter and Gretchen Schmidt. Max never saw either of his natural parents again. He later learned that the Gestapo smashed their way into the small cottage where his family had moved after his father had lost his job and that both his mother and father had been hauled away. Mordechai was on the Gestapo's list as well but the teenager was nowhere to be found.

Nor did Mordechai ever again see his little sister, Rachel, who was twelve years younger. He had asked his parents that last night what was to become of Rachel. Was she to be adopted by the Schmidt family as well? His parents told him that that had originally been the plan but that it had not worked out. They were in the process of making other arrangements for Rachel. Whether those arrangements had ever come to fruition, Mordechai never learned. He had comforted himself in the belief that his parents had been able to send Rachel to live with another family before the Gestapo arrived, but deep down he feared that she, too, had been taken away. His memory of his sister was foggy at best, with the only thing now "real" about Rachel being her deep blue eyes, the vivid color having been burned into his memory from the very first day he had seen her.

Dieter and Gretchen Schmidt were good to the boy, and Dieter would often take him on trips around Germany as Dieter visited the ports where his ships were docked. But, despite the kindness, Mordechai—or Max as the Schmidts insisted he call himself—cried himself to sleep most nights at the thought of never again seeing his parents and, most probably, his sister.

About a year after Mordechai moved in with Dieter and Gretchen, he sensed something was wrong. Hushed conversations were taking place late into the night. People visited under cover of darkness, suspense hanging in the air around them.

"Dad," Max had begged. "What's wrong?"

"They confiscated my trains," Dieter replied, "and my warehouses as well! Soon the ships will be gone and we'll be broke. They'll throw Gretchen and me into their stinking prison for ... " He stopped short of saying "harboring a Jew."

"What can I do?"

"You can do nothing! Nothing at all!" Dieter screamed, his face contorted with rage. "I did your family a favor and now it has turned against me! Without you I can leave anytime, salvage my business. But with you they won't allow it. They say I've disrespected their beloved Führer and they won't provide me the necessary papers."

A few days later, just after midnight, a truck flying the Nazi flag stopped in front of the Schmidt house. Several men jumped out and ran to the front door. Sensing danger, Max slipped out the back and ran toward the woods.

Two Gestapo soldiers were waiting for him. One man clubbed the back of his legs causing him to fall forward, smashing his chin against the hard ground. Max turned his head upward, blood running from his mouth, only to find himself looking into the barrel of a revolver.

"Put that away, you fool," the other man yelled. "This is the boy Major Althoff told us he's been looking for for over a year. Schmidt cut some sort of a deal with Althoff and the kid's the price."

"He's a Jew swine! I say shoot him now. Hell with the Major!"

"Not so fast. We'll be rewarded. Get him into the truck. Hurry, we have more to pick up tonight."

The man standing over Max kicked him in the ribs. "One false move, swine, and I'll shoot you. Reward or not!"

"Helgman!" Smithington's voice broke through to his consciousness. "Are you okay? You're trembling. Here, sit down."

"Oh, sorry. Yes, I'm ... I'm okay. I was just ... thinking about the impact on Leslie bouncing around between foster homes and what it feels like—must feel like—growing up that way."

Smithington studied Helgman intently. "Sometimes it works out and sometimes it's horrible. You never know."

I can attest to that, Helgman thought. "What if I adopt him?" he mused aloud before realizing how absurd and unrealistic an idea it was. But as the thought began to settle in, he felt good about the concept.

"You're not married. I'm fairly certain you can only adopt in this state if you're married."

"What a stupid rule!"

"Lots of things governments do are stupid. But they are what they are."

"I can't leave it there. Any suggestions?"

"Nothing I can think of, but I'll ask around."

Leaving Leslie's room on his next visit, Helgman felt a tap on his shoulder. He turned to face the head operating room nurse. "How are you?" Helgman said. "I almost didn't recognize you out of uniform."

"Uniforms. They do get in the way of things sometimes, don't they," she said. "Can we speak privately for a moment, Dr. Helgman?"

"Of course," Helgman answered, wondering what this could be about.

The woman led the way to a sitting room and motioned Helgman to a pair of small armchairs in one corner. In a voice barely loud enough for him to hear, she began, "It wasn't until you began suturing little Leslie that I realized I knew you. That backward motion gave you away." She blushed. "I'm sorry, I'm not being critical, but it's so opposite from what everyone else does." She took a deep breath. "What I really mean is that...well, that's when I recognized you. I was Dr. Katz's operating room nurse in Pittsburgh."

"Oh, of course," Helgman said. "I *thought* I knew you from before. You're Grace, right?"

"Yes, Grace Passic. You were the best Dr. Katz ever had. He was so proud of you." She studied him for a moment. "I don't think you ever knew how much Dr. Katz thought of you. He would never have told you himself. But we all knew because he would go out of his way to schedule the most difficult procedures when you were on duty." She blushed again. "I'm sorry. I'm blabbering."

"No, no. Please go on. What's on your mind? I sense it's more than to say hello."

"I understand from Dr. Smithington you'd like to adopt little Leslie. I think I can help."

Helgman furrowed his brows and leaned forward.

"I have a good friend in your same situation—I mean unmarried—and she's been talking for years about wishing there was some way for her to adopt a child. She came immediately to mind when Dr. Smithington starting asking around. I told her about you and about Leslie and she went to visit the child. And she's visited him every day since."

"What are you saying?"

"She is willing to marry you so that the two of you can adopt Leslie."

"Marry me? What in God's name are you talking about?"

"Please don't get me wrong or take offense. I'm just trying to help." Grace took a deep breath and pressed on. "Look, there are rumors of ... let me be blunt ... there is no other way to say it. Homosexuality. And, well the truth is ... the real truth is—" She searched for the right words. "Well, my friend's not ... well to say it delicately ... she's not thrilled with men." Grace rushed on. "And so it could work for both of you."

Helgman leaned back and his mouth tightened. "Even if I was as you suggest—which I'm *not* and it's none of your business anyway—this is absurd."

The woman held her ground. "I didn't mean to offend you. The important thing is that if you want Leslie then you'll have to marry to have any chance, right?" Then she added, as if to soften the situation, "There's no law saying you have to stay married."

"And some woman who's never even met me would marry me just like that?"

"We've discussed it."

"Besides the absurdity of this marriage idea, the child isn't normal. Leslie will need extraordinary care."

"That's of no concern to Barbara. As I said, she visits Leslie every day. It's as though he was her child already."

"Absurd," Helgman repeated. He stood up without saying anything further and strode into the hallway.

Grace called after his retreating figure, "Her name is Barbara Stillson. Jewish. Like yourself."

Helgman went straight to his car.

Homosexual. The word asserted itself over and over in Helgman's mind on the entire drive back to New York. He had refused to acknowledge the rumors, preferring to believe that other doctors were reluctant to work with him because they were jealous. But now it was out in the open. The more he thought about it, the angrier he became. He recognized the reality of having to be married if there was any chance that he would be allowed to adopt Leslie, and this added to his anger.

"I've dedicated my life to salvaging the unsalvageable," he fumed to himself. "Children who would otherwise be doomed to live in darkness, pitied by everyone, never able to form normal bonds with people. And this is the thanks I get."

"The hell with them." Helgman was not clear in his own mind about who "they" were.

Life was unfair. He knew it now as Bernard Helgman. He had known it as Max Schmidt in the camp before that. And as Mordechai Stein even before that.

TWELVE

"Uncle Dieter," Stephanie called cheerily as she entered the spacious office overlooking the harbor. "You're looking well. Sorry you couldn't make it to my graduation."

"I wanted to be there, but I couldn't arrive back in time. Bit of a problem in Suez."

"Yes, Father mentioned that. I'm glad it's under control."

"From what I heard maybe it's just as well."

Stephanie knew this was coming and she was prepared. "Father and I discussed my honors speech at length," she replied. "I was simply saying there's a time for young people to do what they think is best for their own lives and don't blindly follow the path set for them by others. I think Father agrees with me now."

"*Family tyranny*?" Dieter shot back. "Offensive words. And after all we've done for you?"

Stephanie took in a deep breath and let it out slowly. "Uncle Dieter, I do very much appreciate what the family does for me. That speech? It's past history. Who pays attention to valedictorian speeches anyway? Senator Kennedy spoke at the commencement, and no one paid attention to him."

"They'll listen once he becomes president."

"I didn't realize you followed politics."

"There's more to running a business than scheduling ships, my dear. Government regulations can make you—or kill you. You need friends in high places."

"But do you think a Catholic could ever be elected President?"

"The country's ready for it, and I'm quite sure Kennedy can be elected. Green Lines will certainly support him if he runs."

"I got to say hello to him at the commencement. Seems like a nice guy but I thought he seemed lost."

"Don't let that fool you. He's one tough customer." Dieter paused for an instant, then continued, his tone more serious. "But you've sidestepped my issue, Stephanie. I'm not happy with what you said. Your father's getting sentimental. Not a good trait in a businessman."

Stephanie would have liked to be able to look directly into her uncle's eyes, the better to read what he was thinking. But he had his back toward her, looking out over the water and watching a tug urge a rust-covered freighter into a berth. "I want to join Green Lines and work with you and Father."

Not until the freighter was made fast to the quay did Dieter respond, still facing the water. "I know what you want, young lady. Everyone in the family has pleaded your case, including your mother. Even your Aunt Gretchen, may she rest in peace, was forever harping on it."

Stephanie started to respond and he waved her off.

"I promised your father I'd meet with you and so here we are. But before we go on, an apology is in order."

"If you mean for implying you are a tyrant, then yes, I do apologize."

"Okay, then. Apology accepted." Dieter turned back away from the water to face Stephanie head on. "Please sit down," he urged, taking his chair behind his desk. Stephanie eased herself into a chair across from Dieter's and waited for her uncle to get on with her job request. But she was in for a rude surprise.

"Now then," Dieter began, "let's discuss your friend, Dr. Helgman."

Stephanie's jaw dropped. *How could he know about her and Helgman?* "What?" She managed. "How do you—"

"Doc McGee. He told me that Helgman was the one who sewed up your forehead when you fell on the island."

"Yes, but—"

"I need to know something. Did you bring Max ... Helgman ... to the island? Or did you just happen to meet him there?"

"He bumped into me. I fell and hit a rock," Stephanie explained. "That's when I met him." Stephanie wondered if her uncle knew that it had happened on the path leading up the hill, but she dismissed the idea. How could he have known?

Dieter did know. Or at least he had his suspicions, but saw no point in pursuing it.

"Anyway, what does Dr. Helgman have to do with my working at Green Lines?"

"It has everything to do with it."

Stephanie screwed up her face in an expression of questioning confusion. She knew, of course, that her uncle and Helgman had known each other in the distant past, but what did one thing have to do with the other? "What do you mean?"

"I know you've been seeing him for a while now, if my sources are to be believed. In any event, I'm willing to take a chance that a girl can succeed in this business and let you in, but only if you promise not to see Bernard Helgman anymore."

Stephanie couldn't believe what she was hearing. *Is there anything this man doesn't know?* It made no sense. But she saw no point in interrogating her uncle about how he knew so much about her private life. She was here to be let into the family business. "Again I have to ask you, what does Bernard Helgman—or him being my friend—have to do with my working at Green Lines? In fact, what does Bernard Helgman have to do with anything?"

Dieter closed his eyes and leaned back, his fingers pinching the bridge of his nose. Stephanie waited as long as she could for an explanation, but none seemed forthcoming. She was about to repeat her question when Dieter opened his eyes and leaned toward her across the desk.

"There's so much you don't know," he said. "Let's just say I have my reasons. In any event, you have a choice to make. Green Lines or Bernard Helgman. You can't have both."

Enough time had now passed for Stephanie to take in the significance of what she'd just been told. And enough time had passed for her initial seed of confusion to develop into full-blown anger. "You have no right to tell me who I can be friends with! This is the United States of America, not Germany!"

"That may be so." Dieter's tone was less harsh than she had expected. "But those are my terms."

Stephanie sat silent—and dumbfounded.

"So what will it be?" Dieter asked after a pause.

Stephanie decided to stall. Maybe her brain could figure out what to do if she just went along for a while.

"Supposing I did agree," she began. "Is this a real job or just a way to keep an eye on me?"

"It's a real job." Dieter ignored Stephanie's petulance. "Your father is planning to retire soon and after I'm gone, you will be the only member of the family who could possibly run this business. Your father and I are sure you have the talent, but no woman that I know of runs a major shipping company anywhere in the world. So we'll see. You will start in the Telex room so you can learn the operation from the bottom up."

"When would I start?" Stephanie pressed, still waiting for a strategy to emerge.

"Tomorrow," Dieter replied. "If it's a deal, I'll instruct Wilhelm Tuckmann to expect you."

So Tuckmann was to continue as her baby-sitter. Tuckmann, a former Gestapo captain, if the rumors were to be believed, was in charge of operations. He was the man who controlled Stephanie's money and who arranged her travel. She had a decent, but sometimes strained, relationship with the man. Other than reporting on her personal life, he had not been too difficult to work with in the past. She was pretty sure he allowed her to overspend her allowance without telling either her uncle or her father. When she was a little girl, he had convinced Dieter to allow him to take her out on the pilot boat and ride back to the dock on a freighter. It had been the *Brigshelm* out of Bremen, she remembered.

Dieter continued to talk, but Stephanie barely heard the words. She was debating whether it was worth giving up the life she had dreamed about since childhood in order to continue her relationship with Bernard. After all, Bernard had made it clear that they had no relationship. But then, why had he come to her graduation? She'd spotted him standing at the back of the hall, but he'd disappeared as soon as she finished her speech.

Then it came to her. It was so simple. Yes, her uncle obviously had ways of tracking her comings and goings, but to this point she'd not been alert to the possibility of his spies—Tuckmann underlings no doubt—lurking in the shadows. She hadn't taken any precautions to keep from being followed because she had no idea that it had been necessary. She already was planning to take the train to New York after visiting with her uncle to surprise Bernard. The ticket was in her purse. If she was careful she could continue to meet with Helgman without her uncle knowing.

At least until she was sure about where she did or did not fit into Helgman's life plans.

"Hello? Stephanie?" Dieter's voice broke through to her consciousness. "Yes or no?"

Stephanie returned to the here-and-now.

"Yes," she replied, now seeing that she could achieve all of her goals—indeed, all of her heart's desires. "Definitely yes, Uncle. Thank you. No boyfriend is worth giving up the opportunity to carry on the family business."

Stephanie reproached herself for her deceit. Except for not allowing her to work in the company, her uncle had been very good to her over the years. However, the choice he'd put before her was unreasonable and unfair. He left her no choice. If it turned out that she and Helgman were not destined to be together, then all the better. But in the meantime ...

"Report at nine in the morning, please," Dieter instructed. "And be sure to address me here at work as Mr. Schmidt. As for your father, it's his business what he wants you to call him."

"Thank you, again, er, Mr. Schmidt." Stephanie rose from her chair and walked toward the door.

"Oh, in case you are planning to continue with Helgman behind my back, let me be clear. I'll find out. And if you do, it won't go well for him. His medical education is not all that it appears to be. A word in the right place and ... and let's just say his life as a doctor will be over."

Stephanie spun around. "You wouldn't—" She caught herself in mid-sentence.

The burning intensity of her uncle's eyes told her all she needed to know.

THIRTEEN

"I'm Barbara Stillson," the woman began tentatively.

Helgman peered at her across his desk, puzzled as to why the woman had no child in tow.

"I'm Grace's friend," she hurried on, not waiting for Helgman to say anything. "You know, Grace Passic? Upstate Hospital? She told you about me."

"Oh, right," Helgman said with no small amount of annoyance. "I told Nurse Passic that I wasn't in the least interested in ... a relationship. Now, if you'll excuse me—"

"But I've come all this way. Please hear me out. You and I both want to raise Leslie. If we don't cooperate he'll spend years in foster care being bounced from family to family. And then what?" Barbara focused on Helgman in an effort to keep control of the conversation. "We can work together to raise him. I'm a good cook. I keep a clean house and I'll be a good mother. And I won't ask anything of you. I have my own income."

Helgman couldn't believe what he was hearing. The woman was interviewing for the position of wife and mother, for God sakes! "There's more to marriage than a clean house," he responded. "It's about living together, sharing experiences, supporting each other."

Barbara continued to look into his eyes. "Relationships grow. It would be no different than an arranged marriage, which sometimes works out just fine. And we both know that the state will never let either of us adopt Leslie on our own whether or not they think any married couple would adopt him."

Helgman couldn't believe it, but he suddenly found himself playing out this scenario in his mind, preposterous though it was. He forced himself to stare back at this woman, willing her to stop talking so that he could take stock of where his mind's eye had taken him. There he was, on a carpeted floor playing with the little boy, perhaps with building blocks, and a woman hovering somewhere just out of his vision.

Was that woman Barbara? Or was it Stephanie?

Stephanie! The phone conversation with her earlier in the week was still raw in his mind. He had at first shared her joy when she told him that her uncle had relented and would allow her to work for Green Lines Shipping. He had also sensed a sadness, and when he had asked her what the problem was she broke into sobs. It took her several minutes to get it out, but there was no mistaking the finality of what she had told him. He knew Dieter was the cause of her sudden change of heart, but he couldn't place what Dieter had said or done to effect this drastic change in Stephanie. What Helgman did know was that any relationship he might have had with her was no longer possible.

Barbara? Stephanie? The realization that both women wanted him but that he couldn't accept either jolted him back to reality. Barbara was there still, but the eyes that were so insistent a moment ago were now more pleading than anything else. Her intentions were good. Admirable, in fact. He had known that all along. But right now, the emotional maelstrom that her arrival and her proposition had stirred up in him was more than he could stand. His mind swirled with the distress he'd already been experiencing in thinking about Stephanie, Dieter, Leslie. Now this Stillson woman. Her very presence so close across the desk was suffocating him. Helgman's clenched hands shot up involuntarily to the sides of his head, as if to squeeze closed the opening into his past that her words had wedged open.

"Get out!" It was all he could manage to say or do.

Barbara reeled back in her chair, her lips open as in mid-sentence. The two of them sat frozen, staring at one another for an uncomfortably long period of time.

"I'm sorry," Helgman said finally, as he struggled to calm himself, appalled at the violence of his own outburst. "You mean well, I know. But this can not be. Please go. I have patients to see." He waved his arm to dismiss her, lowering his head as though to study a file on his desk.

Barbara sat for a moment and when Helgman didn't look up, she got up and walked to the door. She then turned back to him. "I wish there was some way to convince you. I know it's crazy. I had the same reaction when Grace first suggested it. But the more I thought about it, the more I was convinced that it could work. Think of Leslie. He's a special child and he'll need special care. We, you and I, can give him what he needs. He's a good boy. I'm with him every day and he can learn, and I know I can teach him to speak properly. Can't you at least keep an open mind? Think about it? What have you got to lose?"

Helgman looked up. "Listen. I'm sorry I yelled." He then surprised himself by letting her into his inner thoughts just a tiny crack. "I'm not in a very good place right now."

The image he had had just moments before again flashed through his mind—with no Stephanie in the picture this time—and he realized that, through it all and in spite of himself, he was somehow drawn to this woman.

He put out a feeler. "Are you staying in the city?"

"Yes. At least for tonight."

"Can we meet somewhere to talk? Maybe over a late dinner?"

"I'm at the Hilton on Seventh," she said. "But maybe I can audition at your place."

"Audition!" Helgman thought to himself. "That's pretty forward," forgetting what Nurse Passic had told him about her friend being "not thrilled with men".

"Yes, audition. How about if I come to your house and cook dinner? I make a mean spaghetti. I'll bring everything we'll need. Just tell me where and when."

The absurdity of the situation now made Helgman smile. This pleasant but spunky woman had strangely ignited a spark of interest in him. Not an interest in her physically—which obviously was just as well—but in the prospect of them adopting Leslie. He wrote his address on a prescription pad. "It's not far from your hotel. How about seven thirty?"

"Wonderful. I'll be there."

"Right on time, I see," Helgman said, holding his door open.

"Well Doctor," Barbara said, "don't just stand there. Help with these bags. I rang your bell five or six times. I didn't think you were home."

"I was changing ... and cleaning the kitchen if you must know a dirty little secret."

"From what I gather, there are no secrets around here."

When he seemed puzzled, she added, "More than one of your neighbors cracked their doors, checking me out no doubt."

"I forgot to warn you," he laughed. "They're regular busybodies. Nothing better to do with their time."

"I'm sorry if I started rumors for you."

"It'll give them something to think about. Not all bad."

"You have a nice place here. Larger than I thought it would be, judging from the front."

"These buildings are deeper than they are wide. Is that a wine bottle I see?"

Laughing, she pulled two bottles from the bag. "Actually, two of them. Didn't know if you imbibe."

"What do you need?"

"A pot to boil water and something to cook the meat and sauce in. And, oh, a large bowl for salad."

"And wine glasses."

"Aha! There's my answer."

The first bottle was almost empty by the time they moved from the couch to the kitchen. Barbara put up the water and the sauce and seasoned the meat while he prepared the salad.

"You sure are good in the kitchen, Doctor. My father wouldn't step foot in the kitchen, except to pick up his ten o'clock snack that my mother always made before she went to bed." Barbara broke a piece of bread from the loaf and buttered it as she spoke. "Most of what I know about men is from movies and TV. You're certainly not what I expected."

Helgman displayed obvious discomfort with this line of conversation and Barbara retreated to more neutral ground. "Hey, this bread's not bad," she exclaimed. "The guy in the store was right. He was right about the wine, too."

"Where did you shop?"

"Across the street. A place called Tony's Gourmet."

"Good choice. Tony is successful because he gives you a culinary viewpoint. It's the mindset that does it."

"So you believe we're followers, our opinions controlled by suggestions."

"To some extent, yes."

Barbara stood and walked to the stove. "The sauce is just about ready. Let's get the meat sautéing," she said. "Getting back to your comment about suggestion. I agree with you. Very few people know what's right internally. Most people need the opinions of others. I'm not talking about morals, but things like, oh, like the color of drapes in a room. Even more basic, the style of the clothes we wear. We rely on the salesperson, or a friend, to tell us what's right."

"I wouldn't know about that. I don't spend much time shopping."

Barbara worked with her back to Helgman. "It's funny when you think about it though. I take my girl friend, Clare, when I buy a dress. I need her approval. But," she laughed, "I don't even like the way she dresses." She glanced over her shoulder, "Hey, don't just sit there. Make yourself useful. Open the other bottle."

Barbara now talked about her early life, briefly touching on how her family had been dysfunctional. But she talked mostly about how much she wanted to adopt Leslie.

Helgman listened, fascinated by the depth of her concern for the little boy.

"Okay," she called after peering into the sauce pan. "Dinner's ready." She drained her glass, giggled and said, "I'd ask you to cut the bread, but there's not much left. If you'll refill the glasses, we can eat."

"I've had enough," Helgman replied. "I'll just have water."

"You can never drink too much wine. It's good for you. It keeps the French going, even with all that rich food they eat."

"I'm not French and truth is, I don't know what keeps them going."

"Didn't you study nutrition in medical school?"

He filled her glass. "I wasn't aware that we were discussing nutrition." He filled her glass.

Barbara set a plate of spaghetti in front of him, a few strands hanging over the edges. "Be careful, it's hot."

They ate in silence for a few minutes. Then she announced, "This wine is excellent! What's a good spaghetti dinner without a nice glass of wine to wash it down?" She held her glass high. "Here's to us and baby Leslie."

"Whoa. You're getting ahead of yourself. Having dinner is a far cry from getting married or adopting a child."

"How do you think he'll do long term?"

"I expect we'll have to perform a few minor grafts, but nothing major," Helgman replied going along with Barbara for the moment. The grafted skin hasn't been rejected and he's long past where I'd expect an infection to set in. His signs are strong."

"Well, then. He's out of the woods. That's good."

"Yes and no. The brain damage is worrisome. The extent of the damage will take months, perhaps even years, to evaluate. Raising him will be a challenge in any event."

"I'm up for it! I've never backed down from a challenge. I've had plenty of opportunities to run and hide, but I've stuck it out." Barbara studied Helgman. "I had a tough childhood and I want to make it better for Leslie."

"What do you mean by 'opportunities to run and hide'?" Helgman was troubled by something he heard in her voice.

Barbara drained her glass and held it out for more wine before answering.

"It's not a pretty story," she said after taking a long drink, "but if we're to be together, I want you to know everything about me. I had a horrible childhood. My older sister was killed by a car. She ran out into the street after a ball."

Barbara took another drink of wine. "At first it seemed she was just knocked out. There were no bruises, nothing. But she didn't move. Sharon died in the ambulance. My mother blamed herself. And if that wasn't bad enough, my father let her take the blame. I was ten at the time and I remember my mother crying all that night. And the next night. And the next. It seemed she never stopped crying from that time on.

"Then my mother began to drink herself to sleep and my father got angrier and angrier. At first, his anger was directed at my mother. She had closed him off. But then he turned on me. Made me clean the house and scrub the toilets until they glistened. I had to make his breakfast and cook dinners. I could do nothing right as far as he was concerned and he would hit me with his belt and sometimes with his bare hand at the least little thing he claimed was wrong." Barbara was looking down, her moistening eyes fixed on the half-eaten spaghetti. She reached for her glass, only to find it empty—as was the bottle.

"I hated going home," she continued, "but I had no choice. Who was I going to tell? Who would listen to me? Not my mother. She was locked in her room, living her own hell. They would fight, and sometimes he would hit her. I think now she provoked him into it. I think it gave her satisfaction. At least it reinforced that she was justified in keeping him away from her. Their arguments were vile." She stopped talking and wiped her eyes. "You can't imagine how bad it was."

Helgman saw from the way Barbara's body was shaking how much the pain from twenty years ago was still with her. It seemed the wine had made it easier for her to talk, but not even the alcohol could dull the pain.

Her story was a lot like his, Helgman realized. "Unfortunately, I can imagine what you went through," he said softly. "My childhood was not pleasant either."

Barbara wiped her eyes with the heel of her hand and then looked up at him. It appeared to Helgman that she had made up her mind about something. "I'm going to tell you something you can never repeat," she said, her voice barely audible. "Something I've never told anyone before. Promise?"

Helgman nodded, not trusting his voice.

"When I was fifteen, on my birthday, I refused to make dinner. I was being rebellious, I guess. My father became livid and slapped me across the face. When I refused to cry, he pushed me over the arm of the sofa and started slapping my behind. It hurt, but I still refused to cry. I knew he wanted me to beg him to stop, but I resolved not to. It was the only way I could fight back." She stopped talking and looked again at the empty bottle, licking her lips and sucking in her breath as if about to embark on a dangerous mission. "He pulled down my pants and smacked my bare backside with his hand. He kept at it until the pain was so great I couldn't help myself and finally screamed.

"He hit me even harder then. 'You've had that coming to you for some time now,' he growled. 'That'll teach you to defy me!' He struck me again, and then said, 'Your ass is good and red. I think I'll keep it that way.' Then he pulled off his belt and hit me again and again. I begged him to stop. But he just kept hitting me."

Helgman found himself reaching his hand out to Barbara, who took a moment to dry her face with her other hand. Then she continued. "I remember him saying, 'It's glowing. Gives you color. In fact, it's time for your birthday present.' I sensed in horror that he was pulling down his pants—with one hand, I guess—while trying to push my head into the sofa with the other. I tried to get away while I screamed for help. I sort of got away but he caught hold of me. I couldn't break free. He yanked me back to the sofa arm and pushed me forward. I felt his bareness against me."

"Did he ... "

"No. I was saved by my mother. She ran in from her bedroom with a book or something over her head—obviously, she had heard me screaming—and swung at him. He lost his balance, tripped over his pants and fell down. She threatened to kill him if he even so much as touched me ever again. And I think she would have, too. She threw him out and told him never to come back.

"That's my story." Barbara was clearly drained by the experience of telling it. She looked away from Helgman and then turned back.

"My God," Helgman said to himself. He was about to repeat it out loud when Barbara suddenly gave forth with an almost inhuman scream followed by a convulsive bout of wailing. Tears gushed down her face and would not stop. Helgman reached for Barbara's hands. She yanked them away before he could touch her, but just as quickly brought them back to the table and slowly slid them over to his. The wailing gave way to a series of hacking coughs. Those, too, eventually played themselves out, diminishing to a series of sniffles. They sat that way, wordless, for a very long time.

"My God," Helgman said finally, this time out loud.

Barbara nodded. "And you know what? You're the first man I've allowed to even hold my hands. And even with you, I'm terrified." She felt his hands twitch, as if readying to return to his side of the table. "No, don't move them," she said, almost pleading. "It's good. It feels good. Maybe it's because you're a doctor, I don't know. But I can't imagine allowing a man—even a male doctor—to touch me ... you know. The very thought of it gives me chills."

FOURTEEN

For Helgman it wasn't so much the physical abuse he had endured, but rather what he had assisted the Nazi doctors with in the camp infirmary. Various procedures to achieve mass female sterilization were tried. In some cases, ovaries were removed from one woman and implanted in another. "Experiments" the butchery had been called. Not a day passed now when he did not loathe himself for his part in what transpired.

Helgman tried to console himself in the knowledge that techniques he had learned from Dr. Kretzen's books had allowed him to make the last hours of those women's lives more bearable. But they still died terrible agonizing deaths, alone without human comfort in that hell on Earth, on wooden slats splintered from the kicking and thrashing of those who had died before them.

"Barbara, you dear soul," Helgman managed to say to the woman still sniffling across his kitchen table, "I understand. Some things shape us the wrong way and we're helpless to fix them." He gently lifted her hands. "Come, let's go to the living room."

"Gotta clean up when you cook," she replied. "Especially in somebody else's kitchen." She lifted her plate and her uneaten spaghetti slid onto the table.

Helgman took the plate from her. "Here. Allow me. You cooked, I'll bus."

"No. Can't allow that. What will you think of me? Worse yet, what will your housekeeper think?" She reached for the plates, but her leg bumped the chair and she reached out to the wall to steady herself.

"There's no housekeeper. Let's sit in the living room now. Clean up later."

Barbara regained her balance and lifted the empty wine glasses from the table. "Bet you didn't think I could make it this far!" She laughed through eyes that were still red and puffy. "I'm stronger than I look."

"I'd say determined." He took her arm and guided her to the sofa where she slumped into the corner.

Helgman started toward the facing chair.

"Please, Bernard, sit next to me. I won't bite, I promise." She patted the cushion next to her. "Come. If I can do this, so can you."

Helgman carefully positioned himself on the sofa, maintaining what he considered a respectable distance. Yes, he had held her hands, but the table had been between them.

"Now that I've spilled my guts, you must tell me *your* story."

Helgman was silent for a full minute before making up his mind. "I was born in Germany," Helgman began slowly. "In Leipzig actually. We moved to Hamburg when I was little. My father was a lawyer for a shipping company owned by a man named Dieter Schmidt." He winced involuntarily as he uttered the name. "He took me to live with him the night before the Gestapo arrested my parents. A year later the Gestapo came for me."

"My God," Barbara exclaimed. "And then what?"

"There's not much more to tell." Thinking about how he survived in the camp was more than he could handle. Speaking about it was impossible. "I worked in the camp infirmary. That's how I survived."

"I don't understand what you mean by 'worked in the camp infirmary'. You weren't a doctor then. You were ... what eighteen, nineteen?"

"Sixteen, actually, when I arrived. Nineteen when I got out."

"What exactly did you do there?"

"Whatever was required of me to...stay alive and to... get something to eat. Mostly cleaned and ran errands for the doctors."

"Like what?"

"I'm sorry, Barbara, but I've said as much I can. I feel that I'm cheating you after all that you've told me about what happened to you. But I just can't say any more."

Barbara found herself wondering whether all this was a mistake. She was pursuing—hoping for—a relationship with an enigma—a man with secrets and a dark past that she might never learn about. But she decided to put aside her doubts—at least for a while yet. After all, little Leslie desperately needed her, and Helgman was her only hope of making that happen. *Remember, Barbara*, she thought. *You're not one to run and hide. You've stuck it out before and you can make this happen. Just give him time.*

Helgman's hands were resting on his lap. Barbara slowly reached over to put her hands over his, hesitating as if expecting him to pull back.

It was after one A.M. when Helgman looked up. Barbara was sleeping, her head against his shoulder. He debated waking her. Given all the wine she had drunk it was a wonder she'd not passed out sooner than she had.

He gently moved away, trying not to disturb her. Her eyes fluttered open. "What time is it? Did I fall asleep?"

"A little after one. We both did, I'm afraid."

"You said that like it's something to be ashamed of."

"I better call a cab. Too late for you to walk."

"I don't mind sleeping on your sofa. I mean, if that's okay with you."

"I think a cab would be better. Or I can walk you to your hotel."

"Get me a blanket. I'll be fine right here."

He laughed. "What'll the neighbors say? I'll get kicked out of the co-op."

"You serious? I've heard some awful things about New York co-ops, but—"

"Not really." He forced a smile. "I have to leave for the hospital in just a few hours." The statement was accurate, as far as it went. What he didn't say was that Muggs was performing at Upstate and he had to leave at five.

Barbara was disappointed, but concluded that she had pushed him enough for one night. *This went well*, she told herself. *It's only the beginning.*

She gathered up her shoes and her purse and strode to the door. "Okay," she said in as cheery a voice as she could manage. "We'll talk soon. No need to go out with me. In this neighborhood I'm sure there'll be a cab along soon enough." Helgman was about to insist that he wait with her outside until a cab came, but the door had opened and closed before he could form the words.

It was no more than a moment before Helgman felt a chill in the apartment. He thought at first that cold air had come through the open door. But he quickly realized that it wasn't so much that a chill had descended, but rather that a source of warmth had disappeared. A warmth in his home that he had not known since his fifteenth birthday.

FIFTEEN

Barbara walked toward a little table in the back corner of the bar of her hotel, her yellow dress echoing the glow of sun on her cheeks. She had spent the day sightseeing and hadn't received Helgman's message until she got back to her hotel room late in the afternoon. Helgman rose from the table to greet her.

"What a nice surprise," she declared as she reached him. "I certainly didn't expect this."

"I suppose I should say the same. Drink?"

"I probably shouldn't, given all I drank last night. But the occasion demands it. Right?"

"What will it be?"

"I'll stick to wine. Chardonnay. But only if you join me. And hurry. Tell me about Leslie. I can't wait. I've been excited ever since your call."

Barbara's prompt caused Helgman to replay the day's events in his mind. When Muggs had approached the boy earlier in the day, his mouth had opened in a tight grin, which was all that the still raw skin would allow. Leslie's eyes had followed the quarter high into the air, but instead of fixating on it as the other children had done, he focused on Muggs's right pocket where the coin was about to land. When Muggs bent down to kiss the boy's forehead, Leslie had reached up and squeezed the clown's fingers harder than Helgman had thought possible considering his extensive burns. In that instant Helgman's mind was made up. He could not lose this boy.

Helgman returned his attention to the woman sitting across from him. "Leslie definitely has some brain damage," he said. "And truth be told, I believe the child was born with some abnormality. But he's intuitive. He has an uncanny ability to figure things out quickly. Even better, he's healing faster than I expected and with a full range of motion. He grasped my fingers today with surprising force." Helgman involuntarily shuddered when he relived the thrill of it. "Leslie has good sight and motor control and his understanding of cause and effect is advanced for his age."

"Great news." Barbara beamed. "I wish I had been there to see it for myself. I can't wait to get back home and see him."

"What did you do today?" Helgman didn't know what else to say.

"I went to synagogue. I needed time alone. As if going to synagogue can ever be time alone. It's a small congregation that my father told me about."

"Your father? I thought—"

"He's a rabbi."

"Your father," he repeated, confused. "Didn't your father—"

"Oh, I'm sorry. My mother remarried a few years ago. A rabbi. I should have said stepfather. But truth is, he's a real father to me. A wonderful man."

The wine came. When the waiter left, Barbara said, "I have a lawyer friend who says that whoever speaks first in a negotiation is the one who loses. I don't like to lose, so why don't you start?"

"Seems to me," Helgman said, breaking into a smile, "unless I'm mistaken, I just heard you speak. And anyway, what do you mean by 'negotiation'?"

"You know what I mean." She remained silent for a moment. "Are you saying I just lost?"

"That will depend."

"On what?"

"On life, I suppose. On the future. On what we decide to do about Leslie."

Barbara swirled her wine nervously, finally taking a long swallow. "I'm serious. I meant what I said last night. I'll have Leslie no matter what. If you invited me to dinner to talk me out of it it won't work. I've made up my mind."

"Just the opposite, actually. If we don't do this together then neither of us will get him."

"That's the most convoluted marriage proposal I've ever heard," Barbara exclaimed. "That *was* a proposal, wasn't it?"

"Not exactly, no," Helgman replied. "But if it was a proposal, it wasn't anywhere as convoluted as the resulting marriage will be."

"Well, if you didn't propose, then what *did* you do?"

"I guess I'm still thinking it through."

"What else is there to think about? We both know the challenges. And now you know everything about me."

"That's just it. I'm not sure I do. Something in the way you told me about your father has me thinking you didn't tell me everything."

Barbara stared at Helgman for several minutes debating how to respond to his challenge. He was right, of course. She had promised herself before going to his apartment that she would tell him everything. But in the final analysis she couldn't make the words happen. That was a mistake, she now realized. She feared that Helgman's declaration that he was "still thinking it through" was really his way of saying that he was about to pull out altogether. Would her "coming clean" make any difference? If she simply denied hiding anything, would he accept that or would he disbelieve her and, in the face of her lie, abandon the idea of partnering with her and attempt to adopt Leslie on his own? *He's famous*, she concluded, *and may be able to pull strings in high places that I could never get access to.* It was a chance she could not afford to take.

She had to tell him, she decided. Indeed, the words that she had suppressed for so long refused to be denied voice any longer. Thankfully, the waiter had not yet come back because she was powerless to stop the outcry.

"He raped me!" she sobbed. "I lied when I told you I escaped. It's the story I've tried to convince myself of all these years. But the truth is, he raped me. He was about to do it again when my mother came in. She asked if he had violated me. I was so ashamed, I said no. She seemed relieved and didn't question me further."

Helgman started to say something, but she held her hand up. "No. Please let me finish or I might never get the courage again. I got pregnant. I denied it for months and when finally none of my clothes fit, I knew I had to do something. I stole money from my mother and got an abortion. I think she knew I was pregnant all along because she never asked after the money. In some ways, I guess, I see Leslie as the child I lost."

"How awful." Helgman tried to force from his mind the vision of all the women who had died in his arms in the camp as well as those who lived, but could never thereafter bear children.

"I've always blamed myself for the attack," Barbara said. "I don't know what I could have done, but I know I should have done something."

"We often blame ourselves for things that aren't our fault. What's so terrible is that when a person is fired from a job the tendency is to blame the boss or a coworker, but when a woman is sexually assaulted she blames herself. Human nature has a few wires crossed."

"I feel so dirty, so unworthy." Tears coursed down her cheeks. "It's hard to describe the actual feeling. I came to hate the baby. I think that was the worst part. I hated the baby growing inside me and I hate myself now for those thoughts. Most of all, I hate myself for taking its life."

"You don't have to explain, Barbara. I'm familiar with the feeling." He was uncharacteristically compelled to tell her more. "The difference in my case is that I feel as though I volunteered. It wasn't really voluntary, but I blame myself as though it had been." He ached to tell her the full story of his earlier years, of what led him to medicine, but, as usual, the words would not come. "Let's take a walk and find a place for dinner," he finally said, anxious to escape the confines of the hotel bar and the words and thoughts that continued to surface.

They turned left out of the hotel and proceeded toward Broadway. It was a beautiful evening. Couples were walking arm in arm, talking and laughing together. Helgman took Barbara's arm and leaned toward her. "Ever since I came to this country I've envied those people who could walk and talk together like that. You've given me the chance to be one of them."

She laughed nervously and edged closer to him. "Did I just hear that proposal?"

"Since this is a two-way proposition as you pointed out, what's your take? Can we pull it off?"

"Pull it off? If we can pull off getting engaged on our first date, I'd say we can pull anything off." She squeezed his arm. "I never thought I'd say this, but you're a comforting person. I feel safe with you." She laughed. "Listen to me. I'm gushing. I'm sorry. Bernie, I hope this works. I really hope this works."

"I think it can, but let's set the record straight. I'd say that our first date was last night."

She grinned. "That doesn't count. All we did was sleep together." She paused for effect. "Now we're having fun."

SIXTEEN

Helgman stared absentmindedly at the gold block letters on the wall above the receptionist's head: *DAWSON, DAWSON and STEPHANO. Counselors at Law.*

The past three months had been a roller coaster of highs and lows—days of joy interspersed with bouts of self-doubt as he and Barbara worked to merge their lives. She had proven to be a sensitive, warm-hearted woman who was just as passionate for the children she taught as he was for the children he repaired. Their marriage date was fast approaching and while it was going to be a small private ceremony, their checklist still contained myriad details.

One of those details was moving his practice, and his home, to Pittsburgh. He had explained to Barbara that moving to Pittsburgh where she had family would make it easier to build a life together.

Barbara was thrilled with the idea. "It certainly would be easier than raising Leslie in New York City where I don't know anyone."

Helgman called his surgical mentor, Seymour Katz, and broached the subject. Katz listened to the story of the marriage and the pending adoption. Saying he would look into it, the conversation ended without further comment.

Katz had called back later with a surprising, and welcome, proposition. The University of Pittsburgh, actually the University Medical Center, was in the process of establishing a hospital unit devoted exclusively to the treatment of burn victims. Katz had brought Helgman's name to the attention of the UMC chairman, emphasizing Helgman's innovations and particularly the success he was experiencing in the treatment of pediatric burn trauma. Several weeks later Helgman was offered the post of chief of the pediatric burn practice, which he declined, not willing to take on the paperwork required of a department chief. But after weeks of discussion, Helgman agreed to relocate his practice to Pittsburgh in exchange for the opportunity to practice at the new hospital.

"But Bernie, you do more than burn trauma," Barbara had protested when he told her the good news.

"That's why I couldn't head up the burn practice," he explained. "This way I'll be free to work at the burn facility as well as perform reconstructive surgery at Children's Hospital."

That led Barbara to comment that he seemed more excited about moving his practice than he was about their upcoming marriage. "But that's okay," she'd said to him. "I guess that's as it should be."

Helgman's reverie was interrupted when a door to the waiting room opened, framing a middle-aged, slightly overweight man of above-average height. He held out his hand. "I'm Bill Dawson. Sorry to keep you waiting. Couldn't get out of court as fast as I'd planned. Every day's a surprise. Must happen to you more than to me, though."

"I don't appreciate surprises." Helgman began rethinking his choice of lawyer.

"Preparation is the key to avoiding surprises. But sometimes things happen. Come on back and let's talk."

Helgman followed Dawson into the deep-pile-carpeted area where the partners' offices were located. They walked past a case displaying a magnificent Inca artifact collection.

"That's Dad's collection," Dawson said. "A life's work I might add. Most are one-of-a-kind museum-quality pieces he collected over a lifetime with great care and understanding of the Inca culture."

Helgman noted the warmth and caring in the son's voice, both for the art collection and for his father. Seated in front of Dawson's massive desk, Helgman could see, over Dawson's right shoulder, the magnificent Gulf Tower, headquarters of Gulf Oil, several blocks to the east. If nothing else, Dawson's office in the Grant Building in downtown Pittsburgh was impressive.

"I'll come to the point," Helgman began. "I've made inquiries about you and your firm and what I've found is all positive."

Dawson leaned forward while pushing his pad to the side. "How can we help you?"

"I'm about to entrust a lot of money to you, as well as a sensitive secret. This project will require discretion. Can I count on you for that?"

Clearly intrigued, Dawson pulled his pad closer and picked up his pen. "I would hope I am. If you can tell me a bit more I can determine whether you have the right firm."

"Do you, or your firm, have any trouble at all handling Jewish affairs or working closely with Jewish people, or with Shoah survivors?"

The lawyer stood and walked to the window, apparently lost in thought. He turned to Helgman. "Working with Jews ... Jewish people ... is of no consequence for me or this firm. But the word 'shoah' escapes me."

"Shoah—some say Holocaust—refers to the extermination of Jews by the Germans during the war years." Helgman turned his wrist over and held his arm out. "The Nazis called it the Final Solution. Shoah survivors, particularly from a concentration camp called Auschwitz, have numbers tattooed on our arms. We were branded like cattle. Only cattle are treated better, even when being slaughtered."

Dawson, clearly shocked at the sight of the numbers on Helgman's arm, replied, "Dr. Helgman, I can assure you that by the time of our next visit I'll be fully apprised of this Holocaust. I've never seen such a barbaric thing in all my life."

"What I'm about to lay out for you is private and you must agree to handle the work personally."

"I can do that, but some things may require research, or papers drafted. Those tasks are better accomplished by our firm's associates."

"I'll allow you to decide those issues. But full and absolute discretion will be required. I don't want anyone but you to know the details. Above all, my identity is to remain private, known only to you."

"I understand."

Helgman was not yet ready to trust Dawson with the full story, but had decided to get as close to the truth as possible. "I was born and educated in Germany," he began. "I'm Jewish, as you now know. My birth name is of no consequence at this point, but at the age of fifteen my parents sent me to live with another couple and my name was changed. A year later I was taken into the camp."

Helgman waited for Dawson's pen to stop moving before he continued. "After being liberated from the camp a few years later, I spent time in a rehabilitation facility in Switzerland and then came to the United States. While in the camp, I lived in the infirmary where I learned medicine. I then—"

"Pardon me," Dawson interrupted, "but if my notes are correct you left this Auschwitz before you were even twenty. So when did you learn medicine?"

Helgman looked away for a moment before answering. "Self-taught, to help the women in the infirmary. I prefer not to talk about it."

"As you wish," Dawson said, taking his cue from Helgman's body language. "Please continue."

"I finished my medical education here in Pittsburgh under Dr. Seymour Katz. My practice is limited to children, pediatric reconstructive surgery to be more specific. The difficult, the impossible, come to me. Disfigurement shapes a child's life in the early years when personality is forming. For that reason I try to fix the problems years earlier than most doctors are willing to attempt it." Helgman saw that Dawson was studying him intently. "I'm sorry. I get carried away sometimes."

"Listening to you, I'm reminded of a story my father often told. A man once walked into his office. A little man, whose suit appeared as if he had slept in it, and probably he had. He asked my father to help him. He had a vision of how to bring power to the entire southeastern portion of the country. He showed my father sketches of a power system. Dams were to be built, entire towns were to be flooded. Power from the dams was to be distributed to farmers as well as city dwellers. That man's dream helped seven states out of the Great Depression. Years later, my father said to me, 'Son, that's what the practice of law is about. Makes up for the drudge work. The ladies with banking problems. The men with lady problems. I trust someday a man such as that will come into your office. Make certain you are ready.' I assure you I'm ready."

"I'm certainly not such a man. But I do have a dream. Let's get down to specifics. First, and perhaps foremost, my name is never to be revealed. I want to establish an organization and I'll provide money for it from time to time. I'll give you instructions for the use of those funds, but the money must never be traced to me no matter how hard anyone searches. Is that possible?"

"I'll try my best, but I must warn you, nothing is without risks." Tapping his pad with his pen, Dawson said, "I must assume, of course, that everything, I mean the directions that you provide, will be legal. And the money must come from a legal source."

"Of course. I assume if I ever ask you to do something improper you would refuse."

"Indeed."

"The purpose of the organization is to provide money and medical care to women who were treated in the infirmary at Auschwitz or in any concentration camp where human experiments were performed. I've been fortunate and I'll give a large amount of money to the organization." Helgman unfolded a paper yellowed with age, ragged at the edges, and handed it across the desk. "Here is a list of names," he said. "There'll be others from time to time. I don't know where these people are now. Many have died, I suppose. Many are in other countries. I want you to find them or their surviving families no matter where they are. The organization is to take care of them and their families. See they get whatever they may need. I want life made as easy as possible for them. They have suffered enough. They are not to know where the money comes from. Is this something you can do?"

"Yes, although it may be costly," the lawyer replied. "I'm thinking that your goals might be best achieved by setting up a trust." Dawson's mind was racing and he jotted down a list of questions. But instead of asking them, he said, "It's clear this subject troubles you. You need tell me nothing further at this time. I think I can research all I need."

Dawson copied the names from the ancient sheet of paper. When he finished, he scanned the list and frowned. All but two of the names were women's. He started to ask about that, but thought better of it.

"There will be a second organization—I guess another trust, as you say." Helgman seemed unaware of Dawson's puzzlement.

"Another organization?" Dawson was intrigued by the man sitting opposite him with the mismatched tie and the slight tic under his right eye. He wanted to ask about the nasty-looking scar running down the side of Helgman's neck and disappearing under his shirt, but again held his tongue.

"You'll understand in a moment," Helgman said. "Hand me a coin. A nickel or a quarter will do."

Helgman accepted the offered nickel, rolled back his right sleeve and held the coin in the palm of his hand. He then swung his arm into the air, the coin now between his fingers. His arm slowly descended, the elbow held rigid. The coin passed directly in front of Dawson, whose eyes never wavered from it.

Just as the coin dropped below Dawson's shoulder, it fell from Helgman's grasp. Dawson's hand reflexively shot out to catch it. His fingers closed on air.

The coin was gone.

Helgman's hand was still outstretched, his fingers spread wide.

"So, where is it?" Dawson asked, again checking his own hand. "I thought I had it."

"Look under your pad."

Dawson picked up the pad of paper and there was the nickel. "That's amazing!"

"Perceptions, sir. Perceptions. The world operates on perceptions. I dare say that so many of them are false."

"But I don't understand how this ties to what you want from me."

"I'm an illusionist. I use illusions in a clown act. I've been performing for children confined to hospitals. Or rather, I should say, Muggs the Clown has been doing the performing. When Muggs performs, those children forget their troubles, or at least they're distracted for a bit. It works wonders for them and, frankly, for me as well." Helgman waited for Dawson to absorb what he was saying. "I'm prepared to perform a show every other weekend any place in the northeast."

"Okay, every other weekend." Dawson made a note on his yellow pad.

"Yes, the demand is much greater than that, but I'm about to adopt a four-year-old boy and I'm looking forward to spending as much time with him as I can."

"When will all this begin?"

"It began years ago. There are four performances scheduled in the next two months." Helgman wrote several hospital names on Dawson's pad and next to each one added a date. Always a Saturday morning.

"I'll be sure to see at least one of these shows. It'll help me going forward."

"Great," Helgman replied. "And one last thing. To do this right will take more money than I have. So I want you to solicit from doctors at the hospitals where I perform. I won't take any money for my time, but I'll require props, travel expenses, that kind of thing. Muggs is getting quite a reputation and I can't coordinate it properly. Not if I wish to remain anonymous."

"Got it." The lawyer put down his pen.

Helgman stood. "Please don't waste any time getting these organizations formed. Time is not my friend."

Dawson came around his desk and grasped Helgman's hand. "I look forward to working with you, Dr. Helgman. These are ambitious projects."

"I'm sure I'm in good hands." Helgman smiled at him for the first time. "Did I give you back your nickel?"

Dawson looked to the spot on his desk where he last saw the coin. It was gone. He lifted his pad. The desk was empty.

"Your jacket pocket ... left side."

Dawson reached in his pocket and pulled out the coin. He patted his suit jacket. Smiling, he said, "I'm checking to see if my wallet's in place. I swear your hands never moved."

"Check your right pocket."

Dawson retrieved a second nickel and turned to Helgman, a lopsided smile on his face.

"Nobody said the nickel that disappeared is the same one that reappeared," Helgman said. "Misdirection and deception, that's what illusion is all about." His tone turned serious. "Remember, no one, and I mean no one, including my soon-to-be wife, knows I'm Muggs. It's vitally important this be kept private."

Dawson lifted his pad after Helgman had left and found a third nickel.

BOOK TWO

1973

SEVENTEEN

Barbara's stepfather, Kenneth Stillson, had been appointed rabbi of Congregation B'nai Emunah in the hilly tree-lined Squirrel Hill section of Pittsburgh around the time that Barbara and Bernard were married. Squirrel Hill is close to the Oakland and Hill District hospitals where Helgman was to work so the Helgmans bought a three-story house on Beechwood Boulevard—a house with a fenced-in back yard overlooking Frick Park.

At first, the families had dinner together on Friday evenings and often on Saturday morning Bernard would attend *Shabbos* services led by his father-in-law. But as Attorney Dawson became more and more proficient at his task, Muggs's popularity snowballed. Bernard had at first refused to do more than two weekend performances a month, but the demand soared and he often did three and sometimes even four. When Barbara finally protested his being away from home every weekend, he cut back to the original schedule.

When people asked Bernard where he was from, he hedged his answer by saying only that he grew up in Pittsburgh. The truth was, however, that during the time he had worked with Katz he had never once taken a streetcar downtown, or for that matter, anywhere. He had walked back and forth from his boarding-house room on McKee Place to the hospital, passing within blocks of Forbes Field, home of the Pirates and the Steelers, oblivious to its very existence. The old field was now gone, having been replaced by Three Rivers Stadium on the North Side, but that was of no consequence to Helgman. Opening day of baseball was, to him, just another day in the operating theater. He had even failed to notice the cars parked in every driveway and empty lot on Sundays in the fall when the Steelers were at home.

Between his medical practice and the Muggs performances, Helgman was so busy it wasn't until recently—now some sixteen years after the Helgmans had moved to Pittsburgh—that he discovered the amazing Carnegie Museum and only then because Barbara had insisted that they take Leslie to see the dinosaur skeletons that made the museum so famous. On that sunny afternoon Helgman also discovered that he had been living in the shadow of one of the world's leading libraries—a library used to research the Manhattan project at the same time he had been suffering in the camp at Auschwitz.

Earlier in the week, Rabbi Stillson had insisted that the two families spend time together in the city. At first Helgman had resisted, mainly because of a Muggs performance, but Barbara had prevailed and he had shifted the time of the performance to allow him to spend most of the day with his family. On Monday, after they had visited Phipps Conservatory, Buhl Planetarium, and ridden on one of the incline railroads up the side of Mt. Washington, Barbara pulled her husband aside. "I wonder what's gotten into Dad. Over the weekend he's dragged us everywhere he can think of. It's not a bad thing, but it's so unlike him. We did the Block House, Phipps Conservatory, the zoo, and the museum. Oh, I forgot the planetarium and the picnic in North Park. I'm surprised he didn't take us out to Kennywood Park to ride the Thunderbolt. After services on *Shabbos*, he even suggested we go see some clown act at the hospital. You were out so I felt uncomfortable taking Les. I'm sorry now that I didn't go. Dad says the clown is the best."

Helgman's stomach knotted knowing that the rabbi could have been in the spectators. That thought overwhelmed him. Funny, though, that Helgman hadn't seen him.

He turned to respond to Barbara only to find her father standing there. "I understand you're being considered for chief of pediatric surgery," Rabbi Stillson said. "Is that true?"

"I didn't know that was public," Helgman answered in a half-questioning tone. He glanced in the direction of Barbara who was now off talking to her mother.

"No, it wasn't Barbara who told me. I have congregants—doctors—who refer patients to you. They keep me abreast of what's going on."

"I doubt if they'll give me the position."

"Why not?" Stillson asked, his face showing concern. "You're the best there is."

"Hospital politics are not my thing. Stepped on too many toes. Ruffled too many feathers."

"A shame. A real shame. You deserve it."

"Actually, I'm fine the way it is. I don't want extra responsibility." What Helgman didn't say was that Muggs was booked for every other Saturday, usually for performances in two hospitals in the same city. Sometimes Helgman would even consent to a third performance. He didn't have time for administrative duties.

"You know, Bernard, you're a son to me." Stillson said, his eyes growing misty. "The only son available to me." He cleared his throat. "I can't imagine anyone doing the job better than you."

"That's not for either of us to say, I'd have to think. But thanks for the nice words. All my time is taken up with my patients."

"Is that what you were doing Saturday? Repairing an injured child? I couldn't find you."

Helgman went rigid. Realizing he had overreacted, he bent to tie his shoe. "I'm not sure what you mean." He stood to face the rabbi.

"Saturday afternoon after synagogue I visited the hospital as I do every *Shabbos* to see the children. A clown was to perform at two so I called home hoping you and the family could come. Barbara said you were at the hospital. She didn't know when you'd be finished and felt uncomfortable bringing Les without you. Silly of her, but I couldn't change her mind."

Helgman regained his composure. "Sorry Les missed him. Maybe next time."

Rabbi Stillson studied Helgman for a long moment, a quizzical expression forming. He stared directly into his son-in-law's eyes with an intensity that Helgman found unsettling. "You know, there was something about the clown, something very familiar. This was the first time I've actually seen a performance. Yet, I feel as though I know him. Ever have that feeling about someone, only to find that you actually do know them? I think it's the way he holds his head. Tipped to the side the way you do."

"I'm sure all clowns move the same." Helgman forced himself to be calm. "They must learn that in clown school—or wherever clowns come from."

"He plays the hospital many times during the year. Always for the children. I'm surprised you haven't seen him perform."

"I have, actually. Any number of times."

"So why haven't you taken your son to see him? I'm certain the boy would enjoy the performance."

"He's twenty-one. Can you believe it? He's not a boy anymore."

Helgman's attempt to move his father-in-law to a different topic didn't work. The rabbi, for his part, continued his intense focus on his son-in-law's face, making Helgman all the more uncomfortable. "That clown's good, does wonders for the children. I see the results afterwards. Everyone, the children as well as the staff, are, well, upbeat for weeks."

Bernard looked away in a feeble attempt to hide his emotions. He was sure his father-in-law knew, or guessed, the truth. He prayed the old man would respect his privacy and not confront him directly.

"The children try to reproduce his tricks," Stillson went on. "The hospital finds pennies everywhere; in the food, in pillowcases, in bedpans, and even swallowed." Stillson fell silent, as if debating what to say—or how to say it. Then he leaned close to his son-in-law, his voice a whisper.

Here it comes, Helgman thought. He knows the truth about Muggs. How shall I answer him?

"Bernard," the rabbi began, "I have cancer. Six months, they tell me. Possibly a year. Suddenly, each moment is precious. I want to compress what I expected to be the rest of my life into the remaining few months. I was looking forward to retirement and traveling, visiting Israel again and California. It's hard to believe I've never been to California. Always too busy. What was so important, I ask myself. Pending death puts life into a whole other focus." He forced a smile. "I now have twenty-twenty vision on that score."

Bernard clasped the rabbi's shoulders and held tight.

"There are many things I wanted to live to see," Stillson went on. "Now, it seems, I won't have that chance. But, Bernard, I do have one wish. A wish only you can grant."

"I'll do everything I possibly can. You know that." Helgman assumed that his father-in-law was talking along medical lines.

"I want to celebrate my grandson's *bar mitzvah*. It's long overdue."

The request caught Helgman by surprise. His first thought was that the old man had gone mad.

"It's all I have left to look forward to," the rabbi went on. "Please grant my last wish."

Helgman thought a moment. Knowing his son's ability to memorize, he said, "It's possible, I think, for Les to learn the Hebrew prayers and readings a *bar mitzvah* boy is supposed to lead the congregation in. But that's a lot to ask of him. Why put him through it and set him up for possible failure?"

"I've thought about that." Stillson's face was animated. "I can teach him what he needs to know. We can have the ceremony during the Fourth of July weekend. That gives me almost five weeks. It won't be easy—for either of us—but it can be done."

"I have to check with Barbara." Helgman stalled even though he knew his wife would do anything to please her stepfather.

"He *can* learn it," Stillson pressed. "You've said many times he loves tapes. I'll tape everything for him. We'll cut his part way down. You just tell him you'd like him to do it and he and I'll work on it. The young man wants to please. It would be a shame not to give him a chance."

"I don't think it's a good idea," Helgman said. But he understood that the rabbi, armed with the knowledge that Helgman was Muggs, had worked him into a corner. "I'll check with Barbara." He knew that unless Barbara vetoed the idea he had little choice.

Helgman looked over to where the women were standing. Barbara was holding a handkerchief to her face and her body was shaking.

"Her mother is telling her now," the rabbi said. "Bernard, I'll die a content man if I can see my only grandchild called to the Torah."

Helgman bore witness to God's miracles every day. His belief was self-sustaining, free floating, unconnected to organized religion. He thought of God as a given, like any accepted fact. True because it is true, not true because a religion says it's true. However, after Auschwitz he could not bring himself to participate in the rituals of religion. Certainly, not while the vision of tormented bodies haunted him.

Despite Bernard's belief, he knew that this gentle man, the son of generations of rabbis, a man whose life was dedicated to teaching and attending to life's wounds, deserved what little comfort Bernard could provide. Granting the last wish of a dying man was something Helgman simply could not deny.

Resigned to the situation, Helgman said, "Just don't be disappointed if Les doesn't make it."

"Have faith, Bernard. The boy—young man—will do just fine."

"Okay, but let's be sure Barbara approves. Then we'll see what Les says about it."

"Bernard, I appreciate you doing this. It means so much to me." The rabbi threw his arms around Helgman and hugged him.

For the first time since as far back as he could remember, other than lately with Barbara, Helgman did not have the urge to pull away from the touch of another human being.

Later that night, Helgman turned to Barbara, "You haven't said anything for hours. Thinking about your father?"

"He gave me life when I wanted to die. Before he came along, I had nothing but hatred for men ... all men. Without him, neither you nor Les would be in my life." She wiped her eyes. "Thanks for allowing Les to have a *bar mitzvah*. You've given Father more than you know."

"I couldn't say no, but I don't think it's a good idea."

"I'm happy you couldn't." She paused, struggling with her next words. "It's uncanny how much my father is like you. Mother told me things I never knew. Things he never wanted me to know. What he didn't tell you, and what he'll never speak about, is that he lost his first wife and twin sons in Poland."

"He spoke to me as if I were his only son. I can't recall his exact words, but that's how it came out."

"You *are* his only son."

"Wait. Now I remember. His actual words were, 'The only son available to me.' I think he wanted me to ask what he meant, but I was too absorbed in myself to pick up on it."

"I had no idea and neither did Mother." She again wiped her eyes. "He just told her a week ago. She knew he was from Poland. She knew he had lost a wife there. Mother thought she had died from the plague. That's what he told her when they first met. He never mentioned children and she didn't pry."

"He wasn't in the camps, was he?"

"I'm not sure. Underneath that warm smile, he's a private man—very much like you. In fact, it's spooky how much of him I see in you."

Helgman studied his wife trying to determine if she was sending a message. If she was, it was not detectible through her grief.

Softly, Barbara said, "The boys were slain in their cribs. His wife was found on the kitchen floor, her neck sliced clean through. The police had come looking for the Rabbi. He had defied their orders to stop holding prayer services, to stop teaching Hebrew to the children. When they came for him, he was in another village conducting the funeral of his brother, also a rabbi. Word came to him at the funeral and he was told not to go home. He went anyway, to touch them one last time, to say *kaddish* over them. He buried them with his own hands."

"I wish I had known all this." Helgman was upset with himself for not taking the time to have engaged more with his father-in-law and perhaps to have learned what he had just now been told. He wondered how Stillson could continue to embrace a God who allowed such barbarity.

Barbara guessed at his thoughts. "For him to have walked away from his religion would have been to allow them to win. It was not God who caused the atrocities. It was people disobeying God—people abandoning all that is human. Bernie, if only you ... and he ... and the others who survived could talk to those of us who were not there. If only you could trust us enough to tell us what happened—what really happened and not just the superficial stuff. Please, I beg you, tell me what really happened."

"It's too awful. I wake in the night from a dream, and I want to tell you—But I can't. Words just won't come."

"When we first met, you told me what you did for food. We've been married almost seventeen years and I don't know much more about you now than I did then."

"Like you said, I'm not very different from your father."

"Try, Bernie, try," she pleaded. "I don't want to learn your secrets on your death bed. I love you. I won't hurt you."

"It's so deep-down painful that I can't even put it in context. I was forced to do such awful ...." The words froze in his throat. His eyes filled with tears. "I'm sorry. I just can't."

She put her hand on his leg, something she had only recently been able to do without him jerking away. "I'm sorry. When you're ready, I'll be here. How often have I said this to you? Wake me in the middle of the night if that's when you want to talk." She patted him and smiled. "I've always wanted to believe that the secret of where you go on weekends has something to do with your life in Germany. Just tell me you don't have another woman."

"Oh, Barbara! There is no other woman! There never could be. You, of all people, should know that." He now realized how much trust she had placed in him over the course of their marriage. He had been away more than half the weekends since their marriage.

"I'm not complaining, mind you. I promised before we were married that I wouldn't and I keep my promises. Only...."

"What?"

"Only, it gets lonely when you're not home. Les misses you when you are not here and I don't know what to tell him."

"Just what you've been telling him. I'm away on business." Years earlier Helgman had thought the memories would fade with time. But they'd grown stronger, more vivid. What he had done in the camp to survive seemed more monstrous with each passing year. Only during the brief few hours when he became the clown, when he saw the young faces light up, the eyes go wide with wonder, would the camp not be with him. Then and only then was he free of the awful guilt.

Muggs the clown was his only retreat from the torment that was otherwise always with him. He shivered at the thought of losing even a part of that sanctuary.

EIGHTEEN

All week Helgman continued to replay the distressing conversation he had had with Barbara. It wasn't that he didn't want to talk about his early life. He couldn't. Memories of his life before going to live with Dieter Schmidt had been all but wiped clean, either from emotional trauma or from the need for self-preservation. He clung to fleeting images of his own *bar mitzvah*—standing between a group of men and reading prayers; of a *tallis* being draped over his shoulders; of plates of cakes being passed around—as proof that he really was Jewish. But it was all hazy, vague. He had nothing concrete.

Then suddenly he visualized sunshine and recalled the time when laughing came easy and playing in the snow was fun. He remembered his father taking him for a long walk in the woods, just the two of them. He was about eleven years old and they had stopped by a quiet pond. He was tossing stones, making them skip across the water. His father had shown him how to find just the right kind of flat stones and how to throw side arm.

On the way home, his father had said, "Son, bad things are starting to happen. The government is going crazy and we Jews must be careful. Maybe soon things will return to normal. I hope so. But you should be thankful for every day you have." A shadow had fallen across his father's face, but then it cleared. "We're a resilient people," he continued, "and there's at least some good news. Your mother is going to have a baby. Now don't tell her I said anything. She wants it to be a surprise. Don't spoil it for her. Promise?"

The image of a little girl Helgman believed to be his sister came to him occasionally, but the image was always blurry. He had lived with lies and deception for so long that it was impossible to know what was real and what was made up. Barbara was right, he realized, when she had said he was hiding from himself. Or running from something.

"If you can't talk to me," she'd said, "then please find a professional you can talk with."

His mind was on Barbara as he approached his office door. A well-dressed woman stopped pacing the hallway when he stopped to pull out his keys. Absent-mindedly he nodded to her while he unlocked the private entrance to his office suite.

"Dr. Helgman. Bernard," the woman called. "How are you?"

The voice. The face. It all came flooding back in a dizzying moment. "My God. Stephanie! It's been a long time. A lifetime. You're looking well. You're about the last person in the world I expected to see here."

"You're not doing too badly yourself, Doctor." Stephanie laughed nervously. "But then I already knew that."

"What does that mean?"

"I've followed your career in the newspapers. The famous Bernard Helgman. More articles than I can count. I understand a grafting procedure has been named after you. The Helgman—"

"Mesh. The Helgman Mesh."

"You should be proud of what you've accomplished here in Pittsburgh. The new pediatric burn wing and all."

"A lot of doctors caused that to happen. I played a small part."

"The mesh didn't hurt, or so the hospital would want us to believe."

"Us?"

"Green Lines made a contribution. We receive promotional pieces in the mail."

"The children thank Green Lines then. That procedure actually saved my son's life. That's the important thing. It saves lives."

Stephanie's face fell. "Son? I was sure you'd never marry."

"It's a long story. Come on in. We can catch up before my first patient."

When they were seated in his private office, Helgman told Stephanie about Barbara and Leslie, but without going into any detail about Les's disability. Then he said, "But now let's talk about you. Start with why you came here. Don't get me wrong. It's great to see you, but I never expected this. It's been ... let's see ... sixteen, maybe even seventeen, years, right?"

"Why I came? Yes. Well like you said, it's a long story."

"How about the highlights."

"Well, for one thing, I also married. But I'm divorced. I married Bill Nelson, a man I knew in college. Actually, he's the son of my father's banker. He couldn't handle my success with the shipping business."

"Wait. Doesn't your father ... "

"My father had a heart attack and retired. Then Uncle Dieter had a stroke about eight years ago and I took over. Green Lines is doing well."

Helgman guessed from her assured manner that "doing well" was an understatement.

"But there's more, which has to do with why I came."

Helgman's eyebrows rose.

"I've come across all kinds of papers and records since I took over," Stephanie said. "It seems that, for all his bellowing about Jews, Uncle Dieter hated Hitler with a passion. It's all there in a diary I found in a locked drawer in his office."

"A diary?"

"I can only imagine he planned to dispose of it at some point but the stroke happened before he could. It seems Uncle Dieter adopted the son of a former employee. He took the boy just before the Gestapo came for the boy's parents. The boy's name was Maximilian. Actually, I believe Dieter changed it from something else to Maximilian so it wouldn't sound Jewish. The boy lived with Uncle Dieter for over a year and I think I may have met him a few times when I was three or four years old. The truth is I have no real memory of anything that happened in Germany."

Helgman's stomach knotted, but he maintained his composure.

"From what he wrote, and from what I could glean from the company records—what little is left of them," Stephanie continued, "Green Lines owned four warehouses, a small train line, and three ships. It's name was *Lieferservice* then. Railroads were being forced to transport Jews and that's what sent my uncle into a rage against Hitler. According to the diary, he gave up the trains and the warehouses in exchange for exit papers for his family and the families of the captains and crews. He formed Green Lines in Greece and ran the ships under the Greek flag during the war. My family lived in Athens until the war ended and then we came to Boston—and Block Island. I was about seven."

Helgman reached for her hand. The feel of it brought back long-buried memories. "That boy was me," he said. "I was Max Schmidt."

"Yes, I know. Uncle Dieter wrote it in his diary. He gave you up to the Gestapo so he could get our family—and his business—out of the country."

"And I'm still bitter towards him for that. But if I'm honest with myself, I have to say that he did what he could for as long as he could to make my life bearable. There were even some good times for a young kid. In fact, I remember him taking me on those trains to visit the warehouses."

"I presume it was the bitterness that brought you to the bluff. To confront him?"

"And but for our little encounter—and needing to get you sewed up—I probably *would* have confronted him. That was my plan. But once you and I got involved, things became complicated."

"Oh Bernard," Stephanie burst out. "I've loved you ever since. God knows I've tried not to. All the time I was married to Bill I thought of you. That's the real reason my marriage ended. Okay, he had his women. But I drove him to it. I wasn't there for him. You can't love two people—or at least I can't." Stephanie's eyes were red and tears flowed down her cheeks. She made no attempt to dry her face.

"Stephanie. It's too late for all of that. I'm a married man now."

"Yes, so you said. A happily married man."

Helgman knew that he hadn't used the word "happily" in conjunction with his marriage but he saw the conversational maneuver that Stephanie was employing. She was probing—perhaps hoping—that he might respond with some kind of indication that he was not happy in his marriage. He was resolved to prevent the conversation from going in that direction. "How long have you been divorced," he asked, attempting to make Stephanie once again the topic of conversation.

"This week is the one-year anniversary." Her voice was muffled.

"So why come here now?"

"I had a lot of thinking to do. Besides, it's a great way to commemorate the first anniversary of a divorce, right? Look up a person you used to be in love with—and still are."

The phrase "in love with" caused the knot that had been forming in Helgman's stomach to tighten even further.

Stephanie went on. "I promised myself I'd never try to see you, but I couldn't help myself."

"I don't ... I don't know what to say." Helgman reddened. "I wish it had worked out, but it never could have."

An intercom voice interrupted them. "Dr. Helgman, your first patient is here."

"Stephanie, I have to go." And then, in spite of himself, and knowing he was asking for trouble, Helgman invited her to dinner. "You like fish I recall."

Stephanie felt her breath catch in her throat. *He hasn't forgotten me either*, she realized. "Fish sounds great."

"Okay, then. Poli's at six?"

Helgman's steps felt light as he hurried down Shady Avenue. He was angry with himself for running late, but as usual, there were several patients who had required more of his attention than had been scheduled.

He spotted Stephanie the moment he entered the restaurant. "I see my party," he informed the hostess, and he made a beeline for her table. Stephanie stood as he approached. All eyes turned toward the exquisitely elegant woman. The pearls extending down into the plunging neckline of her long dress called attention to a figure that seemed to Helgman more stunning than he recalled from almost two decades earlier.

Stephanie positioned herself to be hugged should Helgman feel the urge. "There you are! You've become at a little more punctual, I see."

Helgman glanced at his watch. "I suppose things never really change. It seems almost yesterday I was apologizing for being late."

When they were seated, she said, "I meant to tell you about an article in the Boston Globe about a month ago. You performed an operation on a little girl, a charity case, in Boston. Her face was terribly burned but you made her beautiful. They did a feature in the Sunday magazine about her fantastic recovery. Magic, it was called. The reporter covering the story happened to catch a clown act at the hospital that very same day and she compared your operating room magic to the clown's magic. The article said something like: *Instead of birds and rabbits, this talented doctor magician made a little girl's face appear.*

"Unfortunately, it doesn't always work out that way."

"You're too modest. I remember that Greek restaurant owner and the story of his daughter."

"Teresa," he said immediately. "You have a good memory."

"Do you remember them all?"

Helgman studied his hands. "Yes. Yes I do. All of them."

"Even the ones who ..."

"Especially them. Yes. Even those."

"God, what a burden you carry. What do you do to relax?"

He searched her face to determine if she was just being conversational or trying to probe. Or had she connected him to Muggs? "Work mostly. I spend time with my wife, Barbara, and Les. He's brain damaged, perhaps at birth, perhaps in the fire that originally brought him to me. He's grown now, but he reads only minimally and can't think abstractly. If he's programmed properly, he'll do what he's been told. When we taught him to take a shower, we didn't think to tell him to turn the water off. Things like that. But he never forgets what he hears and can mimic anything. Even when he was young and I read him a story, he was able to recite it almost word for word after that."

They fell quiet. It was not like the comfortable silence of a long married couple content to enjoy their own private thoughts, but rather the uncomfortable silence of relative strangers struggling to decide on the next safe topic.

"You know," he finally ventured, "I've been thinking of what you said in my office about how your husband couldn't handle your success with the shipping business. You sounded like the world had ended. But you've got everything—an attractive woman who controls a multi-million dollar business."

"Being attractive isn't all it's cracked up to be. Yes, put a smile and a wiggle out there and men come running. But life's more than what's on the surface. You, of all people, know that!"

Stephanie paused to catch her breath and to calm the emotions that were building inside her as she prepared to repeat what she had said to Helgman in his office, hoping this time for a more encouraging response from him.

"Bernard," she cried out, "I don't have the one thing in this world I want more than anything. It's you! Try as

I might I can't—I won't—be able to fill that empty space with anything but you."

Helgman surprised himself with the vehemence of his reaction. "*Your* empty space? What about *my* empty space? You seem to have forgotten that it was you who didn't return my calls after your graduation. Or any time after that. It was painful, Steph. I filled my empty space with a new family and a new life. You have to admit that what you're saying is more than a little strange."

"I know. You're right. But I did it out of love."

"Love? Really?" Helgman shot back, curious to hear the explanation.

"Uncle Dieter threatened to have you ruined. Something he knew about your medical education. And I guess in the interest of full disclosure I have to tell you that he said he would only allow me to join the business if I promised not to see you ever again."

"So you sold out."

"I prefer to believe I protected you."

"Well, also in the interest of full disclosure, whatever that is, I was really calling you out of desperation." He went on to tell her about Leslie and his need to be married to adopt the boy. Then he added, "To be crude about it, I guess you could say I was wife-shopping. I thought that perhaps ... perhaps you would have agreed. At least so that we could adopt Leslie."

"Are you saying you don't love her?"

"I'm not saying that at all." Pausing, he added, "I've already said too much. The truth is neither of us, you or me, deserve any medals. The past is gone."

A busboy appeared to clear their plates. They sat in silence until he had done his job and walked away.

Stephanie spoke first. "I keep thinking if Dieter had stayed in Germany and kept the train line, there's a good chance he'd be dead. I don't know what would have happened to me, being his niece and all and being that my father was second-in-command. I could be dead as well. In any event, I certainly wouldn't have what I have."

"Steph," Bernard said gently, "that's all speculation. Anyway, the only thing that matters is now."

The awkward silence returned until Stephanie prompted Helgman to talk about Leslie.

"The boy has traits and interests that Barbara and I never imagined. Loves animals. Our dog would sleep only with him. When the dog was sick, he'd put his head in Les's lap. The boy can't remain still for two minutes back-to-back, but when the dog got sick Les didn't move the whole time."

"You speak of the dog in the past tense. Did ..."

"The dog was terminally ill and we could not separate the two of them. On the third night, I came home late from the hospital and Les was whimpering in his bed. The dog had died in his arms, but he would not let go. Les slept with the dead dog all night."

"You're making me cry, thinking of it. He sounds like a sweet child."

"We took Les to the shelter to find a new dog. He walked up and down, putting his hands and fingers into every cage, making noises with the animals. Usually, he never speaks. Not in public anyway. That day he called out loudly. 'Daddy, Daddy. All out!'" He wanted them all released. It took us a while to calm him down. Then he retraced his steps and checked every dog over and over. We spent most of the day at the shelter. Finally, he picked out the sickliest dog you ever saw. I thought the mutt wouldn't last the week. Even the manager at the shelter was embarrassed and offered to refund the adoption fee if the dog died. But the dog didn't die. He thrived and followed Les everywhere. The first one was Dog and Leslie named this one Dogdog. They sleep together and play together. Still do, in fact. You can't get the two of them apart."

"Dogdog. I like that. Are animals his only interest?"

"He has a fascination with music. Somehow he's mastered the sound equipment I bought him. He sits for hours making tapes and singing to the music. He can rearrange pieces from many different recordings into new music. And the results are terrific. I remember the first time I listened to one of his tapes. I was expecting—I don't know what I was expecting—but I certainly wasn't expecting to hear something that made sense. His recording flowed perfectly. We started to label what songs were on each tape, but he doesn't need labels to know where the songs are. He just knows."

"What do you mean, he just knows?"

"All you need do is hum some melody. Any melody, and he'll put on a tape that has that melody somewhere in the music. He's never wrong."

"Maybe I could help you find him work in the music field? Some folks owe me a favor or two."

"Who would hire him? He can only do what he's been told to do."

"Please let me try."

"Maybe sometime. But not now." Helgman paused. "While you were talking about your family I thought of something I haven't thought of in a long time."

"What is that?"

"My original ... birth ... name, was Mordechai. Mordechai Stein. I mean before Dieter changed it to Maximilian Schmidt."

Stephanie studied Helgman a long moment. "I understand why you didn't keep Dieter's name, but when you got out of the camp why didn't you go back to your original name?"

Helgman had wondered that same thing over the years but always found it impossible to reconstruct the exact reasons he had done anything in all the turmoil that ensued as he was liberated. He recalled Russian flags going up around the camp, and he recalled stumbling over bodies the Nazis had dumped in their haste to disappear. He had seen the guard he held most accountable for the physical abuse he had suffered. The man was using his bayonet in an attempt to dig under a concrete wall. Helgman replayed the vision of himself yanking the weapon from the torn hands of his former captor, cutting his own face in the process. When the guard managed to get up onto his knees, Helgman drove the blade through the man's neck. Was that murder—or self-defense?

"Are you okay?" Stephanie said. "You look ... more troubled than usual."

"When I got out I was ashamed," Helgman replied. "Ashamed for what I'd done to survive and ashamed because I lived when almost everyone else had died." He choked back his emotion. "I just wanted to start over."

"Bernard, I'm sorry." Stephanie reached across the table to hold his hand. "I'm sorry you had to endure what you did."

Helgman sat quietly for a moment regaining his composure. He then stretched his back and announced, "I hate to say good-bye, but I'm exhausted. It's been a hard week and I've got an early call."

"But it's Friday night. You don't schedule operations on Saturday do you? I hope not."

"I have other business to attend to."

"When my former husband said he was attending to business on weekends, it turned out to be motel time for him and his secretary."

"Nothing like that, I assure you."

"No. Of course not. I'm sorry I even implied it," Stephanie said. "I know you too well."

Staring at her across the table, and hearing her last remark, Helgman realized that she really did still care for him.

And he had to admit to himself that the feeling was mutual—and that it had always been so.

NINETEEN

On the same Friday that Stephanie re-entered Helgman's life, Barbara was kneeling over her flowerbed at the front of the Helgman residence. Les was in his bedroom with a friend listening to music and she was enjoying her quiet time alone. She had begged Bernard to take a few days off, but he had refused, claiming he was booked solid. In fact, she had called his nurse only to find the patient load unusually light.

A woman walked up the front sidewalk and called out, "Hello? Barbara?"

"Yes? Who is it?" Barbara called back in reply and then pushed herself up and turned around. "Grace! Grace Passic!" Barbara threw her arms wide to receive a hug from her friend.

"Grace Simchek now." Grace smiled broadly. "Been married quite a while now. Have two boys, seven and five."

"How wonderful. But what are you doing in Pittsburgh?"

"Moved back here from upstate about ten years ago. I'm *from* Pittsburgh, remember? I worked in the operating room when Bernard was studying under Katz."

"Oh my God, Gracie, I'm so sorry. You *did* call me when you moved back. I've been meaning to invite you over and just never got around to it. You look great. Come on in. Can I get you something?"

"You lie so convincingly, Barbara, but I love it. I've gained at least fifteen pounds and I wasn't a small woman before," she laughed, "in case you hadn't noticed. Glen loves 'em big, or at least that's what he tells me."

They ended up in the living room after taking a quick tour. "You have a lovely house," Grace said. "And I see you love gardening. Things must be going well for you."

"Thank you. Gardening's my outlet. Are you sure I can't get you anything to drink?"

"Water if you don't mind."

"How about a real drink. A scotch maybe, or something mixed?"

"Water'll be fine. Or iced tea if you have some."

Grace followed Barbara to the kitchen. "Married life seems to suit you just fine. Have you gotten over—"

"Come, let's sit on the back porch." Barbara cut off the questions she knew Grace was about to ask. "I hope you have time. We have a lot of catching up to do."

As they sat in the screened-in porch, Grace with an iced tea and Barbara with a double scotch, they took turns running through their respective lives. Barbara dug out a box crammed full of pictures and the two women sat together reviewing the history of Leslie's childhood.

"He's about, let's see, twenty, I guess," Grace said.

"Twenty-one in chronological age. Much younger in development."

"That procedure your husband performed on Leslie caused quite a ruckus. But somehow they patched it up and, as you must know, the procedure he used on Les is now the norm. They even named it the Helgman Mesh."

"Yes, I'm so proud of him."

From the bits Grace revealed, Barbara inferred that her husband Glen worked only occasionally at odd jobs and that they lived on her nurse's salary. "I work pediatrics at the burn hospital, mostly handling your husband's patients. We live in Oakland so it's easy to get to work. It's hard on the kids growing up with their mother gone all the time, but the money's good." She looked around. "Not like this. You have it made. Oh, what I wouldn't give for a back yard like this. And a maid doing the dirty work. Our vacations consist of day trips to Ligonier Mountain. I call our summer vacation 'going to Porchville.'"

"It's not all that it seems," Barbara responded. "No maid. Makes Bernie uncomfortable to have anyone around. Invading his personal space, he claims."

"Oh, I'm sorry. I thought because you've stayed married this long, he was over his ... his problem."

"That's a long story." Barbara replied wistfully.

"Tell me."

"Bottom line is that I have come to love the man."

"Really!"

"I know. Crazy, right? I was afraid of men when we married. You know, we discussed all of that. Bernie took all that fear away."

"That's incredible. I'm happy for you."

"I started to feel the stirrings of it watching him interact with Les. He proved to be such a good father. So patient. And so adaptable to Les's needs. How couldn't you love a man like that?"

"A good father is one thing. A good husband is something else again."

"I know. You're right. He's been nothing but good to me. Well mostly good. He sits with me in the evenings and we talk about his day in the hospital and his latest cases. I tell him about my day. It feels ... comfortable."

"That's a lot more than I get from Glen. Comfortable is one thing, although I'm not sure what you described is love. Sounds like a good friend. What about romance?"

Barbara's shoulders slumped. A moment later, her mind made up, she sat upright as though a weight had been lifted. She took a heavy drink of scotch and waited until it settled. "Oh, Grace, you can't begin to imagine what it's like not being able to touch the man you share your life with. I feel so ... so ... well empty. I know it's not my fault, but there doesn't seem to be anything I can do. There's such emptiness about everything. When the flowers in the garden bloom, it's as if they bloom gray." She swept her arm around, "I keep a good house, but he doesn't notice. I don't think he's ever once gone out to the gazebo. The smell of the flowers seems to agitate him."

Grace hugged her, and with an arm still around her shoulder said, "I thought you didn't want—"

"That's the terrible irony of this. He's been so wonderful to me. He makes me feel special. Except ... except now that I'm over my fear, I want intimacy before it's too late."

"That *is* a terrible irony. I feel so bad for you."

"I know it's wrong to have the urges I do. Bernie's a good man and even without romance, I'm in love with him. But sometimes, late at night, I lay in bed wishing a man, any man, would come to me. I know I sound like a common slut, but I read books and ... and can't get enough of the romance scenes." She bowed her head. "I know it sounds crazy but ... but I want to have a baby before ... before—"

"Goodness! That is—"

"Even worse, I've been fantasizing about men I know. I feel like a tramp because I want sex with any man who will have me. Oh, God, me of all people." Barbara took another long swallow.

"Truth is, hon, sex with Glen isn't the greatest, but it's better than nothing. Just knowing someone needs you makes all the difference."

"I'd give anything for that."

Steering the discussion to other topics, Barbara said, "You know, I once touched the scar on his neck and asked how he was injured. My God, the look that came into his eyes was frightening. He actually began to shake. Sometimes it seems he is getting close to talking, but the words freeze. A certain look comes across his face and the moment passes."

"You know, I feel responsible for you two. Obviously Bernard's problem hasn't gone away. I was hoping it had." Before Barbara could respond, Grace continued, "I'm sorry to further upset you, but you should know—"

"Know what?"

"There's talk at the hospital."

"What kind of talk?"

"Everyone knows that Bernard is unavailable most weekends. And...and there's a doctor—Randy Peters—who was on Dr. Katz's team when your husband showed up and Katz moved him out of the program to make room for Bernard. Well, anyway, Peters has been implying to anyone who will listen that the reason Bernard is rarely available to come into the hospital on the weekends is that he is ..." Grace took a depth breath, then gathering her courage, rushed on, " ... homosexual, and weekends are when Bernard has his liaisons. The talk is getting vicious, and—"

"I can't listen to this." Barbara stood up in an attempt to end the conversation.

"It may be talk, Barbara, but it's beginning to cause problems. Homosexuals are ... well, not welcome in the operating room. Already, some doctors have refused to work with Bernard altogether. That's serious. There's a movement to have his privileges taken away."

"That'll kill him. He lives for his work."

"I can't believe they'll do anything to him. He's too valuable to the hospital. The children's wing was built on money that came in because of him. But I couldn't just sit by any longer and say nothing. Your husband is by far the most gifted surgeon I've ever seen. I've watched him place sutures so fine it looks like pantomime. You never actually see the suture material and the children heal so perfectly."

Silence enveloped the porch. Even the birds seemed muted and far away.

"Sometimes, on a Friday afternoon, I've seen him walk out of an operating room so obviously emotionally drained that I'm sure he'll never return. But on Monday he's back at it, totally refreshed. You can see it in his eyes. Monday eyes I call them. Whatever happens on the weekends does wonders. That's why I was surprised when you told me about your relationship."

Barbara sat up straight. "What are you saying?"

"If he's not sleeping with you," Grace blurted, "then how do you know he's not with someone else, possibly a man?"

"I know my husband well enough to know he's not with anyone, man or woman." Barbara wiped away a tear. "He's driven by something beyond my understanding. When we were first married we tried to sleep in the same bed. I accidentally rolled against him and at first, he didn't move away. Then suddenly his body broke into a sweat. I mean water poured from him. When he stood, the sheets were soaked. He was shaking violently and I thought I'd have to call an ambulance."

"Was he awake? I mean when you were against him, did he know you were there?"

"I thought so at the time, but I've come to believe he was never fully aware." Barbara let out a long breath. "The bottom line is I need my husband to make love to me. Is that so horrible?"

"If sex is so important to you, then divorce him."

"I can't do that to him. I can't."

Grace dug into her purse. "Here, take this card. If your husband agrees, this might do the trick. This guy's about Bernard's age and his specialty is sexual dysfunction. From what I hear, the man performs miracles. Get Bernard to see him. It can't hurt."

Barbara studied the card. "I doubt if Bernie will agree."

"Here's a name for you." Grace wrote on a slip of paper. "This woman works wonders also. Please talk to her before you too make a big mistake."

Barbara felt the churning within her, the feeling she knew only another scotch could suppress. "Can I get you more tea? Or something stronger? I'm going for a refill."

"Water is all." Grace followed her friend to the kitchen. "You know, the fact he's out of town so often without you feeds the rumors."

Barbara poured herself a double and took a long swallow before responding. "It's unusual, yes. But that doesn't mean he's doing anything improper."

"I just hope he survives the rumors. Like I said, it's getting vicious."

"He's a survivor." Barbara took a long swallow before saying, mostly to assure herself, "He's been though worse."

TWENTY

It was after midnight when Helgman arrived home. The restaurant had closed at ten-thirty and he and Stephanie had walked up Murray Avenue to a lounge where they had sipped coffee and talked. He had been tired, but yet had felt strangely alive. They had not seen each other for almost two decades, but it felt to him as if there had been no break at all.

Helgman tried to force his mind to focus on his show in Mars Township the next morning. It was only a forty-minute drive so he wouldn't have to leave until seven. Even seven thirty would work. His spirits, already high, soared as he visualized the children's smiling faces as a bird disappeared in front of their eyes only to appear under a chair. A fish in a bowl would come out of his hat. The fish would remain behind after the show. Several other brightly colored fish would arrive later in the day, as would a large tank and other equipment, all courtesy of Helgman's trust.

Halfway up the stairs to his bedroom, Helgman realized age was catching up to him. The tightness across his chest was getting worse. Sometimes the tips of his fingers tingled. It had been years since he had to think about what his hands were doing. Now, near the end of a particularly long procedure, he had to will his fingers to follow his mind.

He was startled to hear Barbara's voice breaking into his thoughts. He couldn't remember the last time she was awake when he came home so late. He rushed to her room. Barbara was propped against pillows, books and magazines strewn carelessly on the floor. Her reddened eyes evidenced the hours she had spent crying. He kissed her forehead gently and smelled the alcohol, a smell that had become increasingly common in the last few years.

"Are you alright? Is everything okay with Les? Your father?"

"They're fine. I just need to talk to you."

"Okay. What?"

"Grace came by today."

"Grace?"

"Grace Simchek?"

"Woman's the best there is in the operating room. Is something wrong? Why would she—"

"She wanted to talk. Following up with Les. Remember, she's the one who introduced us."

Helgman knew the rumors and guessed what this was really about. He turned away and started toward his room. Long gone were the nights where he could exist on three or four hours of sleep. Now, he felt it if he didn't get six.

"Don't leave." Barbara's voice was unusually strident. "We need to talk. I hardly ever ask anything of you. It's important."

"Give me a moment to wash up," he called to her from the hall bathroom, buying time to gather his thoughts and to be sure there was no residual lipstick from where Stephanie had impulsively kissed him.

Returning to his wife's room, he asked, "So what is it Barbara? I'm tired. It's late. Can't this wait till morning?"

"What morning? You're always gone before the sun rises. I expected you home for dinner."

"I had an emergency."

"It's never different is it? Always some emergency. Don't I ever count?"

"Of course you count. What is it? What's wrong?"

"It's always the same. Another child to repair. My God, you'd think you were the only doctor in the world! You have other responsibilities. Leslie. Me."

"I've tried looking for an associate, but I can't find anyone."

"You're looking for someone as good as you. You'll never find that person. "

"For God's sake, can you tell me what's wrong?" He stood facing her, too tired for mental games. He knew that if this had been a medical emergency, a child needing his care, his mind would be alert and his body would respond. "I'm sorry," he said. "I'm tired. I didn't mean to bark. Now what's bothering you?"

"Your weekends," she blurted. "Like tomorrow. What kind of business takes you away on weekends? I still can't understand where you go—or what you do. And it's been getting worse."

Calmer than he felt, Helgman replied, "I thought we had an understanding."

"That was years ago. Things change."

"Barbara, I'm exhausted. I don't have time for twenty questions."

"Okay, then just answer me *one* question," she sobbed. "Is it another woman?"

"Of all people, you know that can't be true. You think I've been pretending with you?"

"I don't know what to think. A woman needs to know she's loved—that the man she loves wants her, desires her. Sure, you treat me well on the surface, give me material things. But I feel empty. You've eliminated my fear of men. How much clearer do I need to be?" She closed her eyes. "Do you even know the color of my eyes?"

Helgman realized she was right, it had been a long time since he had looked at her, really saw her. "They're green, of course." He also knew her height, the gray in her hair, the small brown spot on her neck. He also knew that of late her eyes were puffy and bloodshot almost every time he saw her. He knew these things as a doctor but not as a husband. "I'm sorry," he said. "I'm sorry. What more can I tell you? What more do you want from me? You're the most attractive woman I know. You still have the most beautiful green eyes I've ever seen. There's no woman I want more than you."

"One more question, then: Is it a man?"

The question hit Helgman as if he had been slammed in the chest with a board and the wind knocked out of him.

"Grace told me there's talk about you at the hospital. Some doctors won't work with you. Maybe that's why you can't find a partner, now that I think about it."

"I know the talk," he managed. "They think I'm homosexual. That comes from Randy Peters. It goes back a long way. I'm losing promising students over it." He paced the bedroom. "I understand this talk coming from them. But my own wife!"

"It's just not right. Disappearing on weekends, keeping everything so secret. Are you ashamed to tell me?" She pulled a pillow against her body. "I sit here imagining all sorts of things. Yes, I see you glancing at the bottle. How else do you think I get through the days when you're out doing whatever it is you do while I'm here crying myself to exhaustion?"

"I didn't realize—"

"You don't want to realize. I need you, Bernie, but you're not here for me."

He sat on the edge of her bed and took her hand. It was the first time he had touched her in months. "I thought we had a deal."

"Things change. Life changes. Do you want out of the deal?"

"You mean a divorce?"

"If that's what it takes to make you happy. I can't go on like this."

"I don't want a divorce, Barbara, unless *you* want out." He was about to add, "There's no one else for me." But thoughts of Stephanie prevented him from saying it. He slid off the bed and walked to the door.

"No. Don't leave. Come back. Sit on the bed. It was nice." She patted the bed where he had been. "I need you to touch me, hold me. I need to know I add something to your life. I need to feel wanted, that I have value. Just let me comfort you."

He lowered his body onto the bed beside her, but keeping a fair distance between them.

"Please," she pleaded, touching him tentatively. "Tell me where you go, what you do. It's okay, whatever it is. I can't bear not to know."

Suddenly, Helgman saw his wife with new eyes. There was something fundamentally wrong. Her speech was slightly slurred and the way she was holding herself was wrong. The realization that his wife was either an alcoholic, or well on her way to being one, hit him. He put his hand over hers and kissed her forehead. "You've lived up to your part of the bargain, but it's taking a terrible toll on you and I'm sorry." He moved closer to her, closer than he had in many years. The almond smell of her hair flooded his senses. It was the same scent that floated in his dreams at night. He buried his face between her breasts, holding her tighter than ever before.

"Bernie," she whispered, "it's not fair how two people can hurt each other so easily without even trying. Why can't we be like other couples? Other men came through the war, even through the concentration camps. They've adjusted. They've married, had children, raised families. That's the ultimate victory over what happened, isn't it? Why can't we be like them?"

Without releasing her, he said, "They all have scars, skeletons, nightmares. Twisted dreams of reality. Some more than others."

He gave a violent shudder. Squeezing his eyes tight, he realized that this was his last opportunity to keep his marriage together. He had to do it. This was the time for the words that had been frozen in his throat for so long to be let out. He shuddered again, pulled his head away, stared into Barbara's eyes, and then again buried himself against her. "Oh Barbara," he cried, now alternating between shuddering and sobbing. "I was housed in the infirmary where horrible things were done to women. I cleaned the floors, scrubbed the walls, and carried dead bodies to the furnaces. I did anything and everything the doctors—or the guards—ordered. I watched as the guards selected women, and sometimes children, as they came off the trains. They lined them up and it was my job to bring them to the infirmary where those butchers brutalized them. My God, Barbara, I marched those poor people to their agonizing deaths. The guards watched my every move, but I had no right to save myself at the expense of those people. I can't let that go. I owe it to each and every one of them to remember."

Helgman fell silent, his ear pressed against Barbara's chest, hearing the beat of her heart. "They'll never hear children laugh, or see flowers, or enjoy their fragrance. Why should I now be allowed those luxuries? Why should I be allowed to enjoy the pleasures of life when I helped take everything from them?"

Now it was Barbara's turn to struggle for words, overwhelmed by not only the pain of what Bernard went through while in the camp, but the realization of what he experienced every day of his life. The sobs that had begun as she learned of her husband's torment became shudders as her own rush of emotions overwhelmed her knowing that he had finally opened up his innermost self.

They held each other for several moments before she regained enough composure to say, "Bernie, listen to me. You can experience all those things for them. Do it in their memory." Barbara held her broken husband tightly, gently rocking, as she had done with Les when he was little and frightened.

"I've tried to rationalize it," he responded to her comforting. "I tried to make myself believe that if I hadn't done what I did then someone else would have. And that's true enough. But the fact remains it was I who chose to do what I did. And it is I who must take responsibility for my actions. There's no other way for me."

"You told me years ago you also saved lives. That's where you learned to suture as you do. The blame isn't yours. It's those who ran the camps. They're the guilty ones, not you."

"I saved some, but not as many as I should have. What right did I have to live? So many died," he cried. "They died and I lived."

"It was your duty to survive. Now you punish yourself for doing your duty?"

"You say that others have come through it, but nobody came through it undamaged. I can look at a person and know whether he or she was in the camps. Even the toughest of them silently cry out."

"Celebrate life, my husband. You condemn the fact you survived, but you should be happy you're alive. Look at the great good you do."

He took a deep breath but failed to overcome the all-pervading sorrow he had felt since being freed from the camp.

"What I did to survive," he said, the words running together, "was a crime against all humanity. I can't change that now, and I can't forget it either." He took a moment to catch his breath. "I must give back all that I took. Every bit of what I now have came because of what I did. My hands, my fingers. They don't belong to me. They belong to the children, to those who died because I couldn't save them."

Helgman picked up his head and looked into her eyes. "Do you understand what I've said? Do you understand what's driving me—controlling me? I can no more control what I have to do than you can control how you feel."

Barbara felt her husband's body go limp and held him tighter. "Bernie," she whispered, "just tell me what you do when you're away. I need to know. Is that so much to ask?"

He wanted to tell her about Muggs, about how his performances freed him—at least temporarily—from the memories. But the thought of digging any deeper into his emotions overwhelmed him. "I'm sorry, Barbara, I can't say any more. Maybe soon, but not now."

Holding him tight against her, savoring the warmth of his body, Barbara was reluctant to press him. "Would I be upset if I knew."

"Not at all. It's nothing either of us will ever be ashamed of. But please believe me when I tell you it's the one thing in my life that allows me to continue."

"The one thing, my dear Bernie, I can't control is that I love you. But I hurt. I need you as a husband. I want to share your bed with you. I want to wake up in the night and see you, hear you, feel you."

He kissed her, this time on the lips. He held her longer than he had ever held her before. Her body felt good in his arms.

When he finally pulled away, she said, "Please do something for me. Grace gave me the name of a doctor who specializes in problems like you have. His name's Solomon Shapiro. She says he's excellent."

"Sol Shapiro? Really? It's too late."

"Please, Bernie. If you love me, please do it for me. Do it for us before it's too late. That would be the best present you could ever give me." She leaned over and kissed him. "And, Doctor, you of all people know that hormones don't last forever. So please do it soon."

"Soon? I've been seeing Shapiro for almost two months."

TWENTY-ONE

T he July Fourth weekend was fast approaching and Ruth Stillson was doing everything she could to keep her mind from dwelling on her husband's failing health. Ruth wished he would take it easy, but he would always respond to her admonitions in the same way, "There will be plenty of time after the *bar mitzvah* to relax," he would say. "How many times in a man's life will he see his grandson called to the Torah? I have prayed I could live to see this day."

"Oh," she exclaimed as the rabbi quietly shuffled into the kitchen, a prayer book in his hand, looking exhausted. "You startled me."

"I've been waiting for you. Come to bed. Finish in the morning."

"You always think I haven't a thing to do in the morning. I have a full day tomorrow."

"Come, keep me company."

"Just let me put the liver away. All this bending, I'm not used to it anymore."

"I was listening to Leslie earlier and his intonations remind me of my father. Such a voice he had. I remember to this day the tears in his eyes when he passed me the Torah. Now it's my turn to pass it on." He brushed away his own tears. "Here I am crying like a baby and the day hasn't even come yet."

"Tears of joy. Strange how we cry both when we are sad and when we are happy."

"Both are powerful emotions. It's nature's way to shed the emotional overload. It'll be interesting to see if Bernard has tears in his eyes. The man baffles me. Never shows emotion. Won't let me call him to the Torah. Says he believes in God, just not in religion. A puzzle he is."

"He's removed all but the faintest trace of Germany from his speech, but I'm afraid he hasn't erased what happened to him." Feeling the need to change the subject, Ruth asked, "*Nu*, you're happy with Leslie's progress?"

"He sounded good, the part that I heard. Barbara says he's in his room and all she hears are muffled sounds. I taped it for him. I've combined three *aliyah* readings into one. He'll read that one and that way we'll have only one *aliyah*—Leslie's. I've made some other modifications as well to make it less confusing for him. Not exactly traditional, but close enough."

"I'm certain God will forgive you," Ruth said.

"I hope so. And, of course, even though we'll have the Torah opened in front of him he won't actually be reading the Hebrew. Just chanting it from memory. I've asked Bernard to bring him to the synagogue in the morning for a run-through. I suppose it'll turn out okay. Now, come to bed. You've been on your feet too long."

Barbara arrived at the Stillson house late the next morning. "I can't believe all this food!" She surveyed the contents of the stuffed refrigerator. "You did this all yourself?"

"I had lots of help," her mother replied. "And that's not all of it. The garage fridge is full and so is the one at the synagogue. We probably have too much food for the number of people who might come, but better too much than not enough. The good news is, I don't have to do another thing. The sisterhood is taking over from here. Your father has been scolding me all week, but I've not seen him so happy in years." Then tears formed. "Oh, God, I'm going to miss him. He puts up a good front, but he's hurting. I can see it when he doesn't think I'm looking." She wiped her cheeks. "I don't mean to spoil things for you."

Barbara gave her mother a long hug. "What's Dad tell you about how Leslie's doing? I know he's in his room with those tapes. But I can't tell if the tape is playing or if it's Les I'm hearing."

"He'll do just fine," Ruth assured her, not exactly answering the question.

"I've never been to a Saturday afternoon *bar mitzvah*. Is it different from a morning service?"

"The afternoon service is short, and there should be only a few people, I hope. We did it that way so that Leslie would be less frightened. And while we are on the subject, how has Bernard been with all this?"

"Actually, other than being a bit concerned for Les, he's fine. I don't think I told you, but Bernie's been reading some books on basic Judaism. Calls it his 'path finder' project. He says he wants to find the path that brought him here."

"What's that supposed to mean?"

"Who knows? Sometimes with Bernie it's better not to ask. Maybe he'll agree to join the family at your house for Passover this year."

"It's a bit late for that, don't you think?" Ruth's tears began in earnest. "I'm sorry, I didn't mean—"

"Oh, mother, I'm sorry. The idea that father won't be with us then is so ... I just can't get my head around it."

"We'll see," Ruth said, absently dabbing at her cheeks with a tissue. "Lots can happen between now and next April."

Rabbi Stillson was in the synagogue sanctuary after lunch on Friday when Helgman and Les arrived at the entrance doors. "Bernard," the rabbi called, "thanks for bringing Leslie. I'm going to run through the service with him. You can stay if you want." Stillson turned to his grandson. "Leslie, are you ready?"

Leslie lowered his head, his eyes focused on his feet. Then he looked up and nodded his head.

"I guess he is." Helgman was not convinced.

"Come on up here, Leslie, and stand next to me."

The young man walked slowly up onto the *bima*.

Rabbi Stillson opened the ark, selected a Torah, and handed it to Leslie so that the boy would be accustomed to its weight when the time came for him to hold it. Confident that Leslie had a good hold of the precious scroll, the rabbi said a silent prayer, thanking God for the privilege of living long enough to hand the Torah to his grandson, a boy not of his flesh, but a boy he loved dearly.

The tears in the corners of Leslie's eyes signaled to the rabbi that the boy understood more of life than people thought. Stillson took the Torah from his grandson, laid it on the reading table and removed the mantle. Then he scrolled it open and watched as Leslie's eyes grew wide at the Hebrew letters inside."

"Leslie, do you recognize the letters?"

Leslie nodded.

"Please use words."

The boy remained silent.

"Leslie," the rabbi urged, "speak to me."

The boy remained silent for another moment. Then he brought his head up. "Yes, Grandfather, these are the pictures like the ones on the paper you gave me."

Stillson hugged him tightly, holding back his own tears. "Yes, these are Hebrew words. The same Hebrew words you have learned from the tape. Are you ready?"

Leslie began to nod, then corrected himself. "Yes," he said. "Les ready."

"Okay. Let's get a signal here. I'll be standing right here beside you all the time. Just watch me. When I rub my chin like this, that will be the signal for you to chant what you have learned from the tape. Can you do that?"

"Yes."

"Okay then. Keep your eyes on me and don't start until I give the signal."

The dancing light through the stained glass windows cast shapes that the rabbi, for the first time ever, imagined as a wedding party moving gracefully through the chapel. For him, the synagogue symbolized the pulse of life; the great hope of a baby naming; the joy of a *bar* or *bat mitzvah*; the deep sorrow of a funeral. Everything came through these doors, down these aisles. Life: ebbing and flowing.

Stillson turned to face his grandson. Although almost six feet, Leslie seemed so small and alone standing patiently beside him, his eyes fixed on the rabbi's every movement. Stillson's hand went to his chin and the boy drew a deep breath.

A moment later, the synagogue filled with the sound of what, to the rabbi, could have been the voice of his own father chanting the melody he remembered hearing as a small child.

A lifetime of memories swept over him: the birth of his own sons; their terrible death; the loss of his first wife; the joy of his marriage to Ruth. A bittersweet smile came to his lips. In spite of all the tragedy, he felt that he was indeed blessed. Tears rolled down his cheeks.

Leslie finished, and not knowing what to do next, froze. The rabbi, shaking off his reminiscence, shouted, "Wonderful! Wonderful! I've never heard it done better. Let's go back to the house. Tomorrow afternoon you can do it for real."

Yes, tomorrow would go well. But as far as Stillson was concerned, his grandson's *bar mitzvah* had just happened.

At eight on Saturday night, the synagogue filled. The synagogue newsletter had mentioned Leslie's *bar mitzvah*, but not many people were expected since it was a holiday weekend in the middle of summer. Surprising, then, that the crowd was the largest the synagogue had ever had for *Shabbos* afternoon service that normally drew only a few families. Extra chairs were brought in amid a crush of people that was more typical of *Rosh Hashanah* than of a mid-summer evening *bar mitzvah*. Ruth gave a silent prayer that they had prepared as much food as they had.

The thought struck Helgman that his father-in-law's illness was probably not the secret the rabbi intended it to be. A nurse, a lab technician, a file clerk, a secretary, or perhaps even a doctor, had passed the information along.

Barbara leaned close to him. "You seem agitated. Are you worried about Les? Or has your pager gone off?"

Before Helgman could respond, the rabbi got up from his large ornate chair at the side of the *bima*. Leslie was sitting in a matching chair positioned right next to the rabbi's and the boy started to get up when his grandfather did. Stillson turned toward his grandson and whispered something while affectionately resting his hands on Leslie's shoulders. Leslie nodded and sat down. Walking to the reading table positioned at the *bima*'s center, Stillson opened his prayer book and recited several prayers in Hebrew. He then looked up to face his congregation. "My friends," he began, his voice hinting at the weakness of his body, "this is indeed a joyous day for me. My prayers have been answered. This afternoon my grandson, Leslie Helgman, son of Dr. Bernard Helgman and my daughter Barbara Helgman, is called to the Torah. Leslie, as many of you know, learns slower than most do, but still he desires to do his part. For that we're grateful."

Bernard looked over to his son on the *bima* and became quickly absorbed in reverie, thinking about his own childhood and the events that culminated in him being here. He was thus only barely aware of what was being said up on the *bima*.

"My friends," Rabbi Stillson had said, "please join me in prayer on page 121 of our prayer books before we proceed with the Torah service and hear Leslie chant today's Torah portion. Let us read Psalm 130 responsively. I'll read each verse in Hebrew and ask the congregation to respond to the Hebrew verse with the English translation."

Barbara picked up her prayer book but her husband did not. The rabbi's voice continued to float in and out of Helgman's consciousness as the images presented themselves in his mind's eye: The last night that he saw his parents, his time with the Schmidts, the atrocities he not only was forced to witness on a daily basis but to participate in, his later life so focused on reversing all the evil he had been forced to do.

Bernard's thoughts were interrupted by the inner echo of something his half-listening brain had just heard. The sounds were fading fast but he was able to grab onto them and refresh them in his mind's ear. It was Stillson's voice in Hebrew and the congregation's English response. The English words were new to him, but the Hebrew words were not. They were, in fact, something that had been indelibly etched in his mind decades before. Not words so much as sounds since he never knew what they meant.

"*Mima'amakim keraticha adonai,*" the rabbi had read. The congregation answered with the translation. "Out of the depths have I cried unto thee."

Bernard, now fully aware of his surroundings, heard himself say, "*Adonai shimah vekoli*" just in time to be in unison with the next verse read by the rabbi.

Barbara stirred in her seat and whispered over to him. "What? Bernie, what did you say?"

But Helgman didn't hear her, nor did he hear the congregation's response, "Lord hear my voice." His mind was somewhere else.

The words were in a voice not his own. It was a voice from another world. One that Helgman could see clearly. He was on his cot at the back of the Auschwitz infirmary. One of the patients was crying out something Bernard knew to be Hebrew. It was the same recitation, night after night. Soon enough Helgman could parrot the whole thing. A prayer, he had presumed. Mannheim. Yankel Mannheim had been the man's name. The man, a skeleton, appeared to be in his seventies or eighties, but Helgman now knew that he likely was no older than forty. "*Mima'amakim keraticha Adonai; Adonai shimah vekoli ...* " Helgman had never learned what it meant. But now he knew. "Out of the depths have I cried unto thee; Lord hear my voice." Now, after all these years, the man's prayer made sense to him. A tear formed at the corner of his eye. Soon his cheeks were wet.

Verse after verse, as the prayer continued, Helgman quietly intoned the Hebrew in perfect unison with his father-in-law, with the congregation continuing its response in English:

"*Tiyena oznecha kashuvot lekol tachanunai.*"

"Let your ears be attentive to the voice of my supplication."

"*Im avonot tishmor ya adonai mi yaamod.*"

"If you, Lord, were to mark iniquities, who, O Lord, shall stand."

"*Ki imcha haslicha lemaan tivare.*"

"For with you is forgiveness ... "

The rabbi and congregation continued on, but Helgman could not. "Forgiveness." A word that had haunted him every day since leaving the camp. Could God—could anyone—possibly forgive him for what he had done? He buried his face in his hands to muffle his sobs as he reached out in his mind, as he had done so many times before, to a God whom he hoped might possibly forgive him.

Now, at least, he had the word—the thought—that might possibly accompany his entreaty.

"Out of the depths have I cried unto thee," his inner voice called out. "God please do hear my voice. And ... please ... please ... forgive ... me."

Would God, in fact, forgive him? He didn't know. He had hoped that all that he had done since leaving the depths of the camp and indeed the depths of post-war Europe might in some way soften the heart of a God who he had so often felt must despise him for the atrocities he had participated in. But would He?

But forgive him for what? Yes, he had killed the guard, but that was in self-defense. Or had it been? His memory of his time in that hell-hole was confused between what he actually had done, what he imagined, what he witnessed, and the stories he had heard during his rehabilitation in Switzerland. The women's tortured faces that once were so vivid in his memory had, thankfully, finally begun to fade. But as the past blurred, so had his memory of his own actions, leaving him with residual guilt and anger, the source of which he could no longer positively identify. He was guilty because he was there. He was guilty because women and children died and he didn't prevent it. How could God forgive?

Helgman felt his wife's hand firmly on his leg. "Bernie, what is it? Are you okay?"

He continued to sit with his face in his hands. Thankfully, Psalm 130 was followed by several more prayers, giving him time to push the memories of Auschwitz away—at least for a while.

"I'm sorry." His voice was barely a whisper. "Maybe I can tell you later."

This was supposed to be a joyous time, Helgman reminded himself. With great effort, he sat up straight, quickly wiped his face, and again looked toward his son. Thankfully, Leslie was looking out at the congregation and hadn't taken notice of his father's distress.

Rabbi Stillson had seen it, though, and he, too, found the need to bring out a handkerchief.

Stillson then continued. "The psalms we just read—and particularly Psalm 130—read like beautiful poetry," he observed to the congregation, "but there is so much there for all of us. If only we will meditate on the words and look inside our hearts.

"My prayer for all of us is that the promise held out to us in the last verse of Psalm 130 will in fact come to pass—that God will, indeed, redeem Israel from all its iniquities."

This was responded to by a chorus of "Amens." The rabbi paused and stared out over the heads of the congregation for a long moment before something of a smile came to his lips.

"But, my dear friends, enough introspection for one afternoon. Let's move to the happy occasion that we've all come here to celebrate." Stillson then turned toward Leslie and motioned for him to come to the reading table. When his grandson was in position, he said, "Leslie, you have the responsibility of cherishing the Torah and passing it on to the next generation. You are a special young man, with special abilities."

The rabbi then turned to the holy ark and opened its curtain. He lifted out one of the Torah scrolls and leaned it on his shoulder as one does a small child.

Turning back to Leslie, he said, "The Torah will be special for you always. It tells us of life and how to behave toward animals as well as toward each other. Here, take it in your arms as you did yesterday."

Leslie reached out his arms and when his grandfather released the full weight of the heavy scroll, he began to stumble forward. The congregation gasped.

Leslie caught himself and stood upright, cradling the precious document as if it were an animal in need of loving care. He put his face against the soft cover and stood facing his grandfather.

The rabbi closed the curtain, recited a prayer and then led Leslie to the reading table where the Torah was to be unwrapped. Taking the Torah from his grandson, the rabbi removed its mantle and unrolled the Torah so that a wide portion lay open. The rabbi then took his place at the corner of the table and whispered to his grandson, "Stand in front of the Torah like you did yesterday."

Leslie did as he was told and then looked up to see that all eyes were focused on him. He remained silent.

When Leslie didn't begin his prayers, Helgman leaned close to his wife. "This is what I was afraid of. The boy is terrified." Then Helgman remembered the chin signal. "Your father hasn't given the signal. He must have forgotten."

People began to cough and clear their throats, but still Leslie said nothing.

Helgman shifted in his seat, touched his own chin several times, and then sat back when the rabbi's hand finally went up to his own chin.

Leslie took a deep breath. Then the words and melody he had learned flowed from him as if he had been chanting them all his life.

The congregation sat stunned. The intonations were perfect. The boy had a sweet voice that captured centuries of refinement of the ancient melody. There was a haunting quality about the sounds he was making that reached back into the mind and evoked long buried emotions, recalling parents and grandparents in the small villages of Russia, Hungary, Poland. For many, these memories were bittersweet, as they remembered the torment their loved ones endured before they fled the Czar and later Hitler.

By the time Leslie finished there were many moist eyes in the synagogue. Barbara's were the wettest of all, but she made no attempt to dry them.

No one moved. No one spoke. They sat in silence and watched as a huge smile formed on Leslie's normally emotionless face. Rabbi Stillson rolled the Torah closed, threw his arms around the boy and pulled him close, the two of them rocking slightly.

Regaining his composure, Rabbi Stillson spoke to his grandson as if they were alone. He ended with, "Leslie, I again tell you that you were perfect. Beyond perfect. I love you and may God bless you always." The rabbi then turned to his daughter and son-in-law. "Barbara, Bernard, please come up and join us. This is a time for a family celebration. Ruth, please join us as well. I trust the congregation will forgive us these few moments."

Barbara stood and took her husband by the hand, whispering to him, "Please Bernie, put your differences with the religion behind you, if just for a moment. This isn't the time to turn away. Les needs your support."

Helgman stood. "Actually, I told your father I'd come up to the *bima*. I wouldn't miss this for anything," he replied. "My only concern is that my cheeks are wet."

"So are everyone else's," Barbara gently reminded him, her hand in his. "It only shows you're human. Not a bad label for someone to have."

Leslie hugged his father, and said, "Did I make you happy? Grandfather is happy. But mother is crying. Is she sad?"

"She's very happy. Those are tears of happiness. You made me very happy as well, Les," Helgman answered honestly. "Happier than you can ever know."

Rabbi Stillson spoke privately to Helgman. "I'm indeed pleased that you will help with the Torah." He had his son-in-law help put the Torah mantle back on, then lifted the Torah and handed it to Helgman. "Come, Bernard, carry it to the ark."

After the Torah had been returned to its place, the rabbi again addressed Helgman. "This has been a truly great day," he said. "A truly great day." He brushed a tear from his weary eyes. "You have a wonderful son." Glancing at Barbara, he added, "And a wonderful wife. Cherish them both always."

TWENTY-TWO

The usual summer slack in Helgman's patient load did not materialize and July passed in a blur of work and performances for Muggs. If anything, August was even busier.

Helgman had spoken to Stephanie by telephone several times. He told her how well Leslie did at his *bar mitzvah* and how the boy had surprised everyone.

Stephanie's normal cheerfulness and upbeat attitude faded with each phone call, replaced by gloom and melancholy. "You have a nice family," she said during one of those calls. "Count your blessings. Barbara sounds like a wonderful woman and it's clear she loves you."

It was just before Labor Day, right after Helgman hung up the phone with Stephanie when his nurse's voice came over the intercom. "Doctor, Mrs. Helgman is on line two."

"He's in the hospital," Barbara announced without greeting. "They took him to Shadyside. Mother says he's not doing well and I'm leaving to go see him. Oh, Bernie, this has come sooner than I had imagined. She says his time is measured in days."

"My God. What do you need me to do?"

"Take charge of Les. I have Millie coming to stay, but she can't be here until after dinner. Ken is here and I don't want to leave the two of them alone for very long."

Ken was Leslie's best friend and they spent a lot of time together. Helgman had been concerned about the relationship for months. Ken was twenty three and it was worrisome that he wanted to spend so much time with someone who was the emotional age of maybe ten or twelve. Until now Barbara had refused to acknowledge a concern.

"I'll cancel my afternoon appointments and be home in an hour."

"Okay, thanks. I'll tell Les."

"Give my best to your father."
"I just pray I can get there in time. Please hurry."

Millie became employed on a live-in basis, having moved into the guest bedroom. Helgman nonetheless canceled all his afternoon appointments for the next several days so that he could be home early. His goal was to send Ken on his way in an effort to reduce the amount of time Leslie spent with him. But Leslie would not hear of it. "Friend," Leslie insisted. "Want my friend!"

The boys had met at the learning clinic. Ken had been a student there himself at one time and was now accepted as a volunteer because he related so well to the children. Ken had a desire to please and he had worked hard while he was a student at the clinic. A house painter had agreed to take on Ken as an assistant. Ken had learned to scrape old paint and repair wood, but his favorite part of the job was cleaning brushes, on which he spent an inordinate amount of time. Occasionally someone would hire Ken to paint on his own. He would make elaborate plans as to how the job would be done and then he would assemble drop cloths, ladders, brushes, turpentine—everything he could think to bring. But something would always go wrong, it seemed. The ladder would fall; the paint bucket would tip over; the drop cloth would pull away from the wall. Even worse, he often brought the wrong type of paint or the wrong color, or he would make some other major mistake.

Ken was tolerated because of his constant good cheer and his willingness to please. He would work tirelessly to fix any problem he caused and in the end, he managed to make every project right.

"Dr. Helgman," Ken began on the third evening, "can Leslie and I paint the basement walls?"

"They were just painted a few months ago, Ken," Helgman answered. "Remember?"

"Sure I remember. But I was telling Leslie that it was time for him to learn a real job. I'll teach him to paint like me. He said no one would trust him. But I told him he shouldn't think like that. He had to try, is what I told him, and he agreed. I'm proud of him. He can do it. He can do anything he puts his mind to."

Helgman had his doubts about this painting project but reluctantly went along with it, even admitting to himself that it might be a positive experience for Leslie. "But don't make a mess," he admonished.

"Thank you, thank you, thank you, Dr. Helgman. Leslie will do a great job. I'll bring the tarps and we can use your ladder. I have brushes and paint. The paint is from a job where I had the wrong color."

"Like I said, just don't make a mess."

Ken stood tall. "Don't worry about us, Dr. Helgman. We will do a good job. I'm a professional painter, you know."

The next day Helgman arrived home to find Millie uncharacteristically agitated. The normally unflappable housekeeper swung her arms toward the basement door and then upstairs in the general direction of Leslie's room. She then quickly escaped to her own room. Expecting a disaster on both fronts, Helgman tried the basement first. *Not so terrible*, he thought. The walls were painted an ugly purple. But at least all was in order. The boys were not down there. He walked upstairs to Leslie's room. Looking through the open door, he was confronted with a scene that made him wish he had stayed at the office. Paint-soaked newspapers were scattered about the room and Ken was calmly wiping purple paint from the wooden floor with a rag. A paint can was lying on its side, mostly empty of its contents. Leslie was standing in a corner staring at his feet.

"Oh, hello, Dr. Helgman," Ken said brightly. "You came home early," he added, glancing up from his steady efforts to clean up the mess. "Nothing to worry about here. Happens all the time in my profession. Have it cleaned up in no time."

Helgman pulled the door shut without saying a word. He returned to the empty kitchen to fix sandwiches for himself and Leslie. He intended to send Ken home so that he and Leslie could be alone.

When the sandwiches were ready he called up to Leslie, but no amount of coaxing could make the boy leave his room. Helgman gave up trying and made a pot of coffee. He ate alone on the porch reading a medical journal. Barbara called shortly after eight to explain that her father was resting comfortably but that her mother was not doing well and that she would be staying with her mother at the hospital.

"Les," Helgman began, after Ken had gone and his son had eaten half his sandwich, "how would you like camping out in a tent? We can buy a tent and put it up in the back yard. If you enjoy that, then we can go camping in the woods. Would you like that?"

"Bears?"

"No bears. We will go where it is safe."

"Want to see bears."

"I asked you about a tent. Would you want a tent?"

"Yes. Can see bears. And wolves."

"Bears and wolves are not in the woods where we're going. We can fish and chop wood and build a fire and cook the fish we catch. I can teach you to chop wood like I did when I was young." Helgman hadn't even thought about fishing since he was twelve. He remembered sitting on the riverbank for hours, a pole in his hand, always fishing just long enough to catch enough for dinner. His mother had been so proud of him then.

"Ken come?"

"Just the two of us, son. We can be together."

"I want Ken to come."

"Not this time, Les." Helgman forced himself to keep calm, remembering that getting angry with Leslie only made matters worse.

"Not go without friend." Defiance in the form of hard-set eyes overtook his otherwise expressionless face.

"Let's talk about it tomorrow. It's bedtime now."

The boy reached out, touched his father's hand, and quickly withdrew it, apparently remembering how his father did not like people touching him.

Helgman pulled the boy against him and hugged him, realizing for the first time that his son was almost as tall as he was. And stronger than he appeared.

The next morning when Leslie continued to insist, Helgman gave in and said that Ken could join them. That seemed to appease the boy and he became excited about setting up the tent. He even forgot about the bears.

"I'll be home from the hospital early today and we can set up camp. Is that okay with you?"

"I tell Ken?"

"You can tell Ken."

The tent lay on the ground ready to go up. "Hey guys," Helgman called, "come over here. I'll show you how to use a knife." When both of them were paying attention, Helgman grasped the knife as he remembered doing as a child and said, "Now be sure to always hold the knife by the handle with the blade pointing away from you." He demonstrated exactly how he wanted the boys to grasp it. "Now each of you take a turn holding it and cutting this rope."

When Helgman was sure they were doing it correctly, he said, "One more thing. Never, never run the blade against your skin to see how sharp it is. Cut a rope or a piece of wood, but never yourself."

They both nodded.

Helgman then had them practice by cutting up the empty boxes from all the gear he had purchased. When he was satisfied they were working safely, he went into the garage to fetch the fishing rods. Returning, he sucked in his breath when he saw Ken in a corner of the yard showing Leslie how to pour fuel into the camping stove. "Be careful with that fuel. Be sure you don't spill it on your clothes or on your skin. Keep it away from your shoes."

"It's okay, Dr. Helgman." Exasperation crept into Ken's voice from all the instructions Helgman had been barking. "It's under control. Working with dangerous chemicals and stuff is what us painters do all the time."

"Still, please be careful." Helgman couldn't count the number of children he had treated over the years for camping burns. Each time he had wanted to scold the parents for being careless, but he always realized that nothing he could say could make them feel worse than they already felt with their child screaming in agony.

"Ken," he shouted across the yard, "you're spilling fuel on your shoe! Please watch what you're doing."

"It's okay. Just a little bit got on my shoe. It'll be okay."

"Don't light that lantern until I'm over there. Do you understand me?"

"Yes, Dr. Helgman. It'll be okay, don't worry."

"I do worry," Helgman called back. "Just please listen to me."

It was then that Helgman saw that they were both standing in wet grass. "Don't light that!" He ran toward them. "There's wet fuel all around you! Don't light that match! Ken didn't I tell you not—"

"You told us not to light the lantern. This is the stove, not the lantern. And it's water, not fuel. I washed the fuel away. We're okay. Nothing's wrong."

Helgman breathed a sigh of relief and turned toward Leslie who was standing with his head down. "You didn't do anything wrong, son," Helgman assured him. "Everything's okay. I'm sorry for yelling."

His head remained down, his eyes fixed on the grass. Before Helgman could say anything more, a voice rang out from behind him. "Hello? Hello there!"

It took Helgman a moment for the voice to register. "Stephanie!" He turned on his heels, hoping that his ears had deceived him. They had not. Stephanie was already advancing into the yard. "What are you doing here?" He glanced toward the boys as his mind began to race: *What's she doing here in Pittsburgh? At my home! How will I explain this to Barbara? At least Millie has the afternoon off.*

"I've got something important to tell you." Stephanie approached Helgman and the boys in the middle of the yard. "And I needed to tell you in person. I found more of my uncle's papers and you won't believe this!"

Helgman was still processing the situation. Didn't they have an unspoken understanding that she wouldn't intrude into his family life? He had no idea what to say at this point, what with the boys standing right there. But it was Leslie who spoke next.

"Lady from Boston," Leslie said, not moving his head.

"What? What did you say Les?"

"Lady from Boston. Here."

"How do you know who she is?"

"Tapes."

Ken broke in. "Leslie listens to tapes for his speech. I taught him how to connect his tape recorder to the phone line," he said proudly. "He recognizes voices. He's never wrong."

Stephanie held out her hand. "You must be Leslie. I've heard a lot about you from your father. My name's Stephanie. And you're right, I'm from Boston."

Leslie looked up, ready to retreat at the first sign of trouble, but took the outstretched hand.

Ken then extended his own hand and introduced himself. "My name is Ken. That's short for Kenneth. Hartly. You can call me Ken. I'm Leslie's best friend. Isn't that right, Leslie?"

"Best friend," Leslie agreed.

"Can we go inside now, Dr. Helgman?" Ken asked. "We want to get some things for the tent."

Helgman nodded, and the two of them ran off.

Stephanie, meanwhile had begun staring off into the distance across the yard. She turned back when Helgman spoke. "I don't think this is smart you coming here," he said, with more than a little edge in his voice.

"I know, and I'm sorry. But listen." She again stared off into the distance as though the story she was about to tell concerned someone far away. "I don't recall whether I told you my father has liver failure—but he does. I found an experimental program at Sloan-Kettering where they take part of a liver from a donor, usually a sibling or a son or daughter. And to make a long story short, Green Lines made a large donation and they agreed to put father in the program."

"What's that to do with you coming here?" Helgman glanced toward the house. Ken and Leslie were nowhere to be seen.

"I'm getting there. I was tested to be a donor but I'm not compatible with my own father. And it's not just that I'm not compatible. The test established that I couldn't possibly be his daughter." She again looked away.

Helgman strained to see into the kitchen to where he thought the boys were.

"My mother confessed. She admitted I was adopted." Stephanie reached into her purse and handed Helgman a scrap of folded paper. "This explains why I'm here. I found it stuck between two pages in Uncle Dieter's diary that, remember, I told you I found in his office. I didn't notice it before."

Helgman unfolded the paper and scanned the neat handwriting, struggling to translate the German. And there it was, about half-way down the page.

M.S. angenommen 21 Mai 1941 (15 Jahre)
S.G. angenommen 25 Mai 1941 (3 Jahre)

"See?" Stephanie exclaimed. "Angenommen" means adopted. M.S. and S.G—that's you and me after we were adopted. Mother told me you and I are brother and sister. Uncle Dieter's diary tells the whole story of him adopting you and arranging for his sister to adopt your sister."

Recalling his own father's words about how the adoption of his sister had not worked out, Helgman was dumbfounded. His anger flared. "This is a forgery! It's impossible."

"Mother swears it's authentic. It makes sense when you put it all together. Why would Uncle Dieter save only one child of his employee? No, he adopted you and arranged for my mother and father to adopt me."

"You're not my sister!" Helgman pressed his eyes closed and fought to bring up an image of his baby sister. But he saw nothing. "Like I said, it's impossible!"

"No. It's not. Why would my uncle's private papers lie? What earthly reason would he have to make up something like that? The ages match. I ask again, why would Uncle Dieter save you and not me, your sister?"

"It's impossible!" Helgman closed his eyes, this time pressing his hands against his temples as if forcing a thought—or an image—into his conscious mind. Then he saw it, but only for a fleeting instant. "My sister had blue eyes. Your eyes are green! You're not my sister!"

"How can you be so sure? You've said often enough that so much of your past is fuzzy, blurry. You may think you remember blue eyes, but you could be wrong. My uncle's paper proves it. Both you and your sister Rachel were taken in by the Schmidt, Grenoble family. Dieter gave me to his sister so it wouldn't be so obvious. I'm Rachel. Don't you see?"

"No, I *don't* see," Helgman snapped back. "Nothing, Stephanie, nothing you can say—and certainly no paper you wave in front of me—will convince me that you are Rachel. I don't trust anything Dieter—"

"But—"

"Stop tormenting me!" Helgman buried his face in his hands in a vain attempt to mask the sobs that were now overpowering him. "You cannot be Rachel. What you have there is the original plan. But Dieter changed his mind. My parents tried to find a family for her but couldn't. Otherwise ... otherwise we would have found each other by now. The Nazis took my sister away when they took my parents. They killed her ... and she's dead."

"How can you be so certain?"

"Because I know! I just know!"

It took several hours for Helgman to regain his composure after Stephanie left. It was only then that his analytical side forced him to look at the situation at least a bit more objectively. Sitting on the porch as he replayed their confrontation, he realized that much of his agitation wasn't about re-living the past and the shock of being confronted with the possibility that his sister had survived the war. He had to be honest. His overpoweringly emotional response to Stephanie's theory had to do, as much as anything, with being confronted with the real possibility of having to give up his fantasies about some day, somehow, being together with Stephanie as lovers. He had to admit that there was little likelihood that the paper Stephanie had presented him would be a fake. Dieter himself had no apparent motive to fabricate the facts that the paper seemed to establish. And if Dieter *did* have a motive for doing so, he wouldn't have hidden the paper between the pages of his secret diary where it might never be found.

And what about Stephanie? He had to believe that Stephanie would rather hold on to the hope, no matter how remote, that he would leave Barbara and come to her, rather than concocting a forgery that would prove them to be siblings and thus forever close off that possibility. Reluctantly, he concluded that Stephanie's version of events did make sense. Could he have been wrong about Rachel's eye color? He had suppressed so much from that time that he now questioned his memory of that detail. Why, he wondered, would his baby sister's eye color be an exception? Maybe they were more hazel than blue. Maybe they had actually been green.

Helgman had been sitting on the porch for quite some time—trying to figure out what he really believed about Stephanie's revelation—when it came to him that he had unfinished business with his son. He stood up, went upstairs to Leslie's room and knocked on the door. He reminded himself to moderate his voice so as not to frighten the boy.

"Les," Helgman began, after being admitted, "do you tape all our telephone calls?"

"No," the boy said, still not looking up.

"Son, you must tell me the truth. I promise not to be upset."

"Mostly," came a muffled response.

"Why?"

"Learn talk."

Helgman was surprised at the response. "Do you mean you learn to speak by listening to the tapes?"

Leslie nodded his head.

"How long have you been doing this?"

Ken, who had come up behind Leslie, began to answer. Helgman cut him off. "No, Ken. I want Les to answer."

Ken's face registered chagrin at the rebuke. "Okay," he said, "if you want. But I usually help him."

"Now, Les. I asked you how long have you been taping our telephone conversations?"

"Year."

Helgman knew the answer to his next question, but he asked it anyway. "How did you learn to do that?"

Leslie glanced over at Ken.

Ken again started to answer but stopped when Helgman shot a look in his direction.

"Ken taught me. He teaches me things."

"What kind of things?"

Leslie, keeping his head down, said, "Make tapes. Record music." He then looked to Ken as if seeking approval to see how he did. Leslie then added, "Painting."

"I helped him," Ken said, "with his grandfather's tape."

At the mention of his grandfather, a frown appeared on Leslie's face. His body tensed.

"What's wrong, Les?" Helgman asked. "What's troubling you?"

Silence.

"It's grandfather, isn't it?"

Silence.

"Tell me, Les. Tell me what's wrong?"

"Grandfather sick."

"Yes, I know. How do you know?"

"Told me," Leslie answered. "Very sick. Grandfather go away. I go to him. Make him comfortable."

Helgman's instinct was to protect Leslie from the trauma of a hospital visit to see a person he loved near death, but he changed his mind when Leslie said, "Grandfather dying. Go away like Dog."

"Okay, Les. We can go in the morning."

The young man's face brightened. "Ken go?"

"No. Ken can't go. This is a private time with your grandfather."

"I'll make him better. Hold him. Be better."

Helgman now worried that Rabbi Stillson's death would indeed be a major setback for his son. But, as he knew all too well, death is a critical part of living. Changing the subject, Helgman announced, "I'm hungry. Time to cook the hamburgers on the grill."

"Good cook." Leslie lifted his head, "Ken showed me."

"Yes, son, I'm sure he did."

"Boys, you have a choice now," Helgman announced after dinner. We can sleep in the tent, but we'll have to get up early in the morning to take it down so Leslie can be with his grandfather in the morning. Or we can take it down now and sleep in our own beds. It's your choice."

The two boys went off across the yard to talk it over. Soon Ken came back and announced, "We'll take it down now. Les is excited about being with his grandfather and he's afraid to sleep out here."

"Can you two take down the tent and put everything away? Or do you want my help?"

Ken threw his head back and said, "We can do it, Dr. Helgman. You can trust Leslie and me to do it."

Helgman took a seat on the porch, anticipating that within a few minutes the ropes would most likely be knotted beyond recognition. He told himself it would be funny if it wasn't so sad. He knew they couldn't help what they were and he also knew it was important for them to make the most of their capabilities. But still, he worried about his son.

Helgman's mind turned back to Stephanie and their earlier conversation.

"I'm sorry it's so painful for you, Bernard," she had said, holding his hand, "It's hard to come to grips with it all, I admit. But everything adds up."

"You think you can tie this all up in one tidy package. But life's not tidy. Especially not my life!"

"What's wrong with tidy packages?"

"Too neat. And besides—"

"What?"

Helgman had remained silent.

"What? I'm waiting."

"Nothing. A passing thought. Gone now."

"Someday, my dear Doctor ... someday you'll learn to speak your emotions. Someday you'll not be so terrified. Someday the barrier between us will disintegrate. I only hope that someday comes sooner rather than later."

TWENTY-THREE

Helgman and his son arrived at the hospital just after eight in the morning. Visiting hours didn't begin until ten, but even though he didn't hold privileges there, the administration extended the courtesy of allowing them in early.

The room marked 'Stillson, Kenneth' held two beds. The rabbi's bed was by the window, his face now so shrunken that his cheekbones and teeth protruded as if they belonged to another, much larger person. The other bed was empty. Helgman was surprised to find his mother-in-law sleeping slumped in a corner chair with no sign of Barbara.

Helgman was struck by Stillson's frailty. Less than two months ago he was full of life. Even as recently as ten days previous he was getting around on his own, albeit a bit slowly. The man now lay with his eyes closed, his body so still that only the monitors confirmed he was still alive.

A poster-sized drawing taped to the wall showed the rabbi peering out from behind a large Torah. His eyes were wide with mock fear, watching a nurse approach with an oversized needle. It had been signed by the children in his summer Torah class.

Leslie marched directly over to his grandfather and took his hand. "Grandfather, I'm here! It's Les. I'm here! Wake up."

"He's sleeping, let him be." Putting her glasses on, Ruth sat up. "Oh, I'm sorry Les. I didn't recognize your voice." She looked up at Helgman. "Nice surprise. I expected Barbara. I'm so glad you brought Leslie. Kenneth has been asking to see him. Come Les sit by me."

A puzzled look flashed across Helgman's face, but he said nothing.

"I'm here for grandfather. Wake up grandfather. It's Les. I'm here!"

"Les," Ruth said, "I'm afraid he can't—"

"It's okay," the old man said through cracked lips, the words barely audible. "I've been thinking about Leslie. Give me a moment to get up. Les, I want to walk with you."

"Helgman glanced again at the monitors. "Dad, it's not a good idea to get up. Please stay in bed."

"People die in bed." Stillson tried to laugh but it came out as a dry cough. "I can't die if I'm not in bed."

Helgman extended his arm over Leslie's head. "I'm not convinced it works that way, but if you insist, take my hand." Helgman anticipated that when Stillson sat up his blood pressure would drop below the monitor's warning level and an alarm would sound. Then it would be the nurse who would force him back into bed.

As if on cue, the alarm went off. "Now just lie back. You can talk to Les right here. We'll leave you two in private." Turning to Ruth, Helgman said, "Come, let's get a cup of coffee."

The nurse appeared and suggested that maybe the rabbi wasn't in any condition to receive visitors right then. "My time here on this earth is limited," Stillson scolded. "I want to spend it with my family. Now please leave me be."

The nurse reset the monitor. "I know rabbis have a special place in heaven, but there's no need to go rushing to get there. Take it easy now and don't be getting out of bed, you hear me?"

Stillson nodded. "I want to be alone with my grandson."

"Okay, but you lie quiet now." She turned to Leslie, "Don't let him get out of bed, young man." She pointed to a cord pinned to the sheets. "Push that button if you need me. I'll be right down the hall. You can hold the water glass for him if you want."

Helgman turned to Leslie, "Your grandmother and I'll be back in a bit. We'll be in the cafeteria on the first floor if you need us. Push the button if you need the nurse."

"Grandfather okay with Les." The boy turned back to the rabbi. "Want water?"

The old man nodded his head and Leslie held the glass so he could sip from the straw.

"We'll be back shortly," Ruth said as they walked into the hall.

When they had left the room, the rabbi had Leslie sit on the bed beside him. "It is important for you to understand that I love you." The old man coughed. "I'll take some more water."

Leslie picked up the glass again, allowing Stillson a long pull on the straw.

The rabbi leaned back on the pillow. "My love for you will always be there. No one can ever take that from you. No matter what ever happens, think of me. You have gifts only a few people possess. And those gifts, with God's help, will do you well. Remember that God loves you as I love you. You are special in God's eyes. He gave you special talents and God watches over his special children."

Neither Stillson nor Leslie were aware of the figure in the doorway. Barbara stood quietly listening.

"Try to understand your parents. They love you as I do." He winced in pain. "Your father loves you dearly, but he has trouble showing love. He has had a very troubled past. But you must love him also."

"Grandfather, I love you very much. I love my mother and my father also very much, but I know some things, too. Some secret things and I think maybe I'm not supposed to say them."

Stillson cupped his hand by his ear. "Les, if you want to tell me, you can whisper it." Leslie bent down and brought his mouth to his grandfather's ear. He was in that position for quite a time before straightening up again.

"Grandfather, I'll miss you very much when you die. When Dog died, I missed him. I have picture of Dog and I talk to him all the time. I'll put your picture next to Dog when you die and talk to you too. I love you even more than Dog."

The rabbi, so much of his life having been spent comforting others in their grief, was now being comforted. Before this morning, he hadn't realized how in touch with life Leslie really was. He pulled his grandson against him and the two of them rocked gently together.

Barbara slipped back into the hall and after a few moments knocked on the door. "Les," she cried, feigning surprise when she came into the room. "How did you get here?"

"Father brought me."

"Where is he? And where's your grandmother?"

"Coffee." The boy was still holding his grandfather's hand.

"Barbara, please give me a few more minutes with Leslie and then I want to speak with you."

"You look tired, Dad. Don't overdo it. I'll be just outside the door. Send Les out when you're ready."

"Time is closing in on me," Stillson said when Barbara rejoined her father sometime later. "I've been postponing this discussion, always waiting for a better time. There is now no better time."

"Don't say that, Dad. Don't talk that way."

"It's true. I've not much time left. Death is not to be feared. I'm at peace." He coughed and sharp spasms of pain racked his body. He lay still for a while before he spoke again. "Secrets. So many secrets. I've never approved of secrets in a family. Yet, we all have so many secrets, so much we don't want even the family to know. I'm as guilty as anyone. But I've come to understand that those who love you figure out the secrets anyway. Answer me a question. Do you know what secrets Bernard is hiding?"

The question caught her off guard. She struggled to form a proper answer.

"It's too late to keep things from me. I'll be gone soon so it won't matter. But please tell me the truth. I'm concerned for you—and for him."

"When he was in the camp he did some things he won't talk about," she said. "It's made him very private."

"Bernard survived longer than most, which probably means that he had to cooperate with the Nazis in some way or other. It doesn't matter. That part of life is accountable only to God. Man cannot judge." A coughing spasm seized him.

Even after the spasm passed, Stillson lay still for a long while before saying in a low voice. "You should understand—even better, Bernie should understand—that God forgives him for whatever he may have done." The old man's eyes closed, his breathing fast and shallow.

"Rest now, Dad. This is too much for you."

The old man's eyes remained closed. "Who is Stephanie?"

Barbara caught her breath. *How did he know about Stephanie? Did Leslie tell him about Stephanie's visit to the house and the phone calls, just as he told me when I called home last night?*

"Yes, Leslie told me." It was as if Stillson was reading her mind. "But what's important is who is she and what's going on, not how I know." Stillson reached out for the water glass and Barbara held it for him while he sucked on the straw. He laid his head back and closed his eyes for a long moment. "I want to help you fix what's broken. I'll die in peace if I know I've helped. I've ignored the signs all too long."

Tears welled up in Barbara's eyes and she didn't know if the words would come out right. She took his hand in hers and his cold skin made her shiver. "Bernie's a good man. He saved Les's life. I watched how he cared for that boy and I fell in love with both of them. At first, it was because I wanted Les. But now I want Bernie as well. He's the best man in the world—after you that is."

Stillson's eyes again closed. "Go on. I'm listening."

"Bernie can't tolerate being touched. Or so I thought anyway. We agreed to be married because that was what the law required for us to adopt Les."

Stillson's eyes remained closed, his face expressionless. His mouth moved, but no sound came.

She wondered how many times he had heard stories like this one. People struggling with their demons, with the demons often winning. "You can't imagine how awful it is to be in love with a man who won't touch you." Barbara wrung her hands. "We sleep in different rooms now, but when we did sleep together he didn't move a muscle all night. It's unnatural."

"The camps were unnatural." Stillson's voice was far away. "Many who survived are troubled." He waited for several spasms to pass. "Stephanie?"

"From what he has told me over the years, she was a woman he knew before he met me. He may actually have been in love with her, whatever love means for Bernie. But something happened." Barbara wiped the tears from the corners of her eyes.

"Being in love with another woman is one thing," Stillson replied. "Sometimes these things can happen, especially when things are not right in a marriage. But doing something about it is another."

"I didn't know until last night when I called home and found that she was at the house—our house. Obviously, to use your words, he *has* been doing something about it."

"When would he get the time? He's always in surgery."

"Weekends. He's gone many weekends, as you know." She thought about the homosexual rumors and realized that something didn't add up. Her husband was uncomfortable with anyone, male or female, touching him—or so it seemed.

"Not the weekends," the rabbi said. "It can't be."

"But it's the only time. His surgery schedule keeps him busy all day. He's in surgery, or in the office, when he says he is."

"Not the weekends," Stillson insisted, his lips drawn tight to let the pain pass.

"Dad, if you know something I don't, please you have to tell me what it is."

"I suppose you're right," Stillson said. "Come, sit by the bed. I need you close to me." He then told his daughter about his suspicions over the years and how Leslie had confirmed just moments before that he had heard his father talking on the telephone about Muggs. "The boy is very much aware. You just have to listen carefully. And not only that. Les said that he wants to learn to be a clown and to perform with his father.

"Barbara, your husband may very well be the world's leading slight-of-hand artist as well as the world's very best children's surgeon. It's a real shame that all aspects of his life can't be as rewarding. And it's even more of a shame he can't share his magic with all of us."

"I try to get him to tell me about his weekends. Oh, how I try. He's just not there. It's as if he'll cease to exist if his secret gets out."

Stillson grasped Barbara's hand. "He's there. Just keep doing what you're doing. Don't give up on him. Bernie is a good man ... a very good man."

"But if he's with Stephanie, then there's no future."

"Don't give up until you know for sure. Ask him. He might not talk much, but he won't lie. I can't believe he's been unfaithful to you. I'm a good judge of character and ... " He put his hand to his head. "I'll bet my ... well, I'll bet my *kippa*." A faint smile came on his face. "You know, where I'm going I don't know if I'll need a *kippa* or not. If Dante is right, I might not need anything to keep my head warm." His body shook, first from his joke and then from the pain.

Barbara turned away from the bed, no longer able to look her father in the eyes. He had more faith in her husband than she had. She was overcome with shame as she tried to rationalize her actions over the past few days—especially her behavior last night after she had learned about Stephanie being at their house.

It had started the previous week, when she had first come to the hospital. A man about her age named Gregory had struck up a conversation with her in the lunchroom. His wife was dying of cancer and had been in a coma for three months. The doctors had told him she would never wake up. Despite the prognosis, he came every night and sat with his wife talking to her, praying for a miracle. But the coma only became deeper. He and Barbara had taken to eating dinner together in the hospital cafeteria. And then two nights ago they had sat for almost two hours, comforting each other and mourning the not yet dead—he, his wife, and she, her father.

"Come, Barbara," Gregory had said the previous night, "there's a great deli a few blocks over. Walnut Street. A ten minute walk at most. We both need a break."

She had taken him up on his offer and while they were waiting for their food, he spoke about his wife. "Before she took ill, we had never really been apart, my wife and I. I don't know how I'll get along when she's gone."

"You'll manage. People do." But the words sounded hollow to her.

"She's terminal. The doctors said she would die months ago. Who knows how long it will be? She's been my life. But she's lost to me now."

Without thinking, Barbara put her hand over his. He looked into her eyes. "That feels good. It's funny how much a human touch means. That's what I miss most, her touching me." He sat for a moment studying her. "Unless I'm mistaken, I'd say you're as lonely as I am. Don't answer if you don't want, but I'd guess your marriage isn't working."

"So much from a touch!"

"It's more than a touch. Your eyes give you away. Until a few moments ago, those were the eyes of a person with unfulfilled dreams. And you've been alone all week."

"Until a few minutes ago?"

"Now they're alive. I'm sorry. Maybe that's my imagination."

Barbara replayed the advice Grace had given her about ending it with Bernard before starting something new. She pulled her hand from his. "Remind me not to touch anyone again," she joked, not entirely sure how she felt. The truth was, her face hurt from smiling, she had just realized, and her heart was beating a lot faster than usual.

Barbara had called home from the restaurant pay phone to check on Leslie. That's when he had told her that the lady from Boston had come to visit. Bernard had told Leslie that Stephanie had come to give him some important information. Barbara was confused and angry when she came out of the phone booth. The more she thought about her husband's former lover at her house the angrier she became.

"Your father?" Gregory asked when she returned to the table.

"My husband."

"Let's go find a bar. Looks like you could use a drink."

Her anger boiled over. "Make that plural drinks."

"That bad?"

"That bad."

They walked along Walnut Street and fell into the first bar they came to. The Pirates were playing and several people, beers in hand, were cheering them on. Gregory directed them to one of several small tables in the far corner and as they sat down, he placed his hands over hers.

"So, what's going on?"

Barbara waited for the waitress to arrive, ordered a double scotch, and was absolutely silent until half-way through her drink. And then it all came out, nothing held back.

A second round of drinks came and disappeared while she was talking.

Gregory listened, never taking his eyes from hers as her emotions spilled out.

The waitress came by to see if they wanted a third round. Gregory waved her away and then turned back to Barbara. "My place or yours?" He was only half joking and certainly half hoping.

"Neither," she replied. "I better get back to the hospital. My mother will be worried."

"Is that what you really want?"

"What I really want, I can't have."

"At least you're being honest." He took her hand. "Come, the air will do us good."

His arm was around her waist as they made their way back toward the hospital. "It feels good to be held," she said. "It's been so very long." At a DON'T WALK sign Barbara turned her head to look up into his eyes. It was all she could do to keep herself from bringing her face around to his and leaning in for a kiss.

She didn't have to.

Gregory swung her around and bent forward, their lips now separated by inches. Barbara pulled him against her, felt his warmth, felt his arms tighten around her back, and, all resolve gone, tilted her head back.

A large number of crossing cycles were ignored as they stood with their mouths glued to one another. Their heads finally pulled apart ever so slightly, but Barbara pulled him against her even tighter. "I shouldn't be doing this," she murmured, but positioned herself to again accept his lips.

Several long seconds later, the WALK sign again switched in their favor. This time they stepped into the street and almost immediately Gregory lurched forward, his hand shooting downward as he bent over to grasp his ankle. "Damn! I twisted it good." He took a step forward and winced.

"My God." Barbara helped him hop back onto the sidewalk. "Do you think it could be broken?"

"I doubt it. But I can't put weight on it."

Barbara pointed to a nearby bus stop bench. "Sit over there for a moment," she instructed. "See how it feels after a bit."

A few minutes later Gregory stood, gingerly allowing the ankle to take his full weight. "Feeling better," he said. "I think all it needs is ice."

"Then let's get you home and get that ice on it." Barbara glanced up and down the street. "Where is a cab when you need one?"

"My car's in that lot over there, but I'm not sure I can drive."

"I'm really in no condition to drive either, but I guess between the two of us, it's going to have to be me. Wait here and I'll bring your car around."

"No way. I'm not letting you out of my sight. And besides, it does feel good to be held."

"Let's go then. Lean on my shoulder and keep your weight off that ankle."

Pulling out of the parking lot, a smiling Barbara had said, "I suppose this is your answer."

Gregory looked at her, puzzled.

"You know. Your question, 'My place or yours?' Well, apparently, it's yours."

TWENTY-FOUR

Barbara returned from her reverie about her previous evening with Gregory and found that her father's eyes were now closed, his breathing regular although shallow. The monitors above his head confirmed that he was not in any particular distress, although there was little doubt that the end was near.

Looking at her stepfather as he lay dying, Barbara reminded herself how lucky she was to have had him in her life.

The rabbi's eyes opened and he spoke in a voice that was faint and barely audible. "You may think I was sleeping, Barbara, but I've been watching you for the last few minutes and I'm deeply troubled. You are in terrible pain. I wish I could mend your anguish, but just as you can't mend Bernard's, I can't fix yours." His body convulsed and his mouth continued to move up and down, but words did not come. It took several minutes before he could continue. Barbara had to lean in close to hear him. "My time has come. My life has not always been pleasant and I've not accomplished all that I've dreamed of. But I'm grateful to God for what I have, for what I've been given." Stillson reached out and touched her, his cold fingers pressing into her arm. "I must tell you that your changing your name to mine was as great a gift as anyone can give another. You have been the best daughter a man could ever have. Take care of your mother and your family." He again waited for the pain to die down. "I love you with all my heart." His voice was the strongest that it had for many weeks.

"I love you, Dad." She bent and kissed his forehead.

Barbara drove her mother and Leslie home, hoping her mother could get a few hours rest. Ruth Stillson was clearly exhausted from the hours of fitful dozing spent in the chair beside her husband. They were sipping tea in the kitchen when the phone rang. Even before she lifted the receiver Barbara knew what she was about to hear. Repeating the news to her mother, they cried in each other arms for several minutes.

"I'd better go upstairs and tell Les," Barbara said after several minutes. "I dread having to do it. He was so attached to Father."

"That boy is stronger than you give him credit for. Go up and tell him."

"Les," Barbara began a few moments later, not knowing how her son would react, "your grandfather has died."

"I know."

"It just happened. How do you know?"

"He told me so. I kissed him goodbye in the hospital."

"He told you?"

"He told me he was going away. Not to be upset."

"Your grandfather was a good man," she said, tears flowing in a steady stream down her cheeks. "I'll miss him very much."

Leslie ran to his mother and hugged her. "It's okay. Put picture of him next to bed. Talk to him. Feel better."

At first she didn't know what he was telling her. Then she remembered how tenderly Leslie always held the picture of Dog and how, when he was upset, he would speak quietly to the picture.

"Mother?"

"Yes?"

"Share picture with you."

"Thank you dear. I'll ask your grandmother for another one. I'm sure she has an extra picture."

"Has two in her bedroom."

It was two weeks after the funeral when Helgman called Stephanie. His feelings for her had abated now that there was the possibility that they were siblings, however remote he thought that possibility was. He told himself that he should call her to apologize for his behavior when she had surprised him in the backyard, but it was really because he wanted to hear her voice.

Stephanie was polite, but sounded distant. He asked what was wrong, but she would only say that she was concerned for him. "I don't know what to make of your ... outburst. It was so unlike you."

"As you might imagine, I've a lot on my mind. None of it good. And ... truth be known," Helgman paused to gather his thoughts, "I don't remember my sister all that well. I visualize her with blue eyes, but even that might be wrong. That's what's so upsetting. How can I have forgotten what my own sister looked like?"

"I've told you before, I can't remember much of Germany either."

"But I was much older. I was—"

"Minds play tricks, Bernard. They just do. Maybe that's what keeps us going. Anyway, I'm actually happy you called. I wanted it to be a surprise for you, but I'll tell you now. Green Lines has rented an apartment for me in Pittsburgh. Place called Gateway Towers. On the river."

"Which river? Pittsburgh has three."

"I don't know ... um ... Allegheny, I guess." Without waiting for a comment, she added, "I knew you wouldn't be overjoyed, so I went on the theory that forgiveness is easier to obtain than permission."

"Honestly, I don't know why—"

"Bernard, hear me out before you get all angry. It's not like I'm moving there. It's just that there's good business reasons for me to be in Pittsburgh on a regular basis."

"I'm listening." Helgman was ambivalent at best about this turn of events. Stephanie being in Pittsburgh would at least give him someone he trusted to talk with other than Barbara and Sol Shapiro. His feelings for Barbara had deepened since he began seeing the therapist, but something had changed and he couldn't put his finger on it. Maybe Stephanie had an insight into what he could do about it. At first he had thought it was his father-in-law's passing that had caused what he thought was depression in his wife. But as the weeks went on Helgman sensed something more; a coolness, an averting of eyes, her bedroom door closed when he came home from the office. They were little things, but taken together, disconcerting.

"This isn't all about you," Stephanie said, "although I must admit if I hadn't been thinking of a reason to be close to you I wouldn't have stumbled onto what I now see as obvious. It's clear to me that we can leverage the company better by individually financing each of our ships. I've worked the numbers and if we allow partial investments by individual investors in each vessel we can increase our tonnage dramatically. This business is about tonnage moved and we'll be able to enter markets faster and turn higher profits. Oil will be key here and I have plans for several supertankers."

"So what's that to do with Pittsburgh?"

"The financial market is strong there. Mellon has made me an offer I can't refuse, as they say. Gulf Oil, U.S. Steel. Two big tonnage consumers. And it's not far from New York City, or Boston for that matter. Short flights."

"If you say so." Helgman's mind was elsewhere, trying to sort out the implications of Stephanie's long-term presence in Pittsburgh. "Financial stuff is not my cup of tea," he finally said. "Actually, it bores me." But he had to admit that Stephanie taking an apartment in Pittsburgh excited him.

"You do your thing, I do mine. Mine's about investments in vessels. Syndication is the term they now use. Syndication is international and Pittsburgh works as well as anywhere else."

"When do you move in—or set it up?"

"Actually, the company already signed the lease and it's being taken care of literally as we speak."

"I can't wait to see it."

"One home-cooked dinner coming up." Stephanie was pleased by Helgman's reaction. "Just as soon as I get there and unpack my stuff."

Barbara sat propped against the headboard of her husband's bed, a half-empty scotch on the bedside table, her bathrobe pulled tightly around her. To say that she was conflicted would be to put it mildly. Her husband was cheating on her. Probably had been for their entire married life, she concluded. But then again, there was obviously something in Stephanie that she lacked and that drew him toward that woman and not to her. So maybe this was all her fault. It was not lost on her that her situation with Gregory was just the same. She was unable to resist the arms of one who fulfilled her in a way that her husband could not—or would not. So how could she fault Bernard for satisfying the very same human desires and in just the same way that she herself had done?

She had convinced herself that in order to keep from going completely insane she had to confront Bernard once and for all and not let him evade her questions as he so often did. At least now she had the startling information that her father had shared with her just before his death. But she also knew, being perfectly truthful with herself, that things with Bernard could not get better unless she broke off with Gregory. Easier said than done, she told herself. Greg was the first man who made her feel like a complete woman. She was not ready—indeed not able—to give that up. What if Bernard did come clean about Stephanie? That wouldn't mean that he could, or would, all of a sudden become the attentive and loving presence in her life that Gregory had become. Suppose that Bernard promised a new beginning for them, with real intimacy, and maybe even made positive steps in that direction? And suppose she terminated her relationship with Gregory to give that a chance? And then what if Bernard slipped back into his old ways? She'd have nothing.

Her plan was to confront Bernard as soon as he came home. Were the weekends just about Muggs or was there a Stephanie component as well? Did she travel with him? Meet him in the various cities where he performed? She needed answers. He couldn't escape to his room to avoid her if she was already there and commandeering his bed. At the same time, she told herself, there was no reason to tell Bernard about Gregory, not now or at any time in the future. If she could make things better between her and her husband, she could simply let her other relationship go, she told herself, and Bernard would never be the wiser. And if this fantasized "new beginning" never materialized, her other life and its comforts would still be intact. As to her guilt about it, if it came to that, she would have to deal with that later. It was too much to plan out all at once and there were too many contingencies to anticipate how things might unfold.

Barbara's heart jumped into her throat as she heard the front door open and Bernard's footsteps on the wooden stair treads.

"I think it's time we spoke about Stephanie," she began, even before he was fully through the door. "Exactly what is your relationship with her? Please be honest with me. It's time we leveled with one another."

Okay. So she had begun. She felt relieved to get on with it, pushing aside the little voice in her head reminding her that although she was demanding that Bernard level with her, she had no intention of doing the same.

"Barbara, I thought we had this discussion. Stephanie and I were raised as cousins in Germany."

"There's more to it than that. Les has told me several times she's your special friend. So I'm just going to plunge ahead and ask this directly. Are you having sex with her?"

"We already discussed this. The answer is no! In fact, she recently showed me family documents that prove that she's my sister—at least according to her. I'm not convinced, but obviously, under the circumstances—"

"Aha. I see. 'Under the circumstances.' Meaning that if she were not your sister—"

"Yes. Perhaps under other circumstances it could have happened. But it hasn't."

"And all this time? Before this supposed documentation showed up? God, Bernie. I hope—"

"No. It never happened. Even before. For the same reason that it hasn't happened with us."

"So not Stephanie. Anyone else?"

"Where's this going? I've done nothing to deserve this cross-examination."

"My father said you would never lie to me."

"I've never lied to you."

"Then where do you go on weekends? Tell me the truth."

"I can't."

"Why not? I don't understand."

"It's my only safe place. The only place I can retreat to for release from the pain. If people know, I'll have nothing. Please understand."

"You're being irrational." She drained her glass. "Germany's the past. Let it go already."

"I can't! It's burned into me. That's who I am. That's who I'll always be. My past is with me every second of every day—except when—"

"When what? It's what you do on weekends, isn't it? We can't go on this way. You have to talk to me."

"Is something wrong? You're not yourself."

"Nothing's wrong that can't be fixed if you would just talk to me." She paused, as if considering her options. "Before he died, my father told me. He knew your secret."

"What did he tell you?" Bernard's face drew tight.

"Does it really matter? What really matters is whether you trust me enough to tell me yourself. *That's* what matters."

Helgman reached into his pocket for a quarter and flipped it in the air a few times. "See the quarter?"

She nodded.

"I'm going to flip it to you. Catch it."

"Is this some kind of test to see if I'm drunk? If so, you can—"

"Just catch it."

He flipped the quarter toward her. Barbara involuntarily reached up and closed her hand around it. Her hand was empty when she opened it.

"I missed it. Where did it go?"

"It's right here," Helgman replied with a grin, retrieving the quarter from behind Barbara's ear.

"Cute. But so what?"

"It's part of what I do on weekends. I put on magic shows for the children at hospitals."

"Finally. That's, of course, what Dad told me, but I needed to hear it from you. Truth be told, *you* needed to be able to tell it to me. You are Muggs the Clown."

"Yes. I'm Muggs."

Even though Barbara had known about Muggs for several weeks—she had even gone to the library and checked old newspapers after her father's revelations—she felt a great weight lift from her shoulders to hear Bernard tell her about Muggs directly. And he had given a plausible account of his relationship with Stephanie. She wasn't sure he was telling her the full truth about that relationship, but she didn't see how she could circle back to the Stephanie topic yet again without, in effect, calling his truthfulness into question. Indeed, she recoiled from the thought of a who's-being-truthful-to-whom discussion given her own duplicitous behavior. It was far less than she had hoped to accomplish this night, but it was a start. And it would have to suffice for now.

"What's that? That thumping noise?"

"Les, I suppose."

Thud.

The sound had come from down the hall in the direction of Leslie's room. Then the whole house shook.

"He's going to hurt himself—or break something. Be back in a minute."

Helgman threw open his son's door, not knowing what to expect. What he saw caused him to gasp. Les was walking upside down on his hands wearing a big red nose below very sad eyes—actually *above* very sad eyes at that moment.

"Les, what are you doing? How many times have I told you to stay out of my things?"

Leslie flipped effortlessly onto the bed and mimicked a bird trying to fly. First, he was a mother bird pushing a baby as hard as she could. Then he became the baby bird trying to summon courage to leave the nest. Despite his anger, Helgman burst into laughter at the bird's antics. The boy's ability to capture the essence of the two birds and to switch between them was exceptional. The baby bird's wings were fluttering ineffectually, appearing to cover its face as if in prayer. Then the little bird leaped high in the air, almost touching the ceiling, its wings wildly flapping. Landing on the floor the bird rolled to a stop and then checked itself for injuries. Climbing to its feet the bird now began strutting around, as if to proclaim he knew all along he could do it.

"That was superb!" Helgman forgot about scolding his son for getting into his things.

The sad eyes became even sadder, the head hung down. Then the bird's face and posture slowly faded into what was no doubt a chicken. The chicken moved off to be by itself, an outcast from the others.

Again Helgman applauded, realizing his son had great natural talent built around his affinity for animals. "Les," he said, "I'm not angry with you, but how long have you been doing this?"

The boy remained silent, peering at his father over the huge red nose.

"It's okay." He put his arm around Leslie's shoulder and tried to comfort him as he did with his young patients.

Finally the boy said, "Ken and I found the bag."

"Well, you're excellent at it." And then, on impulse, he asked, "Would you want to put on shows with me?"

"Could I?" The red nose bobbed up and down.

"If you promise to work hard and learn the tricks. Now go and take the makeup off and I'll wait for you so we can talk. And Les," Helgman called after the boy, "you are to tell no one about this. Understand me?"

While Leslie was gone, Helgman returned to his bedroom and told Barbara that everything was okay but that he needed to spend some time with Leslie. Resolving to resume her conversation with Bernard the next day, Barbara nodded, took herself down the hall into her own bedroom and, exhausted, fell asleep almost immediately. As soon as she had left, Helgman reached into the top shelf of his closet and retrieved a package he had hidden away years earlier. Ripping the package open, he pulled out a painting of a clown. Helgman had reconstructed the artist's daughter's face soon after he set up his practice. "The only time I saw her laugh," the father had said, "is when that clown, Muggs—I think his name was—performed in the hospital. It moved me to paint his portrait from a photo I took at the time. You both helped my daughter to recover, each in your own way, and I wanted you to have it."

When Leslie returned, the two of them hung the picture in Leslie's room. "This clown is named Muggs," Helgman said. "He loves to entertain children. Do you think you could be a clown for children? Sick children? In hospitals?"

"Sick children need help. Not their fault. Les help."

"It means hard work, son. Learning tricks with your hands. Will you work hard?"

"I can, Daddy. I can work hard. I want to be clown."

Helgman produced a quarter and placed it in the boy's right hand between his first two fingers. "Now move the quarter to the last two fingers. You can use your thumb if you want." Helgman produced another quarter. "Watch how I do it."

The quarter seemed to jump across his hand. "I'm sorry," he said. "I didn't mean to move it that fast. Let me show you again."

This time the quarter moved from finger to finger slow enough for Leslie to follow its progress.

Leslie studied his father's agile fingers as Helgman repeated the maneuver over and over. Then he tentatively tried it himself.

The coin dropped to the floor almost immediately. Leslie retrieved the quarter and again it slipped from his hand.

Again and again he tried and each time the coin landed on the floor.

"I know it seems you'll never learn to do it. It took me a while to learn. I'll show you one other thing with the quarter and then I'm going to leave you to practice."

Leslie watched as the coin moved from the palm of his father's hand to the back, held between two fingers. Helgman showed Les in slow motion how to do the same thing.

"Now I want you to practice. Even when you get it, keep practicing. Even I practice every day. It is practice that allows it to work."

"I practice, Daddy. I want be clown like you."

"Like me?"

"Yes, Muggs the Clown."

Helgman was flabbergasted. "How do you know about Muggs?"

"The bag and the telephone."

"Les, please stay out of other people's things."

"How I learn."

"There's a better way to learn. Just practice with the coin and let me know when you're ready."

TWENTY-FIVE

Helgman called from the office at noon the next day. "Any luck, son?" He was anticipating the boy's frustration.

"Nope."

"Have you been working on it?"

"Yep."

"How many times have you tried?"

"Don't know."

"More than a hundred times?"

"Yes."

"More than a thousand?"

"Don't know."

"I told you it was hard. Don't give up. Keep working on it. All of a sudden it'll happen."

"Okay. Les do it."

"Even if you don't learn the trick you can still be a clown. The trick is just extra. You can be a bird, just like you were last night."

"I practice, Daddy. I practice hard."

Later that night, Helgman saw a light under Leslie's door and knocked.

"Okay." There was frustration in Leslie's voice.

"I see you're working on the coin trick," Helgman said, noticing a pile of coins on the boy's bed. "Any progress?"

"No," Les answered, looking down at his feet.

"Nothing to be ashamed about. Here, let me see how you're coming along."

Les reluctantly picked up the coin and it flipped onto the bed.

"Try rotating your wrist a bit." He took the boy's arm and twisted gently. "And hold your palm a little more in the air, like this." He positioned his own hand the way he wanted Leslie's to be.

Les mimicked him perfectly.

"That's good. Now try it."

This time the coin made it all the way across Leslie's knuckles, but dropped on the bed at the end.

"You're almost there," Helgman encouraged. "Do it again. This time close your hand faster."

The coin landed on the bed again.

"You're now actually trying too hard. Relax your fingers. Do this." Helgman held his hand up and flexed his fingers one by one as if he were playing notes on a piano.

Leslie did the same. Then he took the quarter and the coin moved across the back of his hand—and disappeared from view.

"Great!" Helgman clapped his hands in excitement as Leslie did it several more times, all without mishap. "Here," Helgman said reaching inside his jacket for a folded bunch of papers. "I've written a script for you for my next show. It's this coming Saturday. Come to my office at three on Friday and we'll rehearse. The performance is in a little town in the middle of Pennsylvania called State College. You and I'll drive out there after we're finished rehearsing and stay overnight in a motel. All the instructions are written out for you."

"But I can't—"

"It's okay if you're not ready with the coin trick. There are other things for you to do."

The boy's face came alive. "Goodie. Be clown! I practice hard. Be good clown. Work hard."

"I bet you will, Les. I bet you will. Remember, three on Friday."

Leslie walked into his father's office shortly before three o'clock, suitcase in hand. A girl was sitting in the waiting room, a mass of red welts across her face, one eye swollen closed. She had only one ear, the other being a flap stitched closed.

Leslie immediately went over to her and asked, "Want to see trick?"

She turned away from him, as if to hide her damaged face.

Undeterred, he pulled out his quarter and said, "Watch quarter."

Even though she kept her face turned from him, Leslie could see that her good eye was following the quarter. He held up his palm, the quarter facing her. Then he flipped his wrist and the quarter was gone.

He pointed to the ceiling and her head followed. The quarter was on her lap when she looked down.

She laughed, making a strange noise as she did so.

Before Leslie could do another trick, Helgman's nurse announced that the doctor was ready to see her. The girl's mother turned to Leslie. "Thank you, young man. You cheered her up. The doctor is going to fix her face and re-build her ear, but she's afraid she'll always be disfigured. This is the first time she has laughed in a very long time. Thank you again."

Leslie was alone now, waiting for his father. His hands began to shake when he realized Helgman would ask about the coin trick. It had been so easy when it was only the girl and it had felt good to see her laugh.

"Les," his father called. "Come, we can rehearse now. We have to leave soon."

They ran through their routine several times and each time Leslie did exactly as the script was written. Helgman adjusted the routine several times and beamed when his usually slow-to-learn son remembered the new order of things and performed them without a hitch.

"Les," Helgman said an hour later, "we're as ready as we'll ever be. Let's pack up and go. It's a pretty drive to State College. In fact, it reminds me of the countryside around where I grew up. Penn State University is in the town where we're going."

"Goody, goody. Have name."

"What name do you have?"

"You Muggs. Me Muggles."

"If that's what you want, then it's okay with me." Helgman didn't see the humor in the name at first.

"Funny," Leslie said, "using your name and my name together. Muggles?"

"Yes, son. I've got to admit the name is clever."

TWENTY-SIX

Friday was a disaster for Barbara. It was the culmination of events that had begun some weeks earlier when Bernard had told her about Muggs. His confession, as it were, confirmed that her father had been right all along. Bernard had not been using his weekends to see Stephanie or for any other illicit purpose. Even more important, Barbara had detected the possibility of a new beginning—one filled with true affection and, at long last, a physical relationship with her husband.

Leslie's jumping off the bed, or what ever he had been doing, had come at an inopportune time, interrupting, as it had, what she wanted to believe were the pleasant stirrings of a sexual longing by her husband.

Her afternoon liaisons with Gregory—initially an almost every day occurrence—had become few and far between by the beginning of August when Gregory's wife briefly seemed to be emerging from her coma, only to die a week later. Barbara had actually welcomed that respite. Bernard's opening up to her about Muggs and his assurances about Stephanie stirred in her the hope that they could move to the next level—that of physical intimacy. She didn't see how that could possibly happen while she was still involved with Gregory.

Gregory had called her on Sunday. He wanted to resume where they had left off. In fact, he had asked her to leave Bernard and be with him. Barbara had told him that she wasn't sure. They agreed to meet on Friday to talk it all through. But by Tuesday Barbara had already thought it through on her own. She planned to tell Gregory that she had decided to try to make a go of things with Bernard and that she needed to break off their relationship completely.

That was on Tuesday. But as Friday drew closer Barbara began to see things differently. Nothing really was going to change with Bernard, she concluded. Except now,

Leslie would be with him on weekends and she would be even more alone, drinking in her room. She decided that rather than break it off with Gregory on Friday, she would surprise him by showing up with her suitcase.

On Friday morning Barbara asked Helgman if he had plans for Sunday. His response was unusual and disquieting. "You'll know soon enough," he had answered. "It's my surprise to you. Les and I'll be home about five on Saturday and I'll tell you then."

Little did Bernard know that she wouldn't be there when he arrived back home.

Barbara began packing quickly as soon as Bernard and Leslie had left, thankful that, with Leslie gone, Millie had been given the day off. Shortly after ten o'clock, her packing finished, she sat in her living room staring out the window, fidgeting nervously. Her resolve to be with Gregory was now firmly cemented in her mind. But that didn't prevent her from being scared. A florist's van drove slowly down the street and her curiosity was piqued, wondering who the lucky person was who was receiving flowers on a Friday. *Someone planning a romantic weekend,* she thought. It was something she had personally never experienced. But that was all about to change, she told herself.

A young man emerged from the van carrying a bouquet of red roses spilling over the top of a massive paper-wrapped bundle. Barbara's heart sank as he strode up her front walk. "Gregory," she thought in dismay, "how could you?" She had made him promise not to contact her at home in any way. While she had resolved to abandon her husband to be with Gregory, she wasn't yet ready to tell Bernard that she was leaving him for another man. The roses would just be an unnecessary telltale clue.

Barbara's nervousness kept her from seeing how illogical it was for Gregory to have been the sender under the circumstances. If she had thought it through, she would have concluded that the flowers were being delivered to the wrong address. But she wasn't thinking clearly. In a panic, she rushed to the garage, stuffed the flowers into a black plastic bag, and buried them at the bottom of an already half-full garbage can. Lost in swirling thoughts as she returned to the living room, Barbara didn't realize that the florist's gift card envelope was in her hand. She had absent-mindedly pulled it from the wrapping before stuffing the flowers into the garbage bag. Just as absent-mindedly, she stuffed the envelope into her purse lying on the couch.

Barbara checked the time and realized that she was late. She had promised to meet Gregory at noon and it was almost noon already. She rushed around the house, trying to decide on the best place to leave the note she had written to Bernard and at the same time berating herself that she hadn't tended to that task sooner. The note should be in a place that her husband would be sure to find it as soon as he came home, but not where Leslie would find it first. She settled on her own bed, thinking that Bernard would look for her there after not finding her in the kitchen or living room.

Now on the road driving to Gregory's house, Barbara replayed the events of the morning. A vision of the gift card envelope popped into her mind. She saw herself pulling it off the florist's package and holding it as she returned from the garage. Could she have been so stupid as to leave it lying around somewhere? She was about to turn around and return to the house when it occurred to her that she might have put in her purse. She had no recollection of having put it there but....

Barbara opened her purse at the next traffic light and was relieved to see the small envelope tucked into one side of the main pouch. She decided to read the note, thinking that it might help her figure out how to address Gregory's *faux pas* without spoiling things at the very moment of this new phase of their relationship.

Her world crumbled into confusion.

> *Barbara my love,*
>
> *You can't imagine the relief I felt at finally being able to tell you about Muggs and my weekends away from home. I realized afterward how much my keeping that secret from you had infected everything else in our relationship. But I told Shapiro at my last session about what happened and he and I agreed that this is the chance for a new beginning. For us to move forward. I'm finally ready for our honeymoon. A bit belated, but, as they say, better late than never. We leave Saturday night after I get back from my trip with Les. I have a room booked at the Hilton and the*

*rest is a surprise. Plan to be gone five days. Pack
light. I love you. B*

Barbara pulled onto a side street, parked, and slumped
in her seat, her mind racing, trying to decide what to do.
Her marriage was now totally out of sync. Did it even
matter anymore if he wanted to share her bed? She loved
Bernard, but that was meaningless unless he changed. And
hanging over it all was her own deceit.

Trust. Tryst. A single letter difference resulting in
total reversal of meaning. Who was she to demand trust
when she had breached that trust herself? Instead of being
overwhelmed with joy at the flowers and the honeymoon
and all that those gestures promised, she was filled with
remorse, convinced that whatever bond had grown been
between her and Bernard was now irrevocably gone; not
cut with a scalpel, but rather bludgeoned so horribly that
not even Helgman's talented fingers could sew the pieces
back together.

Leslie and Helgman arrived home from State College
shortly after four o'clock on Saturday. The performance had
gone well. Helgman was surprised at how sensitive his son
could be with the children. Muggles had performed his role
well, never missing a cue, sometimes ad-libbing to keep
the laughs going. Leslie had a marvelous sense of timing
and was always in sync with the audience—patients, and
nurses alike. Being a clown was a natural for his son and he
showed every sign of being able to make a career out of it.

Helgman become aware during the drive back that it
was the first time he was excited to be rushing back home
after a Muggs performance. He was eager to share with
Barbara the story of Leslie's bravura debut. And there was
more. Shapiro's counseling was working. A picture formed
in his mind of him and Barbara walking on a warm beach
and dancing late into the night. He had never walked on a
beach in his life. The dancing part was fanciful also. He
had never danced a single step, but music now sometimes
got his feet to tapping and so he told himself that maybe
dancing was something he might actually enjoy.

Barbara had proven to be a good woman and a good mother to Leslie. She took special care to make their home peaceful and relaxing. In truth, he loved her and it was time to devote his attention to completing his therapy and beginning a real married life. Of that much he was certain. His intention was to drive with Barbara downtown to the Hilton, have a nice dinner and, albeit belatedly, consummate their marriage. Then at midday Sunday they would fly to Jamaica for several days. Bernard was more excited about this vacation, his first real vacation ever, than he had imagined he would be.

Driving back from the performance he toyed with the idea of extending the time away to ten days. He was certain Jack Rippore would be more than happy to try his hand at managing the practice on his own in Helgman's absence. Rippore was an extremely talented surgeon who Helgman himself had trained many years earlier and recently brought into his practice after years of searching for someone of Helgman's own caliber.

Once home, Leslie went straight to his room. He wanted to call Ken to tell him about his performance as Muggles. Meanwhile, Helgman went to Barbara's room. She hadn't responded when he called out from the front door to announce their arrival and he assumed she was napping.

The words of the note nearly knocked him over. He reread it several times, certain he had missed something. But there was nothing to misread.

> *Bernie,*
> *Much as things have improved between us, I find I'm still in a bad place. I need time away to think things through and get my bearings. I'm not with my mother, so don't call there. Millie will be back tomorrow..*

Helgman fell onto the bed in a wave of nausea. Just moments before, his world seemed to be expanding with the promise of new beginnings. Now it felt as if it had reversed course and was imploding in on him.

A week went by and Helgman still hadn't heard from Barbara. The practice had slowed, and the only bright spot in his days was his work with Leslie—writing scripts, practicing, teaching new magic tricks. His son was surprisingly quick at picking up new routines and his hands turned out to be quicker than Helgman had expected. He had told Leslie that his mother had decided to take a vacation and would be back soon.

Ten days after Barbara walked out, she called.

"How's Les doing?" There was no apology or explanation. "Do you want me to take him?"

"He's doing just fine. But Barbara," Helgman said, "this has gone on long enough. I want you home. I need you."

Barbara responded with more anger in her voice than he had ever heard before. "You've never needed anyone, Bernie. Why now?" After a moment of silence she said, "Oh, I take that back. When you wanted to adopt Les and couldn't do it without a wife, then you needed me. I can't remember any other time."

"Why the sudden hostility?" Helgman responded, trying to follow his therapist's suggestions. "I've always respected you and treated you properly."

"You call disappearing on weekends without allowing me to know what you were doing treating me with respect? You disappeared last weekend with Les. Is that respect? You even planned a vacation without my input. You have a warped sense of the meaning of respect."

"That was to be a surprise. Our honeymoon."

"A little late." Her tone softened.

"I'm sorry. I really am. The problem was never you. It was always just me. That's past now. I'm ready to move on and I want you with me."

"You think being sorry makes up for the deception, the lies? You went for counseling and kept that from me as well. Now you have Les doing something and you keep that from me. When will it end? For God sakes, Bernie, I'm not even sure I know who you are! Being sorry isn't the issue."

"What is the issue then?"

"Trust. Honesty. That's the real issue. You can't have love without trust. All these years that I thought I was in love with you, I was confused between the real you and my image of you. I was in love with the image. Images evaporate."

"Are you telling me—"

"How can I be in love with a person when I don't know who is showing up at any time. I just don't know who you are."

"Please come home so we can talk. I need you here with me."

"We've never talked, you and I. Oh, maybe when you were deciding on our little business deal. Grace calls it doing your due diligence. And oh yes, daily chit-chat about how the day went. That kind of thing. But we've never really talked about the important stuff. It's always been your decisions on your own. Your way. You put Les in a special school and didn't care what I thought. There's no end to your refusal to include me in your life. They were little things, Bernie, but taken together, disconcerting. It's the little things that make a marriage. The things that happen without thought, without planning. That's what trust is about. All we've shared is an address!"

"That's not fair, we've—"

"Where were you all the years when I needed you? All the years I cried myself to sleep? All the years I sat in my own room with only a bottle of scotch to keep me company? Where were you then?"

He was silent.

"I'll tell you, Bernie. You were nowhere. No that's wrong. You were with your ... lover. You'd still be with her if you didn't think she was your sister!"

"But Barbara—"

"It's late and I'm tired,"

And then she was gone.

BOOK THREE

1973-1974

TWENTY-SEVEN

arbara's walking out was only the first shoe to drop. Ten days later Helgman sat slumped in a chair in the office of his trust attorney William Dawson, his life in ruins. The sequence of events had actually begun a month earlier when Yetta Hertzstein, a former Auschwitz prisoner, had been visiting a friend's child in the hospital. Helgman had come into the room to check on the boy after his surgery. Hertzstein recognized him and told her story to Jeffrey Perkins, the U.S. Attorney. Perkins took the matter to the grand jury, which wasted little time in indicting Helgman on charges of war crimes, immigration law violations and various other offenses based primarily on Yetta's sworn testimony. U.S. marshals then arrested Helgman at his office. Helgman called Dawson, the only lawyer he knew, as soon as he was allowed access to a telephone. Dawson, with the assistance of other lawyers in his office, arranged bail, had bond posted, and instructed Helgman to come to his office the next morning so they could discuss hiring a good criminal lawyer.

This was the first opportunity for the two men to discuss the case in any detail.

"So if you can't represent me," Helgman said, not looking up, "who are we going to get?"

"We'll get to that in a moment, but you need to know some background in order for us to pick the right guy."

Helgman looked up to face him. "Background? What are you talking about?"

"Here." Dawson pushed a multi-page legal-paper-sized document across his desk to Helgman. "You need to read this. Then we can discuss going forward."

Helgman picked up the document and read the title typed onto a large red-bordered label affixed to the cover:

"Go ahead, Bernard, read it." Dawson rose from his chair. "I'll step out for a bit to give you time—and privacy."

Helgman was suddenly alone in the office, his mind alternately racing and freezing as he struggled to focus on the document in his lap. He finally turned to the first page.

Q: (BY MR. PERKINS) Please state your name.

THE WITNESS

A: Yetta Hertzstein

Q: Are you familiar with Doctor Bernard Helgman, a surgeon practicing in Pittsburgh?

A: I am.

Q: Please tell the grand jury in your own words how you know Doctor Helgman.

A: Well, a dear friend of mine, Rita Glatt, has a young son—Joseph—who was involved in an accident that terribly burned his face. Joseph calls me Auntie Yetta. Anyway, I went to visit Joseph in his hospital room and to give some comfort to my friend Rita. While I was there, a doctor came in to check on Joseph. Well, I was shocked when I read the name Dr. Bernard Helgman on his badge.

Q: Why were you, in your words, "shocked"?

A: Because I was in Auschwitz during the war and a doctor named Bernard Helgman was in the camp at the same time as me. Actually, he was in a bed next to me in the camp infirmary and I watched him die there.

Q: You watched Doctor Helgman die in the infirmary?

A: Yes. But I recognized Joseph's doctor.

Q: You recognized him from where? I mean from where did you recognize the Doctor Helgman you saw in Joseph's room?

A. The Doctor Helgman that I saw in the hospital—Joseph's doctor—was not the man who died, but a different man altogether. But he was there.

Q: There? What do you mean "there"?

A: He was there in the camp, in the infirmary. He was much younger then, but I recognized his eyes. He didn't have the scar that he has now, but there is no mistaking those eyes. They're forever burned into my memory.

Q: How did you have occasion to be in the infirmary to see this Doctor Helgman—I mean the Doctor Helgman who treated your friend's son?

A: They did experiments. They called it the infirmary, but it was just a place where the Nazi doctors, butchers, did medical experiments on us. They cut out my ovaries and attempted to replace them with the ovaries from a pig. "You Jews are pigs, after all, so it should be a perfect match." Can you believe that? That's what they said to me as I was lying there.

Q: And this Doctor Helgman was there at that time?

A: Yes. I was in and out of consciousness on the table, but every time I came to, there he was—those eyes—looming over my head and looking down at me.

Q: And his name was Bernard Helgman?

A: We were never formally introduced, if you'll pardon my sarcasm. All I remember is that at some point he turned his head away from me to look across the room when someone called to him. Schmidt. I'm pretty certain they called him Schmidt.

Q: And to the best of your knowledge, then, this Schmidt was one of the doctors who experimented on you?

A: Definitely.

Q: Did you say anything to him in Joseph's room, after you recognized him?

A: No. I pretty much fainted in my chair as soon as I realized that it was him. The next thing I knew, he was gone. But I called the police the next day because I thought they should know this beast—this butcher—was here among us and that they should arrest him. But after I told the police my story they said I should call the federal district attorney's office. That's what I did.

Helgman looked up from the transcript to find Dawson back in his chair. How long the lawyer had been sitting there he did not know.

"I can't believe I was arrested...on this."

"It's our esteemed U.S. Attorney Jeffrey Perkins," Dawson began. "He has his mind set on becoming our next U.S. Senator. He's won over the party bosses, but he needs greater name recognition. Either he quickly makes a name for himself or he's out. You may not follow politics but, in short, you're his ticket to Washington, D.C."

"He plans to make headlines by putting a supposed Nazi war criminal in jail? I'm not—"

"Truth is not his concern. Just the headlines."

"What headlines can he get with me?"

"Let's see. How about: *Senate Hopeful Perkins Set To Prosecute Former Nazi Butcher, Now Child Surgeon?*"

"But I never was a Nazi! I'm Jewish, for God sake!"

"None of that matters. From the publicity he'll generate from this, Jeffery Perkins will become a household name within weeks. This is the stuff that sells newspapers."

"But I'm innocent."

"This is not about your guilt or innocence. It's about politics. Perkins will kill you with sound bites. Our system of justice is not perfect. Judges are not perfect. Even the law isn't perfect. In the end, your fate will be decided by twelve people with prejudices and passions that we can only guess at."

"How long is this going to go on?"

"Perkins will drag this out as long as he possibly can. He doesn't have to win the case, just so long as he doesn't lose it before the election. It will last through the fall, right up until the election."

"And what am I supposed to do?"

"I want your permission to let it be known you're the founder of the Survivor Trust. That it's your money that has paid for medical treatments for hundreds of survivors. We can rally the people who have benefited from your support. That fact alone will stem the tide before it overwhelms you."

"Absolutely not!" Helgman's reaction was visceral. "I didn't fund the trust for my benefit. You're not to breathe a word of my involvement."

Dawson watched as his long-time client jumped from his chair and began pacing the office. "You're making a big mistake, my friend," Dawson warned after Helgman's pacing had slowed. "We can address the subject later when the extent of the difficulties are more apparent, but I believe it's a mistake to not get out in front of this."

"I said no, and I mean no! End of discussion."

"So be it." Dawson knew when to give in, for the present, anyway. "Let's work on obtaining competent criminal counsel. I suggest Geraldo Fleishman and—"

"That radical son of a ... I'll never be associated with that man. His clients are scum."

"As I said, this is a political fight and Fleishman knows how to take on the system. He can grab the headlines away from Perkins."

"I won't be part of that. I love this country and refuse to hire someone who says what he says and does what he does."

"Listen. Unless you fight back, and fight back hard, you'll be destroyed. I'll say it again. If Perkins has his way, you'll never practice medicine again. All that you've worked for will be gone."

"He can't—"

"He can, and he will. Public opinion will demand it. Once this thing gets going, there'll be no stopping it. Let me hire Fleishman. Think of the children."

"I think of nothing else," Helgman shot back. "The children are my life's work."

"That's why you must fight this hard. It's probably only a matter of hours before the hospital suspends your privileges."

"They can't do that.They won't!"

"Of course they can. And they'll have no choice."

"I'm innocent! Doesn't that mean anything?"

"Like I said, the system isn't designed to provide true justice in the face of this type of political crusade. I'm afraid they'll kill you in the papers and on the TV news."

"Whatever happened to innocent until proven guilty?"

"At best, that only applies to the legal system, not to public opinion."

Helgman collapsed back into his chair.

"Bernard, this is serious," Dawson said. "Losing your hospital privileges is the least of it. You've been charged under the federal war crimes act. Many people died in that infirmary. If they tie you to what went on, then they could find you guilty of murder and you can be sent to jail, possibly for life."

"Jail? For life? What the hell are you talking about?"

"You understandably must have been in a fog when I explained all this to you yesterday at the arraignment. Anyway, even if you beat that rap, you still face the possibility of being deported under the immigration laws."

Helgman's head was swimming. "Deported? How? Why?"

"You signed a statement stating your name to be Bernard Helgman. False. You claimed to be a doctor. Also false."

"And so?"

"And so people who get into this country based on seriously false statements are subject to deportation. Even if they can't prove that you actually performed any of the experiments, Yetta Hertzstein's testimony puts you in the room. It will be assumed, at the very least, that you assisted in what went on there. Her testimony suggests you were a part of the Nazi machinery, and cuts against the claim you made when you entered the country that you were an Auschwitz victim."

"My God! Even after all this time."

"And on top of all that, you could be found liable for money damages to compensate the families of those that they say you killed. After they've wiped out your personal accounts to pay those damages they'll try to get to the assets of the trusts as well. Listen, let me call Fleishman before they eat you alive."

Helgman sat silent for a full minute before sitting up. "Who else besides Fleishman?"

"My second choice is a good friend of mine, Wendall Blackridge. He was a justice on the Pennsylvania Supreme Court until about five years ago. Retired after a heart attack. But he still teaches at the law school and is as sharp as ever." Dawson moved across the room to where Helgman now sat slumped in his chair. "I think I can get him for you, but he'll demand that you do exactly as he says. He's the exact opposite of Fleishman. He'll concentrate on the legal papers and keep all the arguing in the courtroom. He will not try your case in the media, that much I can promise. You may win the case, but you may well lose the public."

Helgman looked up. "If you're asking would I follow his advice? The answer is it depends on what he wants me to do."

"That's not the right answer! The right answer is, yes, I'll do whatever he says."

"I can't say that."

"You have no choice if you want to remain in this country and practice medicine. Other than Fleishman, Blackridge is your only real hope of getting through this. I'll be calling in a lifetime of IOUs on this one, so I want your promise to follow his instructions."

Helgman remained silent, his eyes fixed on something in the far distance.

Exasperated, Dawson raised his voice ever so slightly. "Bernard, it's not so difficult a thing to do. Blackridge is the best. He's the Helgman of the legal profession."

"We'll see," Helgman said finally. "I can't promise anything."

"You better make up your mind in short order because there's a lot to do and if there's going to be any response to the press from our side, it's got to happen immediately. Silence will be taken as an admission of guilt. So what's it going to be? Fleishman or Blackridge?"

Helgman slumped down even further into his chair. "Blackridge, I guess."

"Okay."

Dawson reached over to the intercom on his desk and asked his secretary to set up a phone call with Wendall Blackridge. He then turned back to Helgman.

"For what it's worth," Dawson said, "I have no doubt that Yetta Hertzstein is confused. I've known you long enough to know that you couldn't have been the person she claims she saw operating on her."

"Confused, indeed," Helgman thought to himself. "But not in the way you think." Helgman remembered Yetta Hertzstein all too well.

TWENTY-EIGHT

No sooner had Helgman stepped out of Dawson's office when his pager went off. He recognized the number of the hospital administrator, Bill Negley. A call from the nearest phone booth confirmed that Negley wanted to see him in Negley's office. Stat.

"Bernard," Negley began after Helgman arrived about a half hour later, "you're the best surgeon I've ever had the pleasure of knowing. But...."

"I know," Helgman interrupted. "The hospital board, right?"

"They met in a special session this morning."

"How can they do this? I bring more money to this hospital than the rest combined. I've put this place on the map. And this is the thanks I receive in return."

"It's a question of liability."

"That's nonsense. This hospital has not paid out one nickel on account of anything I've ever done."

"You're right, of course. But did you see last night's TV news? The hospital was mentioned prominently in the story, interspersed with clips of Prosecutor Perkins calling you the Butcher of Birkenau."

"That son of ... "

"That's why the hospital had to take action. The papers want a statement and there's a limit on how long I can continue to say 'no comment'. The press is demanding to know why the hospital would allow you to continue to operate on 'our kids,' as one reporter put it. This is bad, Bernard. As bad as I've ever seen it. I hope you got a good lawyer."

"I'm guilty without even a trial! I'm innocent and the hospital is throwing me out without so much as hearing my story."

"Give the board credit. Many of them are admirers of yours. They didn't outright revoke your privileges. They suggested you take a well-deserved vacation."

"I built the children's wing, for God sake! I don't deserve to be thrown out like the dirty wash water!"

"The board's hands are tied. Try to see it from their perspective. Much as they admire you and appreciate all that you've done, they have to protect the hospital at all costs. Your only options are an extended vacation or an outright privilege termination. Believe me, vacation is the best we can do for you. The hospital is going out on a limb even with that. I'm sorry."

Helgman stood and walked to the door. "So, okay. You win. I'm on vacation." He was suddenly more exhausted than he had realized. "But win or lose, I don't ever expect to set foot in this hospital again. Tell that to your precious board."

"Best to not burn bridges. With your permission, Bernard, I'd like to tell them something else—something that will serve all of us better in the long run. I'd tell them, number one, that you're grateful for their doing the best they could under the circumstances and, number two, that you can't wait to get back to work after you've been exonerated."

Helgman thought for a minute before relenting. "Okay, Bill. Whatever you say. At least the second part is right."

"Bernard, I'm sad that it's come to this."

"I appreciate the sentiment, Bill, but don't be sad for me. Be sad for the children."

TWENTY-NINE

"I know it looks dark to you, Bernard," Blackridge said, his large body falling into an over-stuffed chair. Helgman had just arrived at Blackridge's wood-paneled home office where he'd come every day since Dawson had persuaded the retired justice to take the case some two weeks earlier. "But hang in there. We haven't yet begun to fire our weapons."

Possibly because we don't have any weapons to fire, Helgman thought. The old man had said nothing to the press while the newspapers continued to carry front-page interviews with U.S. Attorney Perkins and with self-proclaimed Nazi hunters who had materialized to make their pronouncements. Helgman was more often than not referred to in the stories as the Butcher of Birkenau, a phrase coined by Perkins.

On the other extreme, Helgman had been invited from places as far away as Chicago and Greensboro to attend anti-government, pro-Nazi street rallies, the assumption being that he was, in fact, a Nazi. A demonstration was being organized ostensibly to protest Helgman's innocence, but the march leaders made it clear that their biggest complaint was with the growing number of blacks in city government. Jews and coloreds were not welcome at the rally. Absent from the fray was Wendall Blackridge, who the media now took to calling the Gray Ghost of Times Past.

Helgman's mind drifted off to a meeting he had had the previous day with William Dawson. He had become so upset with Blackridge's low-key approach in the face of the constant media pounding that he was ready to fire Blackridge and hire Geraldo Fleishman after all. He had broached the subject with Dawson, the only person Helgman still fully trusted.

"The damage has been done," the lawyer had answered. "It's best now not to change horses in mid-stream. Blackridge didn't get where he is by being stupid. Do as he says.

The man is uncanny. He prefers winning to churning out press releases."

"But he's doing nothing!"

"Maybe nothing that you can see. He's working the system his own way. Headlines won't help you now that the media barrage has begun. Not even Fleishman could get it turned around at this stage."

"Let's continue with the business at hand, shall we?" It was the voice of Wendall Blackridge, interrupting Helgman's reverie.

The "business at hand" was Helgman dictating his life story into a tape recorder. Blackridge had demanded to know every detail of Helgman's life from as early as he could recall until the present day. It forced Helgman to remember painful details that his emotional survival had required him to forget. As soon as one tape was full, he replaced it with a fresh one. Visions of his sister flashed into his mind along with snippets of his mother and father, all intermixed with horrible images of black-uniformed men standing over women lying on blood-covered wooden tables, their abdomens sliced wide open. On and on, the horrors poured from him as the tapes filled with atrocities too numerous to tally. Never once did a tear come to his eyes, as if his mind were nothing more than a mechanical recorder playing back data stored over his lifetime.

People paraded in and out of Blackridge's home office. Helgman knew that some were typists, but some were obviously young lawyers, mostly men, but also a few women. The lawyers were easy to spot. The men wore suits and ties while the women favored tailored jackets with silk neck scarves. They hardly ever spoke to Helgman, and when they did it was in the most formal and respectful tones.

"Who are all these lawyers scurrying about?" Helgman asked Blackridge one day. "And who's paying their salary?"

"Law students from Pitt and Duquesne, all at the top of their classes. They do the indexing, the coordinating, and the cross-filing. Later, when we're in court and I need a document you'll be amazed at how fast they will produce it. You win or lose on these folks."

"And they work for ...?"

"Me, of course."

"You're no longer in a firm, so where did they come from?"

"Dawson arranged for them. You do realize, don't you, that Dawson's law firm is one of the largest in the country? They have powerful connections, in and out of government. He has made his offices and resources available to us. This is only the tip of the iceberg, I assure you."

"You still haven't told me who's footing the bill for all of this."

"I haven't asked. And my advice to you is don't ask either. If Dawson is concerned about money, he'll bring it up."

"I don't see the big picture here."

"The big picture is 'steady as she goes.' I've kept you away from interviews. The press is starving for news and they are hounding Perkins for stories. The truth is, he's saying and doing legally stupid things. That's good for you."

"The way it looks from where I sit, I'll never work again. How do you call that 'good for me'?"

"The hospital hasn't revoked your privileges, but that means nothing if you're in jail or get deported. If we win this battle you'll be back to work."

"It doesn't appear that we're winning."

"Appearances can be deceiving. I'm convinced I'll be able to put Yetta Hertzstein's testimony in a whole different light based on what you've said on the tapes you've been dictating. My thought is that Perkins will take all discussion of money damages off the table within a week. It's become a political hot potato and he's afraid it'll cause him to lose control of his case. So when the dust settles the only charge that will probably remain will be whether you lied to get into the country which, if they find that you did, is grounds for your deportation.

"And as to that, I've got to say the facts aren't the greatest, unfortunately. You claimed to be Bernard Helgman, M.D. That's two misstatements in one. Whether those are serious enough to warrant deportation, I can't say. It will probably depend as much as anything on what side of the bed the judge got out on. I will say, though, that even if we're successful in making the war crimes count go away, Yetta Hertzstein's testimony provides Perkins with a lot of ammunition to argue for your deportation. He's likely to argue that Hertzstein's story establishes you lied when you presented yourself at the border as having been an Auschwitz internee because your supposed behavior toward Jews in the camp was consistent with being a Nazi."

"It was consistent with survival."

"I know that, and you know that, but will the judge see it that way?"

"So things look pretty grim then?"

"Serious, yes. Grim, no. But let me be frank." The old man paused just long enough for Helgman to realize his lawyer was concerned about something on one of the tapes or perhaps about an answer he had given. "Many actions consistent with survival are not ... shall we say ... legal or ethical."

"What are you trying to say?"

"Just that there is a line—sometimes a very fine line indeed—that one can't cross, even to save oneself. For example, you—"

"I didn't cross any so-called line," Helgman barked, his frustration with the process boiling over.

"Hear me out, please. For example, you can't take another's life to save your own. Unless, of course, that other person is the one who is threatening you."

"I didn't—"

Blackridge held up his hand. "If it turns out that you operated on anyone, anyone at all, even under duress, it won't go well for you. I want your assurance that nothing of that sort occurred."

Even as the vision of the dead guard flashed through his mind, Helgman raised his hand, as if to swear to the honesty of his response. "You have my assurance."

Blackridge studied his client a moment, then said, "Okay, based on your assurance and on what you've said on this tape recorder over these past two weeks, I'm pretty sure that on cross-examination I can make Yetta's testimony work *for* us, not *against* us. In the meantime, we have to prepare for a full criminal defense.

"And one other thing," Blackridge continued. "I strongly recommend that we waive the right to a jury trial. That means that the judge will be not only the arbiter of the relevant law, but he, instead of a jury, will be evaluating the testimony of the witnesses and deciding what to believe."

"Why is that better for me?"

"We've drawn Phillip Walkowski as the judge for your case. I've known Phil Walkowski since law school and he's a straight shooter. As straight as they come. If we have a jury, I expect that the prosecutor will try to distract them from the facts—which I view as being mostly in your favor.

He'll play to their sympathy for Yetta Hertzstein and any other Auschwitz victims who may come forward now that your case has made the national news. Judge Walkowski won't be swayed by a lot of bombast and, if you'll forgive me, bull crap. He'll only care about the provable facts."

"Is there a downside?"

"Well, yes, to be frank. With no jury present, a judge usually allows attorneys more leeway in what the witnesses are allowed to testify to and also the kinds of statements that the judge will allow the attorneys to make in court. The theory is that a judge, given his legal training and experience, is in a position to ignore testimony and lawyer arguments that he decides are irrelevant even after he hears them. It's different with juries. It is commonly believed that once the jury hears something prejudicial it is hard for them to disregard what they've heard. And so potentially prejudicial or irrelevant testimony and arguments are not allowed in the first instance."

"So what's the difference? Either the jury isn't allowed to hear it or the judge hears it but ignores it."

"The difference is that even though there will not be a jury to play to, our esteemed U.S. Attorney Mr. Perkins will still have the press hanging on his every word. They will eat up whatever horrors the judge will allow the witnesses to describe. Again, I don't think Walkowski will be swayed by any of that—not after we've established that you were not the cause of the witnesses' suffering, but rather that you helped alleviate it. But the press will no doubt report in a way that can only be further damaging to your reputation. That's why I think Perkins will also welcome a trial without a jury. It gives him the political leverage he's seeking."

"But if it's going to further damage my reputation, maybe I should take my chances with the jury after all."

"I don't think so. Most of the damage to your reputation has already been done. And let's remember that your reputation will be irrelevant if you get sent to jail or deported."

"My life is in your hands. What can I say?"

"Trust me. We're in much better shape than you believe we are. But let's get back to work. There's still plenty to do and not much time to do it."

"We've gone over this before," Helgman exclaimed when Blackridge pushed a tape transcription in front of him. "In fact, this is the third time I've reviewed this tape."

"Yes, and we'll review it as many times as it takes to get all the facts to line up. The human brain is funny. Sometimes it takes a while for all the things we know to sort out properly, especially when they're as painful as what you experienced."

Exasperated, Helgman asked, "Are we at least making progress?"

"Without a doubt. What you don't know is what these young folks have found in the State Department archives—and from talking to survivors."

"I didn't know you were talking to survivors."

"All across the country. We're conducting interviews in every office of Dawson's law firm and people are still coming forward."

"What are they telling you?" Helgman asked, alarmed at the thought that Dawson let it be known who the benefactor of the Survivor Trust was.

"It's important for us to nail down the facts as you remember them before we expose you to what others recall. I know it's painful to do it this way, but it works."

"Seems backward to me."

"That's how we do it. Now review this transcript and tell me if everything in there is exactly correct. Did you overlook anything? Is there a name you now remember? Think about the infirmary. Was there a break room? An eating area? Who did you see there? Think of guards' names, other orderlies. Everything is critical, no matter how trivial you may think it is."

Helgman reviewed the document yet again. He was surprised to discover that the names of two guards leaped into his memory and he quickly wrote their names on the yellow pad.

Day after day, the routine continued. Dictate, proof, reread, correct, compare, check again. The practice of law, he concluded, was more tedious even than surgery. At least a surgical procedure ends eventually. This process just went on and on with no end in sight.

THIRTY

Blackridge expected Perkins to call Yetta Hertzstein as the government's first witness. After all, she was the woman who had started all this by identifying Bernard as the doctor who had operated on her in the camp. She had never married and was without family. From her deposition, Blackridge knew Yetta was obsessed with avenging what had been done to her in the infirmary.

"Please go easy on her," Helgman begged his lawyer as they continued their trial preparation. "The hatred she feels for me is understandable. I held similar feelings for Dieter Schmidt."

Blackridge peered across the table at his client. "Bernard, you might be the world's most gifted surgeon, but without a question you have an amazing instinct for self-destruction. Please focus on the simple fact that this woman is out to destroy you." The lawyer's tone suggested tolerance tinged with impatience. "Tiptoeing around her will be ... well ... deadly."

"The only thing she has remaining in life is her dignity," Helgman shot back. "I only ask that you allow her to retain it."

"I take it you don't want to plead guilty?"

"Of course not, but what does that have to do with—"

"That's exactly what you'll be doing—pleading guilty—if you continue to tie my hands."

"She's been hurt enough. She means well. She's mistaken, that's all."

"I'm sorry about that, Bernard, but no one is forcing Hertzstein to testify. She put her own hand in the air."

"Just go easy on her."

"It'll depend on her," Blackridge said. "If she is honest with herself then it'll go fine for her." Blackridge paused to allow his words to have their effect on Helgman's thought process. "I've been reviewing the Hertzstein file. There's something missing. Well, not missing perhaps, but confusing. Let's walk through it again."

From the very day that the indictment was announced, the press had been camping out at the Helgman residence, hoping for a sound bite or at least some fresh footage of Helgman coming and going. Helgman learned quickly the value of "no comment" but questions were being shouted not only at Helgman himself but anyone who came to or left the house, including Leslie, Millie, and even the postman. Helgman felt sorry for poor Millie, and grateful that she didn't just quit outright. But his real concern was Leslie, whose equanimity was easily disturbed. Helgman decided to move to a hotel downtown, reasoning that the press would find little value in continuing to stake out his house when they discovered he was no longer there. That, indeed, proved to be the case.

It was late when Helgman arrived back at his hotel room, exhausted from the mental effort of dredging up facts he had suppressed for so many years. With the remembered facts came the nightmares and the sleepless nights. Helgman's nerves were raw, his temper short, and yet Blackridge was unrelenting, grilling him on detail after detail.

Everything Blackridge and Dawson said would happen had now happened. Helgman's office was closed, his hospital privileges suspended, his spirit crushed. And, on top of all that, his family was in ruins. As Helgman thought about the upcoming trial, it wasn't exactly anger he felt at being left unsupported by his colleagues and the hospital he had served faithfully for so many years. It was more a deep disappointment and an isolating numbness. He felt almost as alone today as he had been in the horrific days of Auschwitz.

Then the thought of Muggs leaped to mind, and with it the vision of himself and Leslie, the two of them, working together. He saw faces of children come alive and he knew that even if all else went wrong he would still have Muggs to give meaning to his life. Maybe it was inevitable that he would some day be called to task for his past. Perhaps this was why he had been so secretive of the clown all these years. Helgman took solace from the thought that Perkins and the rest of them couldn't take from him what they didn't know about.

With that comforting thought in mind, Helgman began outlining a new routine designed around Muggs and Muggles, father and son clowns. The clown act would be his future, his salvation.

THIRTY-ONE

The trial was to begin Monday and Helgman struggled to determine how much to tell Les. Blackridge had not required Helgman's presence for most of the week, so father and son had time to perfect their new routine. At Helgman's insistence, Dawson had hastily scheduled performances at two nearby hospitals for Muggs and his friend Muggles.

On the drive north to the Erie Shriner's Hospital for Children, Helgman spoke to his son. "Remember I told you about the trial?"

"Starting soon."

"How do you know that?" Helgman asked, as usual surprised by what his son knew.

"On TV. Judge decides," the boy answered, not looking at his father.

"You're right. The judge will say if he thinks I did bad things in Germany when I was about your age."

"Dad do nothing bad!" Les said, his jaw clenched. "I tell judge you good. Muggs good too. I tell judge."

"Thank you for wanting to help me. But I've got to do this myself."

Les began to speak, his voice hesitant, as it always was when he had something important to say. "I stay with you. You good. I stay no matter what judge says. Tell me what to do. I help."

"Thank you, Leslie. You're a good boy. I'll tell you when I need you."

"Mother not coming home."

"I don't know, son. Let's wait and see."

"She not coming home."

"How do you know she's not coming home?"

"Have boy friend. Not coming home."

"How do—" Helgman thought better of the question but it was too late.

"Hear on phone. Met in hospital. Stay out at night."

"Leslie how many times must we tell you not to listen to people's conversations?"

"Sorry. I hear friend many times asking mother to go away with him. To live with him."

"Leslie, you shouldn't—"

"Stephanie your friend. Mother have friend. Only fair she go live with him."

Helgman realized the boy was not drawing moral conclusions. Instead, he was using fairness as his measure of right and wrong. He reached across the seat and rested his hand on his son's knee. "Let's change the subject. Are you ready for the show?"

Les did not answer. His gaze was now focused on the grey slate rocks lining the hills beside the road. They traveled several miles in silence before Helgman realized the boy's left hand had closed over his own. A tear made its way down Leslie's cheek, hanging on his jaw before falling away.

Helgman's own eyes became moist as the full impact of Les's observation of Barbara worked its way into his conscious mind. The knowledge that Barbara had a man friend certainly put her behavior in perspective. After her father died, she'd stopped drinking. The lingering sweet smell of Scotch had not greeted him when he passed her bedroom on the way to his own. He'd attributed her new behavior to his own sessions with Shapiro and the fact he was paying more attention to her as the therapist had counseled. Now he knew it was something else entirely, something he was not capable of stopping, even if he wanted to.

What Leslie had just told him explained her leaving just as he was ready to move forward. She herself had mixed feelings, he realized. But did it really matter in the end? She had outgrown her fear of intimacy with the opposite sex. But had he? His therapist, after hearing his reluctant and tortured confession of allowing his body to be used by the infirmary guards in exchange for food and access to the medical books, had assured him that sexual preferences would not be affected by such acts of survival.

But Helgman remained uncertain. Perhaps he could be suppressing his sexual orientation even from himself. Uncertainty caused him to discount what Shapiro said about his behavior with the guards. Leslie's relationship with Ken confronted Helgman with the very question he had blocked all these years. Perhaps he himself actually did have predispositions toward men.

Helgman knew he should be angry with Barbara for breaking faith. He also knew he should confront his own emotions and desires—particularly in regards to Stephanie. But the events of the past few weeks robbed him even of the emotion of anger, leaving him with nothing but a paralyzing numbness.

Blackridge paced his office, taking books from one shelf and placing them on another, absentmindedly examining their titles in passing. "Bernard, we're now down to the wire and your story has more holes than a truckload of Swiss cheese. Your parents gave you up to a man called Dieter Schmidt. That man now lives on Block Island. He runs, or did run, a shipping company. According to you, he gave you up to the Gestapo when he left Germany. His sister married a man by the name of Grenoble and the two families left Germany together. The Grenobles brought with them a girl by the name of Stephanie who now claims to be your sister based on papers she found."

Helgman nodded.

"You insist she's not your sister because your sister's eyes were blue and Stephanie's eyes are green."

Helgman nodded again.

"Could you be wrong? Faulty memory? Confused?"

"Possibly," Helgman conceded. "Possibly."

"You were sent to a concentration camp and assigned to the infirmary, you said. You were not put in a barracks with everyone else. They gave you a small cot to sleep on in a back corner of the infirmary. You believe this man Schmidt set up the infirmary arrangement, but you don't know for certain. All you know is that at some point something you did caused you to be hauled in front of the camp commandant who threatened that if you did it again—you don't remember what it was now—he would have you shot, 'orders or not.' According to you, that's how you learned that someone even higher than the camp commandant had given the orders that you were to be treated at least a little more humanely than the other prisoners. That being said, you received only the starvation rations that the infirmary patients were given. So you would have died despite the 'arrangement'. That makes at least some sense. So you actually survived by accepting extra food in return for sexual favors."

"And access to medical books in the library. I wanted food and access to the library so I could learn how to help those women."

"But they died anyway."

"Most, but not all of them. By the end, I had become good enough to save many of them, but not at the beginning. As you know, Yetta Hertzstein was one who survived."

"I suppose that's a bitter irony."

"One of my first successes."

"Even though you are one of the world's finest surgeons, you claim that you never attended medical school but, instead, represented yourself to be a doctor by taking on the identity of a doctor who died in the camp."

"I'm self-taught. From their library. Plus, I trained under Dr. Seymour Katz here in Pittsburgh. Everything I said is true. You believe me, don't you?"

Ignoring Helgman's question, Blackridge went on, "And to make matters worse, you have no papers that prove any of this. Most importantly, nothing shows you as Mordechai Stein, the name you insist you had at birth."

"Mordechai Stein *is* the name I had at birth."

"Even without documents, the testimony of someone who knew you as Mordechai Stein would suffice but you know where we are with that."

The reference was to Dieter Schmidt and his sister, Stephanie's mother, Hilda Grenoble.

Helgman had at first insisted that no contact was to be made with Schmidt; he could not countenance the idea of asking his adoptive father for help of any kind, even if only through his attorney. Blackridge had ultimately convinced Helgman to allow him to contact Dieter, but Dieter summarily declined to be involved, claiming he was too frail and weak to make the trip to Pittsburgh or even to be deposed from his bed.

As to Hilda Grenoble, Blackridge had asked Stephanie to ask her mother what she knew about Helgman's parents.

"You must know who Bernard's birth parents were," Stephanie had said to her mother, "because you must know who *my* birth parents were, and Bernard and I are brother and sister. The paper I found in Uncle Dieter's diary proves that."

"Things are not always what they seem," her mother had replied. "Sometimes there is more than one explanation for things." And then she cut off any further discussion of the topic saying, "I've told you everything that I can."

"Bernard! I lost you," Blackridge said. "Stay with me here."

"Yes. Dieter Schmidt. I know where we are with that," Helgman replied to his lawyer, forcing the conversation with Stephanie out of his mind.

"All in all," Blackridge replied, "to be perfectly honest with you, this isn't the best fact pattern I've ever had to sell. You've heard of Occam's razor?"

"Yes, of course. The principle that the simplest answer is usually the correct one."

"Exactly. Rather than accept your version of events, it's much more straightforward for the judge to conclude that, quite simply, you were an Aryan who obtained medical training in Germany as a young man; that you performed medical experiments in the Auschwitz infirmary just as Yetta Hertzstein claims; and that you attempted to cover up what you did and get into this country by taking on the persona of a Jewish doctor, Bernard Helgman."

"That's not what happened."

"I know. But unfortunately it's a much more plausible story than that of a Jew who gets special treatment in the camp, who has enough time while trying to stay alive, and is so brilliant on top of that, he is able to teach himself so much medicine—strictly from books, mind you, without any classes, or mentoring, or hospital training—that a professor of medicine in this country immediately takes him on as a surgical resident."

"But it's the truth. I passed the Boards with high marks."

"All the more reason to conclude you had formal medical training in Germany. Listen. Be that as it may, it's too fantastic a story to think we can convince the judge that it's true without corroboration when you being Aryan is so much more plausible. If only you'd allow me to settle—"

"No settlement! My name must be cleared at all costs."

"Dr. Helgman," Blackridge replied, his smooth courtroom voice very much in evidence, "When things don't go in accordance with your plan A in the operating room I suspect you don't get emotional. Likewise, in the courtroom.

I expect you to remain calm, thinking through the problem and, if plan A fails, then we go to plan B. Or even plans C, D, E, or F. That's what you do in surgery. Am I right?"

"Of course."

"Then please bring the same discipline to this matter. Especially in the courtroom. Hold your temper at all costs. Perkins would love to get you riled up. The press will eat it up. Just stay calm."

"This is my life we're talking about. I must have my name cleared or I can't practice ever again."

"I certainly understand the importance of this case. I wouldn't have taken it in the first place if I weren't concerned. But the simple truth is, we're dealing with situational ethics. The camps were a wholly different kind of society, one gone crazy, but a society nonetheless. How do we judge that society? By the morals of today, or by the morals of the times?"

Helgman studied Blackridge with a new appreciation for the depth of the man. This was a subject he had privately agonized over since the very first day he had begun to accept favors from the guards.

"You seem surprised," Blackridge said. "I spent my entire life before going on the bench defending people accused of one wrongdoing or another. Some of them have been the most hardened nasty folks you'd ever want to meet. Others, like you, were simply in the wrong place at the wrong time."

THIRTY-TWO

Phillip Walkowski's courtroom was located in a gray
stone building at the edge of Pittsburgh's downtown,
several blocks from the confluence of the Allegheny and the Monongahela rivers overlooking bustling Penn
Station. The massive building housed the post office as
well as the federal courts. The seventh floor courtroom
was packed, a phenomenon usually occurring only for notorious kidnap or murder trials. The room was glaringly
bright, the large window area allowing sunlight to stream
into the courtroom and onto the spectators. The jury box
off to one side, however, was in partial shadow. A brass
railing separated the spectators from the participants. Two
tables in front of the rail held stacks of papers and several
law books.

A door at the right front of the room opened and U.S.
Attorney Perkins walked quickly in and took his place at
the prosecution table. Normally the prosecutor representing
the U.S. government in federal court was one of Perkins's
Assistant U.S. Attorneys. But Perkins had kept this case
for himself for the publicity value.

Prosecutor Perkins was immediately followed into the
courtroom by Wendall Blackridge, who proceeded to the
defense table. Trailing the two attorneys were several clerks
and a uniformed federal marshal. The clerks quickly took
their places behind desks while the marshal posted himself
near the door, his back ramrod straight.

The door again opened and the marshal, his sense of
importance bolstered by the size of the crowd, straightened
his back even further. "All stand," he intoned, his bulging
waistline vibrating. "The United States District Court for
the Western District of Pennsylvania is now in session.
The Honorable Phillip Walkowski presiding."

The black-robed figure of the judge strode purposely
through the door, his arm motioning for those behind the

rail to sit. Prosecutor Perkins and two assistants stood behind the table to the judge's left, the one nearest the jury box while Blackridge stood at the other table with Helgman beside him.

Judge Walkowski took his seat and looked down at the lawyers. "Gentlemen, I believe we're ready to begin."

Blackridge leaned close to his client. "In chambers just a few minutes ago, the judge threw out the reparations count that Perkins had thrown at you. And the jury's gone as well. But unfortunately the war crimes charge is still in."

What happened in chambers was that the judge had been persuaded by the prosecutor's arguments that the statute of limitations does not apply to murder nor to war crimes and so the judge let the war crimes count go forward. He did agree with Blackridge, however, that statute of limitations did apply to the Alien Tort Act and so he threw out the count for reparations. Perkins agreed to a non-jury trial, as Blackridge had predicted.

"And one more thing," the judge had said. "I've heard Mr. Blackridge's 'I'm just a humble lawyer' speech many times over the years. So keep a lid on it please."

"Yes, your Honor. Of course."

"And as for you, Mr. Perkins, I'll not have my court turned into a political rally. Is that clear?"

"Yes, your Honor."

"Now, is there anything either of you wish to say?"

Both lawyers answered in the negative.

"Okay, gentlemen. Let's get this trial underway."

THIRTY-THREE

Judge Walkowski leaned forward in his chair, waited for absolute silence from the packed spectator area, then said, "Call your first witness, Mr. Perkins."

Perkins stood, studied a yellow pad as if he had no idea who he was about to call, then looked up at the judge. "If the Court pleases." He twisted slightly to face a middle-aged man sitting in back of the courtroom. "The government calls Mr. Harold Sumner."

A small man in an ill-fitting suit hurried down the aisle, pushed open the swinging gate separating the audience from the lawyers's tables, and approached the witness chair. He stumbled as he climbed into the chair.

The court clerk approached the witness and instructed the frightened-looking man to place his left hand on the bible and raise his right. "Is the testimony you are about to give the truth, the full truth, and nothing but the truth, so help you God?"

"Yes," Sumner said, swallowing the word.

"Speak up," the judge advised the witness. "We can't hear you if you mumble."

"I said, yes I do."

"No need to shout, Mr. Sumner. Just speak normally. State your name and address please."

"Harold Sumner. Eighteen-oh-five Wildwood Lane. State College, Pennsylvania."

The judge looked to the prosecutor. "Mr. Perkins, please proceed."

"Mr. Sumner, please tell us your occupation," Perkins began, still standing, the yellow pad positioned in front of him on the table.

"I work for the Pennsylvania State Board of Medical Examiners."

"And what is the nature of your work?"

"Well, one of my jobs," the witness began, straightening his tie for the fifth time, "is to maintain records of the medical doctors practicing in the Commonwealth of Pennsylvania."

"What type of records do you maintain?"

"The medical education, physical description, schooling, specialty fellowships, complaints, discipline, things of that nature."

"Mr. Sumner, have you had occasion to review the records of a person going by the name of Bernard Helgman?"

"Yes"

"Could you please tell us why you reviewed his records?"

The witness again adjusted his tie. "Your office requested that I do so."

"And what does the Helgman file show?"

"I need to consult my notes."

"Yes, of course. Take your time."

The little man pulled a sheet of paper from his jacket pocket, unfolded it, and studied it for a moment. "Bernard Helgman is five-foot-eleven inches, has light brown hair, and gray eyes. He was born in Leipzeig, Germany in 1925 and came to the United States in 1947. He was licensed to practice medicine that same year."

"Is there any certification in your files from any medical school that Bernard Helgman had, in fact, attended such medical school?"

"No."

"But you just testified that Bernard Helgman has a license to practice medicine?"

"Yes."

"How did he obtain a medical license if he never attended medical school?"

"Objection," Blackridge said, rising to his feet at counsel table. "The witness has not stated Dr. Helgman did not attend medical school, only that the Board does not have in its records a certification from a medical school. Those are very different things."

"I'll rephrase the question," Perkins added before the judge had a chance to sustain the objection. "Please explain, sir, how a medical license could be issued if the file does not indicate that a person has completed medical school."

"I object again, Your Honor," Blackridge insisted. "There is nothing in the record showing this witness's qualifications to answer questions concerning the circumstances under which one can or can not obtain a medical license."

"Question withdrawn, Your Honor," Perkins responded. "Let me get at it this way. Mr. Sumner, other than Mr. Helgman, are you aware of any licensed doctor in the State of Pennsylvania for whom there is no certification in your files from an accredited medical school?"

"In that time frame, I mean right after the war, there was a shortage of doctors in this country. Field training was sometimes enough to allow someone to sit for the examination. Other than those few years, there is a certification in our files from a medical school for every doctor licensed in the State of Pennsylvania."

"Thank you, Mr. Sumner." And then to Blackridge, "Your witness, counselor."

Blackridge rose at his table.

"Mr. Sumner," he began, "you have told us that there is no certification from any medical school in Dr. Helgman's files, is that correct?"

"Yes, that's correct."

"Is there any other document in your files relating to any medical training that Dr. Helgman may have had?"

Sumner shot a nervous glance in the direction of the prosecutor's table. Perkins raised his eyebrows with an accompanying shrug. Blackridge understood the body language all too well and smiled to himself.

"Yes, there is."

"Might you have brought a copy with you?"

"Yes. It was covered by the subpoena that was served on the Board."

"Would you please tell His Honor what that document is?"

"It's a Memorandum for File dated September 8, 1947 and signed by Dr. Seymour Katz, who was the head of our Board for many years before he died about a decade ago."

"Please tell His Honor what this memorandum says."

Sumner once more looked over at Prosecutor Perkins, but this time found only a blank stare. He took a quick glance at the paper and then looked back up at Blackridge. "It says that Bernard Helgman had appeared before Dr. Katz stating that he was a doctor trained in a medical school in Dresden in Germany but that he had lost all of his paperwork."

"Anything else?"

"Yes. Dr. Katz writes here that he had done his own investigation. He learned that all of the medical school's records were destroyed in the war but he was able to confirm in an exchange of telegrams with the retired head of the medical school that a Bernard Helgman was one of their graduates."

"Anything else?"

"Well, yes. Dr. Katz's memorandum says that Dr. Helgman passed a complete licensing examination that Dr. Katz himself had administered and that Dr. Katz was recommending to the full Board that a license to practice medicine be issued even without Dr. Helgman being able to present any paperwork."

Blackridge shot a look over at the prosecutor before continuing with his next line of attack. "Mr. Sumner," he turned back to the witness, "please tell us this. If letters of praise or accommodation had been sent to the Medical Board would they be in the records you so ably maintain?"

"Yes, sir, they would."

"Are there such letters of praise in Dr. Helgman's file?"

"Yes there are."

"How many?"

"Quite a few."

"More than ten?"

"Yes."

"More than one hundred?"

"I'm not sure. Probably. There is a lot of them—from parents mostly, but many from other doctors as well."

"Is it unusual to have so many letters for a doctor?"

"That depends."

"What does it depend on?"

"Whether the letters are letters of praise or—"

"The letters you are referring to, the ones in Dr. Helgman's files, are letters of praise, are they not?"

"Yes."

"Is it unusual for one doctor to receive so many letters of praise?"

"Yes. Very unusual. Mostly, all we get are complaints."

"If any complaint letters had been received, I mean letters telling of accidents, bad outcomes, morbidity, that sort of thing, would they also be in your files?"

"Yes they would."

"Then your files are pretty complete?"

"Yes they are. I pride myself on keeping accurate records."

"Then, sir, please tell the Court how many complaint letters there are in Dr. Helgman's file?"

"There aren't any."

"So, then, only letters of praise—probably more than a hundred—and no letters of complaint. Do I have that right?"

"Yes, that's right."

"That's all I have," Blackridge said, falling into his seat as though he was exhausted from wrestling the witness to the ground. "No more questions for this witness."

"Any re-direct, Mr. Perkins?"

"No, Your Honor."

Walkowski leaned forward. "The witness is excused. You can leave town if you wish, Mr. Sumner. Thank you for coming."

With a sigh of relief that could be heard at the rear of the large room, Sumner pulled himself upright and quickly made for the door, an undercurrent of laughter following him down the aisle.

Perkins rose, glanced at Blackridge as if to say, "I'll bury you," and turned toward the back of the courtroom. Nodding to a few reporters, he turned back toward the judge and in his most polished voice, intoned, "The prosecution calls Miss Yetta Hertzstein."

THIRTY-FOUR

Helgman's stomach tightened into a knot as he heard the clerk repeat the name in the hallway outside the courtroom. He tried to catch Blackridge's attention but the old lawyer was fumbling through a stack of papers one of his associates had just handed him. Tightness gripped Helgman's chest and a small pain radiated from there into his neck. He heard, rather than saw, a person walking slowly toward the front of the courtroom. The pain intensified when he saw the heavyset figure of the woman whose life he had saved so many years ago approach the barrier.

Perkins hurried over to hold the gate open for her. Hertzstein didn't acknowledge him, keeping her eyes down as she walked to the witness chair.

Perkins walked up close to the witness after she had been sworn in and asked a series of routine questions designed to put her at ease. Hertzstein testified that she had been in a camp in Poland called Birkenau, also known as Auschwitz Two, and while in that camp, she had been operated on in the infirmary.

"Now, Miss Hertzstein," Perkins asked, "do you see anyone in the courtroom today who was in the infirmary when you were there?"

"Yes. That man over there."

"Let the record show," Perkins said, "that the witness pointed to the defendant. Miss Hertzstein, then is it your testimony that the man sitting second from the left at the defense table is a person you saw in the infirmary when you were in Auschwitz?"

"I certainly did see him there!"

"And where was he when you first saw him?"

"He was looking down at me when I was on the operating table."

"And you are positive that is the same man you saw looking down at you when you were being operated on?"

"Butchered! I was butchered by them." Hertzstein took a sip of water. "Yes, sir, that is the same man. How could I ever forget?"

"For the record," Perkins said, "let it be noted that the man this witness just referred to is the defendant, Bernard Helgman." Perkins moved close to his seat, then turned and asked, "Is there any possibility that you are mistaken?"

"Absolutely none!" Hertzstein replied with such vehemence that even Attorney Dawson, who was sitting among the spectators behind Helgman, flinched. "It's him all right. It's because of that swine I could never have babies. Yes, he's the one." She paused to catch her breath. "He butchered me horribly!" Tears streamed down her face.

Perkins handed her a box of tissues and waited while she regained her composure. He then asked, "Miss Hertzstein, have you ever been married?"

"No, sir, I haven't."

"Would you please tell the court why not?"

"What man would want a woman who has been so damaged?"

"I'm sorry to put you through this, Miss Hertzstein," Perkins said solicitously. "You've suffered so much in your life. Thank you for coming here today. We all know how difficult this has been for you and we're sorry for that."

"Inhuman it was. Inhuman!" Hertzstein spit out, all semblance of composure gone.

"Inhuman, indeed." Perkins looked toward the judge. "No further questions."

Walkowski glanced at the large clock on the back wall. "It's time to take a break, but if cross-examination will be short we can wait."

Blackridge unwound his legs from his chair and rose slowly, his hands on the table. "Your Honor, might I suggest it'll be easier on the witness if we just proceed. I don't expect to take very long."

Walkowski looked down at the witness. "It's up to you, Miss Hertzstein. If you wish to take a break, we can adjourn for lunch. If not, we'll just go on."

"Who can eat?" Her voice was surprisingly firm. "Let's get this over with as quickly as possible."

"Mr. Blackridge, please proceed," the judge said.

Helgman leaned close to his lawyer and whispered something. Blackridge whispered back, causing his client's face to flush with anger. A fragmented stream of words from Helgman could be heard by spectators in the first few rows.

"Mr. Blackridge, please proceed," the judge repeated in an impatient tone.

Blackridge stood and edged over to the side of the defense table, as if to distance himself from his client. "Miss Hertzstein, the testimony you just gave the court was, I understand, most difficult for you to relate. I have no doubt that the hearts of everyone go out to you. No one should ever have to face what you have had to endure."

Perkins jumped to his feet. "Is there a question here, Your Honor?"

"Yes, I was about to ask it," Blackridge responded. "And my question, Miss Hertzstein, is this: Do you understand that we are not here today to bring justice to you for what happened in Auschwitz?"

"Don't you think I'm entitled to justice?" Hertzstein responded.

"Just answer the question, please, Miss Hertzstein," Walkowski instructed.

Blackridge continued. "Well, justice, yes. But that is an impossible task. I'm not sure that anyone could provide you with the degree of justice that you deserve. But, Miss Hertzstein, we are here today to find out if Dr. Bernard Helgman, a leading surgeon with an impeccable record of medical achievement in the field of pediatric reconstruction, as this Court has just been told, a man who has dedicated his life to the service of children, was one of the men who performed those brutal acts on you."

Perkins jumped up. "Your Honor, objection. Counsel is making another speech."

"Mr. Blackridge," Walkowski said, "please limit your cross-examination to proper questions."

There was no jury present, so Blackridge knew he had more leeway than normal. "Your Honor, it only seems appropriate that I make my feelings clear before we begin. I, like Mr. Perkins, am outraged at what went on during that terrible time in our history. I just want the witness to—"

"Enough!" Walkowski swept his hand across his body. "Just get on with your questions."

"By all means, Your Honor, thank you. Now Yetta, may I call you Yetta? Is that okay with you?"

The witness nodded.

"Yetta, I want you to think before you answer. Think back to that terrible day some twenty-nine years ago."

"That's all I *ever* do," snapped the witness. "Think about it."

"I appreciate your anguish and I'm sorry for it," Blackridge said, defusing the anger as best he could. "Now visualize for me if you will how many people were in the operating room with you that day."

"I don't have to think. I know. I've lived that day over and over and over. There were five."

"Were they all men?"

"One woman."

"Four men. Correct?"

"Yes."

"Were they all dressed the same?" From his hours upon hours of discussions and review with his client, and from his extensive research, Blackridge knew the answers to these questions.

"I don't understand."

"Were they all wearing, for example, white coats? Or green coats?"

"Yes. Oh, no. One had on a business suit. The others had on gowns."

"A business suit in the operating room?"

"At that point I didn't know it was an operating room. I thought it was a physical examination."

"Tell us what happened."

"The man in the suit was across the room. I really couldn't see him very well. He asked me questions."

"What type of questions did the man in the suit ask you?"

Hertzstein did not answer, but instead glanced toward Perkins.

"Do you understand the question?" Blackridge asked, his voice gentle and even.

"Yes," she said, almost to herself, her gaze focused down into her lap.

"Please speak up, Miss Hertzstein," Walkowski said. "We need to hear you."

"Yes, I said. Yes, I understand the question."

"Good, then please answer the question," the judge instructed.

Yetta Hertzstein continued to look down. "This is personal. I didn't think I'd have to talk about this."

Walkowski leaned forward. "I know this is difficult for you, but you must answer. Will the reporter please read back the question?"

The reporter rolled back the paper tape, cleared her throat, and said, "Question by Mr. Blackridge: What type of questions did the man in the suit ask you?"

Hertzstein turned bright red. Tears ran down her cheeks. "The questions were about ... well, about ... you know, private matters." She looked at the judge, her eyes pleading for help. When none was forthcoming, she again lowered her head. "The questions concerned private matters. Matters not related to this trial."

The courtroom was silent now, all attention focused on the troubled woman. Helgman wrote a note on a pad and pushed it across the table to his lawyer, "For God sake, leave her alone! Don't humiliate her further."

Blackridge, ignoring his client's written pleas, moved close to the witness and pressed on. "Please describe those matters for us."

"If you must know, they concerned my private life before ... before I came to that God-awful place. They wanted to know if I ... I ... had ... had sex before I came to the camp. They wanted to know how many men I had been with."

The spectators waited in silence for the answer, the reporters having their pencils poised to capture every word.

"I told them no. I had not had sex with anyone before I was arrested. The man in the suit asked me the same question many times and every time I said no."

"Was that the end of it?"

"They pulled my legs apart." She dabbed her eyes with a tissue before continuing. "Then the man in the suit was on me. I screamed. He hit me in the face with his hand." She wiped her face again, took a sip of water and, resigned to the fact that there would be no reprieve, continued, "He was yelling that I had lied to him. That I was not a virgin as I had said. I guess he was looking forward to having a virgin and I guess in a sense I wasn't a virgin. The moment the boxcar was opened guards pulled me and several other girls out and dragged us off to the side behind a building. They raped us there."

The reporters scribbled furiously as Hertzstein took a tissue and dried her eyes. "Anyway, he continued to yell that I had lied and then a stick, or something, hit me and cracked my nose. Blood splashed on his shirt and he became even madder. The woman's voice was loudest of all. She also was screaming. She was in a frenzy. The man stormed out and the woman squeezed my breasts several times—she squeezed them so hard I thought I'd pass out. I think she may have bitten me. I still have the marks. When she finished with me, she also left. She's the one who told the others to cut my ovaries out!"

"Let's take a short recess." Turning to the clerk, the instructed, "Be sure the witness has everything she needs. Freshen her water and see to it that no one bothers her. No interviews. In fact, show her to my chambers." He tapped his gavel, rose and disappeared through the side door.

When the court reconvened thirty minutes later, the mask that Yetta Hertzstein had worn for so many years was again in place.

"You may continue, Mr. Blackridge," Walkowski said, "but limit your questions to only those facts that are essential here."

"Thank you, Your Honor. I'll be brief." Indeed, in the hall Helgman had been adamant about no more questions. Blackridge had promised to stay away from personal issues and Helgman had reluctantly given in. "Now Miss Hertzstein. Yetta," Blackridge began, "I'd like to clarify something you said. Was the man in the suit, the man you say was on you, who hit you, was that the man you identified earlier as being in this courtroom?"

Skilled cross-examiners never ask questions they don't already know the answers to. Blackridge had not explored this line of questioning during Hertzstein's deposition because he hadn't wanted to tip off Perkins as to how he planned to neutralize Hertzstein's testimony. But from his unrelenting discussions with Helgman he was positive he knew the answer. Assuming, of course, Helgman had been telling the truth—and that Yetta Hertstein would tell the truth as well.

"No. That swine is not here."

"Do you know who was in charge of the operation?"

"It was obviously that man," she said, pointing directly at Helgman, "looking down at me. Those eyes are burned into my memory forever as they would be into yours if you had been butchered as I was!"

"I understand your anger, and it's certainly justified. However, I believe it is misplaced."

Perkins was on his feet. "Move to strike that comment. Counsel's beliefs are not relevant here."

"Motion granted," Walkowski said. "But remember there is no jury here so we're not following the rules as strictly as we otherwise would." Turning back to Blackridge, he said, "Let's tone it down. Enough playing to the house. Just ask your questions so this witness can be excused."

"Certainly, Your Honor. Now, Yetta," Blackridge said, knowing he was close to an important admission. "I know it's painful to think back to that operating room, but would you tell us where Dr. Helgman was standing during the operation if you were looking up at him?"

"If you mean that man," she said stabbing her finger toward Helgman, "his name's not Helgman! They called him Schmidt."

"We'll get back to that in a moment. But first, please tell us where he was standing."

"How would I know that? My mouth was full of blood. They put a foul smelling cloth over my nose. I couldn't breath. I was suffocating and you want me to tell you where he was standing!"

"Could you guess?"

"Objection," Perkins called out. "Calls for speculation."

"Sustained."

"Would you say he was standing near your face?"

"I suppose so, gathering as how I did see him looking down at me."

"Did he say anything to you?"

"No. He just looked at me."

"Just looked? Were his eyes happy? I mean did they convey to you that he was having fun?"

"No. In fact, they looked sad. Angry almost."

"With a rag over your face and a broken nose, what kept you from suffocating to death?"

"I would have suffocated but I outsmarted them! Someone kept leaning over the table with his arm just next to my head. When he leaned forward I twisted just enough so that the rag over my face caught on his arm and it moved just enough for me to get air."

"That was indeed clever. It saved your life, did it not?"

"Yes I always thought that it did."

"Then it was this very inept person who kept leaning over the table whose arm you used to push the rag aside. Is that what happened?"

"Yes."

"And this inept behavior lasted the whole time you were being worked on?"

Hertzstein looked to Perkins. Getting no signal, she said, "Yes."

"Did you open your eyes at all?"

"I don't remember exactly, but I must have."

"You must have from time to time because you saw the defendant's face. Is that right?"

"Yes."

"Now, let's address the question of the defendant's name if you will. How do you know Helgman isn't his name?"

"Well, two things. First of all, he turned his head when someone in the room called out the name 'Schmidt.' And besides," she continued, "Bernard Helgman was the name of the man who died in the bed next to me."

"I see. How do you remember him so well?"

"He helped keep me alive."

"You mean the man in the next bed got out of bed and helped you?"

"Oh, no! He was too sick for that. He directed a young man, a boy really. A nice young man who was there every night and he helped me. Dr. Helgman, I mean the one in the bed next to me, told him what to do. They talked most of the night. I was too sick to know what they said, but it seemed to me Helgman was teaching the boy what to do. If it wasn't for that young boy I'd have died. He helped keep me warm, even crawled into the bed and lay next to me to warm me. The bed was soaked with my blood, but that didn't stop him. I think his name was Max. That young boy, how can I ever thank him, changed my bandages, gave me water and brought me food. But not this one," Hertzstein cried and pointed to the defense table.

"I've no further questions of this witness.

"Mr. Perkins, you may redirect."

"Thank you, Your Honor. This will be brief. Miss Hertzstein, Mr. Blackridge characterized the man whose arm you used as being inept. How do you characterize that man?"

She thought for a moment and then said, "I've not really thought of that all these years. But now that I reconstruct a bit more, it does seem to me that he may have deliberately placed his arm so I could use it."

Blackridge sat quietly, watching as Perkins, in his zeal to obtain favorable press, marched straight into the trap that had been set.

"Was Dr. Helgman, I mean the man sitting over there, moving about the room or permanently above your head?"

"I don't really know where he was all the time. All I know is that any time I opened my eyes he was above me."

"Were there others above you also?"

"No, he was the only one I saw. Only one person was near my head."

"How old was that person?"

"I don't know. He was young. Like the person who kept me warm at night. About the same age. They looked alike."

Perkins made a pretext of studying notes on a pad, and then announced, "I have no further questions."

Slowly Blackridge approached the witness. He fixed her gaze for a moment allowing her to become comfortable with his presence beside her. Then, as though the two of them were sharing a private moment over coffee, he casually asked, "You said there were others who were out of your sight who worked on you. Did you, in fact, see the face, or even the eyes, of any of the other people who were in the room?"

"I already said I didn't."

"A moment ago you testified that the person standing over you when you were ... being worked on ... looked like the person—the boy—who kept you warm at night. Would you please tell the judge in what way they looked alike?"

Yetta turned her head toward Walkowski, who leaned forward toward her. "For one," she said, "they both had tired, sad eyes. For another, their faces were both gaunt."

"Okay. I have just one final question for you, Yetta," Blackridge said, his voice remaining soft, casual. "Is it possible that the man who was standing over you, the man you have identified as the same man sitting at that table, the man who today is known as Dr. Bernard Helgman, could very well have been the man, then a boy, who placed his arm next to your face so as to allow you to breathe?"

Prosecutor Perkins jumped to his feet. "Objection. Calls for speculation on the part of the witness."

"I'll allow this one," the judge replied, still leaning toward the witness. "Answer the question, please Miss Hertzstein."

Then the room fell silent. The slight whir from the court reporter's electronic transcription device was now clearly heard in the back. Even the judge edged closer to the witness box in anticipation of the answer.

Finally, in a voice barely audible, she said, "It may very well have been his arm."

This time Blackridge did not ask her to repeat the answer. No one in the courtroom had missed it. Nor had they missed the tears streaming down her face. Nor had they missed the questioning glance she made in Helgman's direction. Blackridge extended his hand to help her from the witness box knowing Perkins would not dare protest this display of consideration for the witness by defense counsel.

With a sharp tap of the gavel, court was recessed until two o'clock.

THIRTY-FIVE

Blackridge had set up shop at Dawson's law firm a few blocks from the courthouse. Helgman walked briskly alongside Blackridge as they made their way to Dawson's office for a quick sandwich, after which they would finalize their preparation for the afternoon court session. The hurried movement of people, lost in their own private worlds, made Helgman feel anonymous. It was a sobering reminder that his own drama was just a blip in the vastness of human endeavor. His picture had been in the newspapers and on TV for days, but no one seemed to recognize him. He was on display for all the world to see and ridicule, but yet when it came right down to it, the world had other things on its mind. Except for those who continued to send death threats, nobody much cared about the troubles of some doctor in Pittsburgh.

A feeling of impending doom had loomed over Helgman ever since this had all started and it had become progressively worse as the weeks had worn on. His distress intensified whenever he thought about the testimony that Blackridge insisted that he provide; a narrative consisting of women dying in agony, their bodies sliced and torn apart, of him carrying those tortured daughters, mothers, and grandmothers to the mass crematorium to be turned to ash along with those who passed through the hydrogen cyanide showers and those who perished from sickness, disease, and starvation. Four months was a long time for a Jew to survive at a camp, yet the boy known as Max Schmidt had survived much longer. That fact alone condemned him. Without exoneration by the court, his life was essentially over.

The tension of the morning had been unbearable. Helgman could remain calm in the operating theater, issuing orders in split second fashion even as monitoring devices pinged their messages of impending trouble. However, in the courtroom—with its slowly unfolding drama and with half-truths screaming for immediate reply—he felt trapped and suffocated, panic engulfing him, sucking the very air from his lungs.

Blackridge had handled Yetta Hertzstein well, he had to admit. Allowing the woman to keep her dignity even as she finally admitted that the person standing over her, the one who she identified as Helgman, may have actually saved her life. But the victory was short lived. On the way out of the courthouse, Blackridge had said to him, "The problem now is that other witnesses will be on guard. Perkins will take more care. Remember, this is about who you really are, and in that respect, Hertzstein is merely a sideshow. In the end, we have nothing to really prove your true identity. You took another man's identity and that is what the judge will focus on. This trial is about who you really are, not so much about what you really did."

"If it's not about what I did, then why allow them to say what I did?"

"Because the Court is free to deduce who you are based on your actions. If Walkowski concludes you took lives to save your own he won't spend much time worrying about who you really are."

"What does *that* mean?"

"He'll terminate your citizenship—or worse."

Court resumed exactly at two p.m. and the lawyers immediately become embroiled in procedural issues. By the time those issues were resolved it was four thirty. Walkowski checked his watch and announced, "Too late for a new witness now. Let's pick this up at nine in the morning." He tapped his gavel and the day's proceedings were over.

Helgman and Blackridge spent the remainder of the afternoon and early evening in Dawson's office preparing for the next set of witnesses. The assessment of the day was that Helgman had won round one. Even so, just as if he had been in a boxing ring, he felt as if body blows had been delivered to his midsection with a few to the chin.

Just how much more punishment he could absorb, he did not know.

It was already dark when Helgman started back to his hotel near the river. The streets were mostly empty and Helgman walked briskly while staying alert for any danger. He entered a small park that surrounded his building when a bald man, appearing to be in his late sixties, fell in beside him.

"Bernard Helgman," the man said, "I'm happy I caught up to you."

"No interviews," Helgman said, adhering to his lawyer's admonition. He turned away and increased his stride. The area was well lit and not known as a trouble spot. The man kept pace and Helgman turned to him. "I said no comment. Now please leave me alone."

Instead of backing off, the man said, "Look at me closely, Dr. Helgman. Or should I call you Max Schmidt?"

Now that the slender man's face was directly illuminated by a street lamp, he appeared younger than at first. He was perhaps in his mid-fifties. The man had a wide grin on his otherwise rugged face and something in his manner was eerily familiar.

Hearing himself referred to as Max Schmidt—and the extensive narration he had dictated for countless hours in Blackridge's office brought Helgman's thoughts back to Germany. Then it came to him. Helgman stopped dead in his tracks.

"Oh, my God!" Helgman was all but speechless. The last time he had seen that face it had been atop a body of skin and bones, its eyes sunken deep into the skull, the skeletal body busy cleaning latrines, hauling garbage, and, like Helgman himself, doing what he could to ease the pain of the infirmary inmates. Max had received extra food by giving sexual favors. He had wondered at the time what that other body was doing to survive.

Helgman's hands shot out and grabbed the man's head and twisted it to the side, exposing a scar that ran from the man's ear down the side of his neck.

"Oh, my God!" Helgman repeated as tears filled his eyes and his voice cracked with emotion. He pulled the man close against him. "Oh, my God," was all he could manage as the two of them swayed together oblivious to the sidelong glances of people who hurried past them.

"Kurt! My God, I thought you had died," Helgman finally managed to say. Like him, Kurt had been given a place to sleep in the Auschwitz infirmary. Helgman had come to learn that his own good fortune—if one could call it that—of being allowed to live in the infirmary had been arranged by Dieter Schmidt. How Kurt had wound up in basically the same situation he never did learn. "Kurt," he continued. "I saw you under—"

"I was in bad shape when you last saw me. Nothing the Russians fed me would stay down. I was unconscious for the better part of a month. But enough about me. What about you? Obviously you're alive. When that guard slashed your throat, you fell on a heap of bodies. Blood was everywhere. I was certain you had died. Even so, I tried to find you when I got out of the hospital but couldn't find a trace of you anywhere. Yad Vashem has almost a dozen Max Schmidts, but none of them are you.

"I was taken to Switzerland and then I moved to the States," Helgman said, giving the short version. "If you were in court today, you heard the rest from that guy Sumner at the medical board."

"I *was* there, way in the back row. I came over for the trial. I live in Israel now and I've taken the surname Ben-Moshe. I, too, became a physician and I'm actually now one of the Assistant Ministers of Health. When I read in the international press that the world-famous Dr. Bernard Helgman was being accused of war crimes at Auschwitz I had to come and see for myself. I've been assuming all these years that it was simply coincidental that the Dr. Bernard Helgman that I so often read about in the medical literature had the same name as the Dr. Bernard Helgman who died in the camp. What a surprise to find out that the name was no coincidence; that it was you, the man I knew in the camp as Max Schmidt, my friend and co-conspirator against those Nazi bastards."

The initial excitement of meeting up with his old friend had prevented Helgman from seeing its full implications, but it came to him in a rush that the man standing beside him was his salvation. "You can tell them! Kurt, you can prove I didn't do what they say I did. I told my lawyer all about you, but I assured him you were dead and so we never looked for you."

"Yes, my friend. Of course. But come, let's break bread and catch up with each other. There's so much to discuss."

Over dinner, the two men struggled to cover their lives since they had last been together at Auschwitz. At one point Kurt said, "Max, or should I call you Bernard? It's strange to call someone who you knew so well by a different name."

"I prefer Bernard. Max is long dead."

"How well I understand. I lived for many years on a kibbutz in the Negev founded by survivors. Some of the very same people who passed through the infirmary live there. You would think that because we all went through that horrible experience we could talk about it. But it isn't so. Many are still suppressing it. But, as I'm certain you know, it comes out in strange and unexpected ways. Just this past *Shavuot* as part of the Torah celebration some children ran through the synagogue with wooden guns mock shooting each other. One of the men turned white, gathered his family and ran from the building. We only learned later something that he had never shared with any of us. It turns out he had been sitting in *shul* in Poland when the storm troopers came through and shot his mother and father and his brothers as he watched in horror. He was saved because his father had pushed him down and the father's dead body had shielded him from the bullets."

"If we can't talk to each other, Kurt, who then can we talk with? My lawyer is telling me that I'll have to take the stand and tell my story. I don't know if I can do it— especially if I'm forced to admit what I did to survive."

"Who are they to judge?" Kurt snapped. "By what right can anyone condemn us for surviving that hell! There was no right answer for anyone caught up in that madness. Men allowed their bodies to be used by those animals in exchange for scraps of bread and filthy water. I tell myself I did it to obtain food so that more of us could survive. But the real truth is, I did it so I could survive myself. It took me years to come to grips with that."

"And to try to forget?"

"Not forget. Never! But understand it. You kept yourself alive, my friend. But you kept more than yourself alive. Every person who survived that infirmary is alive today because of you. I know what you had to do to obtain access to those books, how you learned medicine."

Helgman turned his face away. "Kurt, I did it to—"

"No explanations are necessary, my friend. We all did what we had to do. I gave them my body for food, you did it for food too, yes, but also for the medical books."

"I told myself I was doing it to save them—to get food for them, and water. At first, I gave all the food to the patients, but then I started eating some of it myself. That's what I now regret. I wasn't strong enough to resist the temptation."

"You are much too hard on yourself. It's easy now when you have all you need to keep yourself alive to think you could have done anything other than what you did. And that's because the mind doesn't allow us to remember with clarity how horrible it really was."

"You're right. It is so outside our common experience that it's hard to conceive that it could have happened. Yet it did."

"You must speak out. Tell the world what it was like. You have a moral duty to do it. We can't allow this to ever happen again. Ever! And not just to Jews. To anyone who's oppressed."

"I can't do it. I can't. Someday perhaps, but not now."

"Someday never comes, my friend. Someday is now. You have the perfect—what's the word—forum. Use it. Maybe that's what this trial is all about."

"This trial is about a politician trying to make a name for himself. Nothing more." Helgman spit out the words, surprising himself with the hatred he felt toward Perkins."

"Turn it around on him. You can do it by telling the world what really happened. People have a way of sorting out genuine right from genuine wrong, but you must give them the facts. Right now all they have is one side of the story."

"No one will believe me."

"Have faith. God brought you this far. He has plans for you."

"You talk nonsense. God's not orchestrating this. It's politics." Helgman dropped his head. "All anyone will remember are the headlines that have attacked my character from the very day the indictment was announced. My reputation is ruined. I'll be lucky to practice medicine again, no matter how this trial comes out."

"I'm thinking something different," Kurt replied.

"What? What do your mean?" Helgman looked up but Kurt was gone.

THIRTY-SIX

While Helgman and Kurt were discussing their lives over dinner, Wendall Blackridge sat looking out into the night, the lights of the city flickering below him. His office was dark, his staff and associates having been dismissed hours ago. The facts favorable to Helgman from the Hertzstein testimony had not yet hit the nightly news, but every indication pointed to that part of the story being downplayed. The news that sold newspapers and commanded airtime was the war crimes angle—not Helgman's possible humanitarian actions.

With eyes closed, Blackridge replayed the day in court and was pleased with how the cross-examination of Hertzstein had come out. A small victory in a much larger war. The witness he needed most was Helgman himself. But the man remained locked tighter than a bank on Sunday and Blackridge was afraid of putting his client on the stand, his own courtroom talents not withstanding. Even if Helgman testified, the judge was astute enough to pick up on his guilt feelings and it was possible that the testimony could backfire.

The troubling aspect for Blackridge was not being positive he knew who Helgman really was. His assumption from the beginning, the only assumption he could reasonably make, was that Helgman was who he claimed to be. But Blackridge knew all too well that that was not a certainty. Many German officers took identities of prisoners, and it was always possible his client had done likewise. Blackridge was certain his client had not lied to him and that the facts he presented surrounding the infirmary and his participation in what had gone on there were accurate. But from his long years interviewing and cross-examining witnesses he always knew when someone was holding something back. And Helgman, he was certain, was holding back.

Blackridge knew Walkowski was a hands-on instinctive man who prided himself at being a good judge of character. And so he knew Walkowski would want to hear Helgman's account of himself, including how the name change occurred—and why.

All in all, Blackridge concluded that keeping Helgman off the stand would be even more dangerous than putting him on.

The courtroom was again packed, the hallway overflowing with people waiting to gain entrance. The morning papers had carried a picture of Yetta Hertzstein emerging from court sobbing into a handkerchief. As Blackridge had suspected, the press essentially ignored the clear implication from her testimony that the boy who helped her survive was the accused, Bernard Helgman. But something more was up. The number of reporters and TV cameras had doubled.

The principals were in place. The prosecutor looked refreshed while Blackridge appeared to have slept in his suit.

The judge strode through the door.

The spectators rose.

The judge took two steps up to his raised podium, stepped across to his seat, briefly looked over the spectators, then sat down.

The spectators sat down.

The judge's gavel hit the wooden block in front of him.

The second day of the trial had begun. Perkins called a parade of witnesses to the stand, each recounting the horrors occurring in the infirmary at Birkenau Auschwitz and each placing Helgman in the operating room. One such witness was an Otto Landau. He was a slender man who seemed to be about the same age as Helgman. Landau simply testified that he had seen Helgman at Birkenau and at that time, his name had been Max Schmidt. "No big deal," Blackridge had whispered to Helgman. "We've already admitted that."

Other witnesses had more to say, as the trial ground on day after day. There were any number of times when Helgman could hardly restrain himself from screaming out the truth in the face of the muddled innuendo coming from the witnesses. But just as with Yetta Hertzstein,

Blackridge had been able to neutralize any negative testimony on cross-examination and, in some cases, to turn it to his advantage.

For example, a witness named Gershon Schwartzman recounted what happened when he was caught trying to climb over a fence. He told how he was stripped naked even though it was snowing and was made to walk back to the center of the camp, his feet freezing on the ice-covered ground. He was taken to the infirmary and strapped down on a metal table. He told of a man in civilian clothes talking to a woman. He told of three men in the room all wearing blood-streaked white coats. The woman lashed his privates with what felt like a whip while "that man" held his head down, a smelly rag in his hands.

Perkins interrupted the testimony just long enough to ask that the record show that the witness had pointed to the defendant, Bernard Helgman, when he had referred to "that man".

"He was a boy then," the witness continued. "Just a boy. But I remember like it was yesterday. I kept passing out, but I remember his eyes." Schwartzman looked directly at Helgman. "I'll never forget what you did to me."

Perkins observed the reporters furiously taking notes. He knew he had given them a juicy story, but was determined to introduce another angle before they would have to rush out and file their dispatches in time to meet their afternoon deadlines.

"Anything else about that day that you can tell us, Mr. Schwartzman?"

"Yes. I saw him jump on a woman patient."

Just enough to make for a sensational headline, Perkins told himself. *Now let's get these guys out of here.* The prosecutor made a big show of checking the time and then turned to the judge. "Mr. Schwartzman has had a tough time of it, Your Honor, and we shouldn't prolong his distress." He turned to Blackridge. "Your witness."

Perkins had been keeping his eye on the clock all afternoon, pacing the witnesses according to a plan only he knew. He now congratulated himself on his perfect timing.

The reporters, who a moment ago were writing and sketching feverishly, hurried from the courtroom, racing toward the phone bank hoping to make the late edition. They had heard what Perkins wanted them to hear and only a few would remain to hear whatever rebuttal might occur by way of Blackridge's cross-examination.

Indeed, they would have heard a lot.

Blackridge maneuvered the witness Schwartzman into admitting on cross-examination that he had only seen Helgman standing above his head and not actually performing any medical work on him, except after the others had left the room. He also admitted that Helgman had dressed his wounds and that he had healed perfectly with almost no scaring. Reluctantly, he admitted Helgman had given him several drops of water and had come to see him during the night. He couldn't explain how he had healed so perfectly after all that they had done to him. Most importantly, he had no explanation as to why he was even alive.

Nor did any but a few of those same reporters hear what the witness had to say when pressed by Blackridge as to his testimony that Helgman had "jumped on a woman patient." Blackridge had elicited from the witness that the woman's bed was quite far away from the witness's own. He had been in and out of sleep because he was drowsy and couldn't focus well. He admitted that he did not see Helgman actually "jump" on the woman. When further pressed, all the witness could say for certain was that the uncovered woman had been crying out that she was freezing and that some time later the boy was in the bed with her under a blanket, which had somehow appeared. When asked if Helgman might have been the one to get her the blanket or if he had lain down next to her trying to keep her warm, the witness was forced to admit that he really didn't know. He had simply assumed at the time that he had witnessed a sexual attack.

"Did the woman cry out," Blackridge asked, "or say anything like 'stop' or 'get away from me'?"

"Not that I remember."

Judge Walkowski peered over at the witness as though trying to take a measure of the man. He then looked back to his legal pad, eyebrows knitted in an expression of keen concentration, and wrote himself a note.

Meanwhile, Blackridge continued his cross-examination. "Now Mr. Schwartzman, going back to the operating room, did anyone except Dr. Helgman touch you after those other people left the room?"

"No. Not until the Russians liberated us the following day. He was the only one."

"I believe you told us earlier that the woman with the whip had been beating you. Once, twice? How many times did she hit you?"

"Maybe ten, fifteen times. I think I passed out, but I was sure she had cut off my—my penis."

"Well, did she?"

"I thought so at the time. But when the Russian doctors checked my bandages the next day, they said I had been severely lacerated but expertly repaired. In fact, they brought several other doctors over to see it. They marveled over how well I had been stitched."

"And just to be clear, Mr. Schwartzman, nobody other than the defendant, Bernard Helgman, even entered the room after you were mutilated, is that your testimony?"

"That's right."

"Well, then," Blackridge intoned while casting a knowing look in the direction of the judge, "isn't it fair to assume that it was Bernard Helgman who so carefully and skillfully repaired you?"

Perkins sprang to his feet. "Objection, Your Honor. Calls for speculation on the part of the witness."

"I'll withdraw the question. Nothing further."

The courtroom fell quiet. All eyes turned toward Judge Walkowski, who was staring out over the heads of those below him, seemingly caught up in deep thought. It was easily fifteen or twenty seconds before the judge turned his attention to his yellow pad, wrote some notes in a deliberate manner, and continued to slowly shake his head even as he declared that court was adjourned for the day.

THIRTY-SEVEN

T he next morning the trial was lost in a flurry of legal arguments, the significance of which was lost on Helgman. For hours the lawyers marched in and out of the judge's chambers carrying books and files. Blackridge consulted with one of his young associates who hurried from the courtroom, returning an hour later with two large file boxes strapped to a fold-up dolly.

Around noon, the clerk announced a lunch recess.

Helgman walked the few blocks to Dawson's office with Blackridge, neither man saying a word. The mid-day headlines, taken from the previous day's testimony, were devastating. *PHONY DOC ACCUSED OF SEXUAL MUTI-LATION*, one screamed. Another proclaimed, *PROSECUTOR PERKINS UNCOVERS IMPOSTER DOC ASSAULTING PA-TIENT.*

Helgman's picture was prominently displayed beside each article.

"Bernie," Blackridge said, once the office door closed behind them, "this stuff sells newspapers. It doesn't convict you. The trial's a standoff so far. To date, all that they've proven is that you assumed a name, which, in fact, is true enough. They've tried to prove you didn't attend medical school, but Dr. Katz's memorandum seems to have put that one to bed as well. And none of the witnesses have been able to provide any credible proof that you participated in any of the experiments. The burden of proof rests with the prosecution. Perkins will have to convince the judge that you are guilty of what you're accused of beyond a reason-able doubt. All we need to do is plant a seed of doubt in his mind. In point of fact, just reading his body language, I believe that Walkowski has been persuaded not only that you were not complicit in performing any experiments, but that you did everything you could to minimize the victims' pain, limit the extent of their permanent damage and, indeed, keep them alive.

"So then why isn't the trial over?"

"First of all, the prosecution hasn't yet rested their case. They have several more witnesses to call, one of which we'll talk about in a moment. Once that's over with, I can enter a motion for a dismissal on the grounds that the prosecution hasn't shown you to be guilty of anything to a level of certainty that would warrant a conviction. If the judge grants my motion, the trial will be over and we won't have to present any defense. Our defense, in effect, was my cross-examination of the prosecution's witnesses. But even if the judge is inclined to grant my motion for dismissal of the charges, he might hold his ruling in abeyance, wanting to hear your side of the story before announcing his decision."

"I thought I had made it clear I was not going to talk about my time in the camp!"

"I think you need to know the facts of life here. Most of the witnesses we had lined up to testify on your behalf have now backed down. We spent the morning fighting over service of subpoenas on new witnesses. But because of time constraints, I don't believe we'd be able to get it done anyway. In theory, we could just rest our case and renew our motion for a dismissal without you or anybody else testifying. But if the judge has deferred his ruling on my motion, it may mean that he's not as convinced of your innocence as I'm thinking he is. It would be a big mistake in that case to not put on an affirmative defense. Indeed, if you don't tell your side of the story and defend yourself, the judge may wonder if you're hiding something. He's not supposed to do that but, hell, he's only human. It's a chance that we just cannot take."

"Assuming I take the stand. How much do I have to tell?"

"Everything. You can't hold back a thing."

"But—"

"Listen Bernard, you not testifying will only be an option if the judge grants my motion at the end of the prosecutor's case," Blackridge replied, his tone of voice signaling that the discussion was closed. He then looked away for a moment, as if making up his mind about the phrasing of his next question. Leaning in close, he lowered his voice. "And now back to the prosecutor's case, there remains one subject, Bernard, that I hesitate to bring up. But it's critical to moving forward."

Helgman sat quietly waiting for the old man to continue.

"There are rumors circulating around the hospital... rumors...well to be blunt...homosexual rumors."

"How would you—?"

"It's my business to know. And, believe me, it's Jeffrey Perkins's business to know as well. And frankly, Bernard, if there is any truth to the rumors at all you should have been upfront with me."

"I'm not homosexual, no. But how is that relevant?"

"It's not relevant, really. But Perkins has already convinced the judge to hear testimony on that issue on the theory that it goes to your moral character and therefore a general propensity toward doing bad things. I know it's a stretch. In fact, Walkowski was on the verge of disallowing any testimony along those lines when the prosecutor and I met with him in chambers. In the end, though, the judge reluctantly gave in to the prosecutor's arguments that it was at least marginally relevant, saying that he would later determine whether he would at all factor it in."

"And so—"

"And so we need to be prepared with forthright answers when Perkins springs the questions on cross-examination. If you get flustered in the moment—or defensive—it'll be as good as an admission in the minds of the judge and the public. So let's play this out. I'll be Perkins and you answer the questions."

"Really?"

"Really."

"Dr. Helgman," Blackridge began, playing the part of the prosecutor, "are you homosexual?"

Helgman stared ahead, as if deep in thought.

"This is just what I'm talking about." Blackridge leaned forward in his chair. "Any little pause and we're sunk. Let's do this again and this time I want to hear your clear and forthright answers."

"Okay."

"So I ask you again, Dr. Helgman," the lawyer intoned, "are you homosexual?"

"No," Helgman replied, anxious to get this over with.

"Are you in a homosexual relationship?"

"No."

"Have you ever performed homosexual acts?"

"No." Helgman's hands began to shake and he forced himself to remain calm. Then he looked at his hands, his voice barely a whisper. "Not since I left the camp."

"Oh my God, Bernie," Blackridge exclaimed, "I'm so sorry. But maybe now the dam has broken and you can be honest with me. Is that how you survived? Is that why you don't want to testify? This isn't the time to hold back. It could mean your life."

Helgman remained silent waiting for his lawyer to ask another question. But the old man simply sat across from him waiting.

Helgman sucked in his breath. "I did it for food, for medical books. Yes, I'm ashamed to say I did it to survive."

Blackridge took several minutes to digest this development and to run through all that he knew about Helgman, and all the evidence he had seen from the depositions. Then he looked at his client. "Please explain then, why the rumors persist, as if the liaisons were continuing?"

Helgman said, "The rumors stem from the fact I'm away on weekends leading to speculation fueled by those who wish to harm me."

"Away? Where?"

With a resolve that even surprised himself, Helgman told his lawyer about Muggs. About his years as a clown. Explaining that only when he wore the mask of a clown was he truly free of the pain from his time at Auschwitz.

Blackridge nodded, happy that any rumors of homosexuality coud be easily deflected. Checking his watch, he announced, "Time to get back to court."

On the street, Blackridge raised another issue. "I've been receiving checks all along from Bill Dawson for your legal bills. I assumed that the funds came through him from you. But I never thought to ask you why you wouldn't have been paying the expenses directly."

"I hardly have any money."

"One of the world's most successful surgeons has no money? I don't get it."

"Everything I earn, except what my family needs to live on, goes into a trust. Dawson is the trustee."

"A family trust?"

"Actually, years ago it became a foundation, but we still call it the Survivor's Trust. I contribute a good portion of my earnings to the foundation, but others contribute as well."

"What's the trust for? I mean who are the beneficiaries?"

"Two main beneficiaries. Any child who requires special care gets what he or she needs. But the main fund is for survivors. The fund pays for their medical needs and, in fact, any need, medical or not, that a survivor may have."

"Aha. That would explain why your legal bills are being paid for by Dawson. You're a survivor and I suppose Dawson is calling this trial a special need so he can legally expend trust assets for your defense."

"Yes. That's what he told me. I really didn't want to have to divert any of the trust funds away from the real victims, but I've got few assets of my own to pay for all of this. Most of what I have earned over these years has gone to the Survivor Trust."

They had just started up the courthouse steps when the lawyer stopped short and turned to Helgman. "We got sidetracked back there in the office and there's something I completely forgot to tell you."

"Now what?" Helgman sighed, unable to imagine what else Prosecutor Perkins might have in store for him.

"It's one of the witnesses that Perkins has scheduled. He knows that he may or may not get the chance to cross-examine you on the homosexuality issue if we don't put you on the stand. Therefore, he's bringing in his own witness. She's going to be testifying first thing tomorrow morning."

"She?"

"Yes. Stephanie Grenoble Nelson."

THIRTY-EIGHT

"What does Stephanie have to do with all of this?" Helgman demanded, his face coloring.

"Perkins won that argument with the judge. She did well during her deposition, but I'm—"

"You didn't tell me she had a disposition. Why wasn't I there?"

"You were busy and I didn't—"

"I need to talk with her."

"I tried to set up dinner, but her office said she's exhausted from a long business trip. Not taking any calls. She'll be in my office early in the morning, so we can talk then."

"What time is early?"

"Seven."

"I'll be there."

"Get a good night's sleep. Tomorrow promises to be a long day."

Stephanie, in fact, had agreed with Blackridge that it would only serve to distract Helgman more than he already was if he were to know about her upcoming testimony. So she had purposely remained out of town.

She had fallen asleep almost immediately when she got back to her apartment, but dreamed fitfully. Some of the visions were pleasant, but most had ended poorly. In one fragmented sequence, she had been in a park and saw a car's trunk open. Inside was an open bag filled with money. Lying next to the bag was a nail clipper. Her nails were in desperate need of cutting so she put the clipper in her pocket and closed the trunk, leaving the money untouched.

A few steps from the car, a uniformed policeman stepped from behind a tree and handcuffed her despite her protests that the nail clipper was hers. A police siren rang ...

Stephanie sat upright, shaking from the dream, the siren still sounding in her brain. It took her a moment to realize it was her alarm showing 6:00 o'clock. She was due across town in Blackridge's office in an hour.

Arriving less than an hour later, Stephanie was stunned to see how old and tired the lawyer appeared. His shirt was wrinkled and what looked to be dried mustard stains were smeared across the front. A tie lay crumpled in the corner of the sofa.

Taking a clue from her expression, Blackridge said, "Not much time for sleeping these days. Too much to do and too little time to do it." He flipped through his notes, turning page after page of a yellow pad, one of many on the cluttered desk. Finally, he said, "I'm sorry about this, but there's nothing we can do except prepare for the inevitable. I told Bernard you would be here and he should be along any minute. We'll get started without him."

"I still don't understand how I can be of any value to them," Stephanie said, taking a seat across the desk from the old man. "I know so very little."

"On the contrary. You know more than most. You've known Bernard for over fifteen years. The most important fact to remember is that Perkins will try to bait you, to get you angry. You must remain calm. Answer the questions honestly, but above all, don't volunteer any extra information—and don't lie." Blackridge studied his notes for a moment and was about to ask a question when Helgman arrived. "Oh, there you are, Bernard. Take a seat."

"Did I miss any—"

"No, no, just getting started. I was about to tell Mrs. Nelson—"

"Please call me Stephanie."

"Okay, Stephanie. They intend to present evidence of homosexuality to the court. Unfortunately, this country dislikes homosexuals, and it'll play well—at least in the papers."

"Also," Helgman added, "it fits with their characterization of those who performed those experiments at Auschwitz as being sexual deviants."

Stephanie heard the harsh bitterness as Helgman pronounced Auschwitz with more than a trace of his native tongue creeping into his voice. It was as if he were practicing for the day when he would be speaking German again.

"Stephanie, you're a perfect witness," Blackridge said. "Perkins can do no wrong no matter what you say."

"I don't follow. I'd never say anything to hurt Bernard." She paused for a moment, looked at Helgman, then added, "You do know that, don't you?"

Ignoring her comment, Blackridge said, "Let's play this out. Remember they want to prove Helgman's a bad guy, a person not to be trusted. If, as he tells me, he's never had sex with you in all these years, then Perkins can claim that's evidence of homosexual orientation and it fits the mold of the German monsters in the camp. If Bernard did have sex with you, then he's a bad guy because he cheated on his wife. Either way they win."

"You lost me. Bernard and I can be friends and not have sex. That doesn't make either of us homosexual. People don't have sex with a sibling."

"Let's hold that thought," the lawyer said. "But Perkins will have you testify that you and Bernard have been together in your Green Lines apartment, and other places, on many occasions. They will also show that you came to his home when his wife was gone. Then they will ask you when you first met. What will your answer be?"

"We met when I was in college."

"And?"

"And I fell in love with him."

"Now they have you in love with him."

"That still doesn't prove he's homosex—"

"They don't have to prove anything," Helgman again interrupted. "Perkins just puts it out there and the press runs with it. And it's downhill from there."

Stephanie fell silent.

"You'll prove their premise that I'm a bad man. What will you say when you're asked about us making love?"

"It's none of their business!"

"The witness is instructed to answer the question," Blackridge said, playing the part of the judge.

"Then I'll simply say we didn't make love. Period."

Helgman answered, "Perkins will say, you mean to tell the Court, and all these people in the courtroom, and the press that despite the fact that the two of you have been in love for all these years, you never made love? Is that what you want us all to believe?"

"Stop it!" Stephanie turned to Blackridge for help.

"Okay, Bernard, that's enough."

"Overruled!" Helgman said. "Have you ever been married, Mrs. Nelson? Oh, you have, have you? You were married while you loved the defendant. What kind of woman are you, Mrs. Nelson?"

"Stop it! That's entirely enough!"

"Bernard," Blackridge said, "she's right. That *is* enough."

"Stephanie, I wish it were that easy to just stop it," Helgman said. "From what I've seen, they can explore everything they want about you and your past and your relationship with me. You can't make them stop it. Blackridge here can't either, I'm afraid. Whether you like it or not, you'll tell the whole world that you have wanted to make love to me for years and that it was I, even long before I was married, who always pulled away. That's all they need for everyone to draw the inference I'm deviant."

Stephanie turned again to Blackridge. "Is he right?"

"Maybe not entirely," the lawyer replied. "But he's not very far off, I'm afraid."

"There are lots of reasons why we haven't slept together."

"The public doesn't care for lots of reasons," Helgman said. "My wife has left me and that adds to the problem. No, Steph, this is going to be an unmitigated disaster."

"I'll tell them we didn't make love because I thought I was your sister."

Helgman acting as the prosecutor demanded, "But that was only recently, wasn't it, Mrs. Nelson?"

"Well ... "

"And what, Mrs. Nelson, makes you believe that he would have been capable even if he was not your brother? He'll point directly at me so the entire courthouse will focus on me sitting there. Helpless. No, Steph, that's why you're their perfect witness."

"I can't believe it'll be as bad as you make it out to be. It just can't be."

"Worse. Worse than even your worst nightmare." Helgman tried to recall something she had said a moment earlier. The way she had phrased something, but it escaped him. "Something you said triggered something, but for the life of me I can't—"

"I've never heard you so bitter, Bernard. You must have hope for the future. Without a future, we, you—we are doomed."

235

Helgman remained quiet.

"It's the future that drives us to do what we do," Stephanie continued. "Knowing how a child will heal drives you to perform the miracles that you perform."

"The future is gone for me. What do I have to live for? I can't continue my mission, my only mission, my reason for living. What do I have left?"

"Stop that talk. I won't hear of it. My God, Bernard, you've been through worse. We'll get through this."

Blackridge rose and stretched his arms over his head. "If you two will excuse me a moment, I'll freshen up for court. Be back in a few minutes and then we'll be on our way."

When the lawyer left the room, Stephanie turned to Helgman. "To make a very long story short, it now appears to me that Uncle Dieter was playing a lot of games, mostly with the German government, so he could get his key people out. I have to accept the fact that my uncle gave you up to them in order to save all of us. But I do believe he tried to protect you in the camp. I don't think or, to say it differently, I prefer to think, that he didn't know how really bad it was in there."

Pained by reference to the camp, Helgman changed the subject. "I've been thinking about us. You and me. It started when you said you were my sister. I didn't want to believe that because ... well actually because then we couldn't be—"

"Lovers. I was hoping you felt that way, because that's what's been driving me to get to the bottom of this. I just can't live knowing we can't ever be together."

"I want you to know I do love you. I want to be with you. That is, if we clear up this sibling thing. And ... and *if* you'll have me. You know the problems I have. No promises."

"Bernie, I've wanted to share my life with you since Block Island. Seems another life ago. I do love you."

"When this is over, I'll work it out with Barbara. But there may be nothing to work out. It seems Barbara has a male friend who, no doubt, is giving her what I couldn't."

Stephanie watched in silence as the tears flowed down the cheeks of the man she was deeply in love with. Then, without forethought, but with a passion that had been building, she pleaded, "Marry me, my love. Please. Together we're strong."

"You make it sound so easy. Marry you and everything comes out right. There are too many happy endings in the stories you read. I love you, too, but it doesn't come out that way in real life. Not my life anyway." Helgman studied her for a long moment, then added, "Barbara may have left me, but I'm still married. That must be resolved before you and I—"

"Oh, Bernard. We can live anywhere in the world. We'll find a place where they'll welcome you to come repair their children. Green Lines can make a donation and—"

"It's a dream, Steph. A dream. My problems, I mean sexual problems, haven't been resolved. I may not be able—"

"Are you trying to tell me something?" Stephanie's face fell and she pulled her hand away from his.

"Only that I have to resolve my situation with Barbara first."

"I've waited this long. I can wait some more. I love you more than you can possibly know."

THIRTY-NINE

Blackridge returned. "In the few minutes we have remaining," he said. "I'll play Perkins and fire questions at you, Stephanie. Bernard, no coaching please."

"Speak slowly, Stephanie," Blackridge instructed at one point when she rushed an answer, her impatience surfacing. "Even when you know the answer, take your time. Then when you want to take a moment to think about an answer it won't seem so obvious."

The grilling continued until the phone rang. Stephanie welcomed the break. Blackridge swiveled in his chair, and with his back to Stephanie and Bernard, held a muffled conversation. Hanging up, he announced, "Sorry that took so long. We have to go." He searched his desk for a document and finding what he wanted pushed it across to Helgman. "Take a few minutes and review this before you come to court. Stephanie and I'll meet you there. Remember, no matter what she says on the stand, keep your composure."

On the way to the courthouse, Stephanie asked, "How's the trial going? It's getting big headlines and it all seems negative toward Bernard."

"As to the actual legal issues, I don't believe they've scored with the judge. But the headlines mean that Perkins is well on his way to being elected."

"Can't you do anything?"

"I fight with legal arguments, not in the streets with banners and slogans. If Bernard had wanted a street fighter, he could have chosen somebody else."

"Perkins is ruining the career of one of the world's best surgeons. Doesn't he care?"

"Perkins only cares about Perkins," Blackridge responded. "It's the nature of politicians, I'm afraid. Come, let's hurry. I'm not as spry as I once was and we're about to be late. Walkowski will put up with a lot, but being late in his court drives him nuts, just like spectators who chew gum or read the newspaper." He took her elbow and guided her through the crowd near the federal building.

Walkowski banged his gavel at ten o'clock sharp, and Stephanie heard herself say "I do," not more than ten minutes later. Her heart pounded and her mouth was dry. The judge was mostly hidden behind a partition rising from the floor but she knew he was there because of his creaking chair.

Perkins' voice was soft just as Blackridge had told her it would be. "Mrs. Nelson, please state your maiden name."

"Grenoble." *I hope they are all as easy as this.*

"Were you born in the United States?"

"No, in Germany." *Don't volunteer.* She looked to Blackridge as if to say, "I'm sorry." She saw him nod back at her, his lips curled into a wry smile.

"Is your father a United States citizen?"

What the Dickens has my father to do with this?

"Objection, this has no relevance," Blackridge called out.

"I'll allow it as background. But Mr. Perkins, don't overdo it."

"Was your father born in the United States," Perkins asked.

"No."

"Where was your father born?"

This is none of his business. Why am I being subjected to this? Why doesn't Blackridge do something?

"Last question along these lines, Mr. Perkins." Walkowski leaned forward to where Stephanie could see him. "Answer the question, Mrs. Nelson."

"Germany."

"Mrs. Nelson, how well do you know the defendant?"

"Objection. Indefinite," Blackridge said.

"I'll allow the question but you can answer in general terms."

"I"ll repeat the question," Perkins said. "How well do you know the defendant?"

"If you mean Dr. Helgman, I've known him for seventeen years."

"I didn't ask how long you knew him, Mrs. Nelson. I asked how well you knew him."

What an ass. How do I answer the question? We're friends sounds so lame. I love the man is what I want to say.

"Over those seventeen years, I've come to know him well."

"Do you know him intimately?"

Blackridge told me this was coming. It's a private matter. Why is he allowed to ask this in public? "I'm sorry, I don't understand the question." The instant the words came out she knew it was a mistake.

"Surely, Mrs. Nelson, you know what intimate means? You are—were—married, so you have first-hand knowledge of what it means to be intimate, do you not?"

"I have never been intimate with Dr. Helgman in the manner in which you seem to be suggesting. We have had intimate conversations over the years, so in that respect we've been intimate."

"There's no need for hostility, Mrs. Nelson." Perkins continued to use the soft, smooth version of his voice. "We are simply seeking the truth here. Just tell us in your own words then just what your relationship with the defendant has been."

Bastard. I'll use as much money as it takes to defeat this guy in the election. Blackridge should be stopping this. "He's the best doctor, the best pediatric surgeon in—"

"Mrs. Nelson," Perkins interrupted, "I didn't ask for a recitation of his qualifications. His resume isn't on trial here." Several people laughed. "I asked you to describe your relationship with the defendant. You seem reluctant to do so. Is there a problem we should be aware of?"

This man is a rat. Why doesn't the public see through his slick exterior? Why doesn't the judge see what he is doing? Fools, all of them. They love to hear this personal stuff. Vicarious thrills at someone else's expense. "I don't care to elaborate further," she snapped.

"Your Honor," Perkins turned toward the judge, "I respectfully request that you declare Mrs. Nelson a hostile witness. She is obviously not going—"

"I get it, Mr. Perkins." The judge focused on Stephanie. "Mrs. Nelson, no more outburts. Am I clear?"

"Yes, your Honor."

"I'm instructing you to answer the questions that are presented to you. If you don't understand a question you may ask for clarification. But please, no more outbursts, or I will be granting Mr. Perkins's request to have you declared hostile and I guarantee you will find his questioning even less to your liking." The judge then turned to the prosecutor. "Please continue, counselor."

"I'll ask the clerk to read back the question."

The court clerk scanned back through her transcription and then read, "By Prosecutor Perkins: I asked you to describe your relationship with the defendant. You seem reluctant to do so. Is there a problem that we should be aware of?"

"Please answer the question, Mrs. Nelson," Perkins's voice was again soft and friendly, a smile on his face.

"I care very much for Dr. Helgman. We've shared some good times over the years. We talk and he's a great listener. Dr. Helgman is a fine gentleman. And as honest as the day is long."

"You still haven't told us of your relationship," Perkins pressed.

Blackridge was on his feet. "Objection. Asked and answered. Your Honor! Mr. Perkins is badgering the witness. She has clearly answered the question as best she can. She described their relationship. Just because Mr. Perkins isn't happy with her answer is no excuse for badgering."

"Sustained. Move on counselor."

"Mrs. Nelson, tell us please if you have discussed your testimony, I mean the testimony you are now giving, with anyone?"

"Yes. Mr. Blackridge."

"And what instructions did Mr. Blackridge give you?"

Blackridge stood, but before he could say anything, Stephanie responded, "To be honest. To answer all your questions honestly."

Blackridge sat down.

"Mrs. Nelson," Perkins continued, "you have testified that you've known the defendant many years. Seventeen years, I believe you said. Do you know his sexual preferences?"

Even though they had rehearsed this very question, it still caught Stephanie by surprise. It was one matter to sit in a wood-paneled office and discuss private matters but another to do so in public. Stephanie's chest tightened and her face flushed. Her fingers turned white gripping the witness chair. Finally, she managed, "This is a personal matter. I don't discuss such things in public. And if you were a gentleman you wouldn't ask such questions!"

Walkowski sat upright in his chair and glared straight at her. "Mrs. Nelson, he intoned. "If an improper question is asked, Mr. Blackridge will object. Otherwise, you just answer the questions. Do you understand me?"

How does this guy come off lecturing me like a child? He is the ringmaster of this circus. No wonder the system is broken. "Yes, sir. But I see no relevance—"

Walkowski's patience was wearing thin. "Madam, I'll decide those issues. You just answer the questions. Mr. Perkins, continue please."

"Mrs. Nelson, please tell us, do you know the defendant's sexual preferences?"

"Objection," Blackridge called, not bothering to stand. "The question calls for an opinion of a witness not shown to be an expert."

"Overruled. I think the witness is qualified to answer."

"Thank you, your Honor, but I think I can rephrase the question." Perkins turned to Stephanie. "Mrs. Nelson, does your...ahem...friend, Bernard Helgman, enjoy the company of women?"

"I assume so. He and I have always gotten along fine."

The audience snickered and the judge banged his gavel. "No more outbursts," he admonished the spectators, "or I'll clear the courtroom."

When the courtroom quieted, Perkins said, "But you've also told us that the two of you haven't had sex. Does that suggest to you that he enjoys women?"

When Stephanie remained quiet, Perkins said, "Mrs. Nelson, may I remind you that you are under oath to tell the whole truth. We are waiting for your answer."

"Dr. Helgman is a married man. Sex between us isn't the issue."

"I see. Well tell us then, have you and he ever spent a weekend, or weekends, together?"

What is he trying to get at? The only time we've spent together since he's been married was when I went to their house. But Leslie—and his friend—were there. "No."

"Are you in love with the defendant?"

When will this end? This has gone beyond any proper limit and there isn't a thing I can do about it. How do I answer? Remembering Blackridge's advice, she answered, "Yes."

"And is he in love with you?"

"That's something you'll have to ask him."

"Has he told you he is in love with you?"

"Yes."

"So you are in love with a married man. Is that your testimony?"

"I'm in love with Dr. Helgman if that's what you mean."

More snickering.

More gavel pounding.

"Is Dr. Helgman, a married man, in love with you?"

"Asked and answered," called Blackridge from his seat.

"You need not answer the question," Walkowski instructed.

Perkins went on. "Just so I'm clear, Mrs. Nelson. You say that you and Dr. Helgman are in love with each other but you've never had sexual relations with him. Is that your testimony?"

"Yes."

"Is it fair to conclude then that when two mature adults are in love and don't have sex, then something is missing?"

Blackridge objected again. "The question calls for a conclusion that the witness has no way of answering."

"Oh, I can answer," Stephanie retorted before the judge could rule on Blackridge's objection. "I don't see anything missing in what we've done or didn't do. Dr. Helgman is a perfect gentleman."

"Mrs. Nelson," Judge Walkowski said, "there is no need to shout or to get angry. We hear you just fine when you speak in a natural voice."

"I'm sorry, Judge." Stephanie twisted in her seat to face him. "But these are very personal issues that I find offensive to be discussing in public."

"I'm sorry about that," Walkowski answered, his face coloring. "But Mr. Perkins has a right to probe your relationship. It goes to the weight of your evidence. This is an unusual case, under unusual circumstances that happened over two decades ago. I must determine exactly who the defendant is. I'm allowing the prosecutor latitude to establish facts from which I can base my conclusion. Many of those facts were known by people who are now dead. You are one of the few people who has known Dr. Helgman over a long period of time. Please understand we're trying to get at the truth here."

"I understand, but lives are being destroyed in the process. And, in all due respect, I see no relevancy between who he is—or was—and my love life. I find those questions repugnant."

The judge then turned to Perkins. "Mrs. Nelson raises a valid point. The cause and effect, so to speak, are not so simple as you would have the Court believe. Let's take a fifteen-minute recess. I'll see counsel in chambers."

The announced fifteen-minute recess lasted slightly over an hour and when the trial restarted, it seemed to Stephanie that Perkins was more subdued than before the break. The questioning moved away from her personal life to her business life running the shipping company. These questions she fielded nicely.

On cross-examination, Blackridge asked a few questions about the shipping business to clarify that she was now the chief executive officer. That under her guidance, the company had almost doubled in gross tonnage carried. And that profits were up more than three-fold.

"One further clarification, Mrs. Nelson," Blackridge said, "and then we are finished. I know this is difficult for you, but let me please ask you about some of your earlier answers. Earlier Mr. Perkins asked you to explain how it could be that you and Dr. Helgman have had a seventeen year relationship and that you love each other but that you've never had sexual relations with each other. I'm sure you recall that line of questioning."

"How could I forget?"

"Precisely. Well, now I ask you what your inference is from the facts you stated. I mean, do you infer from the fact that the two of you, lovers for seventeen years, haven't had sex to be an indication of Dr. Helgman's sexual preferences?"

"Indeed I do not!"

"Well then, in your mind, what is the explanation?"

"I have thought for the longest time he was my brother."

Eyes went wide as the impact of Stephanie's statement made its way around the courtroom. The pens of the reporters moved furiously and the artists sketching Stephanie worked fast to catch her exact expression.

"I have no further questions." Blackridge took his seat.

Helgman leaned over to Blackridge. "Why didn't you ask her to explain her answer?"

"Hold tight. Perkins can't resist asking. It will be more powerful coming from her in response to his question. This will drive the point home."

"Do you wish to re-direct, Mr. Perkins?"

"Yes, Your Honor, I do." Perkins stood slowly and walked halfway to the witness chair where he then turned his back to Stephanie and said, "Now, Mrs. Nelson you just said you believed you and the defendant are brother and sister. Is that right?"

"Is what right? That I answered the question or that we are brother and sister?"

The spectators laughed and the gavel came down.

"Let me ask it this way. What made think that you were brother and sister?"

"When I took over as executive officer of Green Lines from my uncle Dieter Schmidt, I found a paper in his desk that I took as proof that Bernard, Dr. Helgman, and I were brother and sister."

"Do you still believe that to be the case?"

Recalling her mother's words, 'Things are not always what they seem,' Stephanie looked directly at Perkins and answered, "No, I don't."

Perkins walked back to his table, leaned over and consulted with his associates, both of whom began shaking their heads sideways. He then turned back to the judge. "No more questions."

Walkowski looked toward Blackridge. "Re-cross?"

"None, Your Honor."

"The witness is dismissed," Walkowski announced with obvious relief.

Stephanie stood, her back straight, her shoulders square, her head up. With eyes straight ahead, she walked through the packed courtroom amid whispers and nodding heads from both the spectators and the press.

Behind her, she heard Walkowski announce, "We'll adjourn for the day. Court resumes at nine in the morning."

———

The afternoon headline screamed: *LOVE AFFAIR BE- TWEEN SHIPPING HEIRESS AND IMPOSTOR DOCTOR.*

"I see you have a copy," Helgman said to Blackridge when the two met for dinner. They were waiting for Stephanie to join them.

"I only skimmed the articles on the trial," Blackridge said, "but the gist is clear. Here, let me take a minute and read it in depth." He unfolded the newspaper. "If you catch the waiter's eye, I'll have a glass of the house white wine."

In a bizarre turn of events, Stephanie Nelson, a recent divorcée, took the stand today in the deportation trial of Bernard Helgman, the so-called impostor doctor. Helgman is accused of conducting sterilization, and other medical experiments on inmates, mostly women, during World War II at the detention camp known as Auschwitz. If found guilty, Helgman will most likely be deported to Germany.

Mrs. Nelson, the daughter of Baron and Hilda Grenoble and heiress on her mother's side to the Green Lines shipping fortune, admitted today under sharp examination by Prosecutor Perkins that she is in love with Helgman and has been so even prior to her marriage to Boston banker William Nelson II.

Recently, Mrs. Nelson has taken over running the shipping company from, Dieter Schmidt, her mother's brother.

"Oh, there you are," Helgman said, pushing his chair back and standing to greet Stephanie.

Blackridge refolded the newspaper and placed it on the floor under his chair. "You did an outstanding job today, my dear. You maintained your dignity and that was important."

"I felt abused and the judge was no help." The bitterness in her voice was apparent.

"If you must know, after he adjourned the trial he had both sides in chambers for over an hour. He's not happy with the grandstanding and told Perkins to get on with it. Perkins overplayed his hand and I think that will be the end to any questions or testimony about Bernard's sexuality. Walkowski is allowing greater flexibility than he would with a jury, but he's reached his limit."

"Lot of good that does me!"

"But it helps Bernard. It tells me he's not buying what Perkins is selling. This is a messy business and I'm sorry you had to be put through it."

"No need to apologize," Stephanie replied. "It's not you I'm angry at." She turned to Helgman. "Hey there. Why are you looking so glum? I'm the one who got beat up today."

"Have you seen the paper?"

"No, I've been preoccupied with something you and I need to discuss."

Blackridge placed a glass of wine in front of her and reached for the paper. "I think you should read this."

Stephanie's face grew tighter and tighter as she read and, finally, threw the paper down. "They'll stop at nothing! Is nothing sacred anymore? Why drag my family and my business into this?"

"It's been going this way from the beginning," Blackridge replied, his voice low, almost whispering. "I'm afraid big favors are being called in. It's not about Bernard, really. The purpose is name recognition for Perkins pure and simple. The newspapers are playing into it and at first I thought they were being used. But truth is, most of them are supporting Perkins in the election." Blackridge sipped his wine before continuing. "The reporter on the story you just read overstepped his bounds. You may have noticed Perkins actually stayed clear of using your company's name. He was careful not to mention Green Lines even once. That was no mere happenstance. Someone higher up set the ground rules for this. I suspect heads will roll at the paper. This may have been our first major break in this political theater."

"It's about time," Stephanie said. Turning to Helgman, she said, "You're quiet this evening. What gives?"

"I'm upset for the pain I've caused you."

"You heard what I said on the stand. I do love you. In a way, Perkins did us a favor. It's in the open now. Whatever happens, I'm with you."

FORTY

Helgman had decided to go home that evening rather than
staying in his hotel room, but he never made it to his
bed. Barbara found him asleep on the sofa when she
came into the house just past one o'clock in the morning.
Millie and Leslie had retired hours earlier. She'd been out
with Gregory but had decided not to spend the night with
him, preferring her own bed to his.

Barbara sat across from her husband, watching him as
she had done so many times in their early marriage when
he had come home after a particularly long surgery and
was too tired to make it to the bedroom. After about an
hour his eyes would suddenly come alert and the energy
would flow. He'd bound from the sofa, eat a light dinner
and immediately go to his library to read or write reports.
Barbara had always marveled at his recuperative powers.
Now she only saw a beaten man, his head hanging to the
side as if he would never again have the strength to hold it
upright. *Oh, Bernie, what have they done to you?*

The thought of heart attack flashed through her mind
and she reached to touch him, to feel for a pulse.

His eyes blinked open and he sat up. She waited for him
to orient himself before she spoke.

"Barbara," he exclaimed when he realized who had
touched him. "Where am ... oh, I must have dozed off."

"Shhhh. Let's talk quietly. I don't want Les or Millie
to wake up."

"Sorry. You're right. It's just that I was so surprised
to see you."

"I'll make you some nice tea," Barbara soothed. "What
about something to eat?"

"Tea's fine."

Barbara started toward the kitchen. "You're looking
good," Helgman observed. "Lost some weight."

"Always the doctor. I've been working out." In fact, after the first week in Gregory's bed he had suggested she tighten herself up a bit.

"I've gone the other way." He started to stand and then sat back, his hand to his chest.

"What is it, Bernie? What's wrong?"

"Something I ate. Just heartburn."

"Don't take chances," she called from the kitchen. "If there's something wrong, let's get you to the hospital."

"I'm fine. Nothing a little sleep won't cure."

She stood in the doorway listening for the kettle to whistle. "This isn't a time for heroics. You need to get checked out."

"No, Barbara, I'm fine. And besides, we've got a lot to talk about."

She looked past him to the window. "Yes, Bernie, we do. Your relationship with that ... with Stephanie ... is all over the news." She turned to him, saw the pain on his face and thought he was indeed having a heart attack. But then she realized the pain was for her, for the situation they found themselves in. "It's strange," she said, "hearing about your husband's lover on the TV. It's almost as if I was listening to someone else's life. Detached almost. Like thinking of yourself in the third person." The water coming to a boil caught her attention. "I'll be right back."

Returning from the kitchen, Barbara set a tea mug on the table beside Bernard and took a seat facing him, her own cup now held in two hands in front of her face.

"I feel horrible about this," Helgman began. "I didn't want it to be this way."

"Do you love her?"

"I think so."

"Have you slept with her since we last talked about this?"

"No."

"So she was telling the truth."

"I have to be honest. The only reason it's true is the same reason it's true for us."

"Same story, same ending. Is that what you're saying?"

"It's really not the same story. But I wouldn't be surprised to find it has the same ending."

"I'd think you should figure that out before you do something foolish."

"I understand you've found what you want. So what's the issue?"

"I deserve that, I suppose. Oh, Bernie, I'm so sorry." She brushed away the tears only to have them replaced by more, to the point where his face was a blur. She set her teacup down and reached for the handkerchief Bernard was holding for her.

"I'm sorry," Helgman said, "that came out wrong. I didn't mean it the way it sounded. I just meant that you've found what you want so what's wrong with me trying to do the same?"

"I waited for years for you to want me. I'm not running toward something. I'm running away from the pain. I'd come back to you in a moment if only we could .... No, even if not."

"What are you saying?"

"I love you. Is that plain enough?"

"And the truth is," Helgman replied, "I love you also."

"Well, that settles it." She forced a laugh.

"If only it were so easy ... at this point."

"We can make it work. It's as though you buried parts of your life in the sand, only the blowing winds keep uncovering what's hidden, exposing what was buried. This is the time to dig it all free before it consumes any more of you."

Helgman slumped further into the sofa, his eyes closed, his hands supporting his head.

"It's all right, Bernie." Barbara moved to the sofa and pulled him against her.

Instead of his muscles tightening, she felt his body go soft. She pulled back to look at him, to be certain he was okay. His skin had turned gray, the color drained from him. "Are you certain you're okay? You look—"

"I told you I'm fine."

"I'm afraid for you."

"I've had a tough day. And tomorrow will be even worse." He glanced over at his briefcase lying beside the sofa. "It's all there. Hundreds of pages. My lawyer forced it out of me. From the beginning, every painful detail. You can read it if you wish."

Helgman stood, took a moment to gain his balance, and then slowly walked to his bedroom.

Minutes passed and Barbara did not move, her mind alternating between concern for her husband and worry over her son. For most of the boy's life, her husband had been indifferent, but suddenly this summer something clicked between them and now all Leslie wanted to do was be with his father. She thought back to Leslie as a young boy and how Bernard had for years continued to sculpt his skin as the child grew. Helgman had allowed her to observe him in the O.R. as he carefully removed the scar tissue. She had marveled at how gently her husband's fingers moved, using sutures so thin she never could see them when she changed the bandages.

Her mind turned to Gregory and his easy smile and his willingness to try new things. Yes, he excited her, but she never seemed fulfilled and, for his part, he never seemed satisfied. Her newly found sexual enjoyment was already wearing thin. Being in her own house, with her own husband, with her own son, was real. Being with Gregory was ... well ... just an escape.

Bernard's papers—his life's story—lay untouched beside her. She understood that if she was to help him, she could only do so if she read them. Yet she hesitated, knowing that by immersing herself into her husband's most private thoughts, his pain would become her pain. She wasn't sure she was strong enough to handle it. She closed her eyes and prayed for the right answer to her dilemma. Tentatively, she opened the notebook.

Barbara read the first line declaring his birth name to be Mordechai Stein, born the tenth of October, 1925. It was less than a week until his forty-eighth birthday.

She read the next line. Then the next. And the next.

She sat fascinated as the man she had lived with for so long came alive for the first time. He was playing in the woods, running through the bushes, chasing rabbits and squirrels—not for sport, but for food.

She wept as she read about the children at school throwing stones at him, the teacher doing nothing to interfere. In class, the teacher joined in the torment making him stand at the front of the classroom peppering him with questions he could not be expected to answer. Then paddling him when he came up short.

After his second beating, he vowed to never again be caught not knowing the answer to a question. He went to the school library and devoured every book available.

When Jews were banned from attending school he went every day to the town library, often having to be asked to leave at closing time. When the curfews came for Jews, the librarian allowed him in, but only if he stayed out of sight in the stacks.

The deeper into his life Barbara delved, the more her tears flowed. Bernard had communicated his story as if he had been a disinterested observer, the narrative free of self-pity, the hatred he harbored well hidden.

Then she realized what was coming and pushed the pages from her, not certain if she was up to what she knew would follow. She finally gathered her courage and continued.

Bernard related how after his fifteenth birthday party his parents had told him he would soon be living with another family, the family of his father's former employer. He was to become their son, take their name. His sister was to go with that same family as well, but something changed and she was left behind.

Barbara read about the infirmary and how people died in Max's arms. She learned what he did to obtain access to the medical books and enough food to remain alive. She had no tears remaining for the little girl, Elsa, who Max had tried to save but couldn't.

Barbara turned page after page, almost shouting out loud for joy when the Russian Army trucks rolled into the camp, their flags snapping in the wind. She witnessed Max assume the identity of Bernard Helgman and her own stomach cramped when he described eating his first real meal since being taken by the Gestapo. She followed him as he gradually became a surgeon under the mentoring of Seymour Katz and she was overwhelmed with jealousy when Stephanie came into his life. The rest she pretty much knew and flipped the pages quickly, skimming over the years of their marriage.

As Barbara continued thinking about what she had just read, she began to understand that his secrets were not secrets from her. His secrets had been his only refuge—a small space carved from a world that had always refused him any modicum of privacy, even stealing from him his birth name and all that went with it.

The sun was just showing its first tentative rays when she read Helgman's final words.

"Perhaps my most important legacy is Muggles the Clown," the text read. "My son Leslie has the innate talent for deep emotional expression that I so clearly lack. He is an excellent clown. When it is time for me to leave this earth, I'll do so knowing I've saved at least one wonderful person from what fate had in store for him."

FORTY-ONE

Helgman poured his second cup of coffee and sat down at the kitchen table just as the phone rang. It was Blackridge telling him the court clerk had called to say they would be starting late that day. "Come to the office," the lawyer instructed. "We have some things to discuss."

Barbara came into the kitchen with her bathrobe wrapped around her. "Who was that on the phone?"

"Blackridge," he answered, noting that she had lost even more weight than he had at first thought. "Trial is delayed this morning."

Barbara sat down at the table across from her husband. "Bernie," she began, not knowing how to talk about what he had written, but knowing she had to say something, "you told me part of it. But I never truly understood what you went through. I'm sorry. People send unspoken signals to each other all the time. I'm afraid our signals got mixed up, confused. I doubted you and I'm truly sorry."

"It's my fault. I've been unable to give you the physical, or even the emotional, comfort a spouse is supposed to give. It's not that I haven't wanted to touch you, to hold you, but it's that—"

"I know. I understand. I'm sorry that I did what I did. But I'm here for you now."

"You heard—"

"I heard Stephanie say she loved you. I've asked you this before. I want a straight answer. Do you love her?"

"That's what I've been asking myself. I think I do. But Barbara, I love you as well." He took a long sip of coffee before continuing. "But I ask myself what I'll be like when this is over—however it ends."

"I can't imagine you reverting back. It's out now. Your past, the things that haunt you, the way you've been beating yourself up, the blame for things you had no control over. You're a good person, a really good person. There's no cause for shame."

"You now know what I've done, and you still—"

"More than ever."

"Even knowing what you now know?"

"Even more."

"Who knows if I'll ever be able to—well the truth is I'm impotent and that doesn't go away on command."

"I now understand what's causing the problem. Before, I was responding to my own hurt at being rejected. Now I know it wasn't me you were rejecting."

"And you think it won't bother you going forward? If I don't ... don't ... chase you? You think knowing why will make a difference?"

"Bernie, if it only had been the sex I could have dealt with it. I know I could have. I did for all those years. But it was the rest of it—the never touching, never confiding in me, disappearing on weekends. It was almost as if I were a ghost—seen on occasion but not really there. That's what finally got to me." She looked away and when she turned back said, "You know, your memoirs, the life story I read last night cleared up one thing that has puzzled me from the beginning. It explains why you decided to specialize in burns."

"I just—"

Barbara held up her hand. "How many thousands of bodies were burned while you were in Auschwitz? And you couldn't save even one of them. But you saved our son. Not only medically, but you've given him unconditional love since the first day you saw him. So, yes, I love you. For myself—and for our son."

On impulse, Bernard nudged his hotel key across the table. "That's the key to my hotel room. Room ten-ten in the downtown Hilton. I'll be staying there tonight. I don't know that I'll be able to be physical the way you want, but we can try. If you'll accept me on those terms then come to the hotel and we'll start over. A clean slate. No recriminations. If not, well—"

Barbara laughed. "That's the craziest thing I've ever heard." Then her demeanor turned serious. "You really mean it, don't you?"

"Got the idea from an old movie. Hey, chasing women is new to me."

Barbara was not as amused as her husband seemed to be by his impulsive notion. "And what if you decide you don't want me after all," she asked. "Or prefer Stephanie?"

"Then I won't be there."

"Bernie. This doesn't make a lot of sense. We again began the long process of healing our marriage last night and I certainly want more to come of that. But I don't think it can happen until you're a hundred percent sure it's me you want!"

She pushed the hotel room key back to Bernard's side of the table. "Please let me know when you know."

While Bernie was struggling with his future, Stephanie was dealing with her past. Dieter Schmidt was still struggling with his latest bout of cancer, but she had to see him. She had driven to Point Judith and taken the ferry across to Block Island where her mother picked her up and dropped her off at Dieter's house. Stephanie knew from her mother that Dieter's physician had advised against the visit but Dieter had overruled him.

Dieter was sitting in an easy chair in the corner of his bedroom as she entered. "I understand you're doing well with the business," he said.

Stephanie knew it was difficult for Dieter to concede that she had done as well as she had with Green Lines. "Thank you. Your approval means a lot."

Dieter smiled wanly. "You came on a mission of some kind, I presume. So let's hear it."

Two missions, actually. So here we go.

"Always right to the point." She took a seat in the matching easy chair across from him. "Okay. I need your help."

"You seem to be doing just fine without my help."

"It's help with Bernard's case. He must be found innocent."

"You carried on a relationship with him after promising me you wouldn't. And now you approach me for help. You have your nerve."

"I need your help," she repeated.

"Even if I was of a mind to help you, what is it you'd have me do?"

"Tell the truth. Tell the truth to me and to the judge about who Bernard really is. You hold the facts that can establish his innocence."

"You give me far too much credit. And, besides, as I'm certain your mother told you, and as you can plainly see for yourself, I'm in no condition to travel."

"I'm sure Bernard's lawyer can arrange for you to videotape a statement right from this chair."

"Like I said, you give me far too much credit." Dieter coughed and seemed not able to catch his breath. A nurse rushed into the room and held a towel in front of his mouth. He spit a large wad of mucus onto the towel.

"He has trouble bringing this up," the nurse said. "It's worse when he's agitated I'm afraid. Please don't overtax him. He's frail but making good progress, aren't you dear?"

"If you call it progress to have someone follow you around changing your diapers."

The nurse harrumphed, turned and left the room.

Stephanie saw that it was now or never—for both missions. "So will you help me clear Bernard ... Father?"

Dieter's eyebrows shot up as his jaw dropped. "Father?"

"Mother told me everything. I know she promised you that she would keep everything a deep dark secret. But once Daddy died, she didn't see the point and she thought that I deserved to know."

Schmidt's face went white and he slumped further in his chair. That was all the proof she needed.

"I know everything—or at least almost everything," Stephanie began. "The Steins asked you if you would adopt both Bernard—Mordechai, I should say—and his sister Rachel. But Aunt Gretchen would only agree to taking in one child. That was one problem."

Dieter's eyebrows shot up again, but he said nothing.

"The other problem was me." Stephanie paused to take a deep breath. "Mother said that my birth mother was your former secretary, Anna Gohde. Anna brought me up quietly for three years, but at some point the Gestapo widened its idea of who was defective to include unwed mothers and their illegitimate children. So both problems got solved when Mother agreed to adopt me, and the two of you told the family that I was Mordechai's sister, Rachel." Dieter said nothing, so Stephanie pressed on. "The story was plausible that you had agreed to help your former employee by adopting his son, Mordechai, but how to explain to your wife where I came from? Me being the Steins's other child, Rachel, made sense, but only if mother was in on everything. As it so happened, Aunt Gretchen had become friendly with the Steins at a company holiday party so she actually knew they had a three year old girl. That made your lie about who I was that much easier."

Dieter turned his head away in an attempt to hide his tears.

"Even Daddy thought I was Morcdechai's sister!"

The old man turned back to face his daughter. "Yes, dear Stephanie," he said at last. "That's why I had to insist that you not become involved with him. At some point Bernard would have told your father that he had been Mordechai—Max. Then your father would have had to tell the both of you what he believed to be the case—that the man you were dating was your brother. And then, what? One way or the other the whole fabric of lies that Hilda and I had concocted would have unraveled. And then it would come out that Hilda had lied to her husband about where you came from. And then my affair with Anna...."

Dieter again turned his head away. He coughed, but this time nothing came up.

"Uncle—I suppose Father is the more correct term—I'm not here to judge. You saved my life, so how could I not give thanks. Aunt Gretchen is gone, and Daddy's liver failure finally caught up with him, so there's no longer a need to hide." Softening her tone she said, "I love you. You need to hear that from me. You also need to know I'll stop at nothing to help Bernard. I'm not sure I'll ever know the full truth about you and what you did—and didn't do—but I'll still love you. But I need to know. Did you adopt Bernard and then give him up to the Gestapo to save your own skin?"

"Save my own skin?" Dieter pulled himself up in his chair. "You were right. You're in no position to judge. You, the one person ...."

Stephanie waited until the coughing was again under control. "I'm not judging. I just need to know."

"Listen. Believe me when I say I think of Maximillian-Bernard as a father thinks of a son. It was impossible to get him out no matter how hard I tried. I barely got *us* out. He was the one who had to suffer for us and I've paid the price dearly." The coughing returned. Dieter struggled with something in his throat, put the towel to his face and captured another greenish wad. "All isn't black or white," he continued after reaching for a tissue and wiping his forehead. "You will come to know that no person is all bad—or all good. We each have our weak moments—and our good moments."

"I'm confused."

"I didn't abandon him. I set him up in the infirmary where he could stay warm and get food."

"In a concentration camp? Really? How was *that* possible?"

"Anything's possible. Certain prisoners received special treatment. They called it Canada. I was able to get special treatment for Max. He isn't the only Jew who owes his life to Canada."

"Canada?"

"Never mind that for now. After the war I found out he was alive, but I couldn't face him. Not after what I'd done. But I did arrange for his surgical training at Pitt under a doctor named Katz. That training was, shall we say, a result of very generous donations. Conscience has a very high price, I'm afraid."

"Conscience? You speak of conscience, but it's been almost thirty years and you've still not faced him."

"You're right. But I just couldn't. Could you have?"

"Maybe, maybe not. I'm not the one who sold him off to the Nazis."

"You should thank God you didn't have to make that choice."

Dieter paused to catch his breath. "And there's another thing. The Nazis were not just rounding up Jews. Gypsies, homosexuals, women with illegitimate children, anyone they could get their hands on who was not Aryan or who they branded as defective in one way or another. Need I remind you that you and Anna would have been taken had I not removed you from her. So by giving him up, I saved your birth mother as well as you."

"And what about Max's sister Rachel?"

"It broke my heart to have to tell the Steins that we couldn't take her in as well. A few days later they said they had found another family for her. But everything was in such chaos—"

"And it never happened?"

Dieter slowly shook his head. "Never happened. But the past is gone now." He struggled to catch his breath. "Truth is, I'm relieved you know about Anna. Now we can move forward."

"You treat this like a novel. Let's turn to the next chapter, see what happens. All live happily ever after. Life's not that simple. Bernard's life hangs in the balance."

"There is nothing more I can do." Dieter said between coughing spasms. "I'm an old man, about to die. What more can a man do?"

Stephanie started for the kitchen to fetch the nurse when his faint voice called to her. "Stephanie, come here."

She turned and went to him.

"Do you know how hard it is for a father to watch his own child grow up and not be able to talk to her as a father talks to his daughter?"

"But we did talk, you and I." Tears welled up in Stephanie's eyes and she momentarily couldn't speak. Wiping her face dry, she continued, "How I cherished those times with you up on the hill. Many daughters don't have that with their fathers. I was lucky in that regard."

"Come hold me as a daughter holds a father." Dieter held out his frail hand to her.

Stephanie, her anger dissipating the instant she pressed her face against his, threw her arms around his skeletal body and rocked gently with him. When she could speak, she whispered, "I do love you."

"I love you, too," Dieter managed to say, tears flowing freely down his withered face.

It was only after several moments that Dieter returned to Stephanie's original request. "About this videotape you want me to make. It's far too late for that now." Dieter was now sitting up straighter and had more strength in his voice than she had heard since her arrival. "I'm afraid history has been written with an indelible pen. They will easily brand me a Nazi, which I never was, mind you. The judge will not believe a Nazi would testify to save a Jew. On the contrary, the judge will believe that one Nazi is testifying to save another Nazi. My testimony will convict Bernard, not exonerate him."

Dieter slumped in his chair, again struggling to bring up something lodged in his chest. Stephanie turned away, finding it too hard to watch the struggle. Looking out the window, waiting until the coughing subsided, she caught a glimpse of the bluffs where she and Dieter had spent so many hours in intimate conversation.

Stephanie was far from convinced that Dieter's testimony would not help Bernard's cause. "How about this, then?" she said finally. "Can you at least let Bernard's lawyer decide whether your testimony would be helpful?"

There was no answer.

"Uncle? Father?"

Stephanie came back around to the front of Dieter's chair, and stood motionless as she looked into his face. Then, with tears freely flowing, she gently kissed his forehead and called for the nurse.

FORTY-TWO

Judge Walkowski arrived at the courthouse an hour earlier than usual. Although it was already the fifth day of October, an Indian summer continued in full force with the temperatures forecast for the low sixties. The janitorial crew greeted him with surprised looks as they hurried to finish their early morning chores.

Prosecutor Perkins had completed his case and Blackridge had given the judge a heads-up that today he would be presenting a motion for dismissal of all the charges. If the judge were to grant that motion then Helgman would be exonerated without having to testify or call any witnesses of his own. It was obvious what arguments Blackridge would be making and Walkowski needed some quiet time to review those arguments in his mind so as to better prepare for Blackridge's motion.

On the one hand, Perkins had presented at least a half-dozen witnesses who placed Helgman in the infirmary. Indeed, the judge found that troubling. The old adage, *where there's smoke, there's fire*, played in his head. On the other hand, Blackridge's cross-examination established that none of the witnesses could say that Helgman had been involved in performing any experiments. To the contrary, one could well infer from the cross-examination testimony of Yetta Hertzstein, Gershon Schwartzman and others that Helgman had actually been helping them.

In order to support the case for deportation, Perkins had taken the position that Helgman had lied about being a doctor, which is why he had taken the name of a doctor who had died at Auschwitz. But ironically, that argument actually played in Helgman's favor on the question of the experiments because, if Helgman had not been a doctor, he arguably did not have the medical training to do what the witnesses said had been done. On the other hand, there was the memorandum of Dr. Katz that came out during the cross-examination of Harold Sumner. That document supported the proposition that Helgman did have medical training. Again, ironically, while tending to show that Helgman had not lied about being a doctor when he entered the country, the Katz memorandum lent credence to an argument that Helgman did have the requisite ability to perform the experiments.

The evidence of homosexuality was nothing more than innuendo based on the testimony of the Nelson woman. Walkowski dismissed that out of hand and was angry with himself for not cutting it off sooner than he had. Whether or not Helgman cheated on his wife, or ran with men, was not relevant to the issues at hand, and the judge knew it.

Also irrelevant was the outpouring of mail and of messages on the court's answering machine from the families of Helgman's patients. Chills had run down the judge's spine when he opened the many envelopes and saw the before-and-after pictures sent to him. Even more compelling than the parents' words of praise for Helgman were the images of the children he had repaired. Walkowski knew he was to ignore outside factors, but it was impossible to force from his mind the images of the deformities Helgman had corrected.

In chambers the previous afternoon, Walkowski had casually remarked that he appreciated not having Helgman's patients and their parents paraded before him to offer testimonials on Helgman's behalf. Blackridge had thrown up his arms and replied, "Even if I had wanted to, my client simply wouldn't have allowed it. It's his belief the children have suffered enough."

The burden of proof rested with the prosecutor. If the prosecution's case did not establish to the requisite level of certitude in the judge's mind that Helgman was guilty of any of the offenses he was charged with, then the judge would—indeed have to—dismiss those charges. Yet, he still had lingering questions about this man Helgman who, it would seem, had the name Schmidt while in Auschwitz. Was Helgman a victim or an impostor? Was he a Jew acting in the camp out of desperation, or was he a German worker assigned to the infirmary and now hiding behind an elaborate lie? Maybe none of that mattered if, upon reflection, he were to conclude that the prosecution simply had not made out its case, whatever Helgman's involvement might have been in reality. But it was certainly within the judge's prerogative to hold his decision on Blackridge's motion in abeyance, even if he were to conclude in his own mind that the prosecution's case was lacking.

Who was this Helgman, really? Walkowski just had to know. He was sure that if he denied Blackridge's motion for a dismissal, then Blackridge would have no choice but to put Helgman on the stand in his own defense. Besides whatever questions Prosecutor Perkins might have for the witness on cross-examination, Walkowski could ask questions of his own.

And then he would have his answer.

Millie had spent a quiet evening watching TV while Leslie and Ken entertained themselves in the basement. The promotion for the ten o'clock news had promised full details of the "War Criminal Trial." Millie, not one to turn her back on juicy gossip, hadn't missed a word. Like everyone else who paid attention to the news, she now knew of Stephanie's love affair with Helgman. When the news was over, she turned to go find the boys and send Ken home. She was startled to find both of them standing in the doorway to the living room. "Ken, it's time—"

"I'm just going home, Miss Millie."

"What have you two been doing?"

"Nothing."

"I don't think so. Tell me what you were doing."

"It's a surprise," Ken said. "Leslie has been working on a surprise for his father."

"What kind of surprise?"

"Make him happy," Leslie interjected.

"Make who happy?"

"My father. He's sad. Make him smile."

"Can't tell you any more." Ken stooped to pick up a large gym bag. "It'll ruin the surprise." He then hurried through the front hallway to the door. Millie followed him but he was gone before she could ask any more questions.

Turning to Leslie, she said, "I hope you two are not doing anything you're not allowed to do."

"Tomorrow, make my daddy happy. Go downtown with Ken."

"Downtown?"

"I'm allowed. On the streetcar. Ken knows the way."

That was tomorrow's problem as far as Millie was concerned, hoping Barbara would be home and awake early enough to supervise her son. "Okay. It's time for bed. Want me to make your hot chocolate?"

"Not tonight." Leslie surprised Millie by passing up his favorite bedtime snack and heading immediately up to his room.

Leslie came into the kitchen earlier than usual and found Millie stirring a pot on the stove.

"Good morning, Leslie. I'm making oatmeal. It'll be ready soon."

"Mother? Home?"

"No, dear. She stayed at your grandmother's last night." Millie didn't actually know where Barbara was. "She should be home soon."

As for Helgman, since she began spending the nights at the Helgman residence back when Rabbi Stillson took ill, she never knew when he'd be in the house. He certainly hadn't been home last night.

"Going downtown. With Ken."

"I know, you told me last night. What are you doing downtown?"

"Make daddy happy."

"How are you going to do that? I mean, make your dad happy."

"Surprise."

"Now Leslie, you have to—"

The doorbell rang.

"Ken!" Leslie exclaimed, running toward the front door.

Millie called after him. "Don't you want your oatmeal?"

The door slamming was Millie's answer.

Ken carried the gym bag as he and Leslie walked the three blocks to the bus stop. "This will be fun," he said several times. "You'll make your father very happy."

The bus was already crowded when they boarded. Ken led the way to the back where they stood quietly as more people climbed on. The bus slowly made its way through the Oakland section and then through the Hill District on its way downtown.

Ken looked out the bus window. "I think we're here!" When they were both safely on the sidewalk, Ken pointed to his left. "I think the court building is that way. We'll go over to that park so you can get ready." A fountain off in the distance spewing water high in the air had caught Ken's interest. The two boys headed in that direction.

Ken issued instructions to Leslie once they had crossed the street to the wide grassy area. "Sit on that bench over there. I'll help you make up your face."

Leslie did as he was told. Ken placed the gym bag on the ground and began rummaging through it for the grease paint. He placed several jars on the bench beside Les and then, holding an old mirror, watched as Leslie became Muggles the Clown.

When Leslie was satisfied, he said, "Dress now."

Ken dutifully pulled Leslie's costume from the bag and handed it to his friend.

A moment later Muggles bounded over to the bag, dug through it for something and then jumped up onto the bench. Freed from the close timing required when he worked with his father, Muggles improvised gleefully. He flapped his arms as if they were wings and "flew" to the next bench and then to the next. He purposely missed a bench and tumbled onto the grass, waving what appeared to be a broken wing.

People ambling by had stopped to see what was going on and soon a small crowd had formed. Muggles climbed into a small tree and pretended he was about to fly to the ground. The adults were agog, not knowing what the crazy clown was going to do next.

A policeman appeared. Muggles ran to him and snatched his hat, placing it on top of his chicken head. The policeman snatched the clown's arm, but when the crowd booed he decided to play along and made a pretense of chasing the bird. The clown ran around a bench, finally giving the hat back with a grand flourish, ending in a deep bow. Again, the audience applauded wildly.

"Who's in charge here?" The policeman said when he realized the crowd had overflowed into the street causing a safety hazard.

Ken waved his arm energetically.

The officer walked over. "You with him?"

"He's my friend. Muggles the Clown."

"I don't care what his name is. You got a permit?"

"No, sir," Ken replied. "He's good. Really good. And funny. You need to watch him."

"Can't perform in the park without a permit. He needs to leave."

"But he's not hurting anybody, officer. All good fun."

The policeman turned to watch Muggles for a moment. "Can't argue on that. He's good. But like I said, no permit, no show. Traffic is backing up over there. Captain'll have my head. Hey, duck," the officer called, "come over here, please." He was trying to be as polite as possible, knowing it wasn't good public relations to roust a clown in front of so many laughing adults. But the cacophony of automobile horns was intensifying by the minute. Something had to be done.

When the clown didn't respond, the policeman retreated to his patrol car to seek instructions.

A few minutes later a second police car pulled up and Muggles, seeing the uniformed officers coming toward him, jumped from bench to bench and flopped on the ground as the two officers approached. He was trapped with no way out.

Then Muggles remembered a clown act he had seen where many clowns had climbed out of a police car. Instead of allowing himself to be captured in the park, he ran—actually chicken-waddled—to where the police cars were parked, waving to the audience, jumping on and off benches, and tumbling in the grass as he went.

Muggles pulled open the back door of one of the squad cars and fell into the back seat. An officer who had been waiting in the passenger seat quickly jumped out and pushed the door closed behind him. Muggles banged on the window and pretended he was stuck trying to escape. The crowd howled at his antics.

"Quick," the cop called to his partner, "let's get this guy out of here, before there's an accident." The partner ran around the car, slid into the driver's seat and the car moved away from the curb with clown waving at the crowd out of the window. The folks in the park waved back at him, the children yelling for more. He stopped waving and searched the crowd for Ken. Not seeing him, he sat back in the seat.

After a few blocks the officer turned to his partner. "Danny, pull over. We need to figure out what's going on here." He turned toward the back seat after the car had stopped at the curb."

"Son," the officer said, "take off that nose so we can talk."

Muggles didn't respond.

"Hey. We're trying to help you here. Work with us. It's hard to talk to a duck. Take off that nose."

"Chicken."

"Okay, a chicken. Take off the nose will you, son?"

This time, Leslie did as he was told. He sat facing the men in the front seat, his head down, afraid of what they would do to him.

"What's your name?"

"Muggles the Clown."

"No, son, I mean the name you go by when you're not all dressed up."

"Leslie Helgman," Les responded as he had been taught to do.

The officer scratched his head. The name was familiar, but he could not place it. "Where do you live Leslie?"

Leslie remained quiet. He didn't want to be sent home.

"Come now, son. You can trust us. Where you from?"

Leslie said nothing.

"Hey, enough," the officer's partner said. "Let's take him in and let Sarge figure it out. And then we ... hey, wait a minute! Helgman? Isn't that the guy who's on trial?" He turned to Leslie. "That Nazi doctor? That your father? The guy on trial?"

Slowly Leslie nodded.

"Let's not book him," the first officer suggested, "The family's got enough problems."

"Well, then what?"

Leslie said, "I want to be with father."

"Okay, then," said the officer, his partner nodding in agreement. "Your father's over at the Federal Building. We'll take you there." The car pulled away from the curb and gained speed.

Leslie put his nose back on, pressed his face to the window and waved to everyone they passed. He was having the best day of his life.

FORTY-THREE

Helgman and Blackridge came into court together and sat in the seats they had occupied every day since the trial had started. Helgman leaned toward his lawyer, "Perkins is late. Giving a TV interview, no doubt. What will he do when this is over?"

"That depends on what happens in this trial. He'll most likely be elected if he wins this case. Maybe even if he loses. But truth is he's overplayed his hand. I have it on good authority the party bosses are angry at his treatment of several of the witnesses. Not only that, but he awakened a sleeping giant in the form of your friend Stephanie Nelson. She told me that her company has pumped a ton of money into the other side's campaign in the last twenty-four hours."

"Sounds as if he's on trial and not me," Helgman mused.

"If there's one thing I've learned over the years, it's that desperate men do desperate things."

Barbara entered the courtroom and walked slowly down the aisle, her eyes averted from Helgman's. She was wearing a new dress and with her trimmed down figure looked sensational.

Was she sending him a message? If so, what was it?

Helgman's reverie was interrupted by the bailiff's calling for all to rise as Judge Walkowski hurried to the bench and struck his gavel.

As Judge Walkowski had expected, Blackridge had filed a motion at the close of trial on the previous day, asking the court to dismiss all of the charges. His argument was that the prosecution had failed to present sufficient evidence from which a judge could conclude Helgman was guilty of any crime beyond a reasonable doubt. Blackridge's major point was that even if the witnesses did identify Helgman as having been present in the Auschwitz infirmary, none of them were able to say with certainty that he participated in the operations. So it was Blackridge's position that there was no basis on which the judge could find Helgman guilty of war crimes. Moreover, Blackridge had argued, the testimony of the prosecution's own witness, Harold Sumner from the Board of Medical Examiners, established that the Board had been satisfied that Helgman did, in fact, have a medical degree. Thus the prosecution had not been able to establish that Helgman had lied about his credentials when entering the United States. And as far as Helgman taking on a new name when entering the country, Blackridge had argued that even if that were true, immigrants often gave themselves new names when entering the U.S. That fact alone should not be a basis for deporting anyone.

In rebuttal, Prosecutor Perkins reminded the judge that in deciding a motion to dismiss for lack of evidence, brought at this stage of the proceedings, the court was required to give the prosecution the benefit of every reasonable inference. Echoing the same where-there's-smoke-there's-fire theme that had troubled the judge through the trial, the prosecutor asked the judge to consider what reason Helgman could have had to be standing right at the operating table if he wasn't at least helping in the experiments? Perkins argued that there was, in fact, enough basis to infer that Helgman might, indeed, have been participating in the experiments. Thus, giving every reasonable inference to the prosecutor, it would be improper for the judge to dismiss the case at this point.

Perkins was realistic enough to appreciate that his argument, even if accepted by the judge, would be a stop-gap measure at best. Once the defense finished putting on its case, if any, then the judge would weigh all the evidence without giving either party the benefit of any inferences. At *that* point, in order to find Helgman guilty of any crimes, the judge would have to be convinced of Helgman's guilt beyond a reasonable doubt. Perkins had to admit to himself, based on how the testimony and the cross-examinations had gone, that an ultimate finding of guilt on the war crimes charges was highly unlikely. But he would cross that bridge when he came to it. In any event, winning the case was secondary to his real goal of making a big splash in the press in order to keep his name in front of the public as long as possible during the run-up to the senatorial election.

Perkins made no argument concerning the accusation that Helgman had lied when entering the country. He didn't want to distract the press from focusing on the war crimes angle which, Perkins felt, was the more important way of keeping his name in the public consciousness.

Walkowski was ready to rule on the motion. He leaned forward, looked directly at Helgman, then said, "Gentlemen, I'm going to take the defense's motion under advisement. I'm not denying the motion outright, just deferring my decision for now. Be advised that I might rule on the motion one way or the other at any time based on what I hear during the defense's case, if any."

Anyone able to see Perkins's face knew he was pleasantly surprised. On the other hand, Blackridge had warned his client that this would be the most likely outcome. "The judge is just enough troubled by what he's heard," Blackridge had said, "to want you to give a public accounting of yourself. This is the time to acquit yourself as far as the judge is concerned."

"With that in mind, Mr. Blackridge" the judge continued, "do you have any witnesses to call?"

"We have three witnesses to call, Your Honor. First, Mr. Warner Amsoll, an Auschwitz survivor. Then Dr. Kurt Ben-Moshe, who knew Dr. Helgman in Auschwitz, and who observed first-hand how he helped the infirmary patients. And then we will call Dr. Helgman himself."

"Very well, then. Call your first witness."

Guided by questions from Wendall Blackridge, the witness Warner Amsoll told of his capture and imprisonment at Auschwitz II. He rolled up his sleeve so that all in the courtroom could see the blue numbers tattooed on his arm. In broken English, with a voice devoid of emotion as though he were recounting the tragedy of someone else, he told how he had been taken to the infirmary, made to lie on a filthy cart, his pants cut from him and his testicles removed. There had been no anesthesia, no painkillers, just the brutality of torture.

He told how an orderly named Max, who had been standing over him in the operating room, had later come to him every few hours, sometimes with bits of food but mostly with flavored water. He told how Max had climbed into bed with him to keep him warm.

"This man, who I'm told now calls himself Dr. Bernard Helgman, was named Max when I knew him," Amsoll said. "He is the person who saved my life, and the lives of others around me." Then with tears running down his cheeks, he said, "Whatever or whoever he really is makes no real difference. He was not one of them! I know that as a fact just as sure as I know I'm alive." Amsoll brushed the tears from his eyes and turned to the defense table. "Max, may God bless you."

The silence in the room was palpable and it was only after several moments that the judge turned to the prosecutor. "Cross-examine, Mr. Perkins?"

"Just a few questions, Your Honor."

"Proceed."

"Now Mr. Amsoll," Perkins began. "You say you saw this person Max standing over you in the operating room. Is that correct?"

"Yes, sir."

"What role did this Max play in your operation?"

"I didn't say he played any role."

"But you just testified—"

"He did not assist. He was there. That's all I said."

"What did he do if he did not assist?"

"He held my head."

"Is that not assisting?"

"If he was assisting anybody, he was assisting me. Helping me get through it!"

"But he was assisting, was he not?"

Blackridge leaned over and whispered to Helgman, "Perkins should have stopped. This can only get worse for him."

"Mr. Prosecutor," Amsoll responded. "I'm not sure what you are getting at. Yes, he assisted me, not those butchers! He saved my life and that is what I know. I'm alive today only because of him. Is that not good enough for you?"

Walkowski was about to say something when Perkins addressed the court. "I have no further questions of this witness."

"I shall pray for Dr. Helgman. May God release him from pain." The line went dead.

"We'll take a fifteen-minute recess," Walkowski announced. "And then we'll hear from the next witness."

Helgman stood and wandered out into the hall. Kurt Ben-Moshe, who had been sitting in the spectator's gallery, followed him.

"I understand you've decided to tell your story," Kurt said, his hand on Helgman's elbow. "I was hoping you'd come around. That's good news. I know it isn't easy, but truth is there is no other way for you."

"I'm not convinced it's the right thing to do. Even if the judge grants that motion, I'm ruined. My reputation is gone. Who will send their child to me?"

"You are the best reconstructive surgeon in the world, my friend. That's all anguished parents care about. Have faith."

"Faith? Look at all the good I've done and this is what I get."

"There is always Israel. The people of Israel understand what—"

"But this is the United States. Here they don't—"

"Listen to me, my friend. My government has a proposal for you. One you should consider seriously. Prime Minister Meir has a dream. One of many, I should add. She has her mind set on building a top-notch medical system to provide medical care not only for all of Israel but for our neighbors as well. She believes it is in Israel's best interest to take care of the region."

"What's that to do with me?"

"Come to Israel. You'll be appointed national chief of pediatric reconstruction with appointments to every hospital in the country. This is a teaching position as well. Israel will waive any testing or certification requirements and you can begin your new life as soon as this trial is over. You can resume doing what you've trained for all your life and you can teach others to follow in your footsteps. Under your leadership, there will be a teaching and research program for burn treatment."

"You flatter me, but—"

"There are no buts. Just come join us. Pick up from where you left off."

Helgman's thoughts turned toward Barbara and then to Leslie. "I can't just pick up and go. I need to think about it. To talk with—"

"There is no time to lose," Kurt said, his eyes going cold. "War is imminent. Our enemies are on the borders as we speak. We'll be attacked from all sides; by Syrians and Egyptians both. There will be countless deaths and even more people—including children—burned and mangled. I've been recalled home. And I'm afraid once the fighting begins it won't end for years, maybe generations. There's a real place for you—a real need."

Helgman remained silent.

"Our war—yours and mine—only began in Germany," Kurt continued. "Come help us, Bernard, as you did long ago. Many will be burned and disfigured. You can make a big difference."

"I have a wife, a son. I can't just leave them. Besides, I have been assured that if I'm acquitted I'll be reinstated at the hospital. And I have patients who depend on me here in Pittsburgh."

"My friend, I don't have the luxury of time to debate with you. I need to get to the airport. *Yom Kippur* and war are almost upon us. Good luck with the judge." Kurt pulled a card from his pocket and shoved it toward Helgman. "Take this. Call me at this number when you decide. I didn't know if I'd see you, so I gave Mrs. Nelson an envelope for you. Be well, my friend."

Before Helgman could respond, Kurt disappeared into the crowd.

Helgman stood in the hallway dumbfounded by Kurt's proposal. He didn't know what to think, but now wasn't the time to deal with it. Re-entering the courtroom, he barely had enough time to inform Blackridge that Kurt had left for Israel when the judge strode in.

Blackridge stood up at counsel table after the judge had reconvened the proceedings. "Your Honor, Dr. Ben-Moshe has been called away to Israel on an emergency basis as I understand it. Dr. Helgman will be our last witness after all."

"Call your witness, then."

It was now entirely up to Helgman. He was free to either tell the full unabridged raw story, painting a picture of his early life and what he saw and felt in the camp, or he could give his normal bare bones version. It was either expose the raw nerve of his existence, peeling away all pretext of privacy, or he could hide as he always had in the past.

Just as Helgman was conflicted, so also was Black-ridge, who did not know which Bernard Helgman would come forward.

Helgman placed one hand on the Bible and slowly raised the other. Blackridge stood before him, shoulders slumped as if he had expended his last bit of energy walking up to the witness stand.

"Dr. Helgman," he began, "would you please tell the court who you are? Please begin with your birth."

"My name now is Bernard Helgman. My name when I was born was—"

"We can't hear you," Prosecutor Perkins called out. "Speak up. I'm sure you're about to explain away your misdeeds. Please do so in a voice loud enough for all to hear."

Walkowski raised his voice higher than Blackridge ever remembered. "That's enough grandstanding, Mr. Perkins!" "One more comment like that and I'll hold you in contempt!"

The rebuke had come in open court, not at the side bar as Perkins had expected. All he could manage was a feeble, "Yes, Your Honor."

"I'm sorry, Dr. Helgman," Walkowski said, "Please continue, sir."

During this exchange, Helgman had been looking directly into Barbara's eyes. *Was that Hope? Love? Despair?*

"Thank you, Your Honor. I'll repeat my question for the witness: Dr. Helgman, please tell us about your birth."

Helgman took a deep breath. "I was born in a small town outside Leipzig, Germany in 1925. My name was Mordechai Stein. My father's name was—"

The testimony went on for ninety minutes, during which time no one moved. Slowly, detail by detail, Bernard told how Dieter Schmidt had used him as collateral for allowing the Schmidt and Grenoble families to leave the country. He told of his work in the camp, the horror of what he did to survive.

He was about to skip over what he did to obtain extra food and medical books when he heard Warner Amsoll's testimony in his head. Helgman plunged forward, confessing his sins in open court. It was as if he was asking the world to forgive him for what he had done to survive.

Helgman began his repentance with a full and complete confession. "I sold my body to the guards for food and for medical books. I wanted to learn medicine so I could help those who had been maimed. I learned to suture. The guards used me any way they could think of and all the time they were at it, I was thinking only about what I'd get to eat when it was over."

He gathered strength as he spoke. "I was beyond caring, or so I thought. But every time one of their bodies touched me, I thought I'd rather be dead than give into them once more. But I went back. Night after night, I went back. Their food was keeping me alive, even as their bodies were assaulting me." Then he again looked directly at his wife and said, "Even today the thought of a human body pressed against mine usually sends shivers through me. This is the price I've paid for my survival."

Helgman reached for a handkerchief to wipe the sweat from his forehead and the tears from his face. Many in the courtroom did the same.

Blackridge walked up close to his client. "I have just a few more questions for you Dr. Helgman. First, did you perform any operations on anybody while you were at Auschwitz?"

"The only procedures I performed were to close up the wounds after the butchers left. I did my best to reattach parts and I sutured them up as best as I could."

"But did you perform any of the experiments that we heard about in this trial?"

"No."

Blackridge reached for a yellowed piece of paper on the corner of the defense table. It was another document that Stephanie had discovered in Dieter Schmidt's office.

"I hand you this document," he said to Helgman. "Would you please tell the Court what it is."

Helgman glanced at the paper, then looked at the judge. "This is a letter written by Dieter Schmidt to a Major Braun."

"Are you aware of who this Major Braun was?"

"Only that I heard his name while I was in the camp. I don't think I was ever in his presence."

"Without objection from Prosecutor Perkins, and in the interest of time, I'll summarize the letter and you will tell the Court if my summary is accurate."

By prearrangement, Perkins announced, "Without objection."

"This letter from Herr Schmidt to Major Braun references payments expected from Schmidt to Braun in exchange for allowing you to live in the infirmary. Is that accurate?"

"I didn't learn of the actual arrangement until recently. But yes, I was permitted to sleep on a cot at the back of the infirmary."

"How was that possible? I mean people on the outside giving money to the guards. I assume they were S.S."

"I don't know the details, but I believe it was done."

"While you were there, at the infirmary I mean, what were your duties?"

"Washing the floors, stocking the supplies, getting things for the doctors and the guards."

"General porter duties then?"

"Yes, porter duties."

"So how did it come about that you were bandaging patients—or even at the operating table?"

"It started when they forced me to hold down a woman while they ... they cut her open. She died right there on the table and the doctors just walked away. One of the guards screamed at me to 'get that stinking body out of there.'" Helgman looked to the floor, his hands clenching the railing in front of him. Then he looked back up at the judge. "Those swine wouldn't even allow me to wrap her in the bloody sheet! 'Leave that sheet there,' one screamed, 'we have more coming.' I carried that woman out back and put her in a wheelbarrow as they told me. I don't know what happened then, because I was told to get back to the table to hold down the next woman."

Judge Walkowski leaned forward in his chair. "Okay, counselor, I've heard enough on this topic. Let's move it along please."

"That's all I have for this witness, Your Honor," Blackridge said.

Walkowski turned to the prosecutor. "Cross-examine, Mr. Perkins?"

"No questions, Your Honor."

"Dr. Helgman you are excused," Walkowski instructed. He then turned to the lawyers. "As I told you both yesterday, my plan is to render a decision this afternoon. The Court stands in recess. Counsel, be in my chambers at two. I'll announce my decision at that time." The judge banged his gavel and disappeared from the bench.

Helgman, his mouth hanging half-open, remained frozen in the witness chair confused and utterly exhausted.

FORTY-FOUR

It seemed to Stephanie that it had only been a few minutes—not almost two hours—that she had watched Bernard walk slowly to the stand, a broken man, his hands trembling. She had watched him grow stronger as the words poured from him. His head had come up and his jaw set hard in the way she remembered when he passed in front of her climbing the hill on Block Island, his attention then focused on her uncle.

As his story unfolded, she wept at his torment. He had never even hinted to her what he had done to survive and she was shocked that he was now talking about it in public, laying himself bare for the world to examine. It was so out of character for him that she knew something must have precipitated the change, but she didn't know what it could have been.

Listening to him on the stand reinforced her desire to make a life with him. Bernard Helgman meant more to her than all of her possessions, all of her money. She had been in love with this man for her entire adult life and when he had finally regained his composure and stood up from the witness chair, she had fought the almost overpowering urge to run forward and comfort him, to tell him it would be okay, to hold him close to her.

Instead, she fled to the women's room.

Pandemonium broke loose when the judge disappeared through the doorway, his law clerk trailing a few steps behind. Reporters rushed to file their stories, alerting their editors to be ready for the late breaking news of the actual decision, knowing the judge's timing was set so that the evening papers could carry the story. The timing would be tight, but headlines for either contingency would be prepared and lead stories pre-written for both outcomes.

The reporters who routinely covered the legal beat already had their stories written and Helgman's testimony didn't cause any of them to doubt the outcome. Unless Walkowski acted completely out of character, their day's work was already complete.

Once in the hall, Helgman moved away from the reporters. He made his way through the crowd, took the elevator to the ground floor, and a moment later walked through the massive front door. The air was cool and crisp, a slight wind blowing, as Helgman took a deep breath.

He hadn't yet found Stephanie and while he searched for her on the steps below him, Barbara appeared at his side. "Do you still have that hotel key?"

Helgman's answer was to pull her close and kiss her.

Barbara looked up at him teary-eyed. "Oh, Bernie, it took real courage to do what you did today. I'm so proud of you."

"The real courage came from Warner. Not me."

Suddenly, a commotion formed on the street below them. "That clown's funny. Really funny," someone shouted. "A chicken or something."

People were laughing and clapping. Cars were stopping and traffic was backing up. Horns began to honk.

"Les!" Bernard shouted, turning toward Barbara. "It's Leslie being Muggles!"

Barbara watched in fascination as her son, dressed as a big yellow bird, leaped from the steps and almost landed on a TV camera platform set up at the base of the steps.

The TV crew, astutely sensing an audience-pleasing story, turned the camera toward the chicken. A young woman reporter breathlessly described the clown's antics, ignoring Prosecutor Perkins who waited mid-way down the steps for his interview.

Had the camera been focused on Helgman, it would have captured the biggest smile of his life. The camera would also have captured the image of a tall, well-dressed woman rushing down the steps behind Helgman, her smile fading to disappointment as she witnessed the man she loved with all her heart embracing his wife.

As his parents watched, Muggles produced a quarter and flipped it to the reporter. She reached up to catch the coin, only to find her fist had closed on air. Muggles pointed to the curb where the quarter was wedged into a crack.

"You taught him well!" Barbara hugged her husband again. "Come, let's get down there and end it before he gets arrested—or hurt."

Barbara started down the steps, but a hand on Helgman's shoulder caused him to pause. Stephanie was beside him, tears running down her face. "Bernard," she began, "I can see that I've lost you. All I want is the best for you, but that doesn't make it hurt any the less." She reached into her bag and produced an envelope. "Here," she said, thrusting the envelope toward him. "A man, he said his name was Kurt, asked me to hand you this. I suppose he heard my testimony, and knows our relationship. Anyway, he said he wanted to hand you this himself, but he had to leave in a hurry." She kissed him on the cheek. "I wish the three of you the very best," she said before moving off into the crowd.

Helgman opened the envelope and extracted a bundle of papers. A note attached to the papers read, "Bernard, with the war coming, Israel needs you. I've taken the liberty of filling out an immigration visa application for you and your family. All this needs is your signatures. I'll meet you when you get off the plane and we'll get it processed right away. The Law of Return provides that once you are here, and because you are Jewish, you can obtain automatic Israeli citizenship while keeping your U.S. citizenship as well. The Jewish homeland welcomes you with open arms. Come, finish the work we both started so very long ago. Your friend, Kurt."

FORTY-FIVE

Bernard Mordechai Ben-Stillson, the name Helgman took upon making *aliyah*, stood in the hot sun, a shovel hanging loosely from his left hand, his right arm wrapped tightly around Barbara's waist. He was impatient to begin, not so much for himself, but when his shovel scraped the earth beneath his feet, the children's hospital, the reason for his being in Israel, would finally become a tangible reality. With Mt. Herzl and Yad Vashem as a backdrop, Ben-Stillson couldn't imagine a better place to build a children's hospital.

He was happy that Warner and his family had come to the ceremony. He also was excited to welcome the contingent from the United States—William Dawson, Warner Amsoll, and even Yetta Hertzstein..

Bernard was also impatient because his son had insisted that he come to the ceremony and, as he had said, "Make people happy as Muggles the Clown." Ben-Stillson knew that Muggles couldn't remain in the van much longer, and would burst out at any moment, whether the ceremony was ready for him or not.

A sudden voice resounded over a loudspeaker. "Welcome to everyone who came out today," the voice began. "My name is Kurt Ben-Moshe, Assistant Minister of Health. The Minister has asked me to officiate today because of my strong connection to our honored guests. I'm sorry for the delay. We were waiting for the Prime Minister, but she's been held up and just sent word for us to begin without her. So let me begin."

Bernard thought about his meeting with the Prime Minister yesterday and recalled that she had appeared tired. *It comes with the job*, he had concluded at that time. Now he was worried.

"We are honored today," Kurt continued, "to have visitors from the States and I'd be remiss if I didn't—"

Bernard leaned close to Barbara and whispered, "He'd better get on with it. Les will come out any moment."

"That's what I've just been thinking. I hope Les doesn't get too impatient."

" ... all this," Kurt said, waving his arm around the hillside, "would not be possible without Dr. Bernard Mordechai Ben-Stillson agreeing to join us here in Israel to help build the country. The children are the real beneficiaries here." He turned to Ben-Stillson. "Bernard, do come over here and say a few words. Then please turn over the first shovel of dirt." Kurt turned back to the attendees. "After that, we have a real treat. Muggles the Clown has agreed to perform for us and if he doesn't make you laugh then ... then ... well that's your problem. Bernard, the microphone is yours."

Ben-Stillson walked quickly to the microphone, keeping one eye on the van holding his son. "My dear family and friends, thank you all for coming out here today and especially for being here in this heat. We're dedicating this land today to a hospital in the memory—all too late—of Dr. Bernard Helgman who died in Poland, January 26, 1945.

"We are also planting a grove of trees to honor the lives of the millions who died for no reason other than their religion, or perhaps their sexual preferences. When one thinks of trees, one thinks of roots that grow out of the depths of the earth. Yetta Hertzstein, standing right over here, along with my friend Warner, have themselves come out from the depths. These trees are planted in their honor as well."

Bernard glanced down at the notes in his hand and saw the words *mima'amakim keraticha adonai*—the words to Psalm 130 that he had first heard in the very concentration camp infirmary where Dr. Bernard Helgman had died and both Yetta and Warner had survived. Words that carried a message of mercy—and redemption.

But he was prevented from reading the psalm when the audience suddenly burst into laughter, their eyes alive with excitement.

Bernard's momentary confusion gave way to understanding as his head swiveled in time to see Muggles the Clown, dressed as a yellow bird, land an imperfect back flip, fall to the ground and immediately spring up, the left wing hanging limp at his side.

A collective, "oooh," rose from the crowd.

The bird then tumbled directly toward Bernard. At the last moment before rolling into Bernard's legs, the bird again bounced up, now holding a rope, a lasso tied at the end with a big knot. The loop flew over Bernard's head and the bird tugged as if to pull Bernard away from the audience. Without warning, the big yellow bird again lost balance and fell. The audience gasped as the lasso tightened around Bernard's neck.

Bernard instinctively grasped the rope before realizing that his son was performing the Gordian Knot Trick—the name taken from the impossible-to-untie knot cut open by Alexander the Great. What he didn't understand was how the boy had learned to perform that intricate trick—or to even tie the intractable knot. Involuntarily, Bernard's fingers worked themselves under the loop for protection. What his son had in mind, Bernard could not imagine.

Then, as if it had never existed, the Gordian knot was gone. The rope fell free.

Swelling with pride at his son's clowning skills, Bernard stepped over to where his wife was standing. Pulling her close he felt an unexpected roundness. Tears filled his eyes and emotion flooded his heart. "Barbara," he exclaimed. "Are you ... ? Are we ... ? How long ... ?"

"Ten weeks. Oh, Bernard—my dear Bernard Mordechai Ben-Stillson—this precious new life is a new beginning!"

A collective gasp rose from the crowd followed quickly by shouts of, "*Metzuyan*! Excellent!" Bernard's head jerked around in time to see several people with their arms outstretched, their fingers bent into a half-fist as if they were trying to catch something—something that obviously wasn't there.

"He's better than I ever was," Bernard confessed to Barbara. "How about if he takes my place as Muggs? It's time, you know."

Now it was Barbara's turn to mist up. "A new beginning! Hold me close."

The warmth of Barbara's body pressing against him brought his thoughts back to a night in their bedroom some months earlier. "Yes, my love," he replied. "A new beginning—and a new life."

HA SHOAH – THE CALAMITY

In the late seventies a man sitting across from me at a Jewish Federation meeting told of his escape, as a teenager, from a concentration camp under cover of darkness. The man, a leader of the Jewish community, went on to relate how he and his brother, who had also escaped the camp, spent the remaining war years hidden on a farm by a non-Jewish family. Stories such as his, told by actual survivors, can be found, together with pictures and other important artifacts, at Holocaust Memorials around the world. Some twenty-seven countries have at least one memorial dedicated to those who suffered in the Holocaust. Israel alone has over ten Holocaust memorials, including Yad Vashem in Jerusalem and the relatively new memorial in Tel Aviv which is dedicated: "In memory of those persecuted by the Nazi regime for their sexual orientation and gender identity."

A full list of Holocaust Associations across America and around the world can be found on the web site of Association of Holocaust Organizations — www.ahoinfo.org/membersdirectory.html

The stories of survivors as recorded and preserved in many of these memorials are critical to an understand¬ing of the magnitude of the calamity fostered by intolerance. And while the Holocaust has caused people everywhere to question the very existence of God, and by implication, religion, the survivors have amply demonstrated that it takes more than a calamity to destroy the human spirit—or their religion.

In all, approximately seventeen million people died as victims of Hitler and his followers. The list includes:

Jews	6 million
Soviets & Ukrainians	5 million
Poles	3 million
Romani (Gypsies)	1 million
Disabled in any way	250,000
Jehovah's Witnesses	200,000
Clergy	Thousands
Political Opponents	Thousands

Religious Opponents	Thousands
Learning Disorders	Thousands
Homosexuals & Transgender	Thousands
Blacks (Mulatto)	Thousands

Jews recite the following Kaddish in memory of the deceased. The Kaddish is an affirmation of God and ends with a prayer for peace. I mourn and honor the deceased by reciting the Mourners Kaddish and I trust such a recitation is not offensive to anyone.

Glorified and sanctified be God's great name throughout the world which He has created according to His will. May He establish His kingdom in your lifetime and during your days, and within the life of the entire House of Israel, speedily and soon; and say, Amen. May His great name be blessed forever and to all eternity. Blessed and praised, glorified and exalted, extolled and honored, adored and lauded be the name of the Holy One, blessed be He, beyond all the blessings and hymns, praises and consolations that are ever spoken in the world; and say, Amen. May there be abundant peace from heaven, and life, for us and for all Israel; and say, Amen. He who creates peace in His celestial heights, may He create peace for us and for all Israel; and say, Amen.

May the memory of the departed serve as a blessing for us all.

Personal Notes and Acknowledgments

My daughter, Debra Suzanne Tannenbaum, was the initial editor for all of my published books. Debi passed away unexpectedly not long after she finished editing the manuscript for this book. She would be happy to know that her comments and suggestions have been incorporated into the printed version. May her soul be bound up in the bond of life. Her memory is certainly a blessing to all who knew her.

For a sample of Debi's writing, please go to:

https://youtube/nYpHjYTk90U

My grandparents were fortunate to have already been in the United States when the horrors in Europe began. I, therefore, am blessed to be alive and among those fortunate enough to have parents, grandparents, uncles, aunts, and siblings who did not suffer the worst atrocities imaginable. For that I'm thankful every day.

But I'd be remiss if I did not take note that Dvinsk (now Daugavpils, Latvia) where my ancestors lived had a Jewish population of 11,000 in 1935. At war's end that number had been reduced to thirty-nine. I can only painfully imagine the fate of my relatives who remained behind and whom I never knew. May their souls rest in peace.

My long time friend and colleague Ronald Slusky took time away from his patent attorney practice to read and correct the manuscript as well as pepper me with probing questions. I have come to rely on Ron as a valuable editor, and particularly on his ear for dialogue and timing. His suggestion for the use of Psalm 130 during the *bar mitzvah* scene was brilliant, which in turn, led to a title change. Ron is the author of *INVENTION ANALYSIS AND CLAIMING*, which to my mind, is the best book ever written on patent claim drafting. His seminars are essential for any patent attorney who wishes to excel.

A special thank you goes to Marvilyn Miller who painstakingly edited the manuscript. I have come to rely on Marvilyn's eagle eye and on her patience with the trauma to the English language that I continue to prove I'm all too capable of inflicting.

Thanks also to Dan Davison, Litigation Partner at Norton Rose Fulbright US LLP, for his excellent litigation-related comments.

I also wish to thank Larry Streff, Dr. Stephen Tannenbaum, Leonard Felman, Paul Frazier, Kathlyn Auten, Steve Hathcock, Joyce Faulkner, Rabbi James Gibson, Dr. Gary Solomon, Steven Walden, Lauren Bairnsfather, PhD, Richard Cohen, and Don Crosbie for their valuable input.

Several people agreed to serve as sounding boards for *Out of the Depths*. They have my gratitude for taking the time from their busy lives to read the manuscript and discuss their comments with me in person.

One of these groups met with me at the lovely home of Patti and Nick Jent in Dallas, Texas. My thanks go to the Jents and to Barb and Kevin Jeffries, Sally and Bill Dix, Phyllis Conces, Nancy and David Snodgrass, Mary and Dr. Tom Kimball, Jill Fleming, Julie and Bob Butterfield, and Lisa Pollack.

In Brownsville, Texas, the Hadassah Book Club met at the Temple Beth El to give me their comments. A heartfelt thank you goes to Harriet Light, Elka Jaross, Eva Silverman, Esther Moszkowicz, Lynn Victor, and Peggy Goldfine.

And last, but not in any stretch of the imagination least, words can never express my appreciation for my wife, Mary. She first read an early draft of the manuscript over twenty-five years ago and it is with her unwavering support and encouragement that the book is now being published. Thank you, beautiful woman.

ABOUT THE AUTHOR

David Harry Tannenbaum is a retired patent attorney and lives with his wife Mary and dog Franco on South Padre Island, Texas. David is a past president of Temple Israel (now Beth Israel) in Scotch Plains, New Jersey and a past president of The Jewish Community Center of Central New Jersey. David has also been an active supporter of Jewish Federation in New Jersey.

David is the author, under the pen name David Harry, of the Jimmy Redstone/Angella Martinez mystery/thriller books set in South Texas as well as the literary novel *STANDARD DEVIATION*, a story featuring an Asperger's Syndrome child. When David isn't writing, he enjoys kayaking, biking, and traveling. When David and Mary are off the island, they can usually be found in their old stomping ground of Pittsburgh, Pennsylvania.

David can be contacted at:
RedEnginePressInfo@gmail.com
AuthorDavidTannenbaum@gmail.com
Facebook: DavidHarryTannenbaum
Twitter: DHTannenbaum
Web: DavidHarryTannenbaum.com

CPSIA information can be obtained
at www.ICGtesting.com
Printed in the USA
FSOW02n0251280517
34592FS